DYNASTY 27

The Restless Sea

Also in the *Dynasty* series:

THE FOUNDING
THE DARK ROSE
THE PRINCELING
THE OAK APPLE
THE BLACK PEARL
THE LONG SHADOW
THE CHEVALIER
THE MAIDEN
THE FLOOD-TIDE
THE TANGLED THREAD
THE EMPEROR
THE VICTORY
THE REGENCY
THE CAMPAIGNERS
THE RECKONING
THE DEVIL'S HORSE
THE POISON TREE
THE ABYSS
THE HIDDEN SHORE
THE WINTER JOURNEY
THE OUTCAST
THE MIRAGE
THE CAUSE
THE HOMECOMING
THE QUESTION
THE DREAM KINGDOM

DYNASTY

27

The Restless Sea

Cynthia Harrod-Eagles

LITTLE, BROWN

A *Little, Brown* Book

First published in Great Britain in 2004 by Little, Brown

Copyright © 2004 Cynthia Harrod-Eagles

The moral right of the author has been asserted.

A CIP catalogue record for this book
is available from the British Library.

ISBN 0 316 86104 9

Typeset in Plantin
by Palimpsest Book Production Limited
Polmont, Stirlingshire

Printed and bound in Great Britain by
Mackays of Chatham plc, Chatham Kent

Little, Brown
An imprint of
Time Warner Book Group UK
Brettenham House
Lancaster Place
London WC2E 7EN

www.twbg.co.uk

Select Bibliography

Roy Anderson — *White Star*

Dennis Baldry — *The History of Aviation*

Nancy Bradfield — *Costume In Detail, 1730–1930*

Terry Coleman — *The Liners*

Gertrude Colmore — *The Life of Emily Davison*

Sir Robert Ensor — *England 1870–1914*

M. G. Fawcett — *The Women's Victory and After*

J. Franck Bright — *History of England*

Robin Gardiner — *The Riddle of the Titanic*

Bill Gunston — *A Century of Flight*

Adam Helliker — *The Debrett Season*

Annie Kenney — *Memoirs of a Militant*

Walter Lord — *A Night to Remember*

Harold Nicolson — *King George V, His Life and Reign*

Peter Padfield — *The Titanic and the Californian*

Emmeline Pankhurst — *My Own Story*

R. E. Prothero — *English Farming Past and Present*

Martin Pugh — *The Pankhursts*

Antonia Raeburn — *The Militant Suffragettes*

Bruce Robertson — *Sopwith – The Man and His Aircraft*

Kenneth Rose — *King George V*

J. A. Spender — *Fifty Years of Europe*

Susan Wels — *Titanic*

Anthony Wood — *Nineteenth-century Britain 1815–1914*

THE MORLANDS OF MORLAND PLACE

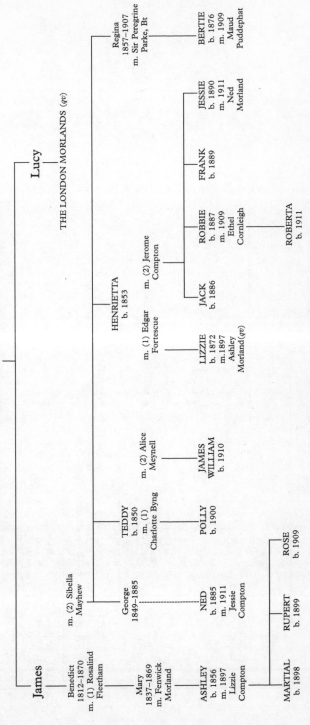

THE LONDON MORLANDS

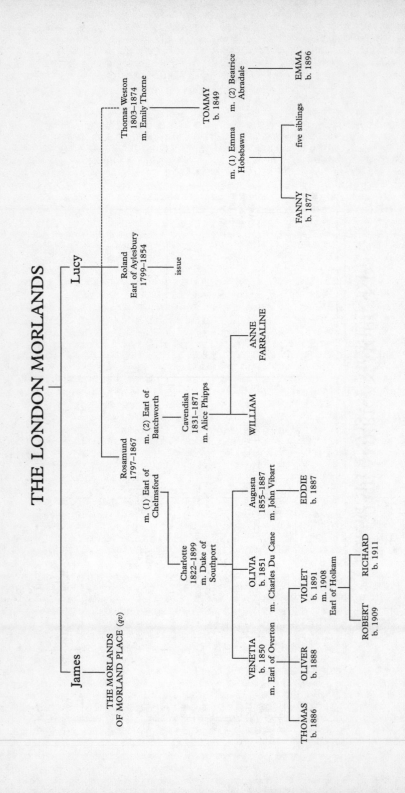

THE AMERICAN MORLANDS

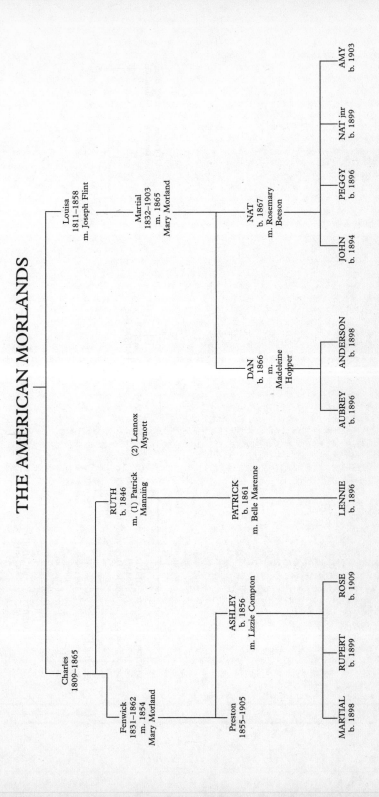

BOOK ONE

At Venture

When round thy ship in tempest Hell appears,
And every spectre mutters up more dire
To snatch control
And loose to madness thy deep-kennell'd Fears—
Then to the helm, O Soul

Last; if upon the cold green-mantling sea
Thou cling, alone with Truth, to the last spar,
Both castaway,
And one must perish – let it not be he
Whom thou art sworn to obey!

Herbert Trench, 'A Charge'

CHAPTER ONE

March 1912

On the evening on which Mr and Mrs Edward Morland of Maystone Villa, Clifton, were to give the first dinner party of their married lives, Ned arrived home late. It had been raining all day – that thin, prickling rain, hardly more than mist, that soaks surprisingly quickly – but as Purvis, the chauffeur, opened the door of the motor for him he found that it had stopped at last. He stepped out into a world of damp, with the steady sound of drips coming through the darkness from the invisible trees all about. The air smelt green and fresh, with a hint of woodsmoke. He thought how nice the house looked, square and solid and welcoming, with its lights glowing through the darkness, and felt a deep, wordless satisfaction at being home.

'Thank you, Purvis. I shan't need you again tonight.'

'Very good, sir.'

The front door opened and his man, Daltry, appeared. He was carrying an umbrella, but seeing no rain descending through the light cast from the door, he put it aside. 'Good evening, sir,' he said, as he helped the master off with his coat.

'I'm a little late,' Ned acknowledged. 'All serene?'

'Yes, sir, except that the drawing-room fire is smoking. The logs were rather damp.'

Close up, Ned saw that Daltry was somewhat smoky about the face. Evidently he had been struggling with it. As the only male servant in the house he was called on in divers ways. Ned knew how lucky he was that Daltry did not object to acting as butler and footman too. Many gentlemen's gentlemen sought other positions when their master married. 'Why are we having a log fire?' he asked. 'What happened to the coal?'

Daltry's face took on a rigid quality, which warned his master off. 'I could not undertake to say, sir.'

'Oh. Where's Mrs Morland?'

'I believe she is dressing, sir.'

'All right. Give me five minutes and then come up and help me dress.' A faint smile touched his lips. 'Better have a wash first.'

Now that he looked around, Ned could not only smell but see woodsmoke, drifting down the hall with the draught from the open door. In the drawing-room, the fire was burning sulkily, but a veil of smoke still hung about the ceiling. A maid was on her knees in front of it – praying apparently, since she didn't seem to be doing anything else to help it along.

'Get a sheet of newspaper to hold up in front of it,' Ned said. 'Don't you know how to do that?'

The maid started and turned. 'No, sir,' she said faintly, and looked as though she would cry. She was very young – she seemed about ten – but more to his surprise she was a stranger.

'Who are you?'

'Susie Grice, sir,' she said, in a petrified whisper. 'I'm new.'

There was no time now for explanations. 'Newspaper. Get one of the others to show you how,' he said, and headed upstairs. A man returning home from his place of work expects order and harmony. Short of moving the furniture around, a wife could hardly serve him worse than by confronting him with unexpected new servants.

Jessie was in their bedroom, standing facing the door, hands on hips, with a preoccupied look on her face. She was not waiting to confront him, however: the thoughtful frown was caused by her corset, and the fact that Tomlinson was behind her, carefully pulling together the two stiff but fragile edges of her gown to do up the fastenings.

4

Jessie's big dog, Brach, who had been lying under the dressing-table, got to her feet, stretched lavishly in front, and came over to greet him with a slowly swinging tail. Brach had belonged to Jessie's late father, but she had pined so much when Jessie married that in pity she had brought her from Morland Place to Maystone. She was a Morland Hound, a breed not really suited to a villa, but Jessie led a vigorous outdoor life, so she had plenty of exercise.

Caressing the dog, Ned regarded his wife. The gown was one they had bought in Paris while they were on honeymoon. It was a dusky shade of pink, a high-waisted, narrow gown of silk with a knee-length Valenciennes lace over-tunic. The tunic hem, the edges of the short sleeves and the bodice were thickly sewn with beads and tiny spars, the weight of which the lace was hardly able to bear, hence its fragility. It was a beautiful gown and Clifton had not seen it yet. She would cause a small sensation at the party tonight, and his annoyance left him at the sight of her. 'You look beautiful,' he said.

Jessie smiled, unable to speak at this critical juncture.

'Right you are, madam,' Tomlinson said, an instant later, and Jessie cautiously let out her breath and felt her body settle into its rigid cage. By day she lived mostly in riding habit, but she was feminine enough to enjoy the sensation of being tightly laced and gorgeously clad.

'I'll never be able to bend,' she said. 'I shall have to be very ladylike if I drop something, and wait for a gentleman to pick it up.' She looked at her husband, who was still fondling Brach's upthrust head. 'You're shockingly late. You'd better go and dress right away. I'm done, all but my hair.'

'Is that all the welcome I get?' he complained. 'After a long day at work . . .'

Tomlinson was quick to react. 'I'll come back in five minutes, madam,' she said, her cheeks red. She slipped out past Ned with her eyes cast down, closing the door behind her.

'It's wicked of you to embarrass the servants,' Jessie said, stepping into his embrace. His skin was cold from outdoors but his lips were warm against hers and, together with the male smell of him and the hardness of his shoulders under her hands, gave her a fluttery feeling. They had only been married three months, and it was still a novelty to her.

'Tomlinson had better get used to it,' Ned said, against her mouth. 'If a man can't kiss his own wife in his own bedroom . . .'

There was a satisfactory silence. When they broke for breath she reached up and touched his fair hair. 'It's stopped raining?'

'Mm.'

'Good. I want everything to be perfect tonight.'

'Why shouldn't it be?' he said, nuzzling her neck. 'We've both been to enough dinner parties to know how they go on.'

'We've both *been* to dinner parties,' she said, breaking away from him, 'but we don't know how they work under the bonnet.'

He was charmed by her metaphor. She could drive a motor-car as well as any man, but you'd never guess it to look at her now, in her Paris gown. He wanted to kiss her again, but she put her hands flat against his lapels to stop him.

'It's all very well,' she said, 'but Daltry will be waiting for you.'

It reminded him. 'No, he won't, he's washing the soot off his face and hands. Why are we having a log fire in the drawing-room?'

'We have to save the coal for the kitchen range,' Jessie said.

'I know there's a coal strike on,' said Ned, 'but my father sent enough across from Morland Place for the fires for tonight.' Jessie's uncle Teddy, master of Morland Place, was his adopted father. 'What happened to it?'

Jessie looked slightly uncomfortable. 'I gave it away,' she said.

'You gave it away?' Ned grew indignant. 'Don't you know what coal *costs* these days?'

Jessie said defensively, 'I told you I was going to do some of my mother's poor-visiting. Well, as I was coming back along Moor Lane I passed Quaker Row, so I called in on the Grices. You know what those cottages are like. You need to keep a fire going in them all the time, and they haven't had one for a week. The water was *running* down the walls. Poor old Grice was in bed upstairs, blue in the face with his emphysema. The air was so cold and damp he could hardly breathe. What was I to do?' she pleaded. 'Mrs Grice has little ones out collecting sticks from the wood, but everyone's doing the same, and what little they bring barely heats a kettle of water. So this morning I told Purvis to take Uncle's sack of coal over to them.'

Ned's annoyance faded, but he looked rather careworn. He couldn't condemn her charitable instinct, though giving away coal at the present time was rather like giving away jewellery. 'You did the right thing, I suppose. But need it have been the whole sack?'

'There was no point in sending just enough for one day. Grice isn't going to be well in that time.'

'All the same—' He frowned, remembering something else. 'Who was that girl downstairs? She said her name was Grice.'

'She's the new housemaid,' Jessie said.

'New since this morning? Don't tell me what's-her-name has left already, the one with the flat face who looks like a fish?'

'Martha.'

'That's right. I thought you liked her.'

'No, Martha hasn't left. Susie's – extra.'

'Extra?'

'She's Grice's eldest girl,' Jessie explained. 'You see, they've spent their savings and Grice is ill and Mrs Grice has to look after the little ones so *she* can't work. So when Mrs Grice said Susie was old enough now and asked if I knew of a place, I said I'd take her on. I know she looks young but she's twelve and Mrs Grice says she's very handy. I'm sure she'll do well because she's so grateful for the job.'

'I'm sure she is,' Ned said. 'Tell me, what else did you do for them? You didn't invite them all to dinner tonight, by any chance?'

Jessie was hurt. 'You don't begrudge my helping them?'

'What would my life have been if it weren't for the kindness of people in our position?' he said, trying to find the right words about tempering charity with common sense. 'It's not a matter of begrudging, but—'

'If you say "but" you must be objecting.'

'Grice isn't even one of our people. Where did he work? The soap factory, wasn't it? They should be looking after him and his family.'

'Well, they aren't. And *Mrs* Grice used to be a housemaid up at Morland Place before she married. That's why Mother keeps an eye on her.'

'She's not *our* responsibility.'

'If you expect me to pass by on the other side—'

'What I expect is for you to ask me before taking on extra staff.'

'I thought the domestic staff was *my* domain.'

'Of course it is, but—'

'And I *thought* I heard you say when we first got married that if I wanted more servants I could have them.'

'I did say that,' Ned said, firmly enough to stop her interrupting again, 'but you don't seem to understand that things are bad at the moment. The miners' strike is having a terrible effect on business. We need to retrench, not go throwing sacks of coal around and taking on extra staff.'

'*One* sack of coal. And *one* extra girl.' Jessie had acted on impulse, but since then had begun to have second thoughts about the wisdom of her actions. Everything Ned had said had already occurred to her. The Grices had to be helped, but the help did not have to come from her. She ought to have alerted Morland Place and left it to them to take coal and offer employment.

But it annoyed her to be questioned about anything she did by Ned. He was her cousin, and she was used to his being the supplicant for her favour, not her critic. She went into the attack with sarcasm. 'Susie's so little, I'm sure she won't eat much.'

'She'll eat the same as the other servants. And then there's her wages to find. And I suppose you'll buy her

her uniform, since I can't imagine she can pay for it herself.'

'Well, if you're going to be so mean—'

'It's not meanness!' Ned cried in exasperation. 'Can't I get it into your head that business is down at the moment, and the price of everything is going up because of the coal shortage? We have to be careful.'

'If things are bad Uncle Teddy will give you something,' Jessie said.

'He won't because I won't ask him,' Ned said sharply. 'He's given me enough already. I shall make my own way from now on, and if I can't afford something we will do without. I won't go begging to him at every setback.'

'You let him give you the coal,' Jessie said.

Ned flushed. 'I *bought* the coal from him,' he said. 'He would have given it to me but I wouldn't let him, and he understood why. Besides, it would be a very different matter to ask him for money. I'm surprised you suggested it.'

Now Jessie was wrong-footed; but anger made her retaliate. 'You seem to forget I have a business of my own. If you can't afford a sack of coal and a new housemaid, I'll pay for them myself out of the profits from the stables.'

'You can't have looked at the accounts lately. There *is* no profit in the stables. The price of fodder is soaring along with everything else, and the bad weather means the grass will be late, so you'll have to keep feeding for longer.' Worry and a feeling of being misunderstood and undervalued fuelled his annoyance, and he went on, 'The stock are eating their heads off and you haven't sold a horse since Christmas. It's not a business, it's a lady's hobby. You might as well keep canaries or do poker-work.'

'It is *not* a hobby!' Jessie cried, stung. 'I haven't sold a horse since Christmas because I sold so many *before*. And I've got Mrs Stinchcombe's mare almost ready, and Mr Hamlyn's polo ponies—'

'If they don't cancel. I happen to know that Stinchcombe's business is in a bad way; and Hamlyn has given up his club membership, so he must be feeling the pinch. The horses are a liability at the moment, and one which I have to

9

shoulder along with everything else. I don't expect you to be grateful, but it's rather hard to be abused for trying to keep us out of the workhouse!'

Jessie was loaded and ready to fire straight back; but something made her pause and hold off, and in the silence she realised with a sinking feeling that they were quarrelling, really quarrelling now. Because they had grown up together they had always had lively arguments, and there had never been any likelihood that she would submit meekly as Aunt Alice did to Uncle Teddy – or even that she would always accept his word as final *after* discussion, as Mother had with Dad.

But this was different. He had hurt her by calling her stables a hobby, and she had been searching about for a way to hurt him back. She noticed all at once that he looked very tired about the eyes, as though he had been worrying as well as working twelve hours a day at his paper mill. And then she remembered something her mother had said to her on the eve of her marriage.

'Never quarrel,' Henrietta had said. 'Discuss, argue if you like, but never use words to wound. And if ever you should quarrel, always be the first to say you're sorry. It's much harder for a man; and if you *were* in the right, he'll know it, and make it up to you.'

So she swallowed hard and tried to find words of conciliation. But before she could speak he said in a tired, quiet voice, 'Don't let's quarrel, Jess. We've guests coming very soon, and I want our party to go well. It's very important for my business. You understand that, don't you?'

'Are things so very bad?' she said, trying to keep her voice steady.

'Oh, it's a temporary dip,' he said, trying to smile. 'But it's been one thing after another lately. The expense of setting up house was greater than I expected, and it came at a bad time, with the strike and so on. We shall pull through, but we need to be careful for a while.'

'Do you want me to send Susie away?' she asked stiffly.

'No,' he said wearily. 'It wouldn't be fair on her not to give her a trial. But don't take on any more waifs and strays, will you? Not without asking me.'

The door opened and Tomlinson came in, so timely that Ned wondered if she had been listening outside for a lull in the storm.

'Shall I do your hair, madam? And, sir, Daltry's in the dressing-room ready for you.'

'Yes, I'm going now,' Ned said, and turned away.

But as his hand reached the doorknob Jessie took an impulsive step after him and touched his arm. 'I'm sorry I spoke crossly and said unkind things. Forgive me?'

It was worth having said it for the smile it produced. There were things he could not say in front of a servant – things he could not do, either – so he put them all into a glowing look of promise, then lifted her hand to his lips and kissed it before leaving her to her maid.

Jessie had been brought up at Morland Place, where her mother Henrietta still lived and was effectively mistress – Aunt Alice did not care to run things. Henrietta had been managing the household at Morland Place for the past fifteen years, and it was a tribute to her skill that Jessie had not realised there was any skill in it. She had thought a house more or less ran itself. It was a revelation to her how much work was involved in giving a dinner party for sixteen.

It was unfortunate that her mother was away at present. Henrietta had gone to London for several weeks to stay with Jessie's half-sister Lizzie. But Jessie had had long talks with her before she left, and they had pored over recipe books together to choose a menu. Jessie's method would have been to choose all her favourite dishes without regard to what was in season, and without knowledge of the work involved in preparing them. Comments like 'You must have some things that can be prepared the day before,' and 'You can't have all those things in the oven at the same time, dear,' opened her eyes to a new world of expertise.

The menu chosen, Henrietta had given her advice about where and when to order the ingredients, drawn up a seating plan from the guest list, and written out an order of precedence, which Jessie had made herself learn off by heart since the subtleties of it were beyond her.

'You and I don't care about that sort of thing, darling,' Henrietta had said, 'but you must remember that a lot of people do, and they are the sort of people who make life unpleasant if you get it wrong. Remember, Ned's business depends to a great extent on how you and he stand in society.'

'It's all such nonsense,' Jessie had complained. 'If he produces the right goods at the right price, what else matters? I know he doesn't care about such things. How could he, when Uncle Teddy doesn't?'

Henrietta sighed and wondered how to explain the realities of the world to her daughter. 'Uncle Teddy's position is very different, and he can afford to please himself. He's the master of Morland Place and wealthy besides.'

Ned, on the other hand, had been born the illegitimate son of Henrietta and Teddy's elder brother George. Despite Teddy's having adopted him, and given him the mill so that he could support himself respectably, there would always be people to remember his origins and hold them against him if he once put a foot wrong.

Henrietta went on, 'Ned still has his way to make, and he has to stand well with people who could make or mar his business. And, darling, it's just as easy to get things right as to get them wrong, if you only take a little trouble beforehand. You want to help your husband, don't you?'

'I suppose so,' Jessie had said, and then, seeing her mother's raised eyebrow, amended it to 'Of course I do.' Though really she felt that doing silly things for a good reason did not make them any less silly, and that rather than 'making up' to silly people one should ignore them.

The work she had done with her mother over the menu had seemed excessive at the time, but afterwards she was glad that she understood the reasons behind it, for when she showed it to the cook she was able to meet her objections from a position of strength.

Mrs Peck was Jessie's second cook already, and they had only been in Maystone Villa two months, since coming back from their honeymoon. The first cook had turned out to be dishonest and Jessie had turned her off. She hoped her new cook was up to the task. Mrs Peck certainly grumbled about having to do a seven-course dinner for sixteen 'so soon', though Jessie did not see how it would have been any more or less arduous at any other time. She supposed it was just in a cook's nature to grumble – the first one certainly had, bitterly and constantly.

'A lot of the things can be done beforehand,' Jessie said. 'And we'll hire waiters to serve at table so the girls will be free to help you in the kitchen.'

Mrs Peck said, 'Extra staff just means more people for me to feed, and more people getting under my feet.' But she was slightly mollified, and as the day drew nearer seemed to pull herself together and become interested in the affair. The maids, Peggy and Martha, were excited about it from the beginning. Though they wouldn't be waiting at table, they would help take the coats, and Jessie overheard them talking about doing their hair differently for the occasion. Even the kitchenmaid Katy, a pathetic, undersized Irish girl with a chronic sniff, was stirred into animation, though the hardest of the extra work would land on her scrawny shoulders.

Dinner was to consist of soup, fish, entrée, roast, entremets, pudding and dessert – the sort of dinner Morland Place might have given, except that there would not be so many choices in each course. Thanks to Henrietta, Jessie had the campaign of action all mapped out in her mind. The cold consommé could be made the day before. The fish was salmon poached in Chablis – top of the stove – served with lettuce. The oyster puffs for the entrée could be made ahead and just needed a minute in a hot oven to 'perk them up' before serving. That left the ovens for the roasts – chicken with tarragons, and leg of lamb stuck with capers. Of the entremets – broccoli, stewed mushrooms and glazed parsnips – the parsnips went into the oven above the roasts while the others were cooked on the stove top along with the sauces. Once the roasts came out the puddings went in – Nassau tart and baked Chaumontel pears – while the rhubarb flummery was cold and made the day before. Dessert was cheese, apples and dried figs: March was a poor month for fruit.

The last thing Jessie had done before she went up to dress was to check the dining-table. Daltry had overseen the laying: having been a footman at a big house before he became a valet, he knew how it should be done. And she gave the flowers in the hall and drawing-room a final tweak. March was a poorish time for flowers, too, but Aunt Alice was very good at flower-arranging and had given her hints. Anyway, she thought the daffodils and hyacinths looked cheerful and nice.

Ned joined her in the drawing-room in a rush just as the first of the guests reached the front door. Peggy and Martha dashed up from the kitchen to help Tomlinson with the coats and Daltry transformed himself into a butler to show the arrivals into the drawing-room. Jessie felt her smile rather stiff and nervous. Beside her, Ned cleared his throat and she realised that he was nervous too. Glancing sideways she saw him insert a finger inside his collar as though it was choking him. How handsome he looked in his evening clothes! Suddenly her nerves disappeared and she was only excited about this evening, pleased to be standing here in her own real home with her own real husband at her side.

With military promptness, the first guests to arrive were Major and Mrs Wycherley, and Jessie was glad because she knew them from her uncle's parties. Major Wycherley was the procurement officer at the Fulford barracks, but she knew him as a keen hunter and polo player. He was a smallish man with beautiful white whiskers, as lavish as the hair on his head was scanty: he was shining above and bushy below like a rock in a meadow. His wife was taller than him and younger, and surprisingly beautiful. Jessie had overheard younger officers speculating on 'how the old boy had caught her'.

'Your gown!' Mrs Wycherley exclaimed, as she took her hand. 'My dear, how glorious! You positively shimmer. Do tell me where you got it.'

'Paris,' Jessie said, pleased with both the question and the answer.

'Tell that at a glance,' Wycherley said, kissing her hand.

'Good to be here, m'dear. Morland – splendid idea to have a dinner party, dispel some of the gloom. Good show.'

The next guests were not quite so welcome to Jessie. Mr Stalybrass was a banker, with no conversation outside his business; his wife a sharp-eyed, discontented woman. She noticed the gown, too, and looked round for something to criticise. 'Did you do the flowers yourself? Ah, the rustic look, so unusual! Yellow is such a difficult colour. I should never have thought of putting blue with it.'

Jessie was old enough to know this was meant to hurt, but too young not to show it had succeeded. Mrs Stalybrass was satisfied and passed on to talk to the Wycherleys in a better humour.

Close behind came Mr Micklethwaite, the principal of Pobgee and Micklethwaite, York's largest law firm. Mrs Micklethwaite was comfortable and wealthily dowdy. She kissed Jessie's cheek and whispered, 'Pay no heed to her, dear, she's such a cat,' then said aloud, 'You look a treat. I don't think I've ever seen such a pretty gown.'

Jessie kissed the round, soft cheek gratefully, glad to have an ally. She had known the Micklethwaites all her life and felt easy with them. The rest of the company was unknown to her and, along with the army, banking and the law, represented York's biggest employers and – more to the point – purchasers of paper: Mrs and Mrs Pickles were railway, the Steads were printing, the Portwaines were in confectionery, and the last-comers, Sir Philip and Lady Surridge, owned several newspapers. These were not the kind of guests she was used to from her uncle's parties at Morland Place, where the company was drawn from landowning, farming, hunting and shooting, and the ranks of old family friends. It was an odd kind of reason for giving a dinner party, to her mind, but her mother had seemed to understand it, and had said that the guests would understand it, too. 'You will be inspected, and if you pass muster the word will be spread that the Ned Morlands are acceptable.'

So as the guests gathered to converse in the drawing-room, she did her best to fit in. At Morland Place the talk would have been about how the wet weather was affecting the lambing and the spring sowing, last week's point-to-point and the letting down of hunters. Here in her drawing-room these comfortable subjects did not immediately arise. The men were talking about the coal strike, by which they had all been affected.

For the past two years a sea of industrial unrest had rolled over the country. One strike after another had checked trade and curtailed profit. First the railway workers, then the boilermakers had gone out; then the terrible miners' strike had crippled South Wales in November 1910. In 1911 it was the seamen and firemen, and they had set off the dockers. Dock strikes beginning in London had spread through August, putting Liverpool and Manchester out of action, and then the railway unions went out as well, paralysing the country and leading to riots: troops had had to be brought in to restore order.

And now the miners had gone out again, and the effects of the lack of coal were being felt all over the country. It was calculated that two million men were idle because of it. Coal prices had gone sky-high. Transport was crippled. Ships were tied up in dock, unable to move. And everybody's business had suffered.

'The Government should take a harder line,' said Mr Pickles. 'Send the army in if necessary – eh, Major?' Major Wycherley bowed slightly in response and said nothing, but his expression showed what he, as a professional soldier, thought of that idea.

Mr Portwaine agreed with Mr Pickles. 'We can't allow a handful of fanatics to hold the country to ransom.'

'But is it just a handful?' Mr Stalybrass said. 'My fear is that if things go on as they are, we shall be overrun. The lower classes are getting too full of themselves, and the longer we allow it to continue, the nearer we come to revolution.'

'Revolution? Oh, surely not, sir,' Ned protested gently. 'The English character—'

'The English character is being corrupted by these damned socialists and agitators,' Stalybrass interrupted. 'The unions are full of them.'

16

'We should never have let them unionise in the first place,' Pickles mourned. 'What's your view, Sir Philip?'

Surridge had been holding aloof from the conversation. He and his wife were inclined to be above their company, and were suspending judgement on the Ned Morlands until they had seen more. So far evidence was mixed. The house was small, and though the servants seemed well trained there were not many of them; but giving a dinner party at all in these straitened times showed either daring or financial resources. He paused a moment, enjoying the silence in which his reply was awaited, and then said, 'It was a mistake to allow socialists into Parliament.'

Encouraged, Stalybrass capped him. 'We should never have given the lower orders the vote. They were quite content before; now they are prey to all manner of agitators and charlatans. Red revolution is what we shall have next, unless we take a firm stand. Red, bloody revolution.' And he emphasised the last words with his fist upon his palm.

On the distaff side, Jessie was out of her depth, for the ladies were talking about their houses and their schemes for decorating and furbishing them. She had grown up to view a house as the place that sheltered you when you could not be out of doors. You were given, or acquired, a few pieces of good furniture, you placed them for your comfort, and then you forgot about them. When the carpet wore through enough to trip you, you replaced it; when the curtains fell to pieces you bought new ones; and when various relatives died and left you a sideboard or a pair of vases you made room for them.

But 'homemaking' as these ladies knew it was something quite alien to her. They seemed always to be restlessly redecorating and rearranging, their ultimate aim to create an overall appearance, to which each separate item contributed. It seemed a bizarre preoccupation to Jessie. She tried for a moment to imagine her mother wondering whether a Georgian side-table 'went with' a Jacobean chest, or caring how her drawing-room 'looked', and failed utterly. Mrs Stalybrass, now, was talking about trying out in her house an 'effect' she had seen in a magazine, with every evidence of thinking it was important. Jessie realised she had entered another world. She was glad when Daltry came in and announced that dinner was served.

As they went through into the dining-room, there was a little flutter and coo of comment at the multitude of candles.

'How nice,' said Mrs Portwaine.

'But I see you have gas in the rest of the house,' said Mrs Stalybrass, making it sound like a criticism.

'Yes,' said Jessie, 'but I think it's nicer to dine by candle-light. My mother says gaslight makes the silver look dull and the food look bad.'

'I'm sure you're quite right,' said Mrs Portwaine. 'We ought to keep up these nice old customs. Gaslight is very well in its place, but the candles in here do make everything look nice.'

Jessie was afraid they were back to homemaking again, but fortunately Mrs Micklethwaite picked up another thread as they all took their seats. 'How is your dear mother?' she asked Jessie. 'I believe she's away from home at the moment? Visiting Mrs Ashley Morland, isn't it?'

'Yes,' Jessie said; and for the benefit of those who did not know, 'My sister Lizzie and her husband and family are going to America, and Mother's helping them pack up.'

'Pack up? Are they moving permanently, then?' asked Mrs Portwaine.

'Ashley has a job to do in Arizona, which he says will take about five years,' Jessie explained, 'but Mother's afraid they'll all like it so much out there they won't want to come back. They have little boys, you see, who are bound to think it all very exciting; and Ashley is American by birth. So Mother thinks she'll never see any of them again, and she wants to spend as much time with them as she can before they go.'

'When do they leave?' asked Mrs Stead.

'Next month. They're sailing on the *Titanic*, on her maiden voyage,' Jessie said, with a hint of pride. There was a murmur of interest. Everyone had read something about the new White Star liner, or seen an advertisement for her. She would be the most luxurious ship ever to sail the seas.

Everyone repeated what they'd read, and envied Lizzie's luck.

'But your uncle is going on her too, isn't he?' Mrs Micklethwaite said.

'Yes, just to New York and back,' said Jessie.

'He was invited by Mr Ismay, the director of White Star,' Ned added. 'Mr Ismay always goes on the maiden voyage of his ships, so that he can see how everything works, and he thought my father would like to go too, seeing that his factories provided all the linens and fabrics.'

'Well, I hope Mr Morland doesn't set too much store on going,' said Mr Pickles. 'With the shortage of coal, it's unlikely she'll sail. If this coal strike isn't settled soon, we shall all be stuck in one place, and nothing will move at all.'

'Even if the strike is settled,' said Stalybrass, 'the shortage won't end. Stocks are all used up, and it will take weeks, if not months, to replace them.'

As the meal progressed, Jessie found how different it was to be the hostess rather than a guest. At other dinners she had been to, she had concentrated on the food whenever the conversation was uninteresting to her. Tonight, as the person responsible, she found she was noticing everything simultaneously. She heard snatches of all the conversations going on. She noted the reaction of each guest to the food and wine. She answered polite questions about the wedding trip while simultaneously noting that one of the hired waiters had a stain on his glove and the other had a dewdrop. She saw out of the corner of her eye every step in the pavane of service, heard in the fabric of sound every extraneous clink, bump, murmur or cough from the servants. When Peggy stuck her head round the door to take a peek at the company and Daltry repelled her with a furious frown, Jessie saw, even though she was looking at Sir Philip at the time and asking him his views on the Irish question.

This new-found ability to see, hear and understand a multitude of things at once made her feel rather clever and grown-up. She was pleased to gather the impression that the party was a success. The food had turned out well, and though Mrs Stalybrass made complaints, disguised as compliments, about its simplicity, she knew it for a good dinner and saw everyone else enjoying it. And the conversation had not flagged for a moment.

She was so comfortable herself that when Ned caught her eye as she lingered over an apple she simply smiled back at him. It took a few glances and gestures of the head towards the door before she realised what he wanted. With an inward sigh – because Major Wycherley had been talking to Sir Philip about polo – she caught Lady Surridge's eye and stood up. She even managed to say, 'Shall we retire, ladies?' just as her mother did, and not feel entirely ridiculous about it.

There followed a tedious interval as she showed the ladies upstairs and then into the drawing-room, and then a further dull period of female conversation. They had got on to servants and children now, and inevitably the point came when someone asked Jessie whether she was expecting a child yet. The question was not put quite so bluntly, but Mrs Pickles – whose husband knew Uncle Teddy very well, as a fellow director of the railway – felt herself sufficiently close to the family to say, 'I expect your uncle is looking forward very much to being a grandfather. I wonder if you have any good news for him yet?'

Jessie, to her annoyance, blushed; but Mrs Stead saved her the necessity of answering by saying, 'Oh, children are a wonderful thing. I have a large family myself, and I always say there's nothing better for using up a woman's time and energy. I can't think what I should have done with myself if I hadn't had a family.'

'Young women these days don't think like that,' said Mrs Wycherley, smiling. 'They don't want to be slaves to the nursery when there's so much else to do.'

'They'll get themselves into trouble, that's all,' said Mrs Stead firmly. 'If a house and a family aren't enough, what'll they get up to? Nothing proper, I can tell you that.'

Lady Surridge rebelled against this domestic agenda. 'A woman of position has many other calls on her time,' she said coolly.

'Dancing, I suppose,' Mrs Stead said disapprovingly. 'This ragtime they all talk about. And picture-shows. And driving about in motor-cars.'

Lady Surridge looked even more crushing. 'I was talking of public service. My various committees take up a great deal of my time.'

'Oh, good works!' said Mrs Micklethwaite, and turned to Jessie. 'The Morlands have always done their share, haven't they, dear? Your mother is an example to us all.'

And so Jessie, to keep the conversation away from babies, told her about doing her mother's visiting, mentioned that she would like some visiting of her own. 'But of course if you don't have an estate, you don't have pensioners to look after, so it's more difficult. I mean, you have to look for good works to do.'

'There is plenty to *be* done,' Lady Surridge said, more approving now. 'I'm sure I could find a place for you on one of my committees.'

At that moment the door opened and the gentlemen came in, bringing with them the whiff of brandy, cigars and a wider world. Sir Philip and Major Wycherley came in together, deep in conversation. Lady Surridge, having regard to the quality of the rest of the men, hastened to ensure their superior company by addressing her husband. 'Don't you agree, Sir Philip?'

'My dear?' he said. He and the major walked over.

'Mrs Edward Morland has a desire to be useful. Don't you think she might join one of my committees? Which one do you think she would best suit?'

Sir Philip looked down at the young woman in the French beaded gown with evident doubt. 'It depends, I suppose, on her interests. *You* have so many, my dear – widows and orphans, education of the working man, better housing, cruelty to animals, first aid.'

Major Wycherley said, 'Mrs Morland had better pick first aid. It's something every citizen ought to know about. It will be needed when the war comes.'

There was a protest at this from several of the ladies within earshot.

'Not the war! No talk of war, if you please. There's nothing more tedious.'

'It will not happen, I assure you.'

'Germany would never attack England. The Kaiser and the King are cousins.'

But the major said, 'War is not only likely, it is inevitable. And it will find us lamentably unprepared.'

'I read a splendid yarn a while back,' said Mr Portwaine. '*A New Trafalgar*, it was called. By a fellow called Curtis, A. C. Curtis. All about the Germans invading England while the Channel Squadron was elsewhere. Stirring stuff. Of course, we trounced 'em in the end, with a new battleship they didn't know we had.'

'What about *The Riddle of the Sands*?' said Mr Stead. 'Have you read that?'

'Is that the one where the chaps come across the German plan to invade England? Yes, I've read that. And there was that one by a fellow with a queer name – can't remember it – called *The Invasion of 1910*. I like a good yarn. Nothing better than reading by the fire of an evening. As my wife will tell you, I'm a great man for books.'

'I read somewhere that there are German spies everywhere,' said Mrs Pickles, with wide eyes. 'Waiters, clerks, hairdressers and so on. Even schoolteachers. They send back reports to the Kaiser, so that he knows down to a bale of hay everything that lies between London and the coast.'

'We had a German waiter last time we went to London,' Mrs Portwaine remembered. 'Dear me! I suppose he must have been a spy – though I'm sure we couldn't have said anything that would help him.'

'Oh, my dear!' Mrs Pickles exclaimed. '*Everything* is a help to them. You simply don't know what use they'll make of the most *innocent* remark!'

'Now I come to think of it,' Mrs Portwaine added, 'there was a German clerk at the desk of that hotel in Leeds where we had dinner with a business acquaintance of Alfred's last month. To think they've reached as far as Leeds already!'

'He wasn't German, Sophy,' said Mr Portwaine. 'He was a Swiss.'

'Well, isn't that the same thing?' said Mrs Portwaine.

'Really, this is the most ridiculous scaremongering,' Sir Philip said. 'Spies and invasions! That dreadful book *The Invasion of 1910* was nothing but the crudest propaganda for introducing conscription and increasing the military budget.'

'I'm against conscription myself, of course,' said the major, 'but we do desperately need to increase the army if we are to avoid it. In the case of an invasion attempt by Germany we would be seriously outnumbered.'

'And then I suppose we would be overrun while we slept,' said Sir Philip scornfully, 'and wake the next day to find ourselves nothing but a small dependency off the coast of Teutonia, forced to eat sausages and sauerkraut for the rest of our lives.'

Mrs Pickles missed the irony, and shuddered. 'Oh, no, not for anything! I can't bear the smell of the stuff. It won't really come to that, will it?'

'I should hope not,' said Mr Pickles. 'Major, surely our British army can't be beaten?'

'The German army is seven hundred thousand strong,' said the major, 'and because all young German men have to serve some time in uniform, they can call on three million trained reservists. Our army numbers about two hundred thousand, most of it stationed abroad – in India, Africa, Egypt and so on – and our reservists about another two hundred thousand. I hardly need to underline the discrepancy. We should start now and put every effort into training volunteers and building up stores of arms and equipment. In that way we might be ready when the time comes.'

'But why should the time ever come?' Mrs Micklethwaite protested. 'I can't see why Germany should want to attack us.'

'They're more likely to attack France,' said her husband, 'as they did in 1870.'

This set the conversation off on to Alsace-Lorraine lines, and the womenfolk soon lost interest. Mrs Portwaine turned to Jessie and said, 'Tell me, Mrs Morland, where did you get that lovely piece of lamb? You must have a very good butcher.'

Jessie wrenched her attention back from Europe and answered, 'It came from Morland Place. I don't think my uncle would forgive me if I bought lamb from a butcher's shop.'

'Quite right too,' said Mrs Micklethwaite. 'The last piece I had from Black's was nothing but string – and I've always thought Black's the best of them.'

'Not Knowles's?' said Mrs Pickles.

'I've not used Knowles since he sent me those mouldy sausages. *Green* they were – I don't exaggerate.'

And the topic of the shortcomings of shops and shop-keepers lasted the distaff side very nicely until carriages were called.

When Ned came in from the dressing-room Jessie was undressed as far as her chemise, and was sitting before the glass while Tomlinson took out her pins. He leaned against the door frame in his spotted brown silk dressing-gown, and Jessie was reminded of the first time she had seen him in it, on their wedding night. Tomlinson withdrew the last pin, and Jessie put her hand over the brush as the maid reached for it and said, 'Thank you. I'll manage now. You can go to bed.'

Tomlinson slipped out, and Jessie began to brush out her hair. Ned said, 'Well, that went off all right.'

'Did you think so?' Jessie asked absently. She was staring at her own reflection, but not really seeing it; tired after the evening, her mind idling.

'Certainly. Didn't you?'

'Mm. But some of the guests were very dull.'

'Never mind. We've done our duty now. The next one can be for our own friends.'

'It had better not be until the strike's over. Mrs Stalybrass thought we were being extravagant.'

'Only with coal,' Ned said, and saw the corner of her mouth twitch in acknowledgement. He was tired too, and happy just to stand there and look at her. He loved the bright tumble of her hair, the smooth column of her neck, the tender shadows that slipped down into her chemise, where the top button was undone. He loved the lift of her arms and the way the movement of brushing made the shadows tremble softly under the fine cotton. A squeeze of passion gripped his vitals as he thought of drawing off that chemise, unveiling the secret, warm, rounded creature beneath. Every nerve of his body carried a memory of her, and of what it was like to love her. He would lay his lips to the tender swell of her breast; she would half close her eyes and he would kiss her eyelids. He loved her eyelids, which were like magnolia petals, curved and white and heavy. He loved her sweet breath and the damp coral cave of her mouth.

He knew she did not love him as he loved her. She had been in love with someone else, someone she could not have. Perhaps in some secret reach of her heart she still kept an image of the lost love. But she had married him; and when she lifted her mouth to his, and those heavy, soft eyelids slid down as if of their own weight, when her arms lifted round his neck and her breasts pressed against him, she was all his, and it made him more than completely hers. As he watched her dreamily brushing and brushing, he wanted to tell her these things, but he was a simple man, with no poetical vocabulary. He reached instead for action, in which he felt more at ease, for he had always had a comfortable knowledge of his body and his skills. He pushed himself away from the door and, as she turned her head enquiringly, held out his arms to her.

Jessie went to him, in a pleasant state of happy thoughtlessness. He looked so handsome, with his hair ruffled out of its daytime sleekness; his shoulders under the brown silk were broad. She loved the touch of his male hands on her bare skin. She wanted him and, knowing that he wanted her too, felt it a good and simple thing. She tilted her head up for his kiss, unaware of how profoundly the gesture moved him.

Lip to lip, he backed her to the bed, his hands working with blind sureness to remove the chemise and his own dressing-gown. Gently he laid her down, paused just for a moment like a swimmer about to slide into warm waters, postponing the moment of bliss; and her hands came up and tugged him down.

Later, hanging above her, he looked down at the seriousness of passion in her face, and knew himself blessed. She had been more than his equal before they married; she had come to him out of strength. There had been no conquering, but her readiness was in her lips and eyes, her openness to him. If she kept a small shrine somewhere for that other man, he did not care. It was nothing. She was his. She murmured something, and his bowels melted in flame. With a helpless small moan he came to her, and she sighed with accomplishment. When it was over, he kissed her quietly and laid his head against her neck. There seemed to him a great stillness at the heart of their relationship, which he reached at moments like this, as a man reaches a haven. His thoughts wound into themselves, slowed and stopped; and he was asleep.

CHAPTER TWO

The 1st of February 1912 had been an important day for Jessie's brother Jack, for it was the day on which the Sopwith School of Flying had opened at Brooklands. Jack had lost his former position as design engineer to Howard Wright when his company amalgamated with the Coventry Ordnance Works. His friend Tom Sopwith had rescued him, offering him the job of instructor at his proposed school.

Jack was a talented flyer, one of the pioneers – his Royal Aero Club certificate was number twenty-three – but he was equally interested in designing and building. Sopwith was a wealthy young man, passionate about aeroplanes and full of energy and ideas. He had told Jack that the job of instructor was only the beginning. The world of aeronautics was expanding so quickly there was no knowing what direction he would move in next – but whatever it was, he wanted Jack with him.

Jack was glad simply to be employed in the field of his choice. He loved to fly, and never tired of the thrill of leaving the ground behind; and when on the ground he enjoyed nothing more than tinkering about with the school 'buses', talking aeroplanes with Fred Sigrist, the engineer, and working out how to improve the performance of the flying machine. The teaching part he had regarded as a means to an end, but he discovered that he had a flair for it, and it was always pleasant to do something well.

His other flying duties were testing the aeroplanes when alterations or repairs had been made, and taking up passengers for pleasure flights. The latter was a lucrative exercise, and good advertisement for the school. Jack had even taken up several females, including, in late February, the wife of Captain Scott, the famous explorer, who even at that moment was on expedition in Antarctica attempting to reach the South Pole. Mrs Scott's trip had featured in the newspapers, with a photograph of her standing with Jack and the machine. Photographers were always hanging around the school for, with or without the presence of eminent people, flying was news. Jack was growing accustomed to seeing himself in the newspapers, though it was often only as an unrecognisable blur in the cockpit.

Another person he had taken up in February was a nice young man called Harry Fairbrother. He had been aeromad ever since Blériot had crossed the Channel, and for more than a year had been working away at his father – a prosperous trader who owned several grocer's shops in Weybridge, Chertsey and Addlestone – to let him have flying lessons. The first breach in the dam had been the pleasure flight, to which Fairbrother *père* had agreed on the 'get the damn nonsense out of your system' principle. But the first taste had only made young Fairbrother want more, and eventually Jack had been invited round to the Fairbrother house for dinner, so that the patriarch could inspect him and decide whether flying lessons would propel his son up the social scale or down.

'I've worked hard for my money,' Mr Fairbrother had said frankly to Jack, over the soup, 'and I'm well respected, but I wasn't a gentleman born and I've little education, so I can never get but so far in society. But my children have had all the advantages money can buy. I want to see them proper ladies and gentlemen, and I'll allow nothing that gets in the way of that. So this flying, now, Mr Compton – is it a genteel thing? It sounds rough and dirty to me, and I can't see what Harry will gain by it.'

Aware of Harry's pleading eyes fixed on him, Jack did his best, and mentioned all the flyers he could think of who were gentlemen in the sense that Mr Fairbrother meant. 'It has been an expensive business from the beginning,' he said, on an inspiration, 'so of course it has tended to be gentlemen of private means who could afford to become involved in it.'

This went down well. Jack was then subjected to a questioning about his own origins, which plainly made young Harry uncomfortable; but Jack was not offended, seeing in Mr Fairbrother only a straightforwardness and determination to get at the facts, rather than impertinence. The last thing Jack would do in normal circumstances was to boast about his family or connections, but for Harry's sake he mentioned that the Morlands were an old landed family, and that his grandfather had borne a coat of arms and had been a close friend of the Earl of Batchworth.

'Well, that sounds all right,' said Mr Fairbrother. 'And you seem a nice enough young man. But teaching in a flying school doesn't sound so high-up. I suppose you've no money, then, in spite of all your grandad's land?'

'Estates pass through the eldest son, sir,' Jack said, avoiding the direct question. 'Other sons and their sons have to earn their living.'

'Aye, well, I don't know that it's such a bad system,' Mr Fairbrother said, brightening a little. 'It doesn't do a man any harm to earn his way.' This was in direct contradiction to what he had said earlier, but as long as he was happy, it looked as though Harry would get his lessons.

Nothing more was said on the subject for the rest of dinner, and the conversation was general. Harry said little, sitting in a dream of bliss. The others at the table were his mother – a plump little brown mouse of a woman – two younger brothers, evidently longing to talk aeroplanes but kept in their place by family discipline, and his sister. Miss Fairbrother did not say very much, but she did not have to. She was ravishingly pretty, and it was all Jack could do to stop himself staring at her. Her hair was flaxen and arranged in elaborate and very distracting curls; her skin was alabaster, her eyes deep blue and frequently veiled by a downsweep of long eyelashes. Whenever he could legitimately address a remark to her, Jack did, and he felt that on those occasions she looked at him not without interest.

At the end of dinner they all retired to the fire in the

drawing-room – no separation of the women in this house-hold, for which Jack was very grateful. He decided there and then that it was a foolish habit and ought to be done away with. In the drawing-room Mr Fairbrother excused himself from conversation by taking up the newspaper, which he said he hadn't had a moment to read during the day on account of his business. Mrs Fairbrother invited Jack to the sofa to sit between her and her daughter, and her three sons gathered round. A more relaxed form of conversation could now take place, as long as they didn't speak too loudly, and they quizzed Jack about aeroplanes and his flying experiences until he protested that it must be very dull for the ladies.

'Oh, no,' said Mrs Fairbrother, 'I love to hear men's talk. Don't you mind me, my dear.'

And Miss Fairbrother, with a devastating flutter of her long eyelashes, said, 'I do find it interesting hearing about your adventures, Mr Compton. You must have led a very exciting life.'

Jack looked back over his life so far and regretted bitterly that it had not encompassed mountain climbing, tiger hunting, jungle exploration and possibly even polar expeditions so that he could keep Miss Fairbrother looking at him like that.

Harry Fairbrother had started his flying lessons at the beginning of March, and was getting on quite well. He was not what Jack would have called a natural flyer, but he was methodical and determined, and Jack was sure he would pass his certificate without difficulty. The relationship with the rest of the family had flourished. Jack had been invited again for dinner and once for tea, and had given the younger boys a guided tour around the Sopwith sheds at Brooklands, and allowed them to sit in the cockpit of the school Blériot so that they could pretend to be the great man himself.

One day in March Jack was waiting at the sheds for Fairbrother to arrive for a lesson. He was smoking a cigarette and chatting to Miss Ormerod. She was a cousin of Mrs Hewlett, who owned the flying school where Jack had taken his ticket, so he had known her for almost two years.

She was quite often at Brooklands, seeming to like hanging around the sheds, talking aeroplanes and watching the flying. Jack's dog, a disreputable-looking mongrel called Rug, was devoted to her.

'I do think it's a waste of your time to be teaching,' Miss Ormerod was saying. 'With the war coming, you ought to be concentrating on designing new aeroplanes.'

'If the war does come, we'll need to have trained flyers ready,' Jack countered.

'Perhaps. But teaching is something others can do. Only an inventor like you can create completely new aeroplanes.'

'An inventor?' he said, laughing. 'Is that what you call me?'

'The man whose mind can create things out of nothing – in a word, who can *innovate* – is the rarest and most valuable person in society.'

'I don't know that I innovate,' Jack said. 'Rather I tinker with things and try to make them better.'

'The wing shape on the Howard Wright biplane was an innovation,' she said. She was surprisingly knowledgeable about aeronautics. In fact, given the amount of time she spent at Brooklands, Jack ought not to have been surprised – but she was a female, after all.

'I'd call that an improvement,' Jack said. They often argued amiably. 'Now, if I could invent a completely new kind of engine – something much more powerful without being heavier . . .'

'You will, I'm sure of it,' said Miss Ormerod. 'Now that the Government is at last taking an interest in flying – oh, did I tell you that my uncle was talking to a Major Trenchard last week, who says that they are definitely going ahead with forming a specialist air division for the army?'

'No, you didn't. About time too! Tell me what he said.'

'They're going to detach the present Air Battalion from the Royal Engineers, and combine the balloons and airships with aeroplanes. And before you ask,' she anticipated with a smile, 'I've no idea how many or which kinds. But he did say there would be two separate sections – or I suppose one could call them wings?'

'One could, as long as there are only two,' said Jack. 'Sections of what?'

'Of the new corps – one attached to the army and one to the navy.'

'Pity. I hoped when they finally grasped the necessity they would make an independent air corps. Most of these army and navy types haven't the first idea about flying. How could they have?' Jack said, with frustration. 'It's a terrible waste of an opportunity.'

'You're too impatient,' said Miss Ormerod. 'Government minds move slowly. It's a great step forward that they're going ahead with the Flying Corps at all. Most military minds can't see what use aeroplanes will be anyway, except for artillery spotting – and even then they think a balloon will do just as well.'

Jack laughed, and stubbed out his cigarette. 'You're right,' he said. 'All the same, they had better learn quickly. There are only about two hundred people in the country with flying certificates, and few of them would be suitable for military flying.'

Rug put up his head and barked, and Miss Ormerod said, 'Here comes someone. Your pupil, I think.' Harry Fairbrother was approaching – with a dainty little figure hanging on his arm. 'And who is *that*?' Miss Ormerod said, in a *sotto voce* of disbelief.

'Fairbrother's sister,' Jack said. 'She is beautiful, isn't she?'

Miss Ormerod didn't answer that particular question. After a pause she said, 'I wonder she should think *that* is suitable attire for an airfield.'

'I think she looks charmingly,' Jack said. Miss Fairbrother was dressed in a pale pink skirt and jacket with a frothy lace jabot at the neck, an enormous hat covered all over with artificial roses, and a spotted veil tied under her chin.

He thought he heard Miss Ormerod murmur, 'Ridiculous!' but there wasn't time to query it as the couple were almost up to them.

'Am I late?' Fairbrother called. 'I'm so sorry. Myrtle decided at the last minute she wanted to come, and then she took ages to get ready. You know what girls are like.'

'The result was well worth any time it took,' said Jack.

Miss Fairbrother smiled. 'Why, Mr Compton, I didn't know you were such a gallant!'

'May I present? Miss Ormerod, Miss Fairbrother. Miss Ormerod, you know Mr Fairbrother.'

'Of course,' said Miss Ormerod. 'How do you do, Miss Fairbrother? You've come to cheer your brother along?'

'Harry's always making such a fuss about aeroplanes, I thought I'd come and see what was so wonderful about them.' She looked into the shed with an air of expecting mice or black beetles. 'Don't you keep them indoors?'

'When we're not using them, yes. But now they're all out on the field, over there,' Jack said.

'Oh. And which one of those things are you going to drive today, Harry?'

Fairbrother winced. 'I wish you wouldn't talk about *driving* them. And they're not things, they're flying machines, or aeroplanes.'

Miss Fairbrother observed them without ardour. 'I don't think they look very romantic. Why are they such a horrid colour? So drab and dowdy.'

'Dope,' Miss Ormerod said.

Miss Fairbrother's eyes opened wide. 'I beg your pardon?'

'Dope is what the canvas is treated with.'

'Oh, do you know about aeroplanes?' Miss Fairbrother looked her up and down. 'How very – clever of you. And what is dope?'

'It's the dressing used on the canvas,' Jack intervened. 'We use sago. That's why the machines are that colour.'

'Sago? Goodness! Well, if I were you, I would use blancmange in future, then you could have them all a lovely, pretty pink. It would look much nicer. I do love pink, don't you?'

Jack laughed, and gave Miss Ormerod a glance that said quite clearly, 'Isn't she enchanting?' And Miss Ormerod gave him an enigmatic look in return.

Fairbrother said, 'Don't stand there talking nonsense, Myrt. Mr Compton wants to get on with my lesson. What will I be flying today? The family tank?' This was what they called the Howard Wright biplane.

'No,' said Jack, 'I thought you might like to try something different today. We're going up in the American Wright.'

Fairbrother was pleased. 'Do you think I'm ready for it?'

'Of course.' Jack turned to Miss Fairbrother. 'Are you going to watch?'

'Oh, yes – if I can bear to. I'm sure I shall have to hide my eyes just at first, in case anything happens. I don't know how you dare to go up in one of those things. You must be so brave!'

'Oh, not at all,' Jack murmured, pleased. 'Now, where can we make you comfortable? I'm afraid the sheds aren't designed with ladies in mind.'

'I'll look after her,' Miss Ormerod said shortly. 'I'll bring that chair through from the galley.'

'I'll get it,' said Jack quickly. It was a wooden kitchen chair that had seen better days. Miss Fairbrother looked at it doubtfully. Everything in the immediate vicinity of an aeroplane seemed to get oil on it, and her pink outfit would show every mark. Quickly Jack took off his leather flying jacket, stripped off his pullover and laid that across the chair. Miss Ormerod gave him a sharp look, to which he replied saying, 'I shall be warm enough without.'

Miss Fairbrother seated herself daintily and Rug came up to sniff at her. She squealed and drew back.

'He won't hurt you. Don't you like dogs?' Miss Ormerod asked.

'Oh, yes, I love little doggies, but not big rough ones. Besides, he looks awfully muddy. I'm afraid he might put his paws on me.'

Jack said, 'I'll take him up with me.'

'Oh! Does he really go up in the aeroplane?'

'Yes. He loves it. I don't usually take him when I'm giving a lesson, but he *is* rather grubby, and he likes to be friendly. Come on, Rug! Are you ready, Fairbrother?'

The lesson followed its usual course, and while he was in the air, Jack forgot everything except the flying. The American Wright had dual controls, and Fairbrother was far enough advanced now for Jack to let him take over for most of the flight. Though a fitful sun was shining, it had little strength, and not enough to counteract the chill of the air rushing by. Jack missed his pullover; but he remembered the early days of flying, when there was no covered-in cockpit, and before special flying clothes had been developed. He remembered stuffing newspaper down inside his stockings for insulation – and still coming down with hands and feet like blocks of ice, all feeling gone from them.

Only when they were coming in to land did he think about Miss Fairbrother again. The way she had looked at him when she said he was brave had caused a definite flutter in his heart. Could she be interested in him? Flyers, he knew, had a certain aura of romance around them, which attracted the ladies. If she did fancy him, what would her father think of it? Old Fairbrother seemed to like him all right, but would he like him as a suitor? True, he didn't have much money, but he did have the blood Mr Fairbrother seemed to admire. He was 'genteel' – dreadful word!

Fairbrother put the aeroplane down with a bounce sufficient to jerk Jack back to the present and his duties, and he gave the nervous youngster calm instructions and helped him guide the machine back to its right place. As soon as they stopped, Rug jumped out and raced round and round barking, his usual reaction after a flight: Jack thought he was testing whether he really was back on solid ground. Then as Jack and Fairbrother jumped down he ran off to find Miss Ormerod.

Miss Fairbrother was on her feet when they reached her, her hands clasped together at her breast, and she flung herself at her brother's neck with a fine, dramatic effect. 'Oh! You're safe! My heart was in my mouth the whole time.'

'What on earth for?' Fairbrother said, disentangling himself. 'There's nothing to it, Myrt. Don't fuss so.'

'Oh, when you came down to earth again and the thing jumped up in the air like that, I thought you were done for. I positively screamed – didn't I, Miss Ormerod?'

'She did,' Miss Ormerod confirmed.

'Oh, Mr Compton, can't you persuade Harry to give up this terrible, dangerous business?'

Jack smiled. 'But consider, Miss Fairbrother, I earn my living teaching people to fly. It would be foolish for me to try to dissuade them, now, wouldn't it?'

'But it's so dangerous!'

'Not really. The American Wright, especially, is very reliable. Accidents do happen now and then, but generally no-one gets hurt. These aeroplanes glide very well, so we get down in one piece all right. And men will always seek out danger, you know. It's in our nature. If we don't find it in one place we'll seek it in another.'

She was gazing into his eyes as he said that, and seemed to find a message for herself in the words. She lowered her eyelashes prettily and said, 'Perhaps I could get used to aeroplanes, if I spent enough time around them. The one Harry was driving just now, what do you call it?'

'It's a Burgess Wright biplane – we call it the American Wright to distinguish it from the Howard Wright. Would you like to come and have a look at it? You could sit in it, if you liked.'

'I would love to come and see it – but the ground looks rather muddy, and I'm afraid . . .' She lifted the hem of her skirt the merest fraction and extended her foot to show the heeled boot of pink glacé kid.

Jack was enchanted. He had never seen such a dainty boot or such a tiny foot. He was filled with the desire to pick her up in his arms and carry her to the aeroplane. What a pity he did not know her well enough for that to be permissible! But her brother could do it. He turned a burning look on young Fairbrother, but the young man did not seem to understand. 'Yes, the ground is soft, and it would be a shame to ruin those pretty boots,' he said. But still Fairbrother did not jump to the rescue, and Jack was forced, sighing inwardly, to say, 'Perhaps when the ground is drier. If you would like to come another time, I should be delighted to show you all the aeroplanes. I would even take you up for a pleasure flight, if you liked.'

'Oh! No, I could never, never go up in one of those things,' Miss Fairbrother said, shuddering. 'Surely you don't take up women?'

'Of course, if they like to go.' He smiled. 'But you'd have to take off your charming hat. It would be snatched away.'

She looked seriously at him. 'But then one's hair would get blown about, and one would get untidy and dirty. No, Mr Compton, I think flying is for men only. But I would love to come and see your machines one day.'

'Any time at all that you like,' Jack said. 'I should be at your service.'

She smiled and extended her hand, and he was so swept away by her femininity that he found himself bowing over it in a way hardly seen, he thought afterwards, in these modern times.

As she and her brother stepped away down the cinder path, Jack sighed and said to Miss Ormerod, 'Isn't she wonderful?'

Miss Ormerod, caressing Rug's ears – she had had a hand on his collar the whole time in case he should try to be too friendly to Miss Fairbrother – said, 'Is she?'

'She's so dainty and sweet. Those tiny feet and hands – almost like a doll's. I can hardly believe she's real.'

'Nor can I.'

Jack detected something a little less than approving in Miss Ormerod's voice and turned to look at her, a little hurt. 'Don't you like her?'

'Like her?' Miss Ormerod seemed lost for words. Then she said, 'Whatever possessed her to come to an airfield dressed like that?'

'I thought she looked lovely.' He surveyed Miss Ormerod's tweed skirt and coat and her neat but strong boots, which could stand a spot of mud, and saw her point. 'Not very suitable, I grant you, but how would she know, when she's never been here before?' Miss Ormerod only sighed at this, and he went on, 'It's a pity she doesn't want to go up, but I suppose a delicate female must have reservations about something so rough and dirty. She's right, really, that it's a man's business.'

'I would,' said Miss Ormerod.

'You would what?'

'I'd go up. But you've never asked me.'

He was embarrassed. 'I'm sorry. I suppose I thought you'd ask if you wanted to. We know each other well enough not to stand on ceremony.'

'Almost like brother and sister,' she said, and he agreed gladly; only thought afterwards there was something odd about the way she said it, as though perhaps she was being ironic.

White Star's *Olympic*, the largest and most luxurious thing afloat, had had an unlucky time since her maiden voyage in June 1911. At the end of that first crossing of the Atlantic she had trapped a tug under her stern while docking and almost sunk it. On her fifth crossing in September she had been in collision with a navy cruiser when leaving Southampton Water and had sustained serious damage to her stern and starboard propellor from the cruiser's under-water ram. And in February 1912 on her way back from New York she had passed over a submerged obstacle on the Grand Banks at twenty knots and shed a blade from her port propellor.

All these accidents meant that she had spent weeks in the graving dock undergoing repairs, and had missed many of her scheduled crossings, causing considerable financial loss to her owners. It had also delayed the completion of her sister ship *Titanic*: there was only one dry dock at Belfast large enough to take them, so they had to take turns in it. After the navy-cruiser accident, the *Titanic*'s starboard propellor, ready but not yet fitted, had been put instead into *Olympic*, and the younger sister had had to wait for a new one to be manufactured.

So it became imperative for the company that a great fuss be made about the maiden voyage of *Titanic* so that as many passengers as possible should be attracted, and the Olympic class as a whole should in future be the ships of choice for the New York crossing. A flurry of advertising brought attention to the revised sailing date for *Titanic* – the 10th of April – and described the ship as even larger and more splendid than her sister, and far more sumptuous in every way than the rival Cunarders, who might hold the Blue Riband for the fastest crossing, but could never hold a candle to the White Stars for luxury.

It was extremely unfortunate, therefore, that the maiden voyage should take place at a time when the coal strike had caused so many travellers to cancel or postpone their journeys. Passengers, simply, were in short supply.

'I'm afraid she's only going to be half full,' Teddy Morland said. He had dined with Joseph Bruce Ismay, head of the White Star line, at his house in Hill Street, Mayfair, and had returned to Lizzie and Ashley's house in Bloomsbury where he was to spend the night before going home to York. 'Ismay tells me they are transferring passengers from other White Star ships to fill up second class. Second class in *Titanic* is better than first class in the older liners, so they won't lose by it.'

'It won't make any difference to us, will it?' Lizzie asked.

'No, no,' Teddy said. 'By George, I tell you I'm looking forward to the trip! My father's the only one in the family who ever went to America, and he went across as a passenger on a cargo ship, so there was no luxury in it for him. How things have changed! And what a wonder of an age we live in. Ships like the Olympic class were beyond imagination twenty years ago.'

Henrietta, sitting by the fire sewing a dress for Lizzie's daughter Rose, who was three, as a going-away present, thought of something and asked, with an unconscious edge of hope, 'But how will they manage for coal? Don't you think the sailing will be cancelled after all?'

'No,' said her brother. 'They'll take the coal off the other White Star ships laid up in port; and *Olympic* is bringing back as much extra as she can carry in bags from New York to transfer to *Titanic*. Don't worry, she'll sail all right.'

Lizzie smiled. 'Mother's really rather hoping she *won't* sail – aren't you?'

Henrietta looked up from her stitching. 'I wouldn't be so dog-in-the-manger. I know how much you are looking forward to going.'

Lizzie knew what was in her mother's mind, but was too honest to hold out false hope. 'If we were to stay in America,' she said, 'you could always come over and visit us.'

39

'It's such a long way,' Henrietta said. She couldn't imagine herself ever voluntarily travelling so far, let alone across the wild Atlantic on a ship, and then by train through a vast land full of wild buffaloes and wilder Indians. 'I'm too old for that sort of thing.'

'Oh, Mother! You aren't old at all!'

'In any case,' Teddy added, 'travelling these days is as safe and comfortable as sitting at home in your own armchair. You don't have to brave hardships and highwaymen, you know, Hen.'

Henrietta only smiled and shook her head. Would she ever see them again, she wondered silently: Lizzie, her first-born daughter, so dear, so clever; and kind Ashley; and the boys, Martial and Rupert, who were thirteen and twelve and clever like their mama; and little Rose? Perhaps they would come back and visit one day; but the children would be grown-up by then, strangers who did not really remember Gran'ma. And a visit was not the same as having your loved ones nearby, to be seen whenever you wanted.

The house was already looking bare, as furniture and belongings that were going to America were packed up and other things sold. They had been lucky that the lease expired in December anyway, and the new tenant wanted to move in early and was willing to pay them for the eight months from May, so they had lost nothing on the house.

'It has worked out so well, it's almost as if it were meant to be,' Lizzie said to Lady Anne Farraline, who called the next day, after Teddy had left.

Anne was a distant cousin. Lizzie had first met her, when a child, at the home of her mother's friend and cousin Venetia, Lady Overton. Lizzie had conceived an instant 'crush' for the dazzling, energetic, articulate young woman. Anne had devoted her life to the cause of women's suffrage, and was so passionate for it she had carried the impressionable Lizzie along with her. As a young woman, Lizzie had had so much intellect and energy, she had needed something more to occupy her than domestic routines. She had given her support to the WSPU, joined demonstrations, and once, to her mother's distress, had served a gaol sentence for protesting at the House of Commons.

It had been a sobering experience; and her duty to her husband and the increasing demands of marriage and motherhood, including the unexpected birth of little Rose, had made her give up active campaigning. Her heart and mind were with the Cause, but it seemed right and proper to her now that her body remained respectably at home.

Anne had never married. Lord Padstowe, who had faithfully loved her through many years of rejection, had finally married someone else and was now a dear and platonic friend. Anne, like her fellow militants, wanted a world in which women were completely the equal of men. Domestic surrender was a betrayal of a woman's intellect and her God-given right of self-determination. If ever Anne had doubted the truth of that, she only had to look at Lizzie – who was clever and well educated – contentedly ordering her household and playing with her baby. Ashley was a very nice man, even quite forward-thinking when it came to women, but he still expected his comfort to come first, and his wife to minister to his needs, not her own.

At the beginning of March there had been a mass stone-throwing protest by the militant suffragettes: the windows of shops, clubs, government offices and the homes of some MPs had been broken. There had been a huge number of arrests, and Christabel Pankhurst had fled to France to escape arrest for conspiracy. Anne had escaped with a few others by hiding under the floorboards of Mrs Garrud's ju-jitsu gymnasium in Oxford Street.

A special meeting of West End firms and traders had been called to discuss how they could save their windows another time. Ashley had had a large notice put in the window of the main office of the Culpepper Shipping Line – his employer – in Piccadilly, which said, 'We are sending people where women have the vote. Avenging angels, please pass over!' It won him amused approval from Anne, who appreciated a joke.

Lizzie said now, 'I'm very glad you are not in prison, dear Anne. I should have hated to leave England without seeing you.'

'I envy you in a way,' Anne said. 'America is so much more advanced than England, when it comes to women. Although,' she added, with a frown, 'I suppose that may not be true of frontier places. I suppose where people are scrabbling for a living in hostile surroundings, the man will still take pride of place.'

'Ashley assures me that where we're going is a perfectly civilised town. I suppose it may be a little wild in between towns, but Flagstaff has restaurants and a theatre and electricity and everything, and the railways are splendid.'

'But still, attitudes in small towns always lag decades behind those in big cities. I'm sure that must be true of America as it is here. Flagstaff will not be like New York or Boston, and the Flagstaffians will expect you to be a good little wife, and not have too much going on inside your head.'

Lizzie smiled. 'Well, I shall certainly try to be a good little wife – and a good little mother. But the burghers of Flagstaff won't be able to stop me reading, writing and corresponding just as before.'

'Oh, won't they?' said Anne. 'You are spoilt, my love, with living in London. In provincial places the other wives will certainly stop you doing anything so solitary as reading, by constantly visiting you to drink endless cups of tea and indulge in pointless chatter. And they'll expect you to call on them in return. And if you refuse to conform you'll become a social outcast and Ashley will take you to task because his business will suffer. Either that,' she added, appearing to reflect, 'or you'll all be eaten by bears.'

Lizzie laughed, and exclaimed, 'Oh, Anne! I love the way you talk. I shall really miss you.' She drew a breath and said more soberly, 'You will write to me?'

Anne looked at her sadly. 'You won't ever come back, will you?'

Lizzie met her eyes. 'I think of the boys, you see, and the opportunities there will be for them in America. Ashley expects us to be there at least five years, and Mart will be nineteen by then and Rupert eighteen, and they'll be at college, and the world will be opening up for them. If they find wonderful careers and decide they want to stay there for ever – well, it would be hard to leave them to come back here.'

'Especially if they marry,' Anne said drily, 'and make you a grandmother. You see how these husbands and families make hostages of women, and drag them in their wake wherever *they* want to go?'

'But it isn't like that,' Lizzie said, rather helplessly, for she always saw Anne's side of the argument, and only *felt* the contrary position. 'It's a matter of love, really,' she said.

Anne smiled. 'Oh, love! Well, you married people always have us there, don't you? You can counter any argument with "love" and we have to bow before the mystery and give you best.'

Lizzie smiled too, and said, 'Well, I *love* you, and I hope you love me enough to come out and visit us when we are settled. Do say you will! Only think what an adventure for you! And of all the people I would want to come, you are the one who could easily afford it. And if you find Flagstaffians ignorant of the Cause, you can make it your task to educate them. You might even find you like it enough to stay.'

'Oh, I think not. Small towns and small minds would drive me mad,' Anne said.

Lizzie looked a little hurt – Anne was not the most tactful of people. 'I didn't think my mind was too small for you even to come on a visit.'

'Darling,' Anne said, eyeing her shrewdly, 'I would love to come and visit you, but would you be happy to include Vera in the invitation?'

'Miss Polk?' Lizzie said, puzzled. 'I hardly know her.'

Vera Polk was a young suffragette, daughter of a shoemaker, who had become a close friend of Anne's, and had even gone to live in her house. It had caused a sensation when Anne had sent away her respectable elderly companion in favour of a girl who by no measure could count as a chaperone. Lizzie had been angered by some of the whisperings of disapproval, which seemed to be aimed at the friendship itself, rather than the question of chaperonage.

She supposed people were objecting on account of Anne's being the daughter of an earl while Miss Polk was a nobody – an attitude she felt was incompatible with the aims of the Movement.

But Anne's question now took her aback. Surely she was not so inseparable from Miss Polk that she could not visit a relative without her? She frowned at Anne. 'Why do you ask? Do you think she would be so eager to come? But surely she could not expect you to take her at such expense just because you are friends?'

'Lizzie, wake up!' Anne said impatiently. 'What I'm saying is that *I* wouldn't want to come without her, any more than, in the same circumstance, you would want to come without Ashley.'

'But Ashley's my husband,' Lizzie said. 'It's very different.'

'What I'm saying to you,' Anne persisted, 'is that it isn't.'

'Isn't what?'

'Isn't different. What you and Ashley are to each other, Vera and I are to each other.'

'Well, I know you are good friends—'

'We are married in everything but law,' Anne said, looking steadily at Lizzie. Since she and Vera had come together, she had met with different reactions among the suffragists. Most of her close circle, the 'hotbloods', were accepting, some even approving, feeling that it was the logical extension of the fight for freedom from man's oppression. Outside their circle there were those who shrugged, those who turned a blind eye, those who were uneasy, feeling that anything that might engender hostility towards the Cause was to be avoided, and those who were downright disapproving.

And there were also those who simply did not see what was under their noses. Lizzie, it seemed, was one of them. The exact nature of Anne's relationship with Vera was beyond her education or experience to understand. Probably the majority of people in the country would fall into the same category. It was something that worked in Anne's favour for most of the time, but she was sometimes frustrated by it, as in the present case. It was ironic, given that Lizzie's first fiancé had had tendencies himself, and had almost been caught up in the Oscar Wilde scandal. But, then, Anne was not convinced that Lizzie had ever understood about Dodie – and since he had redeemed his reputation by marrying a woman chosen by his father, it was possible Lizzie still thought his love for her had failed because of her lack of dowry.

Well, Anne decided, it was not for her to attempt to enlighten her young cousin. Explaining matters to Lizzie was something she shrank from, though she felt she ought to be ashamed of shrinking. But she loved Lizzie and wanted her love in return, and the fear that if Lizzie did understand she might draw back in horror was a great deterrent. So, with an inward apology to Vera, she gave it up, and when Lizzie said, in reply to her last statement, 'I don't understand. Is it a joke?' she smiled. 'Oh, a joke of sorts,' she said. 'I just mean I should miss her if I came out for a long visit with you.'

'Well,' Lizzie said, though still a little doubtfully – for Anne had seemed to be very serious, though about what she was not sure, 'I'm sure we could have Miss Polk as well. Ashley says that American houses are very big, so there'd be sure to be room.' Inwardly she recalled that the one time she and Ashley had met Miss Polk, Ashley had been very disapproving of her afterwards, saying that she was just the sort of brash, rough-speaking, mannerless female that gave the Cause a bad name. Probably Ashley would object very much to inviting her to stay; but she determined to worry about that if and when it happened. She would not let anything approaching a disagreement spoil the last hours she would spend with Anne for, probably, a long time.

CHAPTER THREE

The weekend before their departure for America – which was Easter weekend – Lizzie and Ashley and the children went down to Yorkshire for a farewell visit to the family. So much of their household had been packed up that two days at Morland Place would be a relief from inconvenience and discomfort. Ashley had to return to London early on Monday for business purposes, but suggested that Lizzie should stay with the children until Tuesday and take an afternoon train to London, where they were to spend the last night before catching the boat train on Wednesday morning.

'There's no point in your going back to the house in the state it's in, when you could be comfortable at Morland Place and spend more time with your mother. I shall be working until late in any case.'

'But how will you eat?' Lizzie asked. The cook had left on Friday, and she had secretly been dreading two days of cooking for her family.

'I can eat at the club,' Ashley said. 'Really, it would be a relief to me not to have to worry about you.'

Lizzie was glad to have an extra day and a half in which to say goodbye to the house and grounds she had become so attached to. There was something *about* Morland Place. It was not her childhood home, but it had been her mother's, and she (like Ashley, who was also a Morland) had grown up with stories of it, so enhanced by her mother's wistful longing that she had come to think of it as a sort of Eldorado. Those born to it would always carry it in their hearts.

Uncle Teddy had devoted much of his commercial and

industrial fortune to restoring the house and buying back the lost lands, sold during his brother's disastrous tenure. He now ruled as a benign and generous king in his small kingdom, which encompassed everything he wanted from the world.

With the house and its lands complete, Teddy had concentrated on filling it with as many of the people he loved as possible. When he had taken a new wife, Henrietta had thought she would have to go, on the rule that a house could not have two mistresses. But Alice was a gentle, retiring, and gracefully indolent woman who was perfectly happy for Henrietta to continue running the house, while she devoted herself to needlework, arranging flowers, playing the piano and looking nice.

To Teddy's daughter from his first marriage, Polly, had soon been added a new son from Alice, little James William, now two years old. Teddy had been sorry when Henrietta's eldest and youngest sons, Jack and Frank, had left home in pursuit of their careers, but when the middle son, stay-at-home Robert, had married, he had persuaded him and his new wife Ethel to live at Morland Place. They had now added baby Roberta to the nursery, and Ethel was expecting again.

If only Teddy could have persuaded his adopted son Ned to stay on at Morland Place when he married Jessie, he would have had nothing more to wish for. But Ned had wanted an independent home. Still, Teddy comforted himself, Jessie was at Morland Place so often that he sometimes forgot she was no longer resident; and marriage did not seem to have changed her at all. She was still the same cheerful, straightforward, loving niece she had always been.

Frank came down to Morland Place for the 'farewell weekend', as he dubbed it. While he was studying at University College, London, he had lodged with Lizzie and Ashley. He had become so much a part of the family that he was virtually an elder brother to the boys, had pushed Rose in her perambulator, and had flung himself into Lizzie's suffragette interests. When he finished his degree he had obtained a 'temporary' post as librarian at the London School of Economics, and as Lizzie and Ashley had seemed in no hurry to be rid of him, he had stayed on in their house. He was a brilliant mathematician, but as physically indolent as he was mentally active, so the temporary post and the status of lodger had looked to become permanent. Now, however, he had been forced to find a new place to lay his head. He had taken rooms in Gower Street, and the upheaval had even got him as far as talking about changing his job, though Lizzie doubted he would get further than talking.

'But if you ever do bring yourself to make the break,' she told him, 'you could do worse than follow us to America. Ashley says a young man with a good brain can really make something of himself out there.'

Frank listened to her with a faint smile, then said in that teasing way of his, which always left one in doubt as to whether or not he was serious, that if he saved hard, he could probably raise enough to come out steerage along with the Irish emigrants.

Jack arrived very late on Friday night, and found everyone had gone to bed but Jessie and Lizzie. They were on the sofa in front of the drawing-room fire, chatting in a desultory way, alone except for Brach, who got to her feet and came politely to greet him. The excited Rug spun round her in circles, and dashed back and forth between the women, not knowing whom to lick first.

'Ned and I are staying here for the weekend,' Jessie explained. 'Uncle Teddy said it was silly to travel back and forth when we'd want to be here every minute. And I couldn't wait until tomorrow to see you, dear old Jack.' She hugged him hard. He had been her hero and favourite when they were children. 'Hello, Rug, you old varmint,' she said, receiving the dog's lavish greetings, rubbing his cheeks between her hands in a way that made him swoon with delight. 'Ned sends his regards and he'll see you tomorrow. He couldn't stay awake any longer after a long day at the mill.'

'Nor can I,' said Lizzie, fending off Rug's desire to lick her face. 'I'm sure having ten conversations at the same time is more tiring than running any old mill!' She stifled a yawn. 'Loath as I am to waste any moment of my last hours at Morland Place, I simply can't keep my eyes open any more.'

'Old age,' said Jessie. 'I can't believe you'll be forty this year.'

'Nor can I,' said Lizzie. 'But it will come to you, too, you heartless infant. Wait until you've been married fifteen years and have three children. The day will come when the lure of sleep will be stronger than any desire to see in the dawn.'

'Oh, I pray not,' said Jessie.

'Anyway,' Lizzie said, kissing her brother, 'I've seen Jack more recently than you. I'll leave you to enjoy him in peace. Goodnight, children. Don't forget to see to the fire – remember, the servants have all gone to bed.'

It was not quite true. Lizzie passed Emma in the doorway. She had been nursemaid to Jessie and her brothers, and was now taking care of the new generation of babies in the Morland nursery. She had been with Henrietta's family through bankruptcy and ruin, and was now something of an institution. 'What are you doing still up?' Lizzie said, but didn't pause to hear the answer.

'I came to see if I could get Mr Jack anything,' Emma said. Over the years her broad Norfolk accent had faded gently, but was still evident.

'You came to see Mr Jack,' Jessie amended. 'He always was your favourite.'

'Nurseries don't have favourites, you know that,' Emma said sternly. But the way she looked at Jack belied it.

He crossed the room to give her a hug. 'I'll be here for a couple of days. You didn't need to stay up. I'd have come up first thing tomorrow to see you.'

'But you must be hungry, arriving so late. Mrs Stark has gone to bed, but I could get something cold for you. Or there's some soup left over I could heat up. Or I could make you an omelette. You know how you always liked my omelettes.' When they had been poor, Emma had cooked for them as well.

'Thanks, but I had something on the train,' Jack said. 'You go off to bed, Emma dear, and I promise I'll come and admire your babies in the morning.' He gave her a smacking kiss on the cheek to make her laugh, but she went away reluctantly, still convinced that anyone who had undertaken a journey must be in danger of starving to death unless instantly fed.

When they were alone, Jessie curled up in the corner of the sofa and patted the seat beside her. 'Get yourself a drink and then come and tell me all. I'm not a bit sleepy – are you?'

'Oddly enough, no. I suppose it was the walk from the station that perked me up. Yorkshire air is very invigorating, somehow.'

'It's the Morland Place air,' Jessie said. 'York smells of soot and horses, like everywhere else.' She watched him ply the whisky decanter. 'Pour me a small one.'

He turned with raised eyebrows. 'Jessie! I'm shocked.'

'Oh, fiddle! Just a small one, and never in company. Why should it be exclusively for men? Anyway, what did you think I carry in my flask when I'm out riding?'

'I didn't even know you had a flask,' Jack said, pouring a small whisky for her. 'Soda?'

'No, thanks. I always carry a flask, just in case.'

'In case of what?'

'Emergencies, of course. I suppose it ought to be brandy but I tried it once and couldn't like it.' She received the glass from him and he sat in the other corner of the big leather chesterfield, while Rug settled himself with Brach before the fire with a pleased sigh. The other dogs had already been banished to the hall for the night, so they had it to themselves. 'So how is everything?'

'Oh, going well,' Jack said. 'We've got all four of the school buses working now, and plenty of pupils coming in. Our very first graduate should get his certificate in a week or two – bright chap called Young. And it won't be long before the competition season starts. Tom Sopwith means to enter for everything going, and we'll share the flying between us. And, most importantly of all, we're working on the design of a new tractor biplane that we're going to build ourselves.'

'He did promise you your talents wouldn't be wasted, didn't he?' Jessie said. 'And you always wanted to design flying machines.'

'Yes,' said Jack. 'So all in all, everything with me is flourishing.'

'Everything?' she asked significantly.

'Pretty much,' Jack admitted.

Jessie laughed. 'What's her name?'

'Miss Fairbrother. She's as beautiful as an angel.'

'They always are, Jackie darling!'

'But this one's different.'

'You always say that, too.'

'But I mean it this time. She's tiny and dainty – you never saw such little hands and feet! – and so sweet and innocent. And I really think she likes me.'

'Why shouldn't she?'

'And, before you ask, I know her family and they like me too. I'm teaching her brother to fly, and her father invites me to dinner. He made his fortune in trade, and wants his daughter to marry a gentleman, so *that*'s all right.'

Jessie laughed. 'A gentleman *and* a flyer, what more could anyone want? So, how far has it gone with Miss Fairbrother? Or is it just dinner with her parents?'

'No, she's come to the field several times to watch her brother's lessons and he's brought her to see me flying – though I can't persuade her to let me take her up. And I've taken her out to tea and for a drive twice – in the company of her brother and Miss Ormerod, so it was quite respectable. And I've been invited to a bridge party with some neighbours of her parents, and she's asked me to be her partner. So, you see, it's all going swimmingly.'

Jessie studied her brother's face, remembered previous 'angels' in his life, and said seriously, 'Do be careful, though, won't you? I should hate you to marry the wrong person just because – well, because you were excited and didn't think about it properly. Once you're married, you can't change your mind, you know.'

Jack looked at her with raised eyebrow. 'What is it? Aren't you and Ned happy? Surely you're not regretting it?'

'Oh, Lord, of course we're happy,' she said. 'I don't regret it a bit. Ned's a dear old, kind old thing, and the—' She stopped herself, reddening, on the brink of mentioning the bed thing. 'I mean, marriage itself is lovely. It isn't a bit the way you think, but it's wonderful. And I like playing house and so on. But there's no denying it's a big step. Easily in but not easily out, as the lobster said of the lobster pot.'

'Wise words from an aged sibyl,' Jack said. 'I shall be sure to mark and remember them.'

'Ned and I are all right, because we know each other so well, but what if you married a stranger and, say, had a quarrel and didn't know how to make it up? What then? Although,' she added, when Jack didn't answer, 'I suppose it would be different for you, being a man. There's not much a wife could do to make you uncomfortable.'

Jack smiled. 'You have a strange view of the comparative power of men and women. Miss Fairbrother can punish me instantly with a frown for any little mistake I might make.'

'But that's *before* you're married. Once you've got her properly wed, you'll expect your dinner on the table and retreat behind the newspaper just like all men.'

Jack laughed at that. 'What a picture you paint! Don't tell me Ned has turned into such a caricature already, after three months of marriage.'

'No, of course not,' Jessie said, colouring a little. 'I didn't mean that.' Rug had come to see what the laughter was about, and shoved his head into her hands for more of that delicious rubbing. 'I'm only saying that it's easy to get married without thinking it all through. It isn't just as straightforward as you may think, and I'm glad I did it with someone I knew very well beforehand.'

'Come on, Jess, I know when you're being less than frank. What's happened?'

'Nothing, I tell you.' She made a face. 'We had a dinner party for people important to his business. Oh, it was dull! I had nothing to say to any of them. What sort of people don't ride, and talk about refurbishing their houses all the time?'

'The town-bred middle classes,' Jack said. 'Which, I presume, was what your guests were.'

'But why should people give Ned business just because we have a dinner party and pretend to be like them?'

'That's more than I can answer. It's just the way the world is.'

Jessie sighed. 'I know. I understand I've got to do it, but I think it's perfectly silly.'

'Poor girl!' Jack said. 'What a life!'

'Oh, I'm not so badly off,' Jessie admitted. 'I have the stables and the horses and all the Morland lands to ride over. Imagine having to live in a town! Oh, Jack, you should have seen the boys, Martial and Rupert. They were like dogs let off the leash. I'm so glad Lizzie is staying until Tuesday, so that they can enjoy it here a little longer.'

'I don't think you need to feel sorry for them. They're going on the greatest adventure of their lives – with a journey on the most magnificent ship on the ocean thrown in.'

'I'd sooner be here than crossing the Atlantic on *any* ship,' Jessie said. 'On a train journey you've got the scenery going past, but what will there be for them to look at but miles and miles of water?'

'I think the point about the *Titanic* is that you look inward, not outward. From what I gather she's so big and well appointed you wouldn't even know you were at sea.'

'Well, then,' said Jessie, with some triumph, 'what's the point of going at all?'

'Until the day we design an aeroplane that can fly that far, it's the only way to get to America,' Jack pointed out.

'True,' said Jessie. 'And since that day is not likely to come in our lifetimes...' She stretched and said, 'I'm going to take the boys out riding tomorrow morning. Will you come?'

'That would be jolly – if you've something for me to ride?'

'I'll find you something nice. We have to go early, though – I promised Polly I'd meet her from the train.' Polly was at school in Scarborough.

'Universal aunt, that's you!' Jack smiled. 'When are you going to have some little ones of your own?'

'Now don't you start on that,' she scowled. 'Honestly, the way Mother and Emma eye me up and down every time they see me is positively agricultural!'

On Easter Saturday afternoon the whole family, including Martial, Rupert and Polly, removed itself in three motorcars to the village of Bishop Winthorpe, on the other side of York, for a visit and early dinner at the Red House. This was the residence of Sir Percival Parke, always known as

Bertie, who was the son of Henrietta's late sister. Bertie had had a bad relationship with his father, and so had spent a great deal of his adolescence at Morland Place, and Henrietta always thought of him as her 'extra son'. He had married Maud Puddephat, daughter of an old friend of Teddy's, and she was now expecting their first child.

Maud and Bertie were waiting in the great hall to greet their guests, along with Maud's father Richard, who had retired from business when they married and now divided his time between the Red House and his home in London. He took hold of Teddy's hand to shake it and did not let it go, using it to draw Teddy aside and into conversation. He was not enjoying idleness as much as he had expected and needed the talk of men. Bertie took Henrietta in his arms for a tender embrace, then searched her face and said, 'What is it? I know that look.'

'It's nothing. Nonsense. What look?' Henrietta said unconvincingly, avoiding his eyes.

He continued to survey her. 'Is it Lizzie? You don't want her to go?'

She gave a nervous laugh. 'You always were quick about people, Bertie dear. But don't say anything. I wouldn't spoil it for them.'

He squeezed her hand. 'We'll have a long talk later.'

She moved along to Maud, and Jessie and Ned were before him. He shook hands with Ned and asked how business was going. 'This coal strike must be hitting you as well as everyone else.' And then he looked at Jessie. He had been deliberately keeping his eyes from her until then, though he had known exactly where she was in the room from the moment she entered, and without looking at her had seen every movement and gesture as she gave up her coat and hat to a maid, brushed her skirt straight, looked around her, walked towards him with Ned.

He looked at her, and their eyes met and locked like two magnets that had just passed the critical point. He saw a faint blush rise, but she was otherwise composed, far more composed than he was. She even turned up her face for a cousinly kiss, while Ned watched her with proprietorial pride. Bertie laid his lips to her cheek, and closed his eyes for an instant against the agony of longing that swept over him. But as he straightened he smiled a commonplace smile and said, in what he felt was a completely normal voice, 'You look lovely. New gown?'

'She does, doesn't she?' Ned said quickly, before she could answer. 'Don't you think that colour suits her? It was one we bought in Paris on our honeymoon.'

The word was innocently said, but it stabbed Bertie sharply; as did the quick glance Jessie gave Ned, a small, complicit, everyday look such as passed between young married people who have a newly shared mystery between them. He saw she was happily involved in her marriage, and he forced himself to be glad for her. He would not have her repine, be miserable, long for him as he longed for her. He wanted her to have a normal life, a happy life. But it hurt all the same.

The family spread out, conversation flourished, groups formed and re-formed. The boys and Polly went out to explore the garden. Alice, Maud and Ethel discussed children and confinements, while Richard told Henrietta about his hopes of grandfatherhood. Bertie talked to Ashley and Lizzie about travel and America, and Robbie, Jack and Frank chatted as brothers do who meet after a separation of a few months. Then Maud asked Jack about flying; Frank and Lizzie talked to Richard about the scarcity of accommodation in London; Ned, Bertie and Teddy discussed the coal strike; Ethel and Maud talked about music, Alice and Maud about flower arrangements.

When the children came back in, Bertie offered to show them his stables, and in the most natural way possible turned to Jessie and said, 'Will you come too? I'd like to show you my new Bhutia cross colt.'

Jessie, who had got stuck in a conversation between her mother and Maud about servants, jumped up eagerly, and was across the room in an instant. Ned was subsumed by an offshoot conversation between Robbie and Frank about trains, so Bertie was able to offer his arm to Jessie alone, and with the three children running ahead they went out of the drawing-room and down the side passage to the door most convenient for the stables.

At first Bertie was kept busy introducing each animal and answering the children's questions; but when they had cooed over the charm of the woolly little two-month-old colt foal, bouncing stiff-legged round the large box he was sharing with his mother, they grew bored with the details of breeding that Jessie was so interested in, and wandered off. Now Bertie had Jessie to himself.

He positioned himself, leaning on the partition, so that the light from the outside door fell on her face and he could look at her to his heart's content. The angle of the light threw the scar down her cheek into relief, and he was glad to see that she made no attempt to cover it. In her growing-up years she had developed a series of little movements and gestures that allowed her to hide it from view, but it seemed that since she had married she felt no need any more. He didn't know whether to be glad or sorry about that. It seemed to suggest a contentedness in the married state that he both wanted for her and regretted. He believed she had married Ned to remove herself from temptation – they had sworn to be no more than cousins to each other – but was it possible she had now fallen in love with her husband? Ned was a nice fellow, good-looking and kind, hard-working and honest, and if he was not of the very brightest, the fact that he and Jessie had known each other nearly all their lives would make up for that and give them enough under-standing. Yet Bertie would have thought that knowing each other so well would have precluded her falling in love with Ned romantically – which, he was ashamed to admit, had been something of a comfort to him.

He gazed tenderly at the scar, faint now with age, and hardly noticeable except with the angle of light, and remembered how she had got it, trying to ride her father's stud stallion. Bertie had seen her fall, had got her to safety and, admiring her courage if not her judgement, had visited her often during her long convalescence from the aftermath. He thought with hindsight that he had loved her from that time, that some part of him had been only waiting for her to grow up. But chance and events had kept him from her – the Boer War, his years in India, and then his coming back to England, on his father's death, hardened and disillusioned, to be talked into marriage with Maud by Richard before he'd had time to look around him, before he'd had an opportunity to see Jessie again and remember the special place she held in his affections.

Well, what was done was done. Maud was expecting their child, and Jessie was married to Ned – for all he knew, might be expecting a child herself at this minute. It was hard to think of her doing *that* with Ned – Jessie, who should have been his own. He wanted to cup his hands about her face, to kiss the scar, which seemed somehow peculiarly his own. Most of all he wanted to run away with her to some far place where nobody knew them, and stay there for ever, just the two of them, alone.

Foolishness! He shook his head to get rid of the delicious vision, and Jessie saw the gesture and stopped speaking, looked up at him strangely. The words were out of him before he could stop them. 'Are you happy, Jess?'

She coloured slightly, and he saw the confusion in her eyes. She was not as calm as she had appeared in the great hall – or perhaps being alone with him here had brought back thoughts she had banished. He was ashamed of himself for disturbing her hard-won equilibrium.

'You don't need to answer that,' he said. 'I see you are happy, and I'm glad.'

Jessie continued to look at him, and trembled inwardly. She didn't understand herself. She had married Ned for comfort, and to put herself out of reach of Bertie, but since the marriage she had fallen in love with her husband and was glad of it. Meeting Bertie in the hall she had felt invulnerable and it had made her happy. She had gone with him to the stables sure of herself, glad they could be cousins and nothing more. And yet that one question, and the look that went with it, had thrown her back into the old tormented state she had thought she had left behind for ever. Bertie, whom she had loved all her life! What was he doing to her? What was this feeling? She only knew she must not say his name, or something would break.

Instead she found herself saying, 'Maud looks very well.' It sounded odd in the context, but it was the right thing to say. The sound of Maud's name on the air had a sobering effect. This was not *her* Bertie, but Maud's husband, and soon-to-be-father of Maud's child. She dragged her eyes away from his burning glance, and in an unconscious gesture put her hand up over her cheek, hiding the scar.

The gesture caused him actual physical pain, so that for a moment he couldn't speak. Then he said, 'Yes, she does, doesn't she?'

'I expect you want a boy, don't you?' Jessie said, watching the foal pawing at the straw, pretending to be frightened, jumping away and bucking, then coming back to do it again.

'A boy would be nice,' Bertie said. This was better. Commonplace talk between two cousins. 'She wants to go to London for the confinement.'

Wrong thing to say. It made Jessie look at him again, in surprise. 'Why?' she asked.

'She and Richard believe she'll have better treatment there. I think she's afraid of the baby's coming unexpectedly. Out here it would take hours for the doctor to reach her – or so she thinks.'

'Oh,' said Jessie. 'Well, I suppose that is a point. And you are away from home a lot.'

'Yes,' he said. 'We're lucky that we have Richard to stay with her while I'm away.'

'So when do you go to London?'

'Next week. I'll see her settled in and come back. I can't be from home too long at this time of year.'

Her eyes returned to him. She thought how sad it was for him to be alone, his wife far away, preferring to be in London with her father than at home with her husband. Oh, if we had married, it wouldn't be like that, she thought. I would never have wanted to leave you for a moment. She was glad suddenly of her contentedness with Ned. To be single and lonely would be bad enough, but how awful to be married and lonely!

The children came back, sharp-eyed Polly in the lead. Bertie wrenched his gaze away from Jessie and said, 'It's beginning to get dark. We should go back in. Dinner will be ready very soon.'

Martial said, 'I like this little fellow and his mother best, because they're almost like wild horses. When we get to America, I want to catch a wild horse and train it, like the Indians do.'

'And I want to catch a wolf-cub and train it like a dog,' Rupert said. 'They have wolves in America. It would be fine to have a wolf running at your heels. How everyone would stare.'

'Morland dogs are descended from wolves,' said Polly. 'Aren't they, Jessie? That's why they don't bark.'

Jessie laughed. 'There's a tiny pinch of wolf in there some-where, but it's so diluted by thousands of generations, you'd never know it.'

'Bell and Brach look like wolves, with their yellow eyes,' Polly insisted. 'I do miss Bell. I wish we were allowed to have dogs at school. It's awful having to leave him behind.'

'I bet in American schools they let you have dogs,' Rupert said. 'You'd need them to guard you, in case a bear came in, or Indians, or a mad buffalo.'

Wrangling pleasantly, the children led the way back to the house. Bertie said, 'They're going to be so disappointed when America turns out to be civilised. Every street-lamp and pillar-box will break their hearts.'

'I expect they'll grow up to be solicitors or bank managers, and read the newspaper on the train to work every day,' Jessie laughed. It was just the sort of ordinary conversation two cousins might have.

Morland Place was as full as Teddy could have wanted. Henrietta gave up the big west bedroom to Ashley and Lizzie and took the Red Room, which was Polly's when she was at home. Jessie had her old east bedroom with Ned. Robbie and Ethel had the north bedroom. Jack and Frank had two of the bachelor rooms and Polly had another, Martial and Rupert shared the fourth, and Rose slept in the nursery with little James William and smaller Roberta. And Rug, having been accepted by the Morland Place pack, slept in front of the great-hall fireplace as part of a living carpet of doghood, his chin resting on Brach's flank and Bell's head on his.

Sunday was a quiet day, much of it taken up by two visits to church, as well as prayers read in the chapel by Teddy for the whole household. In between there was a large, late family luncheon – the main meal, to allow the servants a few hours off in the evening to visit their families – which was conducted with the quiet good cheer and gladness that was the mark of the holiest of seasons. Conversation and music filled the rest of the day. Ethel and Alice were both good performers on the piano, Lizzie played a little, and everyone liked to sing. By special request, Jack, Frank and Jessie sang several old songs together as they had used to as children, while Ethel played and Robbie turned for her. Henrietta and Teddy exchanged a glance as the sweet voices intertwined the familiar words with the ancient melodies. It brought back so many memories. As children they had been brought down from the nursery to the drawing-room to sing the same songs to their parents and assembled company, in the far, far-off days half a century ago. Once there had been seven of them; now they were the only two left of their generation.

Teddy retired to the great bedchamber that night contented, feeling how blessed he was. The vast and ancient bed, in which he and his forefathers had been born and in which he expected he would one day die, stood in the shadows like a ship, its hangings like the sails that nightly propelled him across the great ocean of sleep. The fire, recently refreshed, crackled comfortably in the grate, and the bedside candles threw long shapes up the walls and across the ceiling. He preferred candles in the bedroom to lamps. He was used to them and there was something comforting about them. He supposed one day Morland Place would have gaslight, or perhaps even electric light, but he would be happy to see his time out without either of them. He liked things to go on being the way they always had been. His life had seen change enough, and now in his sixties he was content to be home and to have it the way it had been in his childhood, before his mother had died and his father had grown strange, and certainly before his brother George had first altered and then ruined it. He, Teddy, had put things back together, and here he would end his days, he and Hen together as they had been as children, along with as many other family members as he could gather round him.

And his wife, dear gentle Alice, was waiting for him, sitting up by the fire, wrapped in her filmy and absurdly, endearingly impractical dressing-gown. He knew how lucky he was to have won her love. What other woman could he have married who would not have wanted to change things in his home – at the very least to rid herself of his encumbrances? Shy Alice, whom he had always thought was like a delicate fawn, quite incapable of coping with the big, rough world, needed his protection. Her hands were not made for any labour more demanding than embroidery, or her ladylike mind and character to grapple with harder problems than which piece of music to play on the piano, or what flowers to put in the vase on the drawing-room table. She was as helpless and dependent as the canary bird he had bought her and on which she doted. It astonished him that she could have done anything so corporeal as to bring a child into the world.

He crossed the room on the thought, picked up both her hands and kissed them one after the other. They were cold. 'Have you been sitting here long? Why didn't you get into bed? We can't have you catching a chill.'

'I wanted to talk to you,' Alice said.

He saw that she looked troubled, and drew up his chair beside hers so that he could go on chafing her hands. 'What is it, my love? Did Maud's dinner not agree with you? I noticed you didn't eat very much. I didn't care for the mutton myself – too greasy. Bertie's cook certainly hasn't the skill of our Mrs Stark.'

'It's not that,' Alice said, but then she fell silent again. She never spoke much, and seemed to be having difficulty in broaching what was in her thoughts.

Teddy put his mind to it and tried to determine what she was upset about. 'Is it something I've done? Did I forget your birthday? No, that's not until July. Did someone say something to upset you?'

'No, no, nothing like that.' She looked at him with a

61

struggle in her eyes. 'It's – it's your going to America. I wish
– that is – well, I shall miss you very much.'

He smiled and pressed her hand. 'I shall miss you, too.
But it will only be for a few weeks.'

'I wish you wouldn't go,' she said.

He was startled. It was very direct for her, and she had
never asked such a thing before. 'Not go? But, my love, it's
the chance of a lifetime for me. To go across on the most
luxurious ship in the world! And Ashley is going to show
me something of the country before I come back. I'll never
have another opportunity like that.'

She shook her head, blushing and lowering her eyes. 'I'm
sorry. I didn't think. You must go, of course.'

Teddy looked at the top of her bent head, puzzled. 'Why
don't you want me to go? I've been away before on business trips and you didn't mind.' Alice said something, but
her voice was so low, and muffled by her bent head, that
he couldn't catch it. 'What did you say? Dearest, please tell
me. What are you worried about?'

The words, though still low and spoken to the floor, were
distinct this time. 'The sea is so big, and so wild. It's too
dangerous.'

Then he understood. 'You're afraid of the journey? But,
my love, there's nothing to it! People cross the ocean every
day of the year without harm. Ships these days are absolutely
safe. Haven't you heard me talking about the *Olympic* and
her sister ship? How they have watertight compartments, so
that even if they were damaged they wouldn't sink? The
Atlantic is big, but it's not a wilderness. Ships all travel on
the same route, so you are surrounded by other vessels the
whole time. It's like being on a well-used road. It's as safe
as getting into the motor-car and driving in to York – safer,
really, because the big liners have Marconi wireless now, so
they can signal to each other if they need help. Nothing can
go wrong, I promise you. There's nothing to worry about.'

Alice stared at him for a long moment, searching his face.
Then she said, 'I'm having another baby.'

Now Teddy stared; and delight gradually suffused his face.
'Alice! Really?'

'I haven't seen the doctor yet, but I'm sure,' Alice said.

'When is it due? When did—?'

She blushed. 'I think it was in January. After the party at the Winningtons'. Emma says it will come in October, probably.'

He kissed her hand. 'Oh, clever Alice! Another little one! My dear, I couldn't be happier. And are you well? Are you feeling well?'

'Oh, yes,' she said, in her faint, fading voice. 'Except – not liking to eat some things.'

'Oh, quite, quite! That mutton! Well, you shall have everything that you want from now on, no matter what it costs! Ice-cream every meal if you like, and the finest hothouse fruit, and French chocolate. Just say the word, and I'll get it for you. You know,' he added, a little shyly, 'that I'd give you the world if I could. I love you so much, Alice my dear.'

After a silence she ventured hesitantly, 'So – then – you won't go?'

He looked surprised, and then a little dismayed. 'Not go to America? But I've explained to you that there's no danger. And it's only for a few short weeks. I'll be back before you know it, before you even begin to show. Now, darling, don't upset yourself,' he hurried on, as tears began to gleam in her eyes.

'I'm so afraid you won't come back!' she said, in a little gasp of a sob.

'Of course I will,' he said, stroking her cheek. 'This is just your condition speaking, giving you foolish fears. You know how you were the last time, full of fancies. Come to bed now,' he said coaxingly, drawing her to her feet, 'come to bed, and let me hold you, and you'll feel better, you'll see.'

She allowed herself to be coaxed, and after a while, when his big body had warmed her, she began to drift off to sleep, feeling so comforted and safe she was sure he was right and that she had nothing to fear, for he was so very real and solid and *there* that it was impossible to imagine the world without him.

CHAPTER FOUR

White Star had transferred its main transatlantic service from Liverpool to Southampton in 1907. Southampton was closer to London and the Home Counties, which was where most of the first-class passengers came from, and made possible a call in at Cherbourg for the convenience of continental travellers, and another at Queenstown to collect the Irish emigrants who helped to fill up steerage. To accommodate the enormous Olympic-class liners at Southampton, a new double-length dock had been acquired: berths forty-three and forty-four, conveniently next to Harland and Wolff's repair yard.

Titanic arrived at her berth at midnight on the 3rd of April, twelve hours after her sister *Olympic* had departed, leaving behind the sacks of coal she had brought over from New York. Southampton port was crowded with vessels laid up for want of coal or passengers. Competition for dock space was such that ships were moored in pairs or even three abreast, making manoeuvre even more difficult than usual in the narrow channels. But it did mean that there were plenty of hands available and eager to be signed up; and plenty of White Star liners from which coal could be harvested to fill *Titanic*'s stokeholds.

On departure day, the first-class boat train from Waterloo would be arriving at eleven in the morning, but Teddy wanted time to look over everything before the passengers embarked, so having escorted Lizzie and the children as far as London on Tuesday afternoon, he travelled on down to Southampton and stayed the night in an hotel there. There had been a tearful farewell at Morland Place, for despite everything he had said to Alice, and her assurance that she saw the sense of his argument, she still leaked at the eyes so constantly that she could not speak. Teddy had imparted the secret of her condition to Henrietta, and asked her to look after Alice until he came back. He thought that having Alice to fuss over would help keep Henrietta's mind from Lizzie.

With the journey down to Southampton accomplished and the tears left far behind, Teddy was ready to enjoy everything about the experience, and found himself so full of energy that he was up at the crack of dawn on Wednesday. Leaving his man, Brown, to finish the packing and follow at his leisure, he took a taxi-cab to the dock and arrived on board *Titanic* even before the captain.

The vast ship and the dockside were a hive of activity as all the last-day preparations went on. Fresh food was being taken aboard to add to the dry stores that had been loaded already. Crew members already signed up were boarding, to change into their uniforms and begin their duties, while other hands hung about hoping to be taken on as last-minute replacements for those – there were always a few – who missed the boat. Cargo, too, was still coming aboard – Teddy saw a motor-car being swung over high above the deck in slings – and the mail-bags were being loaded for the five postal clerks to sort during the voyage. Carrying the mails gave *Titanic* her RMS prefix and provided a small extra income.

The first person Teddy met as he stepped off the gangplank was Thomas Andrews, managing director of Harland and Wolff, and the ship's chief designer. He was to sail with a 'guarantee party' of eight to make sure that everything was working properly, to correct any minor faults and make notes of anything that needed altering. He and Teddy had worked closely together over the provision of the soft furnishings, and had come to like each other. They greeted each other warmly.

'How is she?' Teddy enquired.

'On the whole, very well,' Andrews said. 'Putting a new

ship into commission is always a strenuous business and, as you know, we've had a pretty tight schedule with this one. But we're getting there, we're getting there. By the time we sail she'll be as nearly perfect as human brains can make her. Would you like me to conduct you round?'

'Very much,' Teddy said; but at that moment Andrews was accosted by a carpenter with a query about berth ladders and an electrician who wanted to report a malfunction in some electric fans, and Teddy said, 'Not to worry, old fellow. I'll look round on my own. I can see you are busy.'

Teddy wandered about the first-class public rooms, watching the last-minute finishing work – a carpet being tacked down here, a scuffmark painted out there, electricians working on light fittings, window cleaners buffing the elaborate mirrors and embossed glass panels. He saw one of the electric lifts being tested, bar stewards arranging their stock and polishing glasses, waiters laying tables for luncheon. He went on deck in time to see the captain arrive – a big, burly figure with a mahogany face and grizzled hair and beard, already dressed in immaculate frock-coat and cap. As soon as he stepped on board the blue duster was run up, signifying that Captain E. J. Smith was in the Royal Naval Reserve.

Suddenly Andrews was back at his elbow, saying, 'I've shaken off my pursuers for the moment. Come and see third class. We're very proud of the standard we're setting. I don't exaggerate when I say I've been in ships where first class wasn't as comfortable.'

Steerage accommodation began on C deck, where third-class passengers had their own promenade deck. 'We're the first line to provide one,' Andrews said. 'In other ships they're virtually battened down for the duration of the voyage, like cargo – no access to the open air at all.'

'Well, this is very pleasant,' Teddy said. Access to the deck was through the bar and smoking-room, which had oak-panelled walls like a cosy public house, and hardwood tables and chairs. On D deck there were two more bars, and a general room – another White Star innovation. It was bright with white walls and pine trim, and furnished with tables and chairs, a piano, and all sorts of cards and games for passing the time. The dining-room also had white walls – in other ships steerage walls were unpainted – and instead of the usual benches and trestles it had proper tables and chairs. Teddy had a look at some of the menus. Breakfast was cereal, kippers, boiled eggs, bread and marmalade and tea or coffee. The midday meal, called 'dinner' in third class, typically consisted of soup, a roast with vegetables, a hot pudding and fruit; the evening meal, called 'tea', was a cooked dish, bread and buns and a light pudding such as stewed fruit or blancmange. Then later on there was a supper of cheese and biscuits, or gruel, and coffee.

Teddy thought of the impoverished emigrants, seeking a better life in America because their homeland had offered them nothing but unemployment and starvation, and almost laughed. 'I don't suppose most of them will ever have seen so much food at one time,' he said. 'They'll think they've died and gone to heaven!'

'As long as the word gets back, and all those who follow them come by White Star,' said Andrews. 'Poor fellows, why shouldn't they have a bit of comfort for once?'

The final touch of luxury was that instead of everyone being crowded into dormitories, there were four- and six-berth cabins. Teddy was especially pleased with the counter-panes for the bunks, which his mill had designed and manufactured. They were of heavy cotton knit, in bright red with the White Star symbol and name woven in white, and he thought they made the cabins look cheerful and snug. 'I shouldn't mind one of these on my own bed at home,' he said, fingering one. 'They look very well.'

Andrews looked at his watch and said, 'I shall have to go now. I'm meeting the chief engineer, and then there's the boat drill.'

'Go ahead,' Teddy said, 'I know you've a thousand things to do.'

Andrews smiled. 'If it were only a thousand, I should be finished in no time.'

The fine spring day broadened. The Board of Trade inspector, Captain Clarke, along with two medical officers, inspected the crew and the accommodation, and then supervised a thirty-minute boat drill. At half past nine the third-class boat train drew up and the passengers shuffled aboard with their jaws hanging in astonishment at the size and splendour of the ship. Members of the press and photographers were arriving all the time, along with a large number of sightseers, so White Star's publicity had not been in vain. Soon the ship was swarming with visitors looking around, riding in the lifts, peering into the public rooms, trying the chairs, inspecting the menus. The ship's orchestra tuned up and settled themselves on deck to play popular songs, ragtime tunes and operetta music, to add to the feeling of festivity.

And then at eleven o'clock the first-class boat train steamed in from Waterloo, and Teddy hurried down to meet Lizzie and Ashley, for the pleasure of seeing their reaction when they first set eyes on the ship. He didn't want to miss a single word or expression.

Lizzie was impressed long before they reached Southampton. The boat train itself was a marvel of luxury, with its rich deep blue upholstery trimmed with gold braid, the dark panelling, the elegant glass light shades, the velvet curtains tied back with gold tassels, the white-jacketed stewards bringing coffee and offering newspapers. 'If the train is like this, what will the boat be like?' she enquired rhetorically.

'You must learn not to call it a boat,' Ashley said. 'It's a ship.'

'Then why is this called the boat train?' she said unanswerably. Ashley retired behind his newspaper again.

They had a compartment to themselves, which was fortunate as the boys were voluble with excitement, and Rose was at an age where sitting still was a near impossibility. She fidgeted about on the knee of the nursemaid, Jenny, who was travelling with them to America, and from time to time, to get relief from her solid young weight, Jenny took her for a walk along the corridor and back. Ashley went outside periodically to smoke, and when the boys grew too restive he took them with him, to let down a corridor window and point out landmarks to them. Lizzie tried to read the magazine Ashley had bought her for the journey, but she was too excited. 'I'm sure I haven't the right clothes for a boat – ship – so fine,' she said to Ashley one time. 'I shall have to pretend that Jenny is my maid as well as Rose's.'

'I don't mind, madam,' Jenny said. 'I could easily help you dress in the evening when my little one's asleep.'

'I could pretend to be your valet, Dad,' Martial said. 'I know how they go on – I've seen Brown laying out Uncle Teddy's clothes.'

'Why can't I be it?' Rupert said at once. 'It's not fair.'

'You're too young,' Martial said, from his fourteen-month eminence of seniority. 'Dad, do people have valets in America?'

'I'm sure they do. Why do you ask?'

'Oh, it just didn't seem a very American thing,' Martial said vaguely. 'I mean, you can't imagine Davy Crockett having someone lay out his racoon hat, can you?

Ashley met Lizzie's eyes across the compartment. 'America is going to be such a surprise to them,' he said.

'To me too,' Lizzie confessed. 'Despite all you've told me, my head is still full of wilderness and Indians and buffaloes. I just can't seem to help it.'

The boys grew ever more excited as the train drew nearer to Southampton, and chattered non-stop; but when they all stepped out of the Customs shed onto the dockside and saw *Titanic* for the first time, they fell silent, awestruck. Lizzie's voice failed her, too. The sheer size of the ship seemed to batter all thought out of her skull.

In length it seemed to go on for ever: from close up under its sides, it was impossible to see all the way to the end. Ashley had said it was more than a sixth of a mile long. And the height! The great black sides reared up into the air like a vast, sheer cliff, pocked with hundreds of portholes, which looked tiny by comparison. Above that was the towering white superstructure; and above that again a glimpse of the four great buff-coloured funnels with the black collars, three of them sending smoke up into the sparkling April blue of the sky – the fourth, Ashley said, was a ventilator.

The size of the ship seemed almost frightening; other vessels were like toys beside it. It was as massive and solid as a building, eleven storeys high and topped by towers as tall again. It's *too* big, Lizzie found herself thinking; and at the same moment, Martial said in a small voice, 'Is it really a *ship*? Mama, how does it float?'

Ashley answered him, 'Very well, my son,' and Lizzie glanced at her husband and saw that, despite the lightness of his tone, he was struck, too.

And then, there in front of them was Uncle Teddy, beaming with delight, a fat cigar between his fingers, looking so familiar and normal that the awe went out of the moment leaving only anticipation and excitement.

'Well, well, well! Here you all are! What do you think, eh? Splendid, isn't she? I've come to show you to your cabin. I've been near enough all over her already this morning, so I know my way about pretty well.'

When they got to the top of the gangplank, they met Bruce Ismay just parting with his wife and children, whom he had been showing over the ship. Lizzie, shaking hands, said at once, 'Oh, Mr Ismay, I must thank you so *very* much for moving us from second class into first class.' They had received the news of this only the night before, from Mr Culpepper. 'It's more than we ever dreamed of.'

'Yes, indeed, sir, it's very, very generous of you,' Ashley said.

Ismay smiled. 'Oh, not at all, not at all! You are by way of representing Mr Culpepper on this voyage, and it's the least I can do. It's traditional, you know, for the head of a shipping line travelling with any of his rivals. If I were to take a Culpepper ship, or a Cunarder, or any other liner, in fact, I should be given a first-class cabin at no charge, and so would Mr Culpepper on any of *my* ships.'

'I still say it's very good of you, sir, and I do thank you,' Ashley insisted.

'Please, say no more. If you will excuse me, I shall just

see my family ashore. Are you going to show your people over the ship, Morland? Good, good. I'm sure these young men,' smiling down at the boys, 'are longing to see everything.'

The first wonder they encountered was the grand staircase, a double flight whose elements flung apart half-way up to form an encircling gallery. It had panelled walls, intricately carved handrails, elaborate pierced-work instead of banisters, and on the middle landing a fine clock set into the wall in a magnificent carved panel. At the bottom the dividing rail finished in a post topped by a bronze cherub holding up an electric flambeau, while the wonder of wonders was that the whole circular structure was covered with a great glass dome, delicately fretted with slender decorative glazing bars, through which the daylight poured down to make the rich woodwork glow and the gilded touches glint.

Everyone had to stop and stare, and after a moment Lizzie said, in tones of wonder, 'How can you have something like this *indoors* on a *boat*?'

Ashley, who had done a lot of sailing in his youth in Boston, winced. 'My love!' he protested. 'It's not a boat and you don't have "indoors" in ships.'

'Oh, don't fuss,' Lizzie said good-naturedly. 'You're missing the point, which is that it's impossible to believe this magnificent structure is somewhere inside a floating vessel.'

'You're right about that,' Ashley agreed. 'It's like the grandest of grand hotels.'

'Or a stately home,' Lizzie capped him. In that moment she lost any sense of being on shipboard. Nor did their cabin, on B deck, do anything to dispel the illusion they were on dry land. They had been given a suite with two bedrooms, a sitting-room and a bathroom and lavatory. All the rooms were large and luxuriously appointed.

'Oh, Uncle Teddy, it's too much! It's absurd!' Lizzie said, almost in tears.

'It is one of the best suites,' Teddy nodded.

'I suppose it's in compliment to Mr Culpepper,' Ashley

said. 'If he were sailing, I expect it's what he would have been given.'

'I dare say,' Teddy said, and then, 'Not to detract for a moment from Ismay's generosity, but the ship will be barely more than half full. Andrews was telling me there've been a shocking number of cancellations – something like fifty in first class. Lord Pirrie was supposed to have been sailing, but he's ill, and J. P. Morgan, who owns the line, cancelled his reservation at the last moment. So there's plenty of room, and to give you this suite really costs nothing. You might as well have it as not – and you need two bedrooms, with the boys.'

The exploration went on. The two bedrooms were decorated in different styles. One was all in dark mahogany and rich crimson. The other – which Lizzie immediately claimed for herself and Ashley – was French rococo, white and gold woodwork inset with panels of silk of deep blue decorated with gold fleur-de-lis. The furniture was Empire style in white and gold, the carpet matched the panels, and the room was so big there was space for a sitting area, with a sofa and two armchairs grouped about a table, and a writing-desk and chair against another wall.

'It's lovely,' Lizzie sighed. 'And isn't everything *new*?' She fingered the bed linen. 'Just think, no-one has ever used these sheets before. We shall be the first people ever to sleep in this bed, ever to stay in this cabin.'

'The first to bathe in this bathroom,' Ashley said. 'Come and see.'

Lizzie followed him in. 'It's far, far better than our bathroom at home,' she said. 'Look at the lovely marble basin, and that huge bathtub – and all those taps! What on earth can they all be for?'

Ashley investigated. 'Hot or cold, salt or fresh, and a number of different sprays and douches. In seven days, I think you need never have the same kind of bath twice.'

'I shall never be out of here,' Lizzie said. 'We must have a bathroom like this one day.'

'I'll build you one in our house in Arizona,' Ashley said, in expansive mood.

They went back into the sitting-room as the steward and stewardess arrived with the luggage. They introduced themselves as Lucas and Walsh. 'The maid and the little girl have the inside cabin just opposite,' Lucas said.

'Shall I see them settled, madam, or would you like me to unpack you first?' Walsh enquired.

'Oh, see to Rose and Jenny, if you please,' Lizzie said. She felt she would sooner unpack for herself than have the strange stewardess examine the deficiencies of her wardrobe.

'I'll leave you to settle in,' Teddy said, 'and go and direct my own unpacking. I'm just down the passage from you.'

'Can we come and see your cabin too?' the boys asked.

'Of course,' Teddy said, 'though there's nothing in particular to see.' They dashed out of the door, and he gave his niece a conspiratorial wink. 'I'll keep 'em out of your way for a bit, if I can. And, by the by, Brown says he's quite willing to take charge of 'em now and then. He won't have a great deal to do for me, and he's fond of children.'

'That's very kind,' Lizzie said. 'Thank him very much for me.'

'I'll come back in a little while and take you all on deck in time for departure. You'll want to wave goodbye to dear old England.'

'I'm sure I shall cry,' Lizzie said.

'I'd be disappointed if you didn't,' said Teddy, and disappeared.

It was all very well to decide to do her own unpacking, but looking around the bedroom Lizzie couldn't see anywhere to unpack *into* – no wardrobes, no chests of drawers. Lucas, coming in with a bag, gave a gentle cough, and revealed that each bedroom had its own wardrobe room.

'Oh, my goodness,' Lizzie said.

'American ladies and gentlemen do seem to travel with a very great deal of luggage, madam,' Lucas said sympathetically. 'I believe it's quite common in America for wealthy people to have separate rooms for their clothes.'

Lizzie turned back to Ashley and said in a low voice, 'Now I *know* I haven't got the right clothes – or nearly enough of them. And I suppose all the other women will

73

have fabulous jewels. Oh dear! I rather wish Mr Ismay hadn't put us up to first class. I think I'd have fitted in better in second.'

Ashley took her hand in a firm grip. 'Now, listen to me. You are to stop this nonsense right now. You are an educated woman and far too sensible to care about such foolishness. Some of the wealthiest people in the world will be travelling in this ship, and you could never hope to compete with them even if I spent every penny I had on furbelows for you. And I should hope you wouldn't want to compete with them, either.'

'No,' she said, sobered by the consideration that she might have hurt his feelings. 'No, of course I don't.'

'Good,' he said. 'We're lucky to be on this ship at all, and beyond expectation lucky to have a first-class cabin. Mr Culpepper meant it to be a treat for us, and it's certainly the opportunity of a lifetime, to be on the maiden voyage of a luxurious liner like this. So I hope you will simply enjoy every minute of it, and not spoil it with worrying about whether your clothes are grand enough.'

'I shall enjoy it, I promise,' Lizzie said, reaching up to kiss his cheek. 'You're always so sensible, Ashley dear, and I shan't think about clothes again.' She was quite sure she would, but she wouldn't be so foolish as to mention it out loud.

When they went up on deck for the departure, Lizzie's resolve was put to the test straight away. She had never seen so many fur coats in one place, while a fair number of diamonds – even at this time of day – flashed back the sun. The ship's orchestra was still playing on deck, competing with a brass band down on the dockside, which was entertaining the vast crowd gathered there to see the great liner cast off. It was a lovely day, the high blue sky just fretted with the lightest of clouds, and there was real warmth in the sunshine. Gulls wheeled about on the light breeze, waiting for the moment when the water would be churned up for them.

Lizzie sniffed the interesting smells of oily water and

seaweed, stack smoke, fresh salt and, nearer to hand, from the passengers, expensive French perfume, cigars, and a hint of mothballs from some of the furs. She suddenly felt absolutely happy. After all the worry and work of packing and planning, she now had nothing to do for seven days but enjoy herself in surroundings of unprecedented luxury. And at the other end of the voyage would be a new life in a new country, full of experiences whose nature she could hardly begin to guess at. She knew she ought to feel sad at leaving her native land – perhaps for ever – but just at the moment there was no room inside her for anything but a quiet, glowing euphoria.

Everyone was crowding up on deck. Brown kindly offered to take the boys away to where they could get a better view and see the crew working to cast off, and Jenny went with him with Rose, as they were getting jostled.

'There's the captain,' Teddy said, and they turned their heads to see him standing on the upper deck by the bridge. 'Isn't he a splendid-looking fellow?'

'The very image of a salty sea-dog,' Lizzie agreed.

With his King Edward beard, his frock-coat, gold braid and gleaming medals, and his wonderful presence, he was just the man to inspire confidence. Teddy stopped an officer hurrying past and said, 'Your captain – what sort of a man is he?'

'Oh, the very best, sir,' the officer said.

'He's the commodore of the White Star fleet, isn't he?'

'Yes, sir, and he always takes out the new ships. He's very popular, with crews and passengers alike.'

'Is he a good seaman?' Ashley asked.

'Oh, *yes*, sir! The finest. There's not an officer alive who wouldn't give his ears to sail under him,' said the officer, with enthusiasm. 'To see him conn a ship up a difficult channel at full speed is an education. And to watch him swing round a bad turn so dashingly, judging it to a nicety, with only feet to spare on either side – well, it makes us flush with pride, sir. But if you'll excuse me, I must be about my duties.'

'Yes, of course, we mustn't delay you,' Teddy said, and the officer hurried away.

Ashley gave the captain one more look and turned away, saying, 'Hm. Might be better, if it was a difficult passage and a bad corner, *not* to go at full speed. That officer seemed to think speed was everything.'

But Teddy said, 'Come, everyone admires the ability to do things more quickly than the next man. If you can perform something perfectly, the next thing is to do it faster.'

Lizzie smiled. 'Yes, and men always do go on about speed.'

'It's how the world progresses,' Teddy said. 'Look, there are the tugs. Four of 'em, I see, to move this great ship. What's the time?' He pulled out his watch. 'Won't be long now. Look, down there, see the visitors going ashore?'

Promptly at noon the air was torn by *Titanic*'s immense triple-toned steam whistle, a sound so loud that it made Lizzie jump and bite her tongue, and sent all the pigeons and gulls on the dockside roofs clattering up into the air. Three blasts on the whistle signalled departure. The ropes were cast off, the tugs took up the slack, and the deck trembled slightly underfoot as the ship got slowly under way. A huge excitement, like gulping in too much air, filled Lizzie, and she felt as foolishly thrilled as any child.

A little strip of water appeared between the ship and the dockside. Below, the crowd were cheering and waving, and Lizzie waved back, though she didn't know anyone down there. But everyone along the ship's rail was waving. She looked down at the pink upturned faces among the dark clothes, and the fluttering points of white where handkerchiefs were being waved. Some people threw flowers into the water. She imagined what a sight it must be for them, the vast, stately ship drawing away, towering against the sky. *We're really going,* she thought. *We're really off!* She glanced at her companions – Uncle Teddy beaming and waving, Ashley looking about keenly at everything – and rather wished the boys were there to jump up and down in sheer excitement on her behalf.

'Well,' Ashley said, 'the departure will be a test of seamanship for someone. The tugs will pull us out into the river, but the dredged channel there is pretty narrow – and I believe only about forty feet deep. No room for mistakes.'

'It's the pilot's responsibility,' Uncle Teddy said. 'I saw him come aboard early this morning.'

They made the turn to port into the river, the tugs cast off, and the ship came under her own power and began to increase speed. Many of the passengers on deck had left the rails now there was no-one to wave to, so the Morland party had more room. Ashley hung over the side, looking down at the water.

'The amount of water we displace must be colossal,' he said, 'and we'll be passing pretty close to the moored ships. I hope our captain doesn't go in for any of his full-speed antics here.'

'We seem to be going quite slowly,' Lizzie said.

She was reading the names of the tied-up ships they were passing. Just up ahead were two more White Star liners – she recognised the livery now. They were moored side by side for lack of space. She could read their names across their sterns. *Oceanic* was tied to the dockside and *New York* was tied up to her. It meant that there really was very little room in the channel, and, as Ashley had said, they were going to pass very close to the *New York*. There was still quite a crowd along the dock, she saw, watching the great new ship go out; and people were still waving, standing in the shadow of the moored vessels.

'Slowly or not,' Ashley said, 'it's still too fast for the conditions. Look at that surge.'

The water displaced by *Titanic* was moving before and to the side of her like a great bulge in the surface of the river. Lizzie saw *New York*'s stern heave up as the surge passed under, and as it moved on forward the ship seemed to struggle in an almost human way, as if trying to get away from *Oceanic*, to which it was close tied fore and aft. And then, with a sound like a gunshot, the ropes securing the two ships to each other snapped, first the aftermost, and then, with a second report, the bow rope. The severed stern rope, which had been stretched taut as an A string a moment before, whizzed across the *Oceanic* like a live thing and Lizzie saw people on the dockside scatter as it whirled among them.

The surge that had forced the ships apart was now driving *New York*'s stern outwards as it pushed her forwards. A gangway between the two ships crashed into the water and splintered. The five-hundred-foot *New York* was swinging her rear into the path of *Titanic*. There were shouts and cries of alarm all along the deck.

'I knew it!' Ashley said. 'I said he was going too fast!'

'We're going to collide!' Lizzie cried. 'Oh, that little tug! It'll be crushed!' The tug *Vulcan* was between the two ships.

Titanic's chimneys belched smoke and the deck vibrated. 'The Captain's stopped engines – now he'll full astern,' Ashley said, staring down urgently at the situation. 'Too late. He won't move her in time.'

New York's stern was still swinging outwards. Her prow, moving forward and being pushed to port by the same action, scraped along *Oceanic*'s side with a terrible scream of metal, taking the paint back to the steel in a long scar.

'Why doesn't that tug push it back?' asked a lady standing beside Ashley.

'He couldn't do it. He'd just be crushed between us,' Ashley answered. He watched as the tug, at full speed, dashed out of the way. Beside *Titanic* it looked like a child's bathtub toy. 'No, I see what he's going to do. If he can get a line over her, he can pull her stern back in.'

There was a tense silence over the deck as everyone watched the drama unfold. It seemed to be happening unnaturally slowly, and Lizzie felt almost as if it were a dream. On land things crashed in an instant; on the water, she discovered, you had time to watch it coming, and it made you feel horribly helpless. The *Vulcan* got a line up to the *New York*'s stern and began to drag her backwards and towards the dock. *Titanic*'s bow moved slowly to port. *New York* was still coming. And then, when there was no more than four feet between the two vessels, *New York*'s way ran out, and she began to respond to the *Vulcan*'s pull. The other tugs were hurrying in to get lines onto the loose ship. The crisis, it seemed, had passed.

Relief raised a chatter from the passengers on deck like starling noise.

'That was a narrow squeak!'

'Oh, there never was any danger. Captain Smith knew what he was about.'

'Good thing we had an experienced man in charge.'

'That was smart work by the captain.'

'He and the pilot kept cool heads, all right.'

The lady next to Ashley said to him, 'You seem to know a great deal about sailing, sir. Why did that ship come adrift? Wasn't it tied up properly?'

Ashley tried to explain to her about the displacement of water, but after a moment she laughed and said, 'It's no use, I'll never grasp it. Still, no harm was done, as it happened. The captain acted quickly and averted a disaster. That's all we really need to know.'

'Yes, indeed,' Ashley said politely. It was not for him to air his opinion of the incident to a stranger.

She looked past him at Uncle Teddy. 'Excuse my forwardness,' she said, 'but aren't you Mr Edward Morland?'

Teddy lifted his hat. 'At your service?' he said enquiringly.

The lady beamed. 'I thought so. I saw your name on the cabin list. I am acquainted with a niece of yours, Miss Jessie Compton. I had the pleasure of meeting her during her come-out with Lady Violet Winchmore. We went to all the same dances and had tea together for ever. And my sister and I stayed in the next cottage to them on the Isle of Wight during Cowes Week. May I introduce myself? I'm Mrs George Penobscot, but I was Amalfia Seavill then.'

Teddy shook her hand. 'Here is another niece of mine, Mrs Ashley Morland, and her husband.'

'Oh, Miss Compton's sister! I heard her talk about you often. How do you do?'

She had such a friendly, open manner that Lizzie shook her hand and found herself beaming in response. Mrs Penobscot was very pretty, with dark curly hair and brown eyes, and was dressed fashionably and very expensively in a silk suit with a large black fox piece (which did *not* smell of mothballs) over her shoulders and a hat trimmed with long marabou feathers. Hers were some of the diamonds

79

Lizzie had noted – a handsome spray at the breast of her jacket glittering between the silky bands of fox. But she seemed too nice and too friendly for the evident wealth to intimidate.

'How is Miss Compton?' she asked.

'Very well. She's married now, too. She married our cousin Ned – my uncle's adopted son – so she's Mrs Morland now.'

'Dear Jessie,' Mrs Penobscot said. 'I do hope she's very happy.' The two men had turned away, leaving Lizzie in private conversation with the young woman. 'She and Violet and I were very close, you know, and we talked all the time about who we would marry. We were sure Jessie would make a good match. She had so many beaux – my sister and I quite thought she'd marry Henry Fossey. He was very much in love with her.'

'Well, so is Cousin Ned,' Lizzie said, amused, 'so I'm sure she is very happy.'

'I am glad. She and Violet were my favourite people in London. I miss London dreadfully. My husband is American, you see,' she said proudly, 'so we live mostly over there, in New York and Connecticut. We come to Europe quite often, but it isn't the same.'

'I suppose not,' Lizzie said. 'I've almost always lived in London, but now my husband and I are going to America, and I'm sure I shall miss it too.'

'We are in the same boat, then,' Mrs Penobscot said, without irony. 'Is your husband American too?'

'Yes, from Boston. He has been working in London, but now his job takes him to Arizona for some years, so I and the children go with him.'

Mrs Penobscot's eyes widened. 'Arizona! What an adventure. I hear the scenery there is quite wonderful. I would so like to see it some day. Do you go straight there?'

'No, we'll spend some time in New York and Boston first.'

'Oh, then you must come and see us while you are in New York,' Mrs Penobscot cried, with evident delight. 'Oh, do say you will! It would be lovely to have someone from home to talk to. Come and stay with us.'

Lizzie laughed. 'You forget there is a large number of us,'

she said. 'Your husband might not like to be descended on by a crowd of travellers, especially when it includes two energetic boys and a little girl at the age to put her fingers into everything.'

'He'd love it,' Mrs Penobscot said firmly. 'George is the dearest creature. You must let me introduce him to you as soon as possible. How nice it is,' she added, 'that we are on a ship, so there's plenty of time for us to become friends.' A slight cloud crossed her sunny face. 'Oh, but how awful of me. I'm assuming too much. I was so glad to meet someone I know – or at least someone who *knows* someone I know – that I didn't think. You probably think I'm an awful fool and dread bumping into me every day.'

'Not at all,' said Lizzie. 'I should be very glad to have you as a friend.'

'Really? Do you mean it? You see, Jessie told me all about you and how *very* clever you are, and I'm not clever at all. But I should so love to have a friend on board. Look here, I'm sure you're too polite to tell me to be quiet and go away, but if you really don't want to be with me, just turn your head away when we meet and I promise I shall take the hint and not bother you.'

She was irresistible, like a merry child. Despite the difference in their ages, Lizzie felt very attracted to her, and thought it would be fun to have another female to talk to, especially one so undaunting in this rich company. 'Do you really not know anyone else on board?' she asked.

'Not as a friend, not to chat to. I know who most of them are, though – the American society ones, at least.' She grinned almost impishly. 'I know all the gossip, so I can point people out and tell you what everyone is saying about them – and, really, I can tell you from the cabin list there are some *prime* candidates on board.'

At that moment a bugler came into sight, walking along the deck playing 'The Roast Beef of Old England'.

'Whatever is that?' Lizzie exclaimed.

'It's the signal for lunch,' said Mrs Penobscot. 'Instead of a gong, you know. Isn't it fun? I must go and find my husband.'

'And I must go and find my children,' said Lizzie.

'There's always so much to do the first day, I don't suppose I shall see much of you,' Mrs Penobscot said wistfully.

'Perhaps we could have tea together,' Lizzie said.

'Really? That would be lovely.'

'Where does one have tea?'

'In the Verandah Café,' Mrs Penobscot said at once. 'We came over on the *Olympic*, and the Verandah Café was where we had tea there, so I expect it will be the same here.'

When Mrs Penobscot had hurried off, Ashley returned to Lizzie's side and said, 'Uncle Teddy's fetching the boys. Have you got rid of that female at last?'

'But I like her,' Lizzie protested. 'She's a nice, good-natured young woman.'

'She talks too much.'

'Well, I like that,' Lizzie said, linking arms with him. 'And I plan to be friends with her.'

'Sooner you than me.'

'You don't understand. A woman needs a female friend.'

He glanced down and squeezed her hand against his ribs. 'If all females were like you, I'd like to have female friends, too. But if it makes you happy, go ahead and cultivate her.'

'She means to ask her husband to invite us to stay with them in New York.'

'He won't when he understands what a crowd we are.'

'That's what I said. I wonder what's for luncheon. I'm starving.'

Ashley laughed. 'Shipboard air. You wait till we've been at sea a few days.'

'Just think,' Lizzie marvelled, 'this is only the first day, and we've got a whole week to come! I'm going to enjoy this so much.'

'That's my girl,' Ashley said.

CHAPTER FIVE

Venetia, Lady Overton, was surprised to receive a visit from MP Tommy Weston. He was a distant cousin of hers and as children they had run in and out of each other's nurseries; but their relationship had been virtually severed when Tommy's marital infidelity had led to the suicide of his wife Emma, Venetia's dear friend. Since then they had had nothing but a distant, nodding acquaintance. In fact, their separate lives were so busy that although they lived within half a mile of each other (Venetia in Manchester Square, Tommy in Brook Street) they rarely saw each other even to nod to.

When the butler told her Tommy was below and asking to see her, she was in half a mind to deny him. She was in her laboratory reading over case histories and comparing them with slides, and didn't want to be disturbed, even for someone she liked. But then she considered that if Tommy had gone so far as to call after all these years (a moment's reflection told her it was twenty, my God, since Emma died) he must have some serious purpose. So she sighed and told Burton to show him into her private parlour.

'Yes, my lady. Shall I bring refreshments?'

'Certainly not,' Venetia said. Burton was new, and did not know the history – though she had no doubt that by the time she saw him again the below-stairs information service would have enlightened him.

She took time to remove her laboratory coat, wash her hands and see that her hair was neat, before walking through the interconnecting study to the parlour. It was a plain but comfortable room, and when she was working at home she always had a fire lit, so it was warm, although the fire had burned down to a glow. Tommy was standing facing it, apparently warming his hands, though the rubbing of them together could have been a nervous gesture, for it was a bright day and hardly cold outside. The walls of the house were so thick that it was always colder inside than out.

He turned as she came in, and she had the width of the room in which to study him as she walked towards him. He was a successful and popular politician, and a wealthy man besides, having inherited his father's fortune and augmented it by wise investment. His clothes and appearance reflected his standing. He was correctly attired in frock-coat, stiff collar and sober tie, and carried his silk hat and gloves – given the coolness of Venetia's reception Burton had quite rightly not relieved him of them. His boots were elegant and his hair well dressed, and everything he wore was of the first quality, as Venetia could see at a practised glance. She was not a careful dresser herself but, thanks to her husband (who had been known as 'Beauty' in his palmy days), she had a good eye for men's clothing.

But time, she noted, had not been kind to Tommy. He had never been a handsome man, though with the vigour of youth he had passed in a crowd, as the saying was; but with age the underlying deficiency of his features had become evident. His skin looked greyish and slack, his eyes were pouchy, his nose seemed to have spread out of what little shape it had ever had, and his thinning hair was unfortunately just the shade of iron grey that always looked dirty rather than distinguished. Still, he was sixty-three, a year older than her, and given his beginnings, she supposed it was a wonder he had lived so long: he had been a sweep's boy until rescued and later adopted in an act of eccentric benevolence by her great-uncle Thomas Weston.

He looked at her with some apprehension and – unusual for a man of such public success – uncertainty. She had not offered her hand and he must have felt it. 'It's very good of you to see me,' he said.

'I assumed you would not have come if it were not something important,' she said.

He was examining her at least as frankly as she had him. 'You don't seem to have changed at all,' he said, in a slightly different voice. 'You look just as you always did. Just as beautiful.'

'Ridiculous,' she said briskly. 'I'm an old woman, and silly flattery has no power to move me.' She knew herself to be as bony as an aged horse, and her burnished hair, always her crowning glory – to her mind her only beauty – was now white. But it was still plentiful, and she had kept her upright carriage, thank God. Her husband still thought her beautiful, and that was all that mattered.

'I didn't mean it as flattery,' Tommy said, quite gravely. 'With some people, age just makes them more of what they always were.'

'I'm sure you didn't come here to discuss my appearance,' she said unencouragingly.

'No,' he said humbly. 'I came to make my peace with you, if you will let me.'

It took her aback. It was not what she had expected, and she had no prepared response. She had to fall back on her natural reactions; and the first was one of curiosity. The second, bouncing off it, was revulsion. Emma was twenty years in her grave, but Venetia was the medical practitioner who had pronounced her dead, and the image, long buried, jumped into her mind unbidden from its hiding-place. Moreover, she had seen Emma shortly before the terrible act, had seen with her own eyes the bitter grief and betrayal that had led her to it.

So she said coldly, 'It has taken you a long time to get here.'

'I've been thinking about coming for the last two years,' Tommy said. 'But, yes, you are right. It took me too long to come to a right mind about what happened.'

'If you expect me simply to forgive you—'

'I'm not sure "forgive" is the right word. What I did was wrong and the outcome was terrible. I don't think there can be forgiveness for that – not on this side of the grave. But I would like to explain – have you understand. Make my peace with you, as I said.' She did not know how to answer, and through her silence he looked at her steadily. 'I know it's a great deal to ask, but will you listen to me? Just that?'

And so, stiffly, she nodded; and then, even more stiffly, gestured him to a seat. He sat as though he hardly knew he was doing it, and perched on the edge of one of the sofas like someone who might have to make a hasty escape at any moment. He did not even put his hat down, but kept it on his knee. Venetia took a seat opposite, and said nothing, waiting for him to begin. She wasn't sure she could have spoken, so many emotions were churning inside her in the wake of the memories that had been stirred.

He looked thoughtfully at the floor for a moment, as if assembling his words – though she guessed he must have rehearsed this scene many times before finally embarking on it – and then began. 'I loved Emma dearly. She was like the other half of me. I suppose you know,' looking up, 'that I had a crush for you for a while. You were like an exotic goddess, far out of reach, hardly of the same world. But Emma was real and human and close. She was like me – we were alike.'

Venetia didn't want to hear this. It was painful. 'I don't—'

He lifted his hand a little. 'Please, hear me.' He gave a small, deprecating smile. 'I've had to learn it pat, or I'd never get through it.' She made a resigned gesture, and he went on. 'My father was against the marriage. He wanted me to get on in the world, and he thought that someone with my difficult background should not marry a woman with an equally uncertain past – and *vice versa*. He thought I would be as bad for Emma as she would be for me. We argued; and then he died so suddenly, and I married Emma, feeling guilty and defiant. It was a difficult start for a marriage, and it made me cling to Emma even more. I grew ridiculously possessive of her, too protective. That's why I quarrelled with you that time, over your advice to her.'

She remembered only too well the names Tommy had called her when he discovered she had given advice on contraception to Emma, beleaguered by too many pregnancies in too short a time. 'You said hard things to me.'

'I know.'

'I thought you a ridiculous prude and a prig.'

'I know,' Tommy said again, disarmingly. 'I thought you were corrupting Emma's purity. And I was horribly embarrassed to think that she had been discussing the intimate side of our life together with you, of all people.'

'Well, she didn't,' said Venetia shortly.

'I know that now. I'm sorry. But I was battling for my career at the time, living on my nerves. I had so much to prove, so much ground to make up, coming from the gutter as I did. And there were always those who were prepared to hold it against me – and to murmur against Emma, which made me mad. I wanted to keep the world away from her.'

'But then,' Venetia said, puzzled, 'if you loved her so much, what made you do what you did – neglect her and then betray her?'

He passed his hand over his face with a groan. 'It was a sort of madness. I can't explain it. I had made my way to the top – as I saw it, through my own efforts, unaided—'

'Unaided?' Venetia said indignantly. 'What about Uncle Thomas and Aunt Emily – not to mention my mother? And the fortune you inherited, and Emma's fortune too? Your connections with our family – without which I'm sure there would have been more talk about your origins than there was.'

'I'm just saying that's how it appeared to me then. I was puffed up with my own success, thought myself no end of a fine fellow, and – here we come to the worst part. I'm afraid you will hate me more than ever, but I want to tell you the truth. When I met Mary, Emma had been in low spirits for some time. She didn't seem to enjoy my success, enter into my plans, applaud me and praise me as I thought I deserved. She seemed to have shut herself away from me. When Mary flung herself at me, and I felt – I felt—' He lifted his eyes to Venetia's, and she saw it was an act of courage and not of theatre, and softened towards him just a very little. 'I felt that such a fine fellow as I was deserved it – deserved not only the trappings of success and wealth, the fine house and clothes and invitations and acclaim, but also —'

'A mistress,' Venetia finished for him, brutally. The slight softening hardened again.

'Yes,' Tommy said frankly. 'That's exactly it. I've never been handsome, or attractive to women. Apart from Emma, no woman had ever shown any interest in me. And here was Mary – handsome and clever and rich – hanging on my every word. I couldn't resist.'

'You didn't try.'

'Perhaps not. It was a kind of madness, as I've said. But I want you to know that I never meant to hurt Emma. I truly didn't think she would mind. I thought she'd stopped caring about me. And I didn't think she would find out. I know that's not an excuse. I wanted Mary, and it was selfish and wrong of me, and what I did was a plain sin, there's no getting away from it. But I never meant Emma to suffer. I always loved her, though I might have forgotten it for a while. If I had known what would happen, I would never, never have done it. I would have died rather than see Emma brought to despair like that.'

He stopped, and when Venetia saw he had finished, she said, 'So this is all your excuse? You didn't mean to.'

He flushed a little. 'It's not an excuse. I don't mean to excuse myself, only explain to you, perhaps have you think a little less badly of me. I did wrong, and someone else paid the price. I can never forgive myself for that. I've tried to make it up since then, in the ways that were open to me. I was a good husband to Beatrice, while she lived.' His second wife, after producing a daughter, had suffered a series of miscarriages that had undermined her health and strength, and she had died tragically young in 1910. 'I tried to be to her what I should always have been to Emma. Since she died, I haven't looked at another woman and never will again. I live for my children and grandchildren now.'

There was silence. Venetia did not know what to say to him, other than that it was all so long ago, and she was too tired to be able to stand reliving the ferment of emotions of that time. She had seen the story from the other side – Emma, having given her vital years in childbearing, feeling tired, unwell and unattractive, neglected by an increasingly successful husband, who no longer needed her now that he had reached his eminence.

Had Tommy *really* felt that in fact it was Emma who had been neglecting him? Well, it was perfectly possible. And, in fairness, many successful men took mistresses, and did not expect it to lead to suicide. She supposed it was Tommy's hypocrisy that had set him aside in her mind: his priggishness over the contraception business, which he had denounced as a sin, set against his willingness to indulge in the sin of adultery when it suited him. A kind of madness, he had said. But all men became a little mad when they married. She had seen it again and again. They worshipped the ground a girl walked on, thought her against all reason perfect, but as soon as they wed her they turned into domestic tyrants and expected the goddess to turn into their own mother. And if she did, they then had a vacancy for another goddess. Perhaps it was in the nature of marriage. Or perhaps it was in the nature of men.

Tommy, at least, had thought about it, had examined his behaviour in a way most men never bothered to. She honoured him for that. She said, 'I don't know what you want me to say to you, Tommy. It was all a long time ago, and it's not for me to forgive or condemn you.'

She saw him look a little relieved, and guessed after an instant's thought that it was because she had called him Tommy. And the thought made her remember that he had been kind to her on many occasions; that he had always been more kind and thoughtful than the generality of men.

'As I said,' he answered, 'I don't ask you to forgive me. Just – understand, and perhaps . . . perhaps draw a line under it.'

'Very well,' she said. 'That much I can do.'

There was an awkward silence. He seemed to have more to say, and did not rise to go. She could not imagine what it might be, and he seemed diffident about broaching it. Did he want some sign of reconciliation from her – an invitation to dinner? Or perhaps he was simply lonely. He had no wife, and all his children had grown up and gone away, except for his daughter by Beatrice – whom they had called Emma, which Venetia had always thought rather an awkwardness.

So for want of something to say, she asked, 'How is little Emma? She's – how old, now? Fifteen?'

'Sixteen,' Tommy said, and his face warmed into animation. 'She's very well. A lovely girl, very bright, and with all Beatrice's beauty. She's at a finishing school in Switzerland – comes home for good this summer. I mean to bring her out next year.'

'I see. And what will you do with her in between?'

'That's something I wanted to talk about with you,' Tommy said. 'I don't want Emma to be flung straight from the schoolroom into the hothouse of a Season, and risk having her head turned. She needs to be introduced gently into Society, to have someone take her about a little, show her how to go on, so that it doesn't all take her by surprise next year.'

'Sensible idea,' Venetia said.

'I hoped that you would be able to put my past behind and undertake it. Not for my sake, but for hers – and perhaps for the good things we shared long ago, before I became a pariah.'

Venetia's eyes widened. 'You want *me* to take her about? No, nonsense. I'm far too old for that sort of thing.' Her eyes narrowed. 'Is this why you've come here and tried for a reconciliation?'

'You make it sound so calculating. I've been thinking about coming to you ever since Beatrice died. Emma's situation has only dictated the timing of it.'

Venetia shrugged this off. 'Well, in any case, as I've said, I'm too old. One of her married sisters would be much more suitable for the task.'

'They're too busy with their own families, and too distant, and they don't have the "in" in Society that you have. You can show her things and tell her things – be a real mentor to her. Your age doesn't come into it. She's very young, still, and I wouldn't want her to be undertaking very much yet – no big parties or late nights.'

'Why not wait until she's older?' Venetia tried. 'Let her act as your hostess for a year or two, and learn that way. She doesn't have to come out the minute she's seventeen, does she? There's plenty of time.'

Tommy looked grave, his eyes seemed to grow distant, as if he stared at something beyond the room. 'Ah,' he said lightly, 'time is something I don't have a great deal of.'

'And what does that mean?' Venetia asked irritably. She was just realising that by arguing rather than saying a flat 'no', she had given ground, and made it harder for herself to get out of it.

'It means that if I don't bring her out next year, I shan't be able to bring her out at all. I've been seeing Sir Crispin Gardiner, the specialist – no doubt you know him. He gives me a year to eighteen months. I'm rather banking on the eighteen months, as you see. I want her to have her come-out. It would be sad for her to be deprived of it.'

Venetia knew Gardiner, both in the flesh and by reputation. There was no need for her to ask the inevitable 'Are you sure?'

Tommy went on, 'I did think that perhaps I ought to bring her out in the Little Season, but that is so very much a second best, and she deserves the best. Venetia, I know it's shocking of me to throw this at you so suddenly, but will you at least let me present her to you? Meet her, think about it, and then decide.'

'Does she know?' Venetia asked abruptly.

'No. I don't mean to tell her, either. If it does turn out to be eighteen months, I can tell her when she's had her Season. I don't want to spoil it for her.'

'And if it doesn't?' He shrugged. 'What happens to her afterwards?'

'I suppose she will have to go and live with one of her sisters – though she'll hate that. They are such very suburban matrons, and she's a very London girl. The only other option is Beatrice's brother and his wife, but that would be even worse. Abradale lives at his club while the House is sitting, and spends the rest of the time in Scotland, and Betty never comes to London at all. And *you* know I have no other relatives. There are the wives of colleagues whom she might prefer to go to, but I don't want to entrust her to strangers. Family matters at a time like this.'

Venetia could see the trap closing, and felt exasperated; but she was sorry for Tommy in spite of everything, and saw his predicament. They had been close once. And she remembered his father, whom she had loved dearly: Emma was *his* grandchild, and one owed something to family. 'Very well,' she said. 'I don't promise anything, but you can bring her to see me.' Perhaps, she thought, if the girl turned out to be presentable – and there was no reason why she should not be – she might find some other suitable matron to turn off the actual business of chaperonage on to, leaving herself with just a supervisory role.

'Thank you,' he said, with all his feelings in his voice. 'I can't tell you how much this means to me. I came here with no expectations. I didn't even think you'd see me.'

Venetia hesitated, then held out her hand, and he grasped it gratefully. His was very cold. Life was too short, she thought – and especially so in his case – to hold grudges. 'You should have come before,' she said. 'At our age,' she added sadly, 'you come to see that there's no sense in prolonging estrangements.'

He looked at her keenly. 'You're thinking about your own daughter, perhaps?'

Venetia's beloved daughter Violet was kept away from her by her husband, Lord Holkam. He had had a political disagreement with Overton and had cut them off in consequence.

'Holkam's a fool,' Tommy said warmly. 'A prig and a fool. And see, once again we men make you women suffer for our actions.'

'Well, Violet loves him,' Venetia said.

'Another man who doesn't deserve the great blessing he's been given,' said Tommy.

As Brown and Jenny, who were getting on very well together, offered to have tea with the children, Lizzie was able to have tea with Mrs Penobscot alone. Ashley declined the invitation to accompany her. 'I suspect I'm going to have plenty of opportunities to enjoy that lady's company over the next few days,' he said. He had some papers to read, after which he and Teddy were going to take the boys to see the engines, on the invitation of the chief engineer, Joseph Bell.

Lizzie stopped at the purser's office on the way, to purchase a postcard showing the *Titanic*, which she intended to send to Morland Place for the amusement of Henrietta and Jessie and the rest. 'If I write it straight away, could it go off with the post at Cherbourg?' she asked. 'I'd like them to get it at home as soon as possible.'

'In that case, madam,' the purser said, 'I suggest you send it off at Queenstown.' He gave a twinkling smile. 'Cherbourg is French, but Queenstown is ours, so the post is more reliable.'

Lizzie laughed and thanked him, wrote the postcard and handed it over, then continued to the Verandah Café. It was a delightful place, very light and airy. All round the walls was a series of white trellis arches covered in green ivy. On one side, they framed fine windows, reaching from floor to ceiling, which looked out onto the glittering sea. Round the rest of the room they were filled in with looking-glass, so the effect was of being surrounded by windows with sea views. There were palms and orange trees in gilded pots dotted here and there, and wicker armchairs and bamboo tables completed the effect of being on the verandah of a grand seaside hotel.

Mrs Penobscot had a table by a window and waved to Lizzie as she stood looking around. 'Isn't it fun?' she said, when Lizzie joined her. 'On the *Olympic* the Verandah Café was terribly popular and it got really too crowded by the end of the crossing. But, of course, nothing's crowded on the first day because everyone's unpacking.' Half a dozen of the tables around them were occupied by groups of middle-aged, prosperous women, chatting and drinking tea. At one table a little girl in white muslin with a blue sash sat swinging her legs and looking horribly bored as her mother gossiped with her head almost touching that of her companion.

A waitress arrived beside them, and they ordered tea. 'The strawberry tarts are very nice,' the waitress suggested.

'Oh, let's have them,' Mrs Penobscot said.

'I rather liked the idea of toasted teacakes,' Lizzie said.

'We'll have both,' Mrs Penobscot announced.

'I can't think how I can even consider tea,' Lizzie said, when the waitress had gone, 'after the lunch I ate. On the way to the dining room, I wondered to my husband what there would be for lunch, and I think his answer should have been "everything".'

Mrs Penobscot laughed. 'I know! It's almost indecent how much one eats on a crossing. I'm sure it's something to do with the sea air. Somehow one can always find room for the next meal – to say nothing of bouillon and hot chocolate on deck, and coffee and cakes at eleven, and afternoon tea, and then a little supper after dancing. I think ship food must be magical in some way because one ought to get as fat as butter but it never happens. Have you done much exploring yet?'

'No, there doesn't seem to have been time. I don't know why, because I can't think what I've been doing.'

'That's another magical thing about ships. Time just disappears. I haven't explored much yet either, but I did just go and have a peep at the Turkish baths, because I really mean to try them this time – if *you* will go with me.'

'Oh! I don't know,' Lizzie began doubtfully.

Mrs Penobscot rushed on: 'They're decorated in real Turkish style. You know, the Mysterious East and all that sort of thing: sumptuous and dimly lit, crimson couches and twiddly Damascus tables and bronze pierced lamps and so on.'

'It sounds rather indecent.'

'Oh, no, not at all! A friend of mine on the last crossing tried it. They have separate times for ladies and gentlemen, of course, and there's a steam room and electric baths and a plunge pool. There's a lady masseur, too, and my friend said that being massaged is simply heaven! If you would go with me, I would be brave enough to try it myself. I must say I long for it! My husband goes to a Turkish bath quite often in New York, and if the men can have it, why not we women?'

Lizzie smiled, and thought suddenly of Anne. That would be an argument she would like. 'Well, I suppose,' she said, 'it would be foolish not to use the facilities of the boat, since we're here.'

'Exactly! Imagine writing home when the voyage is over and having to tell everyone that you didn't do everything there is to do. They'd think you were poor-spirited.'

'Jessie certainly would,' Lizzie said. 'Very well, Mrs Penobscot—'

'Oh, Amalfia, please! One is always much less formal on shipboard – and, in any case, I feel we are going to be very great friends.'

The waitress arrived with an enormous tray and began unloading it. Lizzie noted the leg-swinging little girl's mother and friend still *tête-à-tête* and the little girl more bored than ever, stifling a yawn and allowing her swings to bring her toecaps into collision with the table leg. At present the kicks were gentle and her mother had not noticed them, but if she were not rescued soon . . .

Amalfia noted the direction of her gaze and said, 'How are your children settling in?'

'They're still terribly excited. Ashley and Uncle Teddy are taking the boys to see the engine room after tea. They'll love that.'

'Didn't you want to go?'

Lizzie laughed. 'I wasn't asked. But, no, I think the less I know about the workings of the boat the safer I shall feel. At present I've come to a happy state of not believing I'm at sea at all, which suits me very well.'

'You aren't afraid of the sea? But there's nothing to it! I've crossed four times now. Modern ships are so safe, there's nothing to worry about.'

'So Uncle Teddy says. I'm not really worried, and I've always loved the sea. It's just that I've never been out of sight of land before, and it is a little unnerving.'

'Well, we shall soon be in sight of land again,' Amalfia said, consulting a delicate little gold watch embellished with diamonds. Whatever Mr Penobscot did, he was evidently successful at it. 'This leg of the journey is nothing. We'll be at Cherbourg before you know it.'

They reached Cherbourg at half past six. The port was too small to admit a liner of *Titanic*'s size, so she dropped anchor in deep water just outside. The sun was setting, wonderfully crimson in a pale sky decorated with just a few clouds, which turned pink and then gold-edged purple. Lizzie and Ashley took the children up on deck (Uncle Teddy was off somewhere talking to Ismay), and soon the Penobscots found them, and George Penobscot was introduced. He was a very tall man, well-built, with a fair, open face, a firm mouth and level grey eyes. He was quite a bit older than Amalfia (Lizzie guessed he was about thirty-five) and had the air of a successful businessman – one not to be trifled with, either. But it was plain that he adored Amalfia and she him, which Lizzie thought was lovely to see. She liked him at once, and he and Ashley shook hands and looked each other over in that cautious way men had, then smiled, evidently having liked what they saw. They were soon in a manly sort of conversation, while the females and children watched the fun on shore.

Two tenders came out from the port and lay alongside, and sacks of mail were loaded into one, while into the other stepped about twenty passengers who were ending their voyage there. Lizzie noticed two children, a boy and a girl of ten or eleven, among them, and thought how disappointed they must be to be leaving this wonderful ship.

Dusk was falling, and lights were beginning to show here and there on the indistinct grey bulk of the shore. The sea was calm, the colour of pewter; down below the lights of the ship reflected in it, and here and there gulls bobbed gently on the water, watching the coming and going. The tenders returned, one bringing mail-bags and a tightly packed mass of steerage passengers, many of them emigrants to judge by their poor clothing and huddled demeanour. For them, Lizzie supposed, the next week might be the first time they had ever been at leisure and in comfortable surroundings; perhaps the first time they had had enough to eat.

The other tender brought new first- and second-class passengers, a large number of them – more than a hundred, Lizzie guessed – together with their luggage. Amalfia said they would be wealthy Americans returning home after a European tour. Her continued study of the cabin list proved useful now.

'That's Mr and Mrs Thomas Cardeza – she was Charlotte Drake. They are going to have the starboard side "millionaire's suite", as it's called. They're terribly rich. I've heard tell she travels with fourteen trunks and three crates of baggage. There's Benjamin Guggenheim, the mining magnate, and the two talking together are railroad presidents, Mr Thayer and Mr Hays.'

'Uncle Teddy will like chatting to them,' Lizzie said. 'He's often said he'd like to invest in an American railway.'

'George will introduce him. He knows everyone,' Amalfia promised. 'I'm all agog to see Mrs James Joseph Brown. She's a millionairess and a friend of the Astors, but they say she's terribly vulgar. I can't imagine what the vulgarity consists of, if the Astors like her. Do you think she gets drunk or swears or smokes a pipe?'

Lizzie laughed. 'It would enliven the trip if she did, but I doubt it. People have strange ideas of what's vulgar and what isn't.'

Darkness crept on; the shore disappeared, marked now only by the pinprick lights here and there, and the larger blocks of light of the harbour. It grew cold as it grew dark, and the smell of the water seemed stronger, that flat, metallic smell the sea always seemed to have around harbours, so different from the smell of the waves on a seaside beach.

Lizzie shivered. 'Time to go in, I think,' she said.

'Oh, no, I want to stay here and watch,' Martial cried.

'There's nothing to see, only lights,' Lizzie said. 'And it's nearly dinner time.'

The men joined them at that moment. 'We sail again at eight, according to Ismay,' Teddy said, 'and reach Queenstown about eleven tomorrow morning.'

'I hear you've visited the engine rooms,' Penobscot said. 'I'd have dearly liked to be on that tour.'

'Nothing easier,' Teddy said. 'I can arrange it. I'd be happy to go again myself.'

'Thank you,' said Penobscot. 'And will you all dine with us tonight? It won't be a big dress affair. It never is on the first night. I don't expect the captain will dine down. But we'd enjoy your company.'

Lizzie consulted with Ashley by a glance and said, 'Thank you, we'd like that very much.'

Dinner was pretty much like luncheon, only more so, as Lizzie put it to herself. The first-class dining saloon was vast, a hundred feet long, and capable of seating five hundred and thirty at once. It was light and white-painted with slender pillars supporting a Jacobean decorated ceiling, and had Jacobean leaded windows. The floor was handsomely carpeted, the broad, comfortable chairs were upholstered in dark green, the tables were laid with fine damask and each was lit by a red-shaded lamp. It was quite full when their party arrived, but the carpet and upholstery absorbed the noise, so it was very pleasant.

Dinner consisted of seven courses – hors d'oeuvre, soup, fish, made dish, roast, savoury and sweet – with two or three choices in each. It all seemed very splendid to Lizzie, though Amalfia assured her that the food in the *à la carte* restaurant was of a different order altogether, and that the very wealthy passengers would eat there for most of the voyage. It seemed foolish to Lizzie to pay extra for your food when it was included in the ticket price if you ate in the dining saloon; but she did feel a prickle of curiosity and a desire perhaps to dine *à la carte* just once.

Even as she thought it, Amalfia said quietly, 'I mean to persuade George to dine there at least once. I want to see the Astors and Cardezas in all their glory. Do you think you will join us if we do?'

Bruce Ismay passed their table on his way out of the dining saloon and paused to speak to them. 'How are you liking it so far? Are your cabins comfortable?'

'Everything is perfect,' Lizzie answered.

He looked pleased. 'There are a few minor things here and there that we are taking care of, but a maiden voyage is a chance to learn, and I hope you will tell me if there is anything that could be improved. That is why I am here, you know.'

'I'll try,' Lizzie said, 'but it's hard to imagine anything nicer. You had better ask someone more difficult to please if you want criticism.'

He laughed. 'Have you explored yet?' he asked. 'Have you seen everything?'

'Not by any means. I've only really seen this saloon and the Verandah Café, though my menfolk have been to look at the engines.'

'I would feel privileged to guide you over the ship,' Ismay said. 'You ought to know where everything is in order to get the most out of the voyage. Would you allow me to give you a conducted tour – tomorrow afternoon, perhaps?' His look included everyone in the party.

'Thank you,' Ashley said for all of them. 'We'd like that very much.'

'And I hope you'll dine with me tomorrow night, and tell me your impressions,' Ismay concluded, and with a smiling nod went on his way.

After dinner they retired to the lounge for coffee and brandy, and listened for a while to the concert being given by the ship's orchestra. Then Lizzie confessed herself very sleepy. 'It's early yet, by home standards, but I'm ready for bed.'

'It's been a long day,' Teddy said, 'and full of excitement. I'm not surprised you're tired.'

'Well, I'm not tired a bit,' said Penobscot. 'Can I interest anyone in a hand or two of bridge?'

The other three obliged him, and Lizzie said goodnight and made her way through the fabulous ship to her fabulous cabin. Perhaps it was tiredness, but her sense of unreality was complete. There was no sensation of movement, and it was impossible to believe they were at sea with hundreds of feet of water below them. When she climbed into her great white bed, it was as steady as a rock, and she snuggled down, enjoying the incomparable smell of new sheets. *Never been slept in before*, she thought. She considered just for a moment the dark impenetrable ocean far beneath her and the dark landless air all around her, but just now it didn't seem to matter. *Rocked on the deep, Charlie will sleep*, she thought, the words of the old song coming up from distant memory; and then, unrocked and unconcerned about the deep, she slept too.

In the morning, while taking a first walk around the deck,

they sighted land again, the rugged grey-green coast of south-west Ireland. The sun was shining, the sea so remarkably calm that even the rocks seemed to have lost their menace, and embraced the gentle incoming waves instead of smashing them into spray.

They were not to see Queenstown itself, as it was too small for the Olympic class to dock there. They anchored two miles off-shore, and two paddle-driven tenders took off mail and a handful of passengers, and brought back a mountain of mail-bags and a packed crowd of emigrants for third class.

'It's a wonder there's anyone left in Ireland at all,' Lizzie said to Ashley. They were leaning on the rail together, alone for once. 'Poor things! I hope they have a better life in America.'

'They will,' Ashley said.

'Look at all that mail coming aboard. It shows how many Irish people have relatives in America.'

'A lot of all sorts of people have relatives in America. You'll be getting letters from home soon.'

'Home,' she said, and turned to look at him. 'But I'll have to stop calling it home, won't I?'

'Will you?'

'I don't think you mean us to come back to England once we're there, do you?'

He hesitated, and then said, 'To be honest, I'd be glad to stay out there. In my heart of hearts, I still think of it as home. And there'd be such wonderful opportunities for the children. But I don't want you to be unhappy. I married you in your own country, and the promise was implicit that we would stay. It would be dishonest of me to trick you now into leaving it if you didn't want to.'

Lizzie looked at him steadily, glad of his honesty. 'You mean, if I don't like it there, you'll come back?'

'That's what I mean,' he said.

She smiled. 'There aren't many men who would say that. Women are supposed to follow their husbands without question. "Whither thou goest I will go" – that sort of thing.'

'But we're modern people, with modern ideas.' He

dropped his head closer to hers and said softly, 'And I love you.'

'I love you, too,' she answered.

'So we'll see,' he concluded. 'Perhaps you will fall in love with America and not *want* to come back.'

Well, Lizzie thought, she had her answer – and it was the one she had known in her heart all along. He had said he would bring her back, but if he and the boys and Rose all wanted to stay, how could she make them leave their new land, just for her sake?

They didn't talk again for a while. The great triple-toned whistle blasted the air three times, the tenders cast off and paddled away, and then there was the rattle of the starboard anchor being pulled up, and the slight vibration of the deck as the ship began to make way, turning slowly westwards, towards the New World.

Down on the third-class promenade deck, one of the steerage passengers had brought out a set of Irish bagpipes, and began to play a pibroch as the great liner turned her stern to the old country. The sound of the wailing lament was so melancholy that it made Lizzie shiver. Ashley moved closer to her, and she felt the comforting warmth of his body against hers.

The wake churned brilliantly white in the glass-green water as the ship picked up speed, and a dozen seagulls kept pace with her, flying effortlessly above the after decks, turning their heads this way and that, slipping sideways on the air now and then to a new position, seeming simply to want her company. The low, greyish hump of Ireland diminished as they sailed away, disappearing into the gentle blue-green swell. The gulls turned back, leaving the ship to her lone passage; the sea darkened. Ireland was just a streak on the horizon, looking like nothing more than cloud; and then was really gone.

'And that's the last land we'll see,' Ashley said.

CHAPTER SIX

The strange thing, Lizzie thought, was how easy it was to fall into a routine, which then came to seem like the norm. She supposed it proved the adaptability of the human species, that after a few days a little world had established itself on board *Titanic*, which felt as familiar and comfortable as home.

At home, she and Ashley were not people of leisure, and their early-rising habit enabled them to take a stroll on deck each morning at a time when they could have it almost to themselves.

'I think I like this almost better than any other part of the voyage,' Lizzie said on Sunday morning.

Ashley raised an eyebrow. 'Given all the wonderful, expensive facilities of this ship, and the cost of the ticket?'

'Oh, I mean having you to myself, and the peace and quiet and fresh air,' Lizzie explained. It was a wonderfully clear morning, the sky pale and limpid, though there was a chilly breeze blowing, which made them walk more briskly than on previous days. She looked out to sea, and said, 'There's something wonderfully satisfying about having the horizon so far away. In London one's eye is stopped before it has gone more than a few yards, whereas here you can see for miles and miles.' The sea was dark blue and uninterrupted to the curve of the horizon. 'You can really see that the world is round after all,' she said.

'Didn't you believe it before?' Ashley asked, amused.

'I had my doubts,' she said. 'Oh, this air is wonderfully invigorating! I feel years younger. Ashley, when we're settled in Arizona, do you think we can go for a walk every day like this?'

'We'll be living in a town, you know,' Ashley said.

'Oh, yes. I keep forgetting.'

He smiled down at her. 'Are you having a nice time?'

'The time of my life,' she said. 'No duties or responsibilities, you "at home" all the time, the children taken care of for me, wonderful meals I haven't had to order, and so many pleasant things to do – the only difficulty is in choosing between them.' She squeezed his arm. 'If I were to die tomorrow, I could at least say I have had the perfect holiday.'

'I've enjoyed it too,' Ashley said. 'Work and family take up one's life so much. Not that it isn't a satisfying life, but it has been good to have this time with you – like going back to our courting days.'

'And we've got three whole days more before we reach New York,' she said.

'What have you planned for today?' he asked her.

'Amalfia promised she would play quoits with the children and me on deck before luncheon. What will you be doing?'

'I thought I might try the gymnasium. Penobscot recommends it highly. He says the equipment is first class and the instructor very helpful.'

'You like him, don't you?'

'I've never met him.'

'George Penobscot, I mean, as you very well know! I'm glad, because I like Amalfia *very* much.'

'I see that you do. I'm glad you have made a friend for the voyage.'

'It's more than that. I feel so very attached to her, as though I've known her all my life.'

'Despite the age difference? Like mother and daughter, perhaps?'

'Oh, no, not like that. Perhaps aunt and niece – a very grown-up niece and a very young-at-heart aunt. I do hope we shall be able to go on seeing them in America.'

'Shipboard friendships don't generally survive on shore,' Ashley warned.

'So everybody says. But I think this is different. Can we ask them to come and stay when we get to Arizona?'

'Of course, if they care to come.'

'Amalfia says George is determined to take her to see the Grand Canyon. He says it's something everyone must see once in their lives. And it is somewhere near where we will be, isn't it? So they could come and stay and we could all go and see it.'

'I'd like to see it myself. I never have, except for photographs.'

'Good. I'll talk to her about it today.'

Ashley smiled at her impetuosity. There was something very important to her about Amalfia's friendship. It was brought home to him that for a woman, a husband and children weren't quite enough: there was a definite need for a female friend, the like of which men did not usually feel. Lizzie had been close to Anne Farraline at one time, but as Anne's political views and behaviour had become more extreme, the friendship had faded – and now, of course, Anne was inseparable from Miss Polk. Perhaps Lizzie had been feeling abandoned because of it. He hoped very much for her sake that the friendship with the Penobscots would survive the voyage.

As it was Sunday, the usual daily routine was interrupted by a religious service, held at ten thirty in the first-class dining saloon. Captain Smith conducted it, using White Star's own prayer book, and everyone from all classes attended. Lizzie noticed the awe with which some of the steerage passengers viewed their surroundings: it was the only time they were allowed into the first-class areas. A five-piece orchestra accompanied the hymns, which included the old favourite 'For Those in Peril on the Sea'. Lizzie thought that peculiarly inappropriate, given that they were not fishermen struggling through a raging storm but wealthy people at leisure in a vast and luxurious liner on a calm sea. Everyone sang the hymns with pleasure, enjoying the novelty, and some of the third-class people added harmonies of their own to leaven the polite unison into something rather beautiful.

After the service, as people began to disperse, the Morland

party made their way to where the Penobscots were standing talking to the Thayers, who were travelling with their seventeen-year-old son. Thayer senior and Teddy had become friendly the last few days because of the railway connection.

'Fine service,' Thayer was saying, as they joined them. 'The Commodore's got just the voice for it. Wonderful old fellow, isn't he? Looks the part with that beard and so on.'

'Aren't we supposed to have a lifeboat drill now?' Ashley asked. 'I thought it was a White Star rule to have one each Sunday morning.'

'Oh, I hope not,' said Mrs Thayer. 'I can't think of anything more miserable than standing about on deck in that cold wind.'

'Don't worry, my dear,' Thayer said. 'I've been crossing on White Star for twenty years, and I've never had one yet.'

'I'd have thought it would be rather jolly, winding the boats up and down,' said Thayer junior.

'Quite unnecessary,' said his father.

George Penobscot said, 'Modern ships are as safe as houses. As the saying is, a ship is its own lifeboat.'

'Just so,' said Thayer vigorously. 'If anything should happen, you are much better off staying put on the ship – everyone knows that, who travels regularly. In a storm, a small boat could be overwhelmed by the sea or driven many miles away.'

'Nowadays,' Penobscot added, 'with the Marconi wireless, a stricken ship would call for help, and in a very few hours another ship would come along and take everyone off.'

'And at that point,' Thayer concluded, 'I assure you, you are far easier for your rescuers to find on a big ship than bobbing about in a tiny boat.'

'Well, we don't seem to be having any stormy weather on this trip,' Amalfia said. 'It's been quite lovely every day.'

'Storms don't affect ships like this in any case,' said Thayer. 'Ah, here's the captain.'

Smith had made his way through the throng, stopping to talk in his genial way to everyone, and had finally reached their group.

'Excellent service, Captain,' said Thayer, shaking his hand. 'Just the right length, not too long.'

'Very feeling,' said Mrs Thayer. 'You have such a wonderful voice for it.'

'Thank you, thank you. I'm glad you enjoyed it. What have you good people planned for today?'

Ashley took the opportunity. 'I was wondering whether there would be a lifeboat drill.'

'Eh? Oh, no, not this morning. The wind is too strong. Uncomfortable for the passengers. Not necessary, in any case, with a ship like this.'

'So I was just saying,' Thayer put in. 'Safe as a railway train.'

Everyone laughed. 'Well, I must be about my duties,' Smith said. 'I'm sorry this sharp wind should keep you from the deck, but I'm sure you'll find enough to do inside.'

'I believe we dine together this evening,' said Thayer.

'I have been invited to the restaurant by Mr and Mrs Widener,' the captain said cautiously, not wanting to offend a wealthy customer.

'Just so. George Widener has invited quite a party.'

When the group broke up, Amalfia said cheerfully to the children, 'I don't feel like missing my game of quoits just for a cold breeze. What do you think?'

The boys, who were both by now desperately in love with her, let her know what they thought in no uncertain terms.

'You're very kind,' Lizzie said quietly to her. 'I must confess I was half thinking of cancelling.'

Amalfia smiled. 'You can't get out of it now. But if you like, you can sit covered in a rug in a steamer chair and throw from there, in between sipping your hot chocolate.'

'I'll forgo the chair and the rug – but hot chocolate, now, that sounds like a good idea.'

'It does, doesn't it? Breakfast seems a long way off already. And talking of meals—'

'As one seems to do an awful lot on this boat,' Lizzie put in.

'Quite. Anyway, George and I would like to invite you and your husband and Mr Morland to dine with us tonight in the *à la carte* restaurant.' She beamed with innocent pleasure. 'I was determined to eat there once, and I know you feel the same, so I persuaded him – didn't I, darling?'

'When have I ever refused you anything?' Penobscot said. 'Will you join us?'

'We'd love to,' Teddy said for them all.

Amalfia, Lizzie and the children fetched their coats and went up on deck for the promised game. The wind was already dying down, and though it had been cold it had never been strong enough to break the wave crests. The sea was the same dark blue on all sides, gently heaving 'like a bed quilt come to life', as Amalfia put it.

'You are pleased to be dining with us, aren't you?' she asked Lizzie, as the boys took their throws.

'I'm delighted, of course. Why do you ask?' Lizzie said.

'You looked – I don't know – just a little put out for a moment when I asked.'

'Oh, I'd just thought of something. It was nothing at all, really,' Lizzie said hastily.

But Amalfia would not let it rest, and, as they had become so close in the last three days, Lizzie finally found herself confessing. 'It's clothes, you see. Unworthy thoughts, and I'm ashamed to entertain them, but my wardrobe never was adequate to first-class travel on a boat like this, even when we were eating in the dining saloon. I only have three evening dresses, and the thought of all those millionaires in the restaurant makes me feel faint.'

Amalfia laughed. 'But there's not the least problem in the world. You and I are very much the same size and shape, and I have heaps of things, more than I shall wear before we get to New York. Do let me lend you something.'

'Oh, really, no, you're very kind, but I couldn't.'

'Why ever not?' Amalfia said, her eyes wide. 'We're friends, aren't we? In fact, I feel you're almost like a sister to me. To tell the truth, I never got on as well with my sister Florence as I do with you – we were too different. Oh, *do* let me lend you a gown! It would make me very happy.'

'I don't know what Ashley would think,' Lizzie said, weakening.

'If he's anything like George, he won't even notice,' said Amalfia. Lizzie knew he would. She had too few things for him not to know them pretty well. Amalfia clasped her hands together. 'I have the perfect thing for you – my sea-green silk. I've never worn it, because when it came home I decided the colour didn't really suit me, but it would look perfect on you. Look here, you must let me lend it to you. Come to my cabin this afternoon, after lunch, and we'll try it on.'

'Mother, it's your turn,' Rupert complained at that moment. 'I wish you wouldn't *talk* so when you ought to be playing.'

The interruption allowed Lizzie to drop the subject of the gown without actually having agreed or refused. But as the game progressed and the morning wore on to lunchtime, she found that her curiosity and Amalfia's determination had settled between them on the trying-on after luncheon; and she was too much of a realist to think that she would refuse to borrow the gown having tried it on.

While Lizzie was playing quoits and Ashley was exercising in the gymnasium, Teddy had been having an informal meeting with Bruce Ismay and Thomas Andrews about the *Titanic*, and the passengers' reaction to her. When it was over, Andrews went off to his cabin and Ismay and Teddy strolled out on deck together, intending to have a turn or two before luncheon. The wind had dropped away completely and the air was now quite still; the little swell it had caused was also subsiding.

'Quite remarkably good weather we're having for our maiden trip,' Ismay remarked.

'Yes,' said Teddy. 'It's good to see the sun after the wet spring we've been having.'

As they came up to the companionway that led to the bridge, they saw the captain coming down, and stopped to talk to him. 'Another ice warning,' Smith said, handing Ismay a piece of paper. 'From the *Baltic*, this time.' *Baltic* was another White Star liner.

Ismay spread it out so that Teddy could read it with him.

To Captain Smith, Titanic. Have had moderate, variable winds and clear, fine weather since leaving. Greek steamer Athinai reports passing icebergs and large quantities of field ice today in lat 41° 51" N, long 49° 52" W. Wish you and Titanic all success – Commander.

Ismay looked up from the note to the captain. 'So we shall come up to it – when?'

'Tonight some time. It's a little north of what our position will be, but of course one has to make the allowance for the southerly drift.'

'I see. Very well,' Ismay said, and he and Teddy continued on their way, Smith going in the other direction.

'Ice?' Teddy queried.

'Icebergs, growlers, field ice – it's quite usual in April in the North Atlantic,' Ismay said. 'However, it has been a very warm spring in the far north – the warmest for thirty years, they are saying – so more ice has broken away than usual, and it's appearing further south than usual. That's all.'

'Did the captain say *another* ice warning?'

'There was one this morning from a Cunarder, saying much the same thing. It's the beauty of the Marconi system – ships are able to send each other advance warnings of weather conditions and hazards and so on. It's as though one had eyes and ears everywhere.'

Teddy smiled. 'Yes, I can see that. Practically makes the captain redundant, eh?'

'Oh, not quite that,' Ismay said, with a smile, as they headed for the dining saloon. They found Amalfia and Lizzie just going in.

'Oh, good,' said Amalfia. 'Our husbands have disappeared and we thought we were going to have to eat alone. You will come and join us, won't you?'

'With pleasure,' said Ismay. 'What have you been doing this morning?'

'Braving the elements and playing with the children on deck,' said Amalfia. 'But the wind seems to be dropping now.'

'Yes, it will be a pleasant afternoon, I think,' said Ismay.

'But it must be going to get colder, mustn't it?' Teddy asked, and said to the ladies, 'The captain had a warning of ice up ahead.'

Ismay looked startled and felt in his pocket. 'Dear me, I still have it. I put it in my pocket without thinking. I must give it back to Captain Smith.' He took it out and showed it to Lizzie and Amalfia.

'How will this affect us?' Lizzie asked.

'Oh, not at all. You won't feel the cold inside the ship, I assure you.'

'Won't we be late into New York? Won't we have to slow down?' Teddy asked.

'No, there's no need,' Ismay said. 'Ice is not a danger except in thick weather. Provided it stays clear, we can carry on as we are. It's quite customary to keep up speed in ice fields, you know. It's better to get out of it as quickly as one can.'

Lizzie said, 'I wouldn't mind if you did slow down. I'm enjoying myself so much, I feel as though I never want to reach New York.'

'Oh,' said Amalfia, 'but you've promised to come and visit us, and I do so want you to see our house.'

'We shall be in New York on time,' Ismay promised. 'It would cause too many people too much inconvenience if we were late. Punctuality is important with a ship this size.'

'When you think what a distance we have to cross,' said Lizzie, 'it's amazing that you can predict so exactly when we'll arrive.'

Teddy smiled. 'Yes, when my father crossed, back in the sixties, he hardly knew which *week* he would arrive. How times have changed.'

In the afternoon the breeze which had cancelled lifeboat drill died away so completely that the only air movement was caused by the ship's passage through it. There was not a cloud anywhere, sky and sea reflecting each other in perfect deep blue, and through the clear air the sun fell with welcome warmth.

Lizzie took Rose for a walk on the deck, pleased to have her to herself just for once. Rose had taken a great fancy to Amalfia, on account of her beauty and gaiety, to the extent that she had now renamed her doll in her honour, and when the walk was suggested she was at first reluctant to accompany her mother without either of the Amalfias she adored. Once on deck, however, she trotted along happily, chattering about her tiny, huge concerns.

'Do you like it on the boat?' Lizzie asked.

'Yes, I *do*,' Rose said, with emphasis.

'What do you like best?'

She thought a moment. 'I like best when we played with the fing like a stick and Martial frew the rope and Rupert frew the other bit.'

'You mean when we played quoits?'

Rose nodded, and then chuckled appreciatively. 'Rupert frew it in the sea, nearly, when he went his turn.'

'Threw, darling, not frew.'

'Mummy, will we play it when we get to 'Merica?'

'No, I don't think so. It's a game you only play when you're on a boat. But there'll be lots of other games, just as nice.'

Rose considered this. 'Will we go on a fing like when we went in the motor that time?'

'Which time was that, darling?'

Rose frowned. 'I can't fink it. When the ants came.'

'When the ants came?' Lizzie was floored.

'Yes,' Rose said impatiently, 'when we frew a kike, and the ants came, and we had cake and fings and orange in a bockle.'

'Oh, you mean a picnic!' Rose's confusion of 'flew' and 'threw' was catching. Lizzie could not now remember what it was you did to kites. 'Yes, we'll have lots of lovely picnics in America, and there are lots of exciting places to have them in, too, much more exciting than Hampstead Heath.'

'I like egg in my sandwich in a picnic,' Rose said judiciously. 'But not grass.'

That meant egg *seule*, not egg-and-cress, Lizzie knew. They came to the taffrail and she lifted Rose so that she could stand on a rail and look over the side. She was silent a while, and then, 'Mummy!' came the familiar imperative. 'Why aren't there any fings on the sea?'

'You mean other boats? Oh, there are, lots of them, but

111

they're too far away to see just now.' They had passed other ships during the voyage, but for the moment the ocean was as empty as the sky from horizon to horizon. They seemed all alone in a circle of heavenly blue that went on for ever. They might have been the last creatures left on earth. She imagined the globe they had worked from at school, thought of the large curve of Atlantic that separated the comfortable masses of Europe and America, and thought of what a tiny speck *Titanic* would have made on that. It might have been frightening if it weren't such a lovely day.

'No, not boats, I mean,' Rose said. 'Fings like on the sea at home, when we went to the beach. With white on them.'

It took Lizzie a moment to get this one. 'Waves, you mean? Oh, because the sea is too smooth for them just now. You see, when the wind blows—'

But Rose generally asked questions for the sake of speaking, and wasn't yet much interested in the answers. She interrupted with the demand, 'Down, please.'

Lizzie lifted her down, and Rose took her hand and drew her firmly along the deck. 'We go see the sweetie lady,' she pronounced.

This was a lady who spent every afternoon on deck, well muffled in a steamer chair, with a tin of jujubes in her pocket, and always offered one to the pretty little girl with the golden curls when she came past. Lizzie had to admit that Rose was a delightful picture in her sailor dress and hat, with white socks and shoes. It was rather a shame, she thought, that probably the only memories Rose would retain of this trip of a lifetime in the grandest ship ever to float were a game of quoits and a tin of sweeties. What it was to be young!

'Mummy, does the sweetie lady live in the chair always, in the night? Is it a picnic when she has the tea and fings and toast, what the man brings her in the white coat?'

Catching questions like a slip-fielder, Lizzie walked slowly down the deck under the amused and admiring eyes of the lounging passengers.

'I don't know if you've noticed,' Ashley said at dinner, 'but this ship has a definite list to port.'

'Has a what?' Amalfia asked.

'It leans,' Penobscot translated. 'That way.'

'Yes, I have noticed that,' said Teddy.

'I noticed it when we were leaving Queenstown,' Ashley said. 'I supposed vaguely it was to do with the sea running – not that there was much of it even then – but now there's no wind and the sea is quite calm and yet this brand new ship still lists persistently to port. It's odd.'

'You should ask one of the officers about it,' Teddy said. 'There's sure to be an explanation.'

'Oh, I did,' Ashley answered. 'He said it was probably because they had used more coal out of the starboard bunkers than the port, and that it would even itself out later on the voyage.'

'Well, there's your answer,' said Teddy.

'But it's an answer that doesn't answer anything. *Why* would they use more coal from one side than the other?'

'I can't imagine. Are you worried about it?'

'No, of course not,' Ashley said. 'It doesn't matter. It's just a puzzle, and I don't like puzzles.'

The mood in the restaurant was very gay. The Wideners' party – which included both the captain and Ismay – was making as much happy noise as breeding permitted, and the effervescence spread to the other tables. They were talking at one point about the plan for the next day of firing up the remaining engines and seeing how fast the ship would go. Ismay said he thought she would beat *Olympic*'s best time, and soon there was speculation all round the restaurant, and friendly bets being taken as to what speed would be reached.

'If they have a speed trial, does that mean we'll get to New York early?' Lizzie asked.

'Oh, no,' said Ashley. 'They'll have to slow down later on to get us there at the right time. We couldn't get in early, because the dock wouldn't be ready for us.'

The food in the *à la carte* restaurant was, as promised, quite different from that in the dining saloon, more what one would expect at a very expensive restaurant in London or Paris – in fact, the chefs and waiters were not White Star employees but supplied by Gatti's. Lizzie was aware that she looked right for her surroundings in Amalfia's sea-green silk. It was a beautiful gown, with a demi-train and a heavily beaded bodice, as was the fashion, and it made her feel very grand. Amalfia had been wrong, though, in thinking that Ashley would not notice it. As soon as he had come into the bedroom and seen her in it, he had frowned and asked where it came from. Lizzie answered him with increasing hesitancy, seeing he did not like her explanation.

'I hope you aren't going to allow this trip to make you discontented. It was supposed to be a special treat, but if it makes you think meanly of your everyday situation—'

'Oh, but it won't! Of course not! I'm only borrowing a gown on this one occasion because everyone will be very grand, and I've worn all I have with me already. It's not discontent, dearest, just – just being practical.'

'Practical?' Ashley looked at her a long moment. 'I don't like you to borrow. It looks as though I can't provide for you.'

'I should never have thought of it for myself,' Lizzie said hastily. 'Amalfia offered, and was very insistent about it.'

'Oh, she forced you to, did she?'

'I didn't say that. I could have refused, but she so wanted to do something nice for me, and it would have been making a big fuss over it to say no. It didn't seem that important. Ashley, please don't be angry. We weren't expecting to be travelling first class, that's all.'

'I'm not angry,' he said. 'I didn't think you cared about –' he waved his hand over her '– fripperies, that's all.'

'Fripperies?' she exclaimed. 'Do you know what a gown like this costs?' The humour came back into his eyes, and she relaxed. 'Don't you think I look nice?'

'No,' he said, stepping closer. 'Nice doesn't begin to be adequate. You look magnificent.'

So that was all right.

As soon as the sun had started to go down, the temperature had begun to fall. When Ashley and Lizzie went for their late stroll on deck after dinner, he insisted she get a coat first. 'It will be chilly.' But it was more than chilly: the air took their breath away when they stepped out of doors.

'The temperature must have plummeted since this afternoon,' Ashley said. 'It can't be much above freezing point now. I suppose it's because the sky is so clear – no cloud cover to keep the warmth in.'

They walked to the taffrail together, arm in arm. 'It's so still,' Lizzie said. 'No wind at all. I never thought it could be like this out at sea. One always thinks of the Atlantic as being grey and stormy.'

Ashley looked down at the black water, where the lights of the ship reflected in it, rippled by the ship's movement; and then beyond. 'Flat calm,' he said. 'I've never seen anything like it. There isn't the slightest swell.'

'It's as still as a mill-pond,' Lizzie agreed.

'I wonder how often you see conditions like this out here. It must be pretty rare.' He sniffed the air. 'Can you smell that?'

'Smell what?' Lizzie asked. The air was so cold that she could see her own exhalations. She imagined her breath turning instantly to frost and falling glittering to the deck.

'Don't you smell that flat, black sort of smell? That's ice. We must be almost up to it now. They said we'd get into the ice field tonight.'

'Ice doesn't have a smell!' Lizzie laughed.

'Oh, yes, it does,' Ashley said. 'You forget I did my sailing around Boston. It gets very cold there in winter, and I know the smell of ice as well as any sailor.' He looked down at the surface of the water again. 'We must be doing twenty knots or more. I wonder the captain doesn't slow down, knowing there's ice ahead.'

'He knows what he's doing. He must have done this crossing hundreds of times. And you know what Mr Ismay said – that there's no need to slow down when the weather's clear. It couldn't be clearer than it is tonight.'

'That's true,' said Ashley.

Lizzie gazed up at the immense beauty of the night. The sky was so clear that the stars stood out brilliantly, shining like diamonds against the depthless black. There was no moon, so they seemed all the brighter: enormous and, to a town-dweller, amazingly numerous, crusted across the sky in a blue-white dazzle, faintly reflected in the still, glassy sea. Against such splendour, the chill of the air was exhilarating.

'It's breathtaking, isn't it?' she said at last to Ashley.

He turned his head to look down at her. 'It makes one feel glad to be alive.' His expression was tender, and Lizzie instinctively squeezed closer to him. 'I'd like to remember this always,' he said. 'Not just this night, but this feeling.'

'We will,' Lizzie said, turning up her lips for his kiss. They were alone on the deck. 'Every starry night in Arizona,' she said, 'we'll remember this one.'

Lizzie was woken by a jarring movement of the mattress under her, accompanied by a strange grinding sound that went on for some moments. She lay with her eyes open in the dark, listening; replayed the sound in memory. Not a little noise close by, she thought, but a distant noise, and therefore, presumably, a bigger one.

She felt Ashley stir beside her. 'Are you awake?' she whispered.

'Yes,' he said. 'Did you feel that?'

'What was it?'

'I don't know.' They lay in silence for a minute. There was a slight vibration of the ship, and then nothing. Ashley got out of bed and went to the porthole. 'We've gone astern,' he said. 'Now we've stopped.'

He left the porthole and put on his dressing-gown. Lizzie was beginning to feel sleepy again, as the blissful warm nothingness she had been jerked from called her back.

'What's the time?' she murmured, almost without moving her lips.

'Twenty to midnight. You go back to sleep. I'm going to see why we've stopped,' he said, and she was happy to close her eyes and let him.

He crossed the sitting-room and stepped out into the corridor. Everything seemed as usual. The lights, lowered for night, were burning all along the passage; there was no sound or unusual movement. He walked along a little, and coming to a cross-passage met a steward coming in the other direction.

'What's happened?' he asked.

The steward was reassuringly unperturbed. 'Nothing at all, sir,' he said. 'Nothing to worry about.'

It was an automatic answer, and Ashley persisted: 'Yes, but what was that noise? Why have we stopped?'

'I don't know, sir,' the steward admitted. 'P'raps we might have dinged something. But it's nothing at all to worry about, not in this ship. You can go back to bed, sir.'

Though the man had no answers for him, he was obviously not the least worried, and Ashley turned away and went back to the cabin. But he was wide awake now, and put on a lamp and sat down to read and listen for any further disturbance.

Ashley had not long disappeared when Teddy came out into the corridor, with his dressing-gown over his night-clothes, and after walking hesitantly down the corridor a few yards, met Ismay, similarly attired.

'What's happened?' Teddy asked.

'I don't know,' said Ismay. 'I felt a jolt – a jarring sensation.' He looked worried. 'I wonder if we've shed a propellor blade.'

Their eyes met and they both thought of *Olympic*, her accident on the Grand Banks, and the lengthy stay in the Belfast dry dock that followed.

'I hope not,' Teddy said. 'That would be shocking hard luck.'

'I just asked a steward, but he knew nothing. I'm going to put my coat on and go up to the bridge. Will you come?'

'Gladly. I'll get my coat too,' said Teddy.

Minutes later they were making their way through the ship towards the bridge. There were still quite a few passengers up – mostly men, who had been smoking and playing cards in the smoking-room. Everyone was asking everyone else what the noise had been and why they had stopped. Stewards were bringing fresh glasses of whisky, emptying ashtrays, and answering, 'I don't know, sir,' to various questions.

When they reached the bridge, the captain was standing in the chart-room, fully dressed, looking as calm as a rock, talking to First Officer Murdoch, the officer of the watch, and Fourth Officer Boxhall. He looked round as Ismay and Teddy appeared, his expression concerned but not alarmed.

'What's happened?' Ismay asked without preamble.

'We've struck ice,' said the captain. 'Murdoch hard-a-starboarded and reversed engines, but we were too close to avoid it.'

'Ice?' said Ismay.

'An iceberg, sir,' said Murdoch. 'I closed the watertight doors at once.' The ship, Teddy knew, had the newest system where a single electric switch closed all of them together.

'I sent young Boxhall to have a look,' said the captain. 'He was just going to report. Well, Mr Boxhall?'

'I can't see any damage, sir,' the young officer said, 'but there must be some. There's water in the orlop forrard of number-four bulkhead.'

'Is that bad?' Ismay asked.

'I'm afraid it may be, if the water's risen that far,' said Captain Smith. 'It's a great nuisance. Mr Boxhall, you had better work out our present position, in case we have to call for help. When was the last fix taken?'

'Seven thirty, sir. Mr Lightoller took it.'

'You'd better work from that by dead reckoning. Quickly as you can, please. Ah, Mr Andrews.' He turned as Thomas Andrews came onto the bridge. He was fully dressed.

'Mr Pitman asked me to come to the bridge,' Andrews said. 'He says we've hit an iceberg. I was working in my cabin. I didn't hear anything at all.'

'The water's up to the orlop. You and I had better go below and make an inspection,' said the captain. 'We need to know the full extent of the damage.'

They hurried out. Teddy and Ismay stood to one side and waited. 'Does this mean we'll be late getting into New York?' Teddy asked.

'I think it certainly must,' said Ismay. 'The pumps will deal with the leak, but we will have to go slowly if the hull is breached. If it's bad, we may have to have the passengers taken off.'

Teddy nodded, and kept a sympathetic silence. Taking the passengers off would mean paying them compensation. After the troubles *Olympic* had gone through in her first year, it seemed now that *Titanic* was going to lose money as well, and on her very first trip. What wretched luck! It was a good thing, he thought, that the ultimate owner, the hot-tempered and dictatorial J. P. Morgan, had cancelled his trip.

It was not long before Smith and Andrews returned to the bridge. Andrews looked white and shocked. 'There must have been some kind of underwater spur on the iceberg,' he said. 'It's opened a rent in the ship's side, no thicker than my finger, but it must be three hundred feet long. At least five of the forward compartments are damaged below the waterline, perhaps six.'

'But the ship's plates are an inch thick,' Ismay protested.

'Whatever it was, it opened her like a sardine tin.' His eyes went round the group, gathering their attention. 'She's lost.'

'Lost?' said the captain. 'You mean – we're going to sink?'

Teddy said, aghast, 'But she can't sink. What about the watertight compartments?'

'They can't save us in this situation,' Andrews said. He looked as though he felt very sick. 'All they can do is give us a little time. We could survive with one or two of them damaged – even four – but not five.' He swallowed. 'You see, they don't go all the way up to the top deck. As the weight of water pulls her down, the water will go over the top of the bulkhead and flood the next compartment, then the next, and so on.'

'What about the pumps?'

'They can't cope. She's making water too fast. She'll go down by the head. There's nothing we can do.'

There was a moment of awful silence as each of them grappled with the reality. The unsinkable ship was going to sink. She was really going to sink. All this beauty, Teddy thought, would end up at the bottom of the sea. The tragedy of it tightened his throat.

The captain was the first to pull himself together. 'Well, we had better get a message away. There must be plenty of ships in the vicinity that will come and take us off. How much time have we, Andrews?'

Andrews turned away and, leaning on the chart table, began scribbling figures on a piece of paper. He straightened, checked his figures, and turned back to the captain. 'An hour and a half,' he said. 'Possibly two. Not much longer.'

'But—' the captain said, and stopped. He seemed, for the first time, as stricken as his ship. He had to clear his throat before he could speak again. 'We'd better send out the CQD, find out what ships there are nearby. I'll go to the wireless room myself. Where's that position, Mr Boxhall?'

Boxhall handed him the scrap of paper and he hurried away. Ismay muttered something about going to get dressed, and hurried out after him. Teddy and Thomas Andrews followed more slowly.

'I can't believe it,' Teddy said. 'This beautiful ship!'

'God, what a thing to happen!' said Andrews.

'I don't understand how an iceberg could do so much damage,' Teddy said, almost pleadingly. 'I mean, the *Olympic* had a forty-foot-high hole in her side when she collided with that cruiser, and she limped back to port. I remember Ismay telling me the passengers all sat down to luncheon immediately afterwards.'

'That was a vertical hole, not a horizontal one,' Andrews said. 'Ships are designed to withstand colliding head on, or being hit by something else head on.' He shook his head in a goaded way. 'It's ironic, but if Murdoch had not put the helm down, if he had hit the iceberg with the point of the bow, there would have been some damage, but nothing desperate. But one can't blame him. It's a natural instinct to try to avoid a hazard.' He turned away from Teddy. 'I must see what I can do,' he said. 'I advise you to get dressed, and get your family up and dressed, too. Tell them to put their warmest clothes on.' And he was gone.

Good advice, Teddy thought. There would be some standing around on the freezing deck to endure before they transferred to whatever ship came to rescue them. Warm clothes all round must be the priority – and perhaps a flask in the pocket wouldn't come amiss.

CHAPTER SEVEN

There were quite a few people on deck now. They had evidently not yet been to bed for they were in evening dress. All were talking in an interested way about the situation, and the words *ice* and *iceberg* were common currency. Word had spread. Teddy heard one man saying he had seen a crushed mass of ice packed up against the porthole as they passed. Their breath and the smoke of cigars wreathed on the air. It was bitterly cold, and now that there was no wind of passage from the ship, it was possible to appreciate for the first time how utterly still the air was. The sea was like black glass.

There was quite a noise coming from up forward, and Teddy went to see what it was before going below, in case it was a development of importance. But when he got to the taffrail and looked down, he saw it was only a group of steerage passengers on their own promenade deck. Masses of ice had fallen in lumps on the deck, presumably dislodged from the iceberg by the impact, and high-spirited men were playing an impromptu game of football with it. There was a strange smell in the air, presumably coming from the ice: a clammy, dank odour, like something from a particularly damp cellar.

Teddy turned away. Around the horizon there seemed to be a number of lights of other ships, which was reassuring, though it was impossible to tell how far away they were. Two hours, he thought. They had two hours. How fast could ships sail? *Titanic* had been making better than twenty knots, but could other ships match that, even in an emergency?

121

How far was the horizon – twenty miles? Or was it more at night? Or less? He wished he knew more about maritime matters. Say a ship whose lights he could see was twenty miles away and set off at full speed towards them, it must surely get here within an hour and a half? At worst they might have to spend a little time in the lifeboats, but there was nothing really to worry about.

He went inside, and found a great many more passengers about, some dressed, some half clad. The card players had resumed their games; drinks were being served; conversations were animated. The incident had given them all something to talk about, a new and absorbing topic. Everyone seemed to want to tell what they had felt and what they had seen, and no two accounts were the same.

'It was just as though the ship ran over a thousand marbles,' one lady said. 'A tremendous din.'

'It sounded like someone tearing a strip off a piece of calico, nothing more,' said another. 'You could hardly hear it.'

'It was extraordinary. The iceberg looked exactly like the Rock of Gibraltar,' said a gentleman with a red face and a large moustache. 'Must have been two hundred feet high – colossal thing.'

'Nonsense, sir,' said an elderly, white-haired man. 'Saw it m'self with my own eyes. It was quite squat, hardly as tall as the ship, and wreathed in fog.'

'Oh, there was no fog in the case, sir, I assure you! The air's as clear as a bell.'

Passing another group, Teddy heard an ample lady saying anxiously, 'My husband says a sailor told him we might have to get into the lifeboats, but he assured him we would be back on board in time for breakfast.'

'Lifeboats, nonsense!' another lady replied. 'What do they need of lifeboats? This ship could smash a hundred icebergs and not feel it. Ridiculous!'

'My steward told me we would be delayed for about two hours and then steam on to New York,' said a man.

'It would be foolish to get into a lifeboat and then come back on board. It's far too cold to be bobbing about on the sea,' said a lady.

'Well, I certainly shan't get into any lifeboat,' drawled another man. 'Everyone knows you're safer staying on board the ship. A ship is its own lifeboat, that's the saying.'

Teddy went on. He was walking down the corridor towards the cabins when a terrible noise began up on deck that stopped him in his tracks. He couldn't think what it was. A steward came out of a cabin behind him and he whipped round to ask him what the noise was.

'They're letting off steam from the boilers, sir. Reducing the pressure. Just a precaution.'

'Precaution against what?' Teddy asked.

'I really couldn't say, sir,' said the steward, a little perplexed. 'I just look after passengers. I'm not a sailor, sir. But it's nothing to worry about, that I do know. You're safe as houses in this ship.'

Such was the man's confidence – such had been the confidence of everyone he had passed – that Teddy began to feel rather strange, and even wondered for a moment whether he had dreamed the whole scene on the bridge. But then he remembered Andrews's face, his white, shocked expression, and hurried on. He knocked at the door of Ashley's suite and went straight in. He was glad to see Ashley awake and up.

Ashley put aside the papers he was reading and got to his feet. 'What is it?' he said. 'Do you know something?'

'I've been to the bridge,' Teddy said, and told what he knew. 'The damage is too great, despite the watertight compartments. She's going to sink. Andrews says she has only two hours at the most to live.'

Ashley looked stunned, shook his head in amazement, but he did not waste time in argument. He had the greatest respect for Thomas Andrews, and if he said *Titanic* was doomed, then it must be so. It passed belief; but it must be so. 'What is being done?' he asked.

'They're sending CQD by the ship's wireless, and another ship will come and take us off. We must get everyone up and dressed, and in their warmest clothes. It's bitterly cold out there.'

'Very well. I'll go and tell Lizzie, and then go across and wake Jenny and have her dress Rose. Will you wake the boys for me? Start them dressing, then go and dress yourself,' Ashley advised. 'Come back when you're ready. I think it best if we stay here until the rescue ship arrives, and then go up together. No sense in getting cold until we have to, or risking being separated.'

'Quite so,' Teddy said. Though he was by far the elder, it seemed natural for Ashley to take charge. He was, after all, a sailor and a shipping man, and this was his sphere.

The boys were hard to wake, and complained about being dragged from their downy cobweb of dreams. 'Come along now,' Teddy said, 'it's an adventure. Get up and get dressed – and you'd better put on two jumpers, one on top of the other, and then your overcoats too, because it's very cold on deck.'

'Are we going on deck?' Rupert asked sleepily. 'Is it a picnic?'

'No, but you might have a trip in a lifeboat. Won't that be exciting?'

Martial was properly awake now, and had got as far as sitting on the side of his bed in his pyjamas. 'In a lifeboat? Why, Uncle Teddy?'

'The ship's been damaged and it won't be able to take us to New York after all, so we'll have to transfer to another ship,' Teddy said.

'How was it damaged?' Martial asked.

'Was it the Germans?' Rupert asked, sitting up with an excited bounce, shaken out of sleep at last. 'Was it a bomb? Have we gone to war? Are we sinking?'

'Never mind all the questions, just get up and get dressed,' Teddy said. 'Help your brother, Martial.'

'I can dress myself,' Rupert said, spurred by the proposed indignity to scramble out of bed. Teddy saw them make a start, told them sternly to be quick and not waste time talking, and hurried over to his own cabin, where Brown was waiting for him.

'You're dressed,' Teddy discovered with surprise.

'I anticipated I might be needed,' Brown said. 'I heard the noise of the boilers being let off, sir, and I know what that means.'

'Do you?'

'I read about it, sir, in a newspaper story. They do it to prevent the boilers from exploding when they – when it – when the seawater rises far enough to flood them.' He met his master's eyes. 'We are sinking, sir, aren't we?'

'Yes,' said Teddy. The word had a terrible finality, and lay on the air in its own silence.

'How could it happen?' Brown said, but it was not a question, only an expression of sorrow.

'I must get dressed,' said Teddy.

'I have your clothes ready for you, sir. I thought the flannel shirt, and the tweed suit, sir, would be warmest.'

'You think of everything, Brown,' Teddy said. 'What would I do without you?'

He turned away but Brown called him back with a low, urgent question. 'Sir – is there danger?'

'No, I don't think so. Only discomfort. A crossing in a small boat, perhaps, to the rescue ship.'

Brown let out a held breath. 'If you will permit me, sir, when I have dressed you, I would like to help Jenny with the children.'

'That would be an excellent plan. Go ahead. I can dress myself.'

Brown went away. Teddy dressed quickly, putting on a woollen waistcoat over his shirt and under his jacket. His overcoat was lying waiting across his bed – excellent Brown! He found his silver flask, filled it from the decanter on the side table and slipped it into the pocket; sought out his deer-stalker with the ear-flaps and crammed that into the other pocket. Finally he put on his watch, and glanced at the time before crossing to the other cabin. It was nearly half past twelve. He felt a moment of trepidation. Fifty minutes had passed, somehow, since the sound of the collision had woken him up, and Andrews had said two hours at most.

He had barely returned to the sitting-room of Ashley's suite when Lucas and Walsh arrived, looking hastily dressed, but perfectly calm.

'I beg your pardon, madam, sir, but the captain has ordered all passengers to put on their life-preservers and go on deck. It's just a precaution, madam, nothing to worry about.'

Lizzie was helping Brown to adjust one or two deficiencies of the boys' attire. 'Very well, thank you, Lucas. You see we are dressed and ready.'

'Yes, indeed, madam. Walsh and I would have helped with the children if you had rung.'

'That's quite all right,' Lizzie said. 'But as we are ready, we would prefer to wait here, if you don't mind.'

Lucas looked doubtful. 'The captain's orders are for everyone to go up on deck, madam.'

'I don't want to expose the children to the cold night air unless it is necessary.'

'Look here,' Teddy said, 'I'll go up and see what's what, and then come back and report. How would that be?'

Lizzie was grateful, and the steward looked happy to be handing over responsibility.

Teddy felt too restless to remain in the cabin, and was glad of the excuse to go above. It was as he walked along the corridor that he noticed for the first time a longitudinal slope to the carpet beneath his feet. The ship was definitely down by the head, and a little finger of cold alarm worked its way down his spine. But when he reached the public rooms, the atmosphere was so relaxed that he was swung the other way again into confidence. In the dining saloon the waiters were laying the tables for breakfast. A contingent of the ship's orchestra, some in white jackets and some in blue, had set themselves up at the end of the lounge and were playing jolly tunes: they had just finished 'Alexander's Ragtime Band' and were beginning on 'Oh You Beautiful Doll'. People were wandering about, gathered in groups to talk, sitting with drinks or with hands of cards; some in evening-gowns and dinner jackets, some with coats over their nightclothes – he saw one large woman with a fur coat over her nightgown, and bare feet. Some were wearing lifejackets, some were carrying them, some were helping each other put them on. Stewards were trying to urge people up on deck, and there was a procession moving slowly up the grand staircase, but many were grumbling about the disturbance and a great many downright refused to be moved. Two ladies strolling arm in arm were accosted by a steward almost under Teddy's nose, and he heard them laugh and say, 'We know quite well the ship can't sink, and we're *not* going to go down into one of those little boats, so there's no use asking us.'

Feeling rather as though he were in a dream – for everything was a bizarre mixture of the familiar and the strange – Teddy joined the stream going on deck. A steward passing him against the flow said, 'Your lifebelt, sir – you ought to have your lifebelt on!'

'It's in my cabin,' Teddy said placatingly. 'I'll go and get it later.'

The steward was left behind as the crowd moved upwards. The man beside Teddy said, 'Damned lot of nonsense, if you ask me. They say the captain's ordered out the lifeboats! All very well takin' precautions, but it's damned cold out there, damnit. Better off stoppin' inside. Not like the Commodore to make a fuss.'

Up on deck the crowd spread out and it was possible to see how few people had actually obeyed the order. There was some activity around the lifeboats, but it did not seem either urgent or purposeful, as if the sailors did not know what to do, or did not believe there was any necessity for it. Teddy went to the rail and looked down. The great ship, an island of light in the blackness of the moonless night, sat curiously still in the water. The noise of steam emission was dying away now, and instead of its din there was the chatter of voices. The surface of the sea, seventy feet below, seemed a tremendous way down. It looked cold and black, and the thought of being out on it in a tiny boat in the vastness of night was a lonely and frightening thing, when here you were on the big, warm, lighted, friendly ship.

The ship's band were coming from the entrance to the grand staircase with their instruments, moving their operation from the lounge out on deck, perhaps in the hope of persuading the passengers to do likewise. Teddy turned and walked aft along the deck. He was on the port side, and noticed that the deck under his feet was listing over to the

127

starboard slightly, as well as down towards the prow. Two of the officers, Lightoller and Moody, were working with some seamen at one of the lifeboats. As Teddy reached them he saw Lightoller look up towards the bridge and, following the direction of his gaze, saw the captain standing there, looking down.

'Should we start getting the lifeboats away, sir?' Lightoller called.

The captain stared for a moment, as though he had not heard. Then he nodded slightly. Lightoller seemed unsure if this were an answer to his question. 'Sir?' he said.

'Yes, Mr Lightoller,' the captain called back. His voice sounded remote, and cracked a little, as though he had not used it for a long time. 'Women and children first,' he said, and turned away.

'Right, you men,' Lightoller said.

Teddy interrupted him. 'What news of a rescue ship? It's not really necessary to take to the boats, is it?'

'Excuse me, sir. Step aside, please. We have work to do here,' the officer said brusquely.

'I know, but just tell me—'

'Stand aside, please, sir, I said!'

Teddy found himself almost elbowed aside. He shrugged and went on down the deck, looking for another officer who might have more time for him. He didn't want his loved ones to be exposed to a little boat in the freezing night if it were not necessary.

He went down the after staircase, and at the bottom of the first flight he met Thomas Andrews coming from the corridor leading to the lounge. His heart lifted at the sight of him. 'Thank God,' he said. 'Someone I can talk sense to. What's happening, Andrews? I see lights of other ships all around us. When are we going to be rescued?'

Andrews's face was grey and stricken. He looked like a man mortally ill, and as he seized Teddy's forearm in a grip that hurt, Teddy felt really afraid for the first time.

'Listen to me,' Andrews said. 'Get your people up and get them into a lifeboat. Do it now. There isn't going to be any rescue.'

'No rescue? But—'

'*Listen* to me! There's no-one near enough. They've been sending CQD and the new signal, SOS, for half an hour. The nearest ship to answer is a Cunarder, the *Carpathia*, and she's coming at full speed, but she's nearly sixty miles away. She will not reach us in time. Do you understand? The ship will be gone long before she gets here. She's sinking fast and there's no hope of rescue.'

'It's the boats, then,' Teddy said.

'Yes, the lifeboats.' Andrews put a hand to his brow for a moment, covering his eyes. When he lowered it his expression was stark, his eyes haunted. 'There are two thousand, two hundred souls on this ship. Fully loaded, the lifeboats can take about twelve hundred.'

Teddy stared. 'You mean – you mean there aren't lifeboats for everyone?'

'There's no requirement for it in law,' Andrews said helplessly. 'No-one ever thought . . .'

The horrible truth began slowly to sink into Teddy's consciousness as it had obviously already done to Thomas Andrews. The ship was sinking. Rescue would not come in time. There were spaces in the lifeboats only for twelve hundred people. A thousand people – a thousand! – were doomed to die. Teddy grasped after some hope, some solution. 'Lifebelts?' he said.

'The sea temperature is twenty-eight degrees,' Andrews said. 'A man couldn't live for more than a few minutes in that water.' The gripping hand tightened. 'Get your life-jacket on and try to get into a lifeboat. That's my advice to you. Get your people away and try to save yourself.'

Teddy stared at him, as if there *must* be something more, as if this could not *possibly* be all there was. 'What about you?'

Andrews only shook his head. His hand slackened and dropped from Teddy's arm. He started to turn away, then turned back. 'Keep this to yourself,' he said. 'You understand, if it gets out – there's no knowing what might happen.'

Teddy felt a sickness settle in the pit of his stomach. He understood. A thousand people on board were doomed to die. If it became known, there might be panic, fighting around the lifeboats, the weak trampled by the strong, boats damaged or overturned, perhaps, in the struggle. That must not happen.

He had seen how many people simply did not believe the ship could sink, and would refuse to get into the boats. Many had gone back to their cabins; others had not risen from their beds in the first place. It was better to let them die in ignorance than risk mass panic and riot. Smile, and let them select themselves, unknowing, for death, since so many must die anyway. He felt sick.

He thought of the captain's words, 'Women and children first.' Yes, that was the way of it – had to be. Save the women. The men must sacrifice themselves. He thought suddenly, piercingly, of Alice, and the child she was carrying. He would never see her again; never see his child born; never return to Morland Place. Tears flooded his eyes, and he had to gasp to hold them back. Oh, he didn't want to die! He wished Andrews had not given him this burden of knowledge, the same burden that was making Andrews look ill and grey. But he had it now, whether he wanted it or not; and he had something to do, a duty to perform – a family to save. He straightened his shoulders, braced himself, and with a nod to his doomed friend, he turned and hurried towards the cabins.

When he got to Ashley's suite, he found everyone gathered in the sitting-room. Lizzie was playing Snap with the boys. She was deliberately making a muddle of shuffling, dropping cards everywhere, to amuse them. The sound of their laughter added one more bizarre element to the unreality Teddy felt. Rose, her face swollen with sleep, was in Jenny's arms, leaning against her shoulder, watching with solemn, drowsy eyes.

Ashley jumped to his feet as Teddy came in. 'What's happening? I heard what sounded like a rocket being fired.'

'Yes, they've started firing them off, signalling to other ships.'

'Why, what's wrong with the wireless?'

'Oh, nothing, but not all ships have wireless, you know.'

'Of course I know that. But surely—'

Teddy decided in that moment not to tell Ashley. 'A ship is coming to the rescue – the *Carpathia*, one of the Cunard line. But as a precaution, the captain has ordered the women and children into the lifeboats. So we must go up now,' he said. Nobody moved, and he added, with a sense of panic that he had to fight down, 'Right away, do you understand. We have to go *now*.'

Something in his face communicated itself to Ashley, for he turned to Lizzie and said, in a voice of magnificent calm, 'Well, if it's the captain's orders, we must obey. Come along, my dear, set an example. Come, boys – Jenny.'

Lizzie looked into his eyes, and then turned her glance fleetingly, piercingly, on her uncle. 'Very well,' she said. She held out a hand to Rupert, ushered Martial in front of her with the other, and left the cabin.

The angle of the corridor floor was steeper now, Teddy noticed, as they trooped along it. Passing the door to the Penobscots' cabin, Lizzie exclaimed, 'Oh, Amalfia! We must make sure she's all right. They might not have heard.'

Knocking on the door produced no result, and Teddy opened it and looked in. Lights were on but there was no-one there. 'They must have gone up,' he said.

When they reached the public rooms, the crowds had thinned a little as many people had either gone on deck or back to their cabins, but there were still plenty about, wandering rather aimlessly or talking in groups; the inveterate card players, still without life-preservers, dealing and laying. Teddy heard a steward, placing a glass of brandy beside one of them, say, 'On the house, sir. Captain's orders.' The player looked up briefly. 'Things that bad, are they?' he said, without much interest, and looked back down at his hand. 'Two clubs.'

Lizzie looked around anxiously, but she could not see the Penobscots. 'Oh, where are they? I wish they had come to us. If we have to get into the boats, I want to be in the same one as Amalfia. Can you see them anywhere?'

'There are a lot of people at the purser's office, madam,

collecting their valuables,' said Jenny. 'Perhaps they've gone there.'

'I don't want to go without Amalfia,' Lizzie said. 'I must find her.'

Teddy was growing anxious. Time seemed to be running away with them. It was ten to one. How much longer could they stay afloat? He thought of the water creeping up remorselessly inside the hull. There was no time for this! He *must* get them away.

'I'll find them,' he said. 'You go on, get up on deck. I'll find them and bring them to you.'

'Will you, Uncle Teddy?' Lizzie said. 'Oh, you are kind.'

'Go on now,' he said. 'I won't be long. They're bound to be somewhere about here.'

She went on with the children, and Teddy caught Ashley back and said, in an urgent undertone, 'Get them into a boat. Don't wait for anything. Get them away safely, whatever happens.'

Ashley gave him a searching look, and a lot of thoughts clicked together in his mind. 'My God,' he breathed.

'*Go,*' Teddy said desperately.

Ashley clasped his hand briefly but fervently, and hurried after his family. Teddy watched them for an instant until they were swallowed up in the crowd, knowing he would never see them again. Then he turned the other way.

The Ashley Morlands headed up the grand staircase. Brown had Martial by the hand now, while Lizzie held Rupert's. As they stepped out onto the deck another rocket went off with a whoosh, making the boys gasp with surprise as it exploded high above in a burst of white stars.

'Fireworks!' Rupert cried excitedly. From the other side of the ship came the sound of the orchestra playing dance tunes. 'It's like a party,' he concluded, with wonder.

'Don't be a dope,' Martial said sternly, but there was a tremble of excitement in his voice, too. 'Are we really going down in a boat?'

'You are,' said Ashley. 'And you must help take care of your mama and little sister.'

They had come out on the starboard side of the ship. Above them, the great starry sky spread its jewelled canopy, fabulously clear and bright. Below on the smooth black sea, just beyond the reflected lights of the ship, a first lifeboat was in the water, had pulled a little way off and was standing by. Ashley thought it seemed to have very few people in it. A second was in the process of being lowered, forward of the first. The officers responsible on this side of the ship were First Officer Murdoch and Fifth Officer Lowe – Ashley had met all the officers when Ismay had given them a tour of the ship, so he knew their names. As the lifeboat splashed into the water and the falls were cast off, Murdoch leaned over and called down, 'Mr Pitman! Pull away and hang around the after gangway. Good luck, old man!' Then he and Lowe and the seamen they were commanding walked along the deck to the next boat.

Ashley and his family followed. There seemed to be very few people around. Most of those on the boat deck were further aft, or over on the port side, where the band was playing. Far more had gathered on the deck below, A deck, which was more sheltered from the cold, and more familiar to them. The officers made boat number three ready, and then Murdoch turned to the waiting crowd. They looked back at him, quiet, polite, ready to do as they were told. Among them Ashley noted a little boy fast asleep on the shoulder of his nurse, his arm tight around a toy polar bear, and a gentleman, attended by a black servant, clutching a Pekingese dog to his breast. He also recognised the Cardezas, the wealthy couple who had taken the starboard side 'millionaire's suite', standing together with their maid and man.

'Come along, then,' Murdoch said. 'Let's have the women and children first.'

The women in the group went forward, or were urged forward by their menfolk, and were helped, or lifted, into the lifeboat. Lizzie managed to hang back until last, and even when the officers turned to her, she hesitated, looking up and down the deck. 'I wish I knew where Amalfia was. Aren't we going to wait for her?'

'There isn't time,' Ashley said. 'You must go now.'

'But I don't want to go without her.'

'Come along, please, madam,' Murdoch said, not impatiently, but firmly.

'Uncle Teddy will find her and make sure she's all right. Go on, now. Don't worry.'

She and the boys were helped in. Jenny passed Rose over, then climbed in herself. Lizzie looked back at Ashley with sudden fear. 'What about you? Aren't you coming too?'

Ashley looked around. There were no more women or children anywhere in sight, just the group of men and crew members standing silently watching. He looked at Murdoch.

'By all means, go with your family,' Murdoch said, 'but please be quick.'

'Are you sure? Is it all right?'

'Yes, carry on,' said Murdoch, and when Ashley had jumped gladly in, Murdoch beckoned to the other husbands and the unattached gentlemen standing nearby. 'Get in, gentlemen, please.'

They climbed aboard, together with a number of crewmen, and a group of firemen who had come up from the boiler rooms and were lingering hopefully nearby. Now there was no-one in sight on the deck but Brown.

'Come on, Brown,' said Ashley.

Brown hesitated, looking unhappy, torn between his loyalty to his master and his desire to be with the children. 'I can't leave my master, sir,' he said. 'I'm sorry.'

'If you're not boarding, please step aside,' Murdoch said. 'We can't waste time.'

The boat was not completely full – Ashley guessed there were around fifty people in it, about twenty-five women and children and the rest male passengers and crew members. 'Get in, Brown,' he called out. 'Your master sent you with us, it's what he wants. Mrs Morland will need your help – and Jenny.'

Mr Cardeza's servant, who was nearest to the boarding point, looked up at Brown and silently shifted a little sideways, as if making room for him. It seemed to decide Brown, who almost lurched forward as though some restraining tether had been cut. He climbed into the boat, but he sat hunched, his expression one of great misery. There were tears on his face, and he looked suddenly very frail.

'Right,' Murdoch called to the seamen, 'lower away.' The boat began to jerk slowly downwards. Murdoch leaned over and called down to the seaman in charge of the boat, 'Moore, I'm going to lower you as far as A deck, so you can board some more passengers from there.'

'Aye aye, sir.'

But when they stopped at A deck, they found it closed in by the weather screens that had been added to *Titanic* at the last moment in Belfast, to prevent promenading passengers being troubled by spray. Ashley stared at the people on the other side of the glass, looking bulky with their white canvas life-jackets over their coats, standing quietly watching. He met the eyes of a woman in an enormous fashionable hat, decorated with ostrich feathers and trembling jet beads and ornaments; and she smiled nervously, almost placatingly, like a child who fears, but does not understand, something going on among the grown-ups.

Seaman Moore had a conversation with a colleague on the deck, then called up to Murdoch, 'They can't get the screens open, sir. It needs a special spanner. Someone's gone to get it, but he hasn't come back.'

Murdoch said something to Lowe that Ashley did not catch, and then he called down, 'We can't wait any longer. We'll lower you as you are.'

After a moment the boat jerked again, dropping a foot or two. The woman on the deck gradually disappeared from view, but her white face and blank expression, under her expensive hat, stayed printed on Ashley's mind like an after-image of light as they moved slowly down the side of the ship. At every level they passed portholes, catching glimpses of empty rooms within, each like the lighted stage in a theatre, waiting for the actors to come in. The boys were quiet now, their excitement depressed by the strangeness and tension they felt from the adults around them; Rose and the little boy with the bear slept on their nurses' laps. It was very cold, and Ashley could smell the ice on the sea below them. He wished he had thought to bring gloves with him.

When they hit the water one or two of the women cried out in alarm, but they were soon quiet again. There was no urge in anyone to talk. There were more than enough crew members in the boat to manage her, but it took them time to free her from the falls. Ashley, with a sailor's experience, realised it was because the sea was so calm: there was no swell to lift the boat and slacken the ropes momentarily to allow them to be unhooked. But it was done at last, and the seamen unshipped the oars and began to pull away.

Lizzie's hand crept into Ashley's and he looked down at her. Her eyes were wide and full of tears. 'Uncle Teddy – Amalfia – will we see them again?'

'There are lots of other boats,' he replied. 'I'm sure they'll be all right.' He saw her accept the comfort without necessarily believing it; she took a deep breath and controlled the quivering of her lips.

They both turned their eyes back to the ship. 'It looks so beautiful,' Lizzie said. Outlined against the starry sky, every porthole and saloon ablaze with light, it was a thing of enchantment, made yet more magical by its uncanny stillness, and the regular whiz and dazzling white explosion of the rockets. It looked so enormous, so stable, that it was impossible to believe anything could be wrong with it – so Lizzie thought, until they were far enough off to see the terrible, unnatural slope downwards towards the bow, made more dramatic by the line of lighted portholes, which should have been parallel to the sea's surface, but instead went down to meet and disappear under it. The sight made Lizzie shiver, and it was nothing to do with the cold. The shock of understanding at last what was to happen had numbed her, so that she couldn't feel fear, only an enormous sorrow. The seamen stopped rowing and rested on their oars, the boat stopped moving, and then there was nothing to do but sit on the icy black water and watch the ship die.

Teddy searched the public rooms for the Penobscots, but without success. A little more sense of urgency seemed to be permeating the crowds, and a long queue had formed at the purser's office to withdraw valuables from the ship's safe. It was an orderly queue, and the purser and his assistants were dealing with the requests quickly and efficiently, but the sight of it only added to Teddy's feeling of unreality. It was a quarter past one. How much longer could the ship survive? It was more than an hour and a half since she struck. Why were these people bothering about their jewels and banknotes? He wanted to shake them, to scream at them, to make them understand the truth – but he must not. His fatal knowledge was sickening him.

He recognised an American lady, Mrs Benson, in the queue and, remembering that the Bensons knew the Penobscots well, stopped to ask if she had seen them.

She spoke first, breaking off chattering to her maid to exclaim, 'Oh, my, Mr Morland, did you ever know the like of this? Dragged from our beds at this unearthly hour, and now they're saying we have to go down into the lifeboats! But I told Robert I could *not* go without my diamonds. They were my mother's, you know, and it's the sentimental value – though they're worth a clean fortune as well! What do *you* think is going to happen? You must know more than we do, connected with White Star as you are. My friend Millie Wilmington told me not to come on this ship because she said there are always inconveniences on a maiden trip, but I never thought anything like this would happen. How can a ship this size be damaged by an iceberg? And I suppose we'll be late getting to New York now, which is such a nuisance because it's my niece's wedding on Saturday and she lives all the way up state and I depended on having some shopping before I go.'

When Teddy could edge a word into the flood he asked about the Penobscots, and she said at once, 'Oh, I've seen them. They were in this same queue, but a long way ahead of me. She has that lovely emerald set, you know. I told her it was—'

'Do you know where they are now?' Teddy interrupted firmly.

'I expect they've gone up on deck. She had her fur on – the sable – so I expect that's where they've gone.' Teddy

137

would have moved away but she clutched his arm and said, 'I was wondering if I ought to go back and put *my* fur on. I was afraid it might get spoiled if we had to go in a boat, but now I wonder if I mightn't need it as it's so cold. What do *you* recommend, Mr Morland?'

Teddy looked down at the hand, curved like a claw, heavy with diamond rings, digging into his sleeve, and was filled with revulsion and panic. He dragged his arm roughly away, and meeting her startled eyes said, in a low voice, 'I recommend you to go *now* and get into a lifeboat. Leave your damned diamonds. What use are they?'

He hurried away, but heard her behind him say, '*Well!* The manners of some people.'

He found them at last down on A deck, forward on the port side. They were standing at the back of a large crowd, which consisted of other eminent first-class passengers, including the Astors, the Wideners, the Thayers and the Ryersons, together with various servants and children, who were all waiting patiently behind the weather screens, looking at a lifeboat that was dangling tantalisingly outside.

Amalfia greeted him eagerly. 'Oh, Mr Morland! I'm so glad to see you. But why aren't you with the others? How are dearest Lizzie and the children? Are they going to get into a lifeboat? I must say I think it's a great deal of foolishness. We shall look pretty silly rowing about in the cold and then coming back on board.'

Teddy said quietly, 'There will be no coming back on board. I assure you it is essential you get into a lifeboat. Lizzie and the children will already have gone. She wanted me to make sure you did the same.'

Amalfia searched his face. 'You can't mean that the ship really is sinking? I've heard some people say so but I thought it was all a nonsense.'

'Yes,' Penobscot agreed. 'This ship can't possibly sink.'

'I'm afraid it's true,' Teddy said. 'The iceberg made a hole in her bottom too big for her to survive. You must get your wife into a lifeboat, Penobscot. What is happening here?' He looked at the dangling vessel.

Amalfia answered: 'Oh, they lowered it for us to board from here and then found they couldn't open the screens. One of the officers, Mr Lightoller, told us to wait here while he sent a crewman off to get the special spanner that's needed.'

'I see. Well, when he gets back, he'll get the boat away all right, so make sure you are in it.'

'What will you do? Didn't you say Lizzie and the others have already gone? Won't you stay and come with us?'

Teddy said gently, 'There won't be room for me on the boat. It's women and children first, you know.'

Her eyes widened. 'But – you mean—' And she looked at her husband. 'George?'

'Women and children first,' he said. 'That's the way it has always been. But I'll get you away safely, my darling, I promise you.'

'No,' Amalfia said. 'I'm not going.'

'It's perfectly safe,' Teddy said at once. 'The sea's quite calm.'

Amalfia turned towards him, her eyes bright with tears. 'I'm not afraid. But I won't leave George. How can you think it?'

'You must go, darling,' Penobscot said.

'Lizzie made me promise I'd see you safely off,' said Teddy. 'You won't make me break my promise, will you?'

Amalfia straightened a little, and she suddenly seemed ten years older in her bleak dignity.

'You needn't try to humour me,' she said. 'I understand your concern, but I won't get into a boat without George.'

'My dear young lady,' Teddy began, 'you don't fully appreciate—'

'But I do,' she interrupted. 'I'm not a fool. I understand what all this is about now.' She put her hands into her husband's and looked up into his face. 'I love you, George, and I'm not going to leave you. We'll take our chances together.'

Penobscot's face seemed to grey as he saw her determination. Teddy saw him swallow, as he seemed to come to a decision. 'My darling, outside a lifeboat there is no chance for us. Tell her that it's so, Mr Morland.'

'It's true,' said Teddy heavily.

'You must go,' Penobscot went on gently. 'If you stay with me you'll die.'

'I know,' said Amalfia.

'You know? Then how can you refuse? I have to know you are safe. You must do this thing for me. You must live.'

'What would my life be without you?' she said calmly. 'How could I live, knowing I had left you here, remembering this for ever, imagining–' she swallowed '– imagining your last minutes all alone? If we cannot live together, then we will at least die together.'

'Oh, my love,' Penobscot said shakily, and closed his eyes against tears.

She managed a quivering smile. Teddy saw that she was very afraid, but still she tried for lightness. 'You never know,' she said, 'something may happen. We may get off together somehow. There's always hope, as long as we are together. Don't send me away, George. I don't want to live without you.'

For answer he kissed her forehead, and drew her against him, putting a sheltering arm around her. 'Let's go and find a quiet place,' Amalfia said. 'Away from these crowds.' She looked at Teddy. 'Tell Lizzie I'm sorry. I was so glad to be her friend these last few days, and I wish it could have gone on for ever. But she'll understand.'

'I'll tell her,' said Teddy, with a heavy heart. She did not understand, or had forgotten, that he was as doomed as they were.

She looked up at her husband again. 'Tell her I'm happy,' she said, 'and not at all afraid.'

Teddy watched as they walked away up the deck. He felt suddenly the loneliness of death. He needed to be with someone he knew. He turned away and went to look for Ashley, to make sure that Lizzie and the children had got off safely. At least they could comfort each other a little, he thought.

He went up the grand staircase again and out onto the boat deck on the port side, where the ship's band was playing tunes from Gilbert and Sullivan operettas. Another rocket shot up into the sky and burst into stars. He began to push slowly through the crowds, looking for Ashley. A lifeboat was being loaded by Lightoller and Moody. A crowd of men stood watching as the women were helped in over the side. Most were being very stoical about parting, but one woman clung to her husband and sobbed, and had to be forcibly detached and lifted in. Another woman put her arm round her and comforted her.

When there were no more women to hand, Lightoller ordered the boat to be lowered; but it was only half full. What was the man about? Teddy thought of Amalfia and George Penobscot, and of Ashley – of Colonel Astor down below on A deck, whose adored young wife was heavily pregnant – of all these men standing by, who had kissed their wives and obediently stood back. He felt a desperate anger on their behalf. Empty places on the boat – lives needlessly thrown away! He pressed his fingernails into his palms to control himself, and as the working party moved on towards the next lifeboat he managed to push his way through the crowds and catch Lightoller's sleeve. The officer turned.

'For God's sake, man,' Teddy said in an low, urgent voice, 'don't send the boats off half empty! You could have got a score of men into that last one.'

'It's women and children only,' Lightoller snapped. 'Captain's orders.'

'But the captain said women and children *first*, not women and children *only*. I heard him. He can't have meant you to—'

Lightoller interrupted: 'I can't allow special treatment for you, Mr Morland, no matter who your friends are. Please stand aside and let me do my duty.'

Teddy flushed with anger. 'I wasn't asking for myself, but for these gentlemen whose wives are in the boats.'

'Women and children only,' said Lightoller again. 'It's the rule of the seas, sir, and my specific orders.'

Teddy saw immovable stubbornness in his eyes. 'Then won't you at least hold back the boats and order a search for the women?' he begged.

'There is no time for that. I must get the boats off as quickly as possible.'

'But you can't condemn people to die just because—' Teddy began.

The officer cut him off angrily: 'This is wasting time. Stand aside, sir, and don't interfere with the working of the ship, or I'll have you clapped in irons.'

He looked fierce enough to do it. Teddy thought of being locked up below in the ship's last moments and quailed before the image. He dropped his hand and Lightoller walked on with his working party. Teddy turned away, and the group of gentlemen left on the deck parted round him, some giving him curious, others distasteful looks. He ignored them, deep in thought.

The ship was far down by the head now. It was half past one. There was not much time left, and by his guess half the lifeboats were away, yet there must be hundreds of women still aboard. He felt desperate to do something, not only to help but to keep the sick dread at bay. He thought of Lightoller's determination on 'women and children only'. Did the officer not know the true situation? Or was it that, knowing everyone could not get off, he preferred to let all the men die rather than have to choose between them? Perhaps it was neither of these things, but simply that he was clinging in a desperate situation to something he knew. None of them, he supposed, could be thinking very clearly. What had he himself done, after all, but wander about pointlessly, numbed with shock and fear, as much adrift as everyone else?

Well, he could change that, at least. He could do something useful while there was still time. He shook his head to clear it, and went back inside to look for women.

CHAPTER EIGHT

Among the patches and lumps of ice and growlers, the sea was dotted with lifeboats, all pulling away from the stricken ship. Every time they came near to one, a woman would call out in a distraught but somehow hopeless manner for her husband. 'Charles! Are you there, Charles?' Lizzie's hand was in Ashley's, gripping it hard, but it tightened still more whenever the pathetic cry went up.

He remembered that Murdoch had told the boat before this to stand by. Given that this one was not near full, he called out to Seaman Moore, 'Shouldn't we stand by closer to the ship, in case there are more people to be got off?'

Moore's answer was quite firm. 'No, sir, we have to keep our distance. It's the suction, you see, when she goes down. It could pull us right under with her.'

'He's right, sir,' said one of the other seamen.

One of the male passengers said, in a panicky voice, 'These fellows know what they're doing. Leave 'em be. We're all right where we are.'

The Pekingese was shivering violently, and its owner opened his coat and folded the animal inside, with only its head sticking out at the top. Ashley noticed that his native servant was shivering too, having come originally, he supposed, from a warmer clime.

The bright ship was so far down by the head now that the boat deck was only about twenty feet from the water at the forward end. It would make launching the remaining boats easier, he thought – except that she seemed to be listing quite badly to port, which would make it harder to load passengers from that side.

'How could it happen?' Lizzie asked him, out of a long train of thought of her own. 'If the iceberg was big enough to do all that damage, how could they not have seen it? They must have had lookouts.'

Ashley roused himself to answer her. 'There's no moon. An iceberg is dark, you see, dark against dark unless light shines on it. And the best way to spot a berg is by the waves breaking at its foot, but there are no waves either. There's a flat calm.'

'No waves, and no moon,' Lizzie said. A combination of chances, then, she thought. Just an accident – the sort of accident that made you think God had planned it that way, for some purpose of his own. But what, and why? She remembered dinner in the restaurant, Amalfia gay and laughing in her emeralds, Lizzie in the sea-green silk, all of them happy and without a care, the bright lights, the white-jacketed waiters, the luxurious furnishings. It seemed so long past, like something in history. Could it really have been only a few hours ago?

'What's the time?' she asked, but her voice came out too quietly and Ashley didn't seem to hear her.

A military-looking gentleman slipped a flask out of his pocket, but seeing her looking at him – her eye attracted only by the movement – he changed his mind and put it away again. Did he think she disapproved of drinking, or was he afraid he might have to share it? Time seemed agonisingly to have stopped, leaving one with nothing to do but think such exhausted, pointless thoughts. Faintly across the water came the sound of music – the band still playing on deck. It was like a mysterious, weirdly beautiful nightmare.

Teddy went through the public rooms again, but though there were people about – not so many of them as before – they were all men. The first-class passengers seemed to have resigned themselves and to be determined only to meet their end like gentlemen. Where were the women? Had they all gone to the boats, or had some gone back to their cabins?

He could hardly perform a cabin search. Perhaps there were still women in the second class. He went on down to B deck and walked uphill with some difficulty towards the after end of the ship where there was a second-class smoke room behind the *à la carte* restaurant. The restaurant was empty; the tables were half laid, and glasses that had fallen off onto the floor had rolled until various legs of furniture had impeded them. As he stepped through the door a domed silver trolley – the sort that had a spirit lamp underneath for keeping joints hot – passed the critical point and began to trundle down the slope towards him. Teddy stopped at the sight of it – mentally exhausted as he was, he could not think what to do about it – but the inherent instability of its castor wheels made it veer sideways, hit a column and overturn with a metallic crash. Almost in the same instant a stack of plates slid from a serving table onto the floor and several broke. Teddy proceeded cautiously, as though the furniture might rise up and bite him, and passed through onto the second-class stairway and thence to the smoking room. But it, too, was empty, though there was smoke in the air, cigarette and cigar ends in the ashtrays, and empty tumblers on tables. As he stared around, one that had fallen on its side rolled over the edge and crashed to the ground. Despite the slope on which he was standing, it was hard to connect these movements with the ship's list. It was as though inanimate objects were coming to life, taking advantage of the humans' plight.

Where now? He tried to cudgel his brain into remembering the layout of the second- and third-class public rooms. He thought there was something on C deck below this – the second-class library, was it? – and, ah, yes, right aft on C deck were the third-class smoke-room and general room. That would be a fertile hunting ground. Surely that would be where the passengers would gather, if they hadn't gone up on deck. He went back to the staircase and started down it, fighting the sense of horror that was building in him at the prospect of going further down, when his animal instincts were screaming at him to go up. Suppose the lights went out? God only knew how they were still burning. If they went out and he was left here in the blackness! He would never find his way up. His heart was pounding. He gulped air, longing for outside, longing for the bitter night and the stars, for however long was left to him. If he must die, let it be seeing the sky, not trapped below in muffling, unnatural darkness.

But there must be women somewhere. He waited a moment, clinging to the banister rail until his legs stopped trembling, and went on. At the turn of the stairs he saw something glinting below; a few more steps, and he saw it was water. The water had reached C deck! It made a tide-mark across the staircase hall, and even as he watched it crept insidiously, moving further aft. D deck must be under water then – D deck where the first-class dining-saloon was, the second-class lounge, the two third-class bars. And the cabins, all the cabins on D, E and F, and those forward on C, were now under water. If people had been in them, asleep, they would be drowned by now. A howl rose in his throat: he could feel it, and fought against it, the desire to howl like an animal. He had to hold on.

Then he heard voices – high, frightened, female voices. They were coming from the corridor that ran forward, giving access to cabins – all first class, if he remembered rightly. He turned towards them; stepped down into the water and splashed towards them, feeling the icy clamminess soak through his boots and stockings and then his trousers. He crossed the staircase hall and entered the corridor, the water up to his knees now. He called out, and was shocked to hear his own voice, reedy and trembling like an old man's. He forced it down, and shouted again, more normally: 'Is anybody there?' An indecipherable clamour was the response, a splurge of human cries. 'Where are you? Come this way!' he called. 'Come quickly.'

There was more calling, and it had a desperate note. He waded on, afraid, as the water went over his knees; and then someone emerged from a side passage ahead of him, a woman in a cloth coat holding a small child. She turned her face towards him, white and shocked, and made an inarticulate sound of relief.

'This way, come this way!' he called.

'Thank God, oh, thank God!' she cried. More women were emerging behind her, and a man, elderly, white-stubbled, with a cap pulled down tight and a cheap, shiny suit. Third-class passengers, without a doubt.

As they saw him, they all began to clamour at once.

'Thank God you found us!'

'Can you show us the way out, mister?'

'We got lost. We've been wandering about for hours.'

'The water keeps comin' up and comin' up.'

'Oh, Jesus, can you get us out, sir?'

There were seven women, the man, the child in arms, and two boys of about ten; the women were wet to the waist, the boys to their chests. Teddy said, 'Come this way. Follow me,' and turned in his tracks. They hurried after him, still all talking at once, trying to tell him what had happened, but he hardly heard them. When he reached the staircase again he got up onto a dry stair and turned to them. 'You women and children must get up on deck at once and get into a lifeboat. Are there any more of you?'

'We don't know where they are. We got lost,' said the woman with the child. 'We saw some people but they didn't speak English. Down below, that was. They went the other way. And the water kept coming up. Our men were in the smoke-room, but we can't find it.'

'It's that way,' Teddy said, gesturing. 'I'd better go and warn them. Can you find your way up to the boat deck?'

'No, no! Don't leave us. We'd get lost again. For pity, sir, show us the way.'

The old man came forward, almost shyly, reached out a hand but did not quite dare to tug Teddy's coat to get attention. 'Is that the way of it, sir?' he said, in a soft voice like mist rolling down a field. His eyes fixed on Teddy's earnestly. 'Is it women and children only?' Teddy nodded, unwilling to pronounce sentence. 'Then it's no use to me. Would ye ever take the women up above, sir, to the boats? I'll go to the smoke-room and warn the men. No use of you wasting time doin' it.'

'No, Grandad, you've got to come with us,' said the

147

woman with the child, her voice sharpening. 'Sure they'll let you on. You're just an auld one.'

'I can't show you the way, Mary dear. Go on with the officer, all of ye, and I'll get and tell the men. Go on now, there's no time to waste.'

That at least was true. The water was right across the hall now. Teddy said, 'You must come at once. Quickly, quickly.' He led the way, hardly knowing if they would follow; but the old man took himself off briskly, to release them, and in fear of being left behind the other women followed Teddy, surging past the one holding the child as she stared after the old man. Then she turned and followed too.

Teddy led them up and along and up, in a panic himself to be outside again, and they stumbled after him, silent now, intent on keeping up. Thank God, here was a staircase he recognised; he almost ran up it and then they were out in the icy air, under the stars. The women gasped as it went into their lungs and cut through their poor clothes; Teddy felt the cold lacerate his wet legs. Along the deck he led them, and there was a lifeboat being loaded, First Officer Murdoch in command.

'Women here!' Teddy called, hurrying along, his voice cracking. He felt so tired he could hardly speak. 'Women and children! Women here!' He was so afraid the boat would go without them – as if it were an animate thing, and full of spite, like the rolling glasses and slithering plates below.

Murdoch turned, blessedly calm, a rock of authority, and said, 'Come along, ladies. That's right. This way.'

Teddy found his legs had stopped of their own accord at the sound of Murdoch's voice. He stood like a horse with his head hanging as the women almost ran past him, eager to embrace rescue before it changed its mind. Teddy wanted to help get them aboard but he didn't seem able to move. He saw Ismay was there, helping some other women – second class by the look of them. Enough people helping, he thought numbly. Go below and get some more. Third-class smoke-room. May be women there. He turned and almost staggered back along the deck, in through the first-class entrance and down the stairs.

When he reached B deck, movement in the first-class smoking-room caught his eye and almost instinctively he turned towards it, went in through the door. At one table Major Archie Butt was still playing cards with three companions, including Arthur Ryerson, whom Teddy had last seen standing on A deck with his wife as she waited for the screens to be opened. They glanced up at him, and then down again, as if he could have nothing to say that would interest them. Over by the fireplace Teddy saw Thomas Andrews, standing staring at the wall. Andrews would know, he thought. He would know where the women might be.

Andrews did not turn or move as Teddy approached. Close up, Teddy could see that he was not staring at the wall but at something not in view, at his thoughts or memories.

'Andrews, where is everyone? They're sending the boats off half empty, but I can't find any more women.'

Andrews did not move. 'Can't tell them apart,' he said.

Teddy stared. 'What? What do you say?'

Andrews's focus changed minutely, and he lifted a hand to the clock, which stood centrally on the mantelpiece. 'Did you ever notice, on the *Olympic*, the tiny flaw in the enamel of the clock face? Just here.' He opened the glass at the front, and ran his forefinger down the right side of the face.

Teddy put his hand to Andrews's shoulder and shook it gently. 'You're not making sense. You must help me find the women. Help me.'

Andrews turned to look at him at last, and if his expression had been bleak before, it was frightening now: it was a face that had looked into hell.

'I can't help you. Put your life-jacket on. Save yourself, if you can. That's all.'

Andrews wasn't wearing a life-jacket. 'Won't you even try for it?' Teddy asked.

'I designed her. She's my ship,' he said, with finality. He turned away, and taking out his pocket watch, checked it against the clock, and then delicately corrected the latter by a minute.

Teddy was about to speak again when he heard voices – female voices – from the direction of the staircase. He turned, caught a glimpse of female shapes, and hurried in that direction. Out in the hall were two women, a mother and grown-up daughter perhaps, dressed with outdoor clothes over nightdresses, the hems of which were wet. They were clutching each other's hands, and their eyes moved about wildly like those of frightened calves in an abattoir.

'You women!' Teddy called as he hurried towards them. 'What are you doing here?'

The older woman looked at him wordlessly, weeping. The tears slid from her eyes without effort or convulsion. The younger woman looked frightened and said, 'I'm sorry. We're from second class, but we couldn't find our way up. The water – the water—' The memory of it seemed to stall her tongue and prevent her finishing the sentence.

Teddy waved it away. 'Come on, come with me. You must get to a boat.'

They fell in behind him with exhausted, silent gratitude. Teddy glanced back just once at Andrews. He was closing the glass on the front of the clock. He didn't look as though he would ever move again.

On the boat deck, Teddy hurried to where he had last seen Murdoch, and found him organising the launching of a collapsible lifeboat from the vacated davits of one of the standard vessels. There was a crowd of women and children – Teddy would have guessed twenty-five or thirty – to which he attached his own two. Bruce Ismay was still there, helping to shepherd the women. He and Teddy exchanged a weary glance but did not speak. Teddy wondered if he looked as bad as Ismay did.

The lifeboat was swung out and they were starting to help the women to climb in when there was a noise of stampeding feet and shouting, and a crowd of men came running up the deck. They seemed to be from third class, by their clothes, and their expressions were wild.

'Here's one!' someone shouted, and they surged towards the boat.

'Stand back there!' Murdoch shouted. One of the men shoved past him and grabbed the falls. 'What d'you think you're doing?'

'We're taking over this boat,' someone shouted in reply. The man on the rope was repelled by one of the crewmen already in the boat, and the other grabbed up an oar ready to fend off intruders; but several were now trying to board, climbing up on the taffrail, swinging over on the falls, and the rest were pressing in behind, struggling with the crew members on deck. A woman screamed. Teddy was hit hard in the back, whether deliberately or by accident he didn't know.

'Get back, get back!' Murdoch was shouting. 'You'll wreck the boat!'

'We've a right to save ourselves!' someone yelled at him.

A woman near Teddy was knocked over and would have fallen underfoot if he hadn't caught her and hauled her upright. He grabbed the collar of the intruder nearest him and tried to drag him back, but the man was big and strong and pulled himself free. He turned his face towards Teddy for an instant, and Teddy cried, 'Let the women on first, God damn it!' but he didn't seem to understand. He was very swarthy, so perhaps he did not speak English; or perhaps, like so many others on the ship, he was simply dazed into incomprehension by shock. He shoved Teddy away with a hand flat to his chest and went on pushing forward.

The lifeboat was making alarming grinding noises against the ship's side, and the women already in it were screaming. The ropes supporting it were stretched flat under the weight of men hanging on them; disaster seemed inevitable.

But then Murdoch managed to drag out his pistol, and fired three shots into the air. The effect was dramatic. At once all shouting and struggling stopped. Murdoch stood square and grim, facing the mob with the blaze of his own personality.

'Get back and let the women and children through or, by God, the next shot won't be in the air!'

The crew members took advantage of the still moment to grab and heave off the intruders on the rails and falls. Everyone else seemed to be holding his breath; and then one of the men – the ringleader, presumably – shouted,

151

'There'll be another boat somewhere. This way, lads!' And they were off again, breaking from a shuffle into a run as they emerged from the crowd and careered down one of the cross walks to the other side of the deck.

Murdoch stuck his pistol into his belt and said, 'Let's get this boat loaded. Quickly now!'

No-one needed any second urging. Teddy and Ismay helped the crewmen board the women and children, then a group of shocked, soaked and black-faced firemen, and then four Chinese men from steerage, who in their complete incomprehension were as helpless as children, and not much bigger. The crewmen got in – one of them, Teddy noticed, was the barber from the barber-shop who had trimmed his hair a day or two before. And now there was no-one in sight anywhere on the deck.

Murdoch looked at Teddy. 'Mr Morland,' he said. Teddy shook his head, more to clear it than in negative, but Murdoch said, 'You've done enough, sir. Come along.'

The women he had conducted up the stairs smiled nervously and reached their hands out to him, and Murdoch took his arm to help him up. The huge effort with which he had been holding himself in control, suppressing his horror and dread, wavered and seemed likely to collapse. 'Come on, sir,' Murdoch said, and, understanding his difficulty, added with surprising gentleness, 'What good will it do to add another death to the tally?'

And Teddy stepped forward and down into the boat. Ismay stood alone on the deck now. 'Come on, Mr Ismay,' said Murdoch.

'I can't,' he said. 'There must be women still on board.'

'I'm going to lower this boat *now*,' said Murdoch impatiently. 'Get in, sir. What's the point of wasting a space? It's no part of your duty to go down with the ship.'

Teddy lifted his head at that. Murdoch, he saw, intended to do just that thing. 'Ismay,' he called. 'Someone has to tell the story.'

And Ismay climbed down and sat beside him, his face rigid and his eyes fixed.

'Lower away,' said Murdoch. 'You're in charge, Rowe.

There are some lights on the port bow. Pull towards those.'

It was hard to lower the boat, because the ship was listing so far to port now that here on the starboard side the lifeboat no longer hung clear. Two of the crewmen had to push it clear with oars; but the descent was short. It was a horrifyingly small distance from the boat deck to the water.

The crewmen took the oars and began to pull, and Seaman Rowe steered first clear of the ship and then round towards the port bow. When they cleared the prow, Teddy could see lifeboat four still dangling at the level of A deck, and thought with shock of the women and children he had left waiting patiently there for the crewman to come back with the spanner. But relief surged through him when he saw that they were loading it now. The screens must have been removed, for a woman in a fur coat was being helped over the side into it; he could hear Lightoller's voice clearly across the still water, though he could not make out his words. He thought with sharp pain of Amalfia and George Penobscot. Perhaps Penobscot would have persuaded her to change her mind. There had still been time. He wondered, too, about Ashley. He had not seen him in all his wanderings about the ship. How could he have left him there? He should not have got into this boat without him. What had he been thinking of? How would he face Lizzie, if he survived?

But perhaps Ashley would still get off. There were only the other three collapsible boats left on board now. He could see men working on the aft portside collapsible, which was stowed on the roof of the officers' quarters – tiny black figures against the stars. Teddy thought he saw the captain come out of the wireless house and walk back towards the bridge. At the bow end, B deck's portholes were under water, and only the slope up towards the stern prevented the sea covering the forward well-deck, but it would not remain clear much longer. Lights of the flooded decks still shone under the surface; but the stern had begun to lift now with the weight at the head, and in the after end of the ship he could see the lights right down as far as F deck clear of the water. That's where the missing passengers must be, he thought, in cabins in the after part of the ship.

There was silence in his own boat. No-one spoke, or even cried; the only sound was the creak and splash of the oars, and the occasional grunt from an oarsman. Seaman Rowe, his back to the stricken ship, steered for something he was staring towards. Teddy turned his head to look, but could see nothing. One of the oarsmen asked Rowe something, and he replied, 'It's a sailing ship, I think.' A pause, another question. 'They don't have wireless.'

And then silence reigned again.

By two o'clock, the water was up to B deck amidships. The forward portside collapsible lifeboat was got away, but the aft collapsibles were still being struggled with. There were more people on deck now, visible as black clumps here and there, milling about aimlessly. Then at ten past two the bow dipped under the sea at last. Water rushed over the forecastle, and the ship made a sudden lurching movement as the forward end was pulled under. Faintly over the water came the sound of screams, and in the lifeboats they could see a rush of people on all decks towards the stern, like a black wave. Here and there a tiny black fleck starfished down into the water, dislodged, or jumping. As the water crept up the decks and the stern began to lift out of the water, the people on board scrambled further and further aft, while some of those who had fallen into the sea caught onto any part of the ship they could reach and tried to clamber up again out of the icy water.

'Oh, God,' Lizzie said softly. 'Oh, God.' She thought of Uncle Teddy, and gripped Ashley's hand harder.

'Mama?' said Rupert, in a trembling voice, and she put her free arm round him to comfort him, but could think of no words that would help.

The maid of Mrs Hays, a Frenchwoman, was reciting the rosary, softly and rapidly, over and over.

Then with a ghastly, slow relentlessness, the stern heaved itself up out of the sea, massive as a building, rising like a monster of the deep, water pouring from it in cataracts. With a hideous rending of tortured metal the foremost funnel toppled forward; they could hear the explosive sound of the steel cables that supported it as they snapped and lashed through the air; there were screams from people in the water as the funnel fell on them.

The stern went up and up, two hundred and fifty feet of it, rearing into the sky. Those on board scrambled for foothold, handhold; screamed as they slid backwards down the deck; clung in clusters, like swarming bees; hung from the taffrails, from each other; fell in twos and threes, in clumps, shaken off like fruit; fell in single starlike loneliness into the dark. The ship's gigantic propellors lifted out of the water, shockingly naked, and there was a terrifying, stupefying noise, something between a roar and a groan, as everything inside her slid and crashed and fell forward, massive equipment tore loose, smashing against the bulkheads, bursting through them. It was horrible, like a long drawnout cry of agony from the dying ship.

And the brilliant lights went out at last, with a suddenness that made Lizzie catch her breath. They flickered on again, a ghostly crimson glow, and then went out for ever. The new darkness made it hard to see anything, until the eyes adjusted; the ship was just a black shape where the stars were not. The stern remained poised, perpendicular, while from it came the crying of those on board, merged together into a continuous faint wail. Then the ship screamed again as, torn by forces beyond bearing, she split amidships, metal ripping away from metal, massive deck boards bursting upwards, flying like splinters, superstructure tearing away. The front end was gone. The stern fell back into the water, sending up a great white wave, hurling those clinging to the rails into the sea, and then at once began lifting again as the water gushed into the torn-open end. At an angle, all that was left of her slipped under the surface, with a gurgling, moaning sound, like a stricken animal; quickly now, trailing steam, ending with a sound like a gulp as the water closed over her.

She was gone. Where the giant ship had been there was nothing but a few wraiths of steam over a sea like black oil; and above, the great pitiless wheel of the cruel stars.

*　　*　　*

155

Though there was stillness where the ship had been, there was not silence. Hundreds of people – men, women and children – had gone alive into the freezing water, and now their cries came through the darkness, magnified by the clarity of the air to a pitiful ululation, as they called out names, called out for help that did not come from God or man.

Collapsible C was fully laden, and Seaman Rowe steered resolutely away from the scene, but still Teddy was moved to say, 'Can't we go back? We might rescue one or two. Surely there's room for a few—'

Rowe's reaction was sudden and angry. 'A few? There's hundreds out there! They'd swamp us, sink the boat, and we'd all die as well. Is that what you want?'

'No, no, but—'

'There's no "but" about it. We can't help them. That's that.'

'He's right,' said one of the women, in a high, hysterical voice. 'They'd kill us all! Listen to him!'

'I have people back there,' Teddy said. The pitiful wailing across the water was making his hair rise and his mouth dry.

'We've all got people, mister,' said a man, quietly.

'I'm in charge of this boat,' Rowe said fiercely, to a murmur of agreement from the other passengers, 'and what I say goes. We're heading for the lights of a ship. That's my orders, and that's what we're doing.'

Ismay sank his head into his hands. Beside him Teddy stared at Rowe, wondering about his anger, and as the man turned his head slightly he saw, reflected in the starlight, that there were tears on his face. It was not callousness: the rage came from the knowledge that there was nothing they could do to help.

A similar debate occurred on the lifeboat where Ashley asked the same question – but with more urgency, for their boat was not nearly full.

'What's the capacity of this boat? It'll take seventy, surely, and there can't be more than fifty of us. We could save twenty people.'

'You don't understand,' said Seaman Moore, at the tiller. 'If we went back they'd *all* try to get in. They'd capsize us.'

'But they're *dying*,' Lizzie cried. 'We have to go back.'

'What this fellow says is quite right,' said Mr Cardeza. 'We'd be capsized for sure.'

'My husband's a noted oarsman,' said Mrs Cardeza, 'so he knows about boats.'

'Fifty of us would die,' Cardeza went on, 'and for what?'

'I can't bear that noise,' said another of the women, putting her hands to her ears. 'Why won't they be quiet? How long will it go on?'

Mrs Hays's maid began praying again. Mrs Hays, who seemed to be in a state of shock, cried again, weakly, 'Charles! Where are you?' which for some reason caused Mrs Cardeza's maid to burst into tears.

'Don't go back! I don't want to die! I don't want to die,' she sobbed.

'Be quiet,' her mistress said to her sharply. 'We aren't going to die. We're not going back there.'

'Can't you shut her up?' someone muttered uncharitably.

Ashley tried once more. 'Please,' he said to Moore. 'By the time we get there, most of them will be too weak to swamp the boat. We can't just let them all die without trying to help.'

There was an anxious chorus of dissent, through which Mr Harper's voice rose clearly. 'Even if you could get anyone out of the water,' he said, 'they wouldn't survive. Soaked through as they are, they'd die of cold before we were picked up by a ship.'

'That's true,' said Cardeza. 'We'd be risking ourselves to no purpose.'

'Besides,' said Mr Dick, 'there are other lifeboats much less crowded than this. Let *them* go back, if anyone is going to.'

A current of feeling seemed to be growing against the Morlands, and quite a number of people were glaring at them, as though it would not take much to spur them to attack. Lizzie felt a flutter of fear. In their present over-wrought condition, there was no knowing what people might

157

be capable of. They might throw them overboard. She squeezed Ashley's hand in warning.

Moore closed the argument by saying, 'I'm not going back. I'm in charge of this boat and that's my last word.'

There was no more talking, only the muted sobbing of the maid and the whisper of the rosary. There was nothing to block out the terrible sound of the people in the water crying out and moaning as the cold gripped them. Those who had been saved had no choice but to listen to those who were doomed, with nothing to distract the mind from the knowledge that the crying was gradually fading away, as one by one they died, frozen to death, alone in the black water.

Teddy emerged from a long hell of thought to find that there was silence everywhere, except for the occasional cough or sniff from his companions. The crewmen were still rowing, but without effort, as though the rhythm had simply become a habit. He straightened up and looked around, and found that there were no other boats nearby, nothing to see in any direction but the darkness. He felt suddenly and powerfully how small they were, a minute speck on the face of the waters, alone in the vastness of the Atlantic.

He looked at Rowe, who seemed slumped slightly over the tiller. Had the man fallen asleep?

'I say,' he called. Rowe looked up at once – no, he had not been asleep, only lost as Teddy had been in baleful thought. 'I say, shouldn't we keep in sight of the other boats?'

Rowe seemed to have to rouse himself for speech. He made a false start, rolled his tongue round his mouth and lips and began again. 'We were told to pull for that ship,' he said. He looked ahead, and then all round, straightening himself for a better view. 'She must have been moving, because we never got any closer to her.'

'I don't see any lights now,' Teddy said. 'Can you see anything?'

Rowe seemed reluctant to answer, but at last, after staring for some time, he said, 'She must have gone over the horizon. We've lost her.' He gave Ismay a nervous glance, as though he might be reprimanded for inattention to his job, but Ismay was far gone into a shell of shock. He looked at Teddy then, as though hoping for new orders, now the old ones had failed.

Teddy did not want responsibility, but he wanted to survive, now so much had been sacrificed. He said gently, 'I was only thinking that we ought to try to get back to the other boats. It will be easier for the rescue ship to find us if we're all together, won't it?'

Rowe appreciated having the apparent decision passed back to him. 'Yes,' he said. 'We'll never catch that ship now. We'd better turn about.'

'Can you find the way back?' Teddy asked, even more gently.

'I've got a compass,' Rowe said. 'I'll just reverse our heading.'

He met Teddy's eyes. Who knew where the other boats would be? They might have rowed in another direction, or simply drifted away. Still, it was important to be as close as possible to the position of the foundering, because that was where the rescue ship would go first. Rowe gave the order and the oarsmen turned the boat about and began to head into a different piece of blackness.

Teddy became aware that the older of the two second-class women was shivering uncontrollably. She and her daughter were worse off than the third-class women, whose clothes were at least coarse enough to give them some protection: they were in their nightgowns, and their over-coats were designed for fashion rather than hard wear. He felt suddenly guilty in his warm clothing, despite the icy numbness of his feet and legs. He began to try to struggle out of his overcoat – no easy task sitting down.

'Ismay,' he said, 'help me, will you? Ismay, old fellow!'

It took several attempts to break through to his friend's consciousness and make him understand what was wanted. Ismay helped him, leaden-eyed, not querying by so much as a look what he was doing. They were all so far gone in shock, cold and exhaustion that Teddy's effort to divest himself drew no eyes to him. When he had got the overcoat

159

off, he gave it to the younger woman, who was nearer to him. 'Make her put this on,' he said. 'Your mother, is it?'

The girl stared, stupid with cold, and then said, with an obvious effort, 'Yes. Yes, my mother.'

'She's cold. Make her put this coat on. Do it right up. And,' he remembered, 'there's a hat and some gloves in the pockets. *You* should put those on. It will help a little.'

'Thank you,' she said, rather blankly, then roused herself to do his bidding. She had to dress her mother like a child, and the woman stared uncomprehendingly while it was done. Then the young woman did what Teddy suggested and put on the hat and gloves. He nodded approvingly. She turned back to him, searching his face for information. 'You're very kind,' she said.

'I should have thought of it before,' he said. 'I suppose we all . . .' He made a hopeless gesture to signify their state of mind.

'I'm very grateful,' she said. She hesitated, and then said, 'Our name's Hemming.'

Teddy saw that she wanted to offer him something by way of thanks. His hand made an automatic, foolish gesture towards the hat he was not wearing, and he pulled it back and said, 'Mine's Morland.'

She nodded, looked at her mother, who seemed close to sleep now she had stopped shivering so violently, and then looked away into the darkness. 'They're all dead, aren't they?' she said softly.

He didn't answer. There was no need.

A little wind got up, and the sea became choppy, adding to the misery. The cold was bitter, and the darkness seemed as though it would go on for ever. Everyone in the boat was sunk in a fitful doze from which they were roused every few minutes by discomfort, to the hideous recall of what had happened. Their weary minds tried to escape, and every return brought a repeat of the scenes of horror they had witnessed. Lizzie dreamed of the little boy and girl she had seen leave the ship at Cherbourg. In her dream her own children were with them. She saw them turn back and wave to her, and felt an agony of grief that she would never see them again. Then she would wake for a moment, to the realisation of the truth, and doze again, falling back into the same dream.

Ashley jerked awake to find all feeling gone from his feet and hands, so much so that for a moment he couldn't move them at all, and when he did they felt like dead flesh, not belonging to him. He tried to flex them to get the blood moving again, and stared around. Something was different. What was it? There was a different smell in the air. And – yes, the stars were a little fainter, the darkness diluted by the first hint of grey. Dawn was coming – that's what the smell was. He remembered it from his sailing days. He struggled his watch out of his pocket. Half past three. In an hour it would be light – thank God! And what would they see then? He straightened his aching neck and looked around. Some distance away, to the south-west, he could just make out the shape of another lifeboat, a denser black in the darkness. And far off to the east, where there was the most light to see by, he could see a little group of boats, which had lashed themselves together. No-one else was in sight.

As the greyness increased he saw that they were still surrounded by ice, lumps like boulders, small bergs, and, further off, just visible now, some bigger ones, drifting slowly, like mountains on the march. There seemed very little debris in the water, just a deckchair or two, some lifebelts, the occasional piece of wood: the ship had taken everything with her when she went to the bottom.

The woman next to him – Mrs Speddon – woke with a jerk, looked around her, and then groaned. 'I thought I'd dreamed it,' she said. Seeing Ashley awake, she said, 'How long before the ship comes to rescue us?'

'I don't know,' he said. 'It can't be long now.'

She shivered. 'I don't believe they'll ever find us. In all this sea, how can they find us?'

'They know our position,' Ashley said; but he thought, they know where we *were*. Who knows how far we've drifted? And there were no supplies on the boat, no food and little water. How long could they afford to wait to be found?

161

She seemed to hear his thoughts in the tone of his voice. 'They'll never find us,' she said. 'We're just going to die in this boat.'

One of the firemen nearby said, 'Oh, they'll find us, don't you worry. Every ship in a hundred miles is coming. They'll be all over us by morning, you'll see.'

Mrs Speddon did not answer, as though it were a matter of no importance. Ashley saw she had resigned herself to death, was sinking down towards it as towards welcome sleep. Shock, fear, exhaustion, and, above all, cold would take their toll if spirits weren't kept up. People could just lie down and die. He sought for something to say to her, and then offered her his own comfort. 'Dawn's coming. Don't you see it's getting lighter?'

She didn't answer, sinking back into her torpor.

Lizzie stirred, woken by his voice, perhaps. She made an indeterminate noise of query, which turned into one of complaint. 'Ooh, my feet are so cold,' she said quietly to Ashley. 'What time is it?'

'Half past three.'

'Is that all?' she moaned softly. 'I thought it must be later than that. It feels like such hours.' She felt her husband stiffen and said, 'What is it?'

He was staring away into the darkness. She looked, too, but couldn't see anything.

'I thought I saw—' he began, and then his head jerked up. 'Yes! Look, over there. It was a rocket, I'm sure it was.'

'I don't see anything,' Lizzie said.

'It's very far away. Right down on the horizon.' They both stared, straining their eyes hopelessly into the darkest part of the sky. There was nothing.

Then a streak shot up into the sky and burst into green sparks. 'I see it!' Lizzie cried.

'That's one of ours, one of the lifeboats,' said Ashley. 'Can't you tell by how near it is?'

Lizzie felt so sick with disappointment she really thought for a moment that she might retch. 'You shouldn't have raised my hopes,' she said.

'No, no,' he said quickly, 'that wasn't what I saw. I saw

a white rocket a very long way off. Obviously the man in charge of that lifeboat saw it too, and replied.'

'Then – you mean—'

'Yes. Someone is coming. And they're not far off now.'

Gradually the others in the boat began to wake, and the word went round like a little trickle of warmth into their cold, shocked hearts: hope, more welcome than hot food would have been just then. The faint greyness of the sky increased, the stars sinking back into it one by one; in the east the first yellowish stain of dawn appeared. Around them the sea was bleak with ice, and they could see more than a dozen giant bergs, a mountain chain dwarfing their humanity. Ashley wondered whether one of them might be the iceberg that had killed the ship. There would never be any way of knowing.

Now the approaching ship's signal rockets were clear to see, tinier but not less real than the lifeboat's green replies. They came at regular intervals. Everyone in the boat had seen them. Moore took the tiller again and ordered the crewmen to the oars, and they began to row towards the rockets. With something real to head for, the men pulled on the oars with vigour. Ashley asked to have a turn, to warm himself up. Cardeza joined him, and they found each other's rhythm and pulled steadily. Rowing, they had their backs to the approaching ship, and it was impossible to resist craning round for a glance now and then. First, in the darkest part of the sky, Ashley thought he saw a ship's green navigation light; then the possibility of a shape, just a more solid centre to the greyness; and then an undoubted ship. Slowly she grew over the horizon as they pulled gratefully towards her. Some of the women were crying, but no-one spoke.

Ashley was relieved at the oar by a crewman and climbed carefully over to his previous seat. He was able to see that the rescue ship had grown much closer during his spell. She was hull up, now.

Mr Harper spoke, to no-one in particular: 'She looks so small,' he said, 'with her one funnel.'

She did. The last ship they had looked at from this boat had been a giant, the largest ship ever launched; this one, by comparison, was like a child's toy. But as they drew nearer to her, no ship on earth would have seemed more beautiful.

There was no more talk. Time seemed to slow down, agonisingly now that rescue was in sight. From the ship's being fully visible there was a long period when it did not seem to get any closer. From a long way off, they saw a lifeboat reach her, and people climbing or being hauled up the sides. Lizzie ached with longing to be safe, to be warm. She watched each tiny rising figure hungrily.

Then, it seemed quite suddenly, the ship was near enough to read the name on her bow, *Carpathia*. And then she was looming over them, black and solid, and there were people on deck staring down, a silent crowd lining the rails, a row of pale, round faces. There were ladders hanging down her side, flapping slowly with the rocking of the sea, slings being prepared for those who could not climb.

They reached the side of the ship, Moore making the boat fast and grabbing the end of the rope-ladder. He said, 'Women and children first,' and the now familiar words tore away the warmth of relief in Lizzie's mind and exposed the hideous memories beneath.

Rose was still asleep, and she took her out of Jenny's arms, needing very badly to touch her saved child. The little children were lifted to the deck in canvas sacks, and Martial and Rupert managed to climb up the rope-ladder, but when it came to Lizzie's turn, she could not make her feet and hands obey her, and she had to be hauled up in a bo'sun's chair.

On deck she could not stand at first. A kind-faced woman put a blanket round her, helped her up and supported her until she could make her legs take her weight. She saw one of the young officers from *Titanic* – Boxhall, wasn't that his name? – standing nearby with one of *Carpathia*'s officers, and he smiled at her, a welcoming but dead-weary grimace. *Carpathia*'s officer had a young, shocked face; he asked her her name and wrote it down. The boys were there, and Jenny again holding Rose, who was beginning to wake, looking puzzled and sleepy and a little cross. The kind lady wanted to lead them all away but Lizzie said inarticulately, 'My husband – in the boat.'

The officer said, 'Don't worry, I'll send him to you. Go along with this lady now.'

'Come along, dear,' said the lady. 'We're in the way here.'

So Lizzie let her lead them away. She couldn't think properly, or speak. Everything seemed tiny and far away, as though seen through the wrong end of a telescope; her limbs were someone else's. In a large passenger saloon, somebody sat her down and said, 'Here, drink this,' and thrust a mug of hot coffee into her hands. She looked at it for a long time before she could make herself realise what it was; and then it seemed somehow bizarre to the point of insanity that she who had seen what she had seen should now be looking at something as ordinary as coffee in a thick white earthenware mug. She was very thirsty and wanted to drink it, but for the moment she could not remember how it was done.

The lifeboats were widely scattered, over a five-mile area, and it took time to get to all of them. The last boat reached *Carpathia* at about half past eight, and when everyone was aboard and it was known that all the boats had been accounted for, *Carpathia* turned and began to steam back towards New York. She was a small ship, and had not the facilities for all the extra souls on board for the longer trip to Europe.

Carpathia's own passengers, agog with horror, excitement and compassion, helped the crew to receive the shocked survivors with blankets, hot soup, coffee and cocoa and, for the worst off, items of their own clothing. The ship's doctor, helped by doctors from among the passengers, examined and treated injuries. At first the survivors could only sit, staring numbly at nothing, having to be helped to drink the reviving soup that had been prepared for them. But as they began to realise they were rescued, the questions started, and the questing. There was only one thing to ask, though it was attached to a hundred names: is so-and-so here?

The extent of the tragedy gradually became known, the appalling figure filtering through as *Carpathia*'s officers compiled the list of those who had come on board. The exact total fluctuated a little, but it was around seven hundred. Fifteen hundred people had died, drowned or frozen to death in the icy sea. The survivors filled the two public rooms and spilled over onto the decks, and as the day wore on there was a slow milling of people through the crowds, looking for friends and relatives and asking after them: have you seen him? Did anyone see her?

There was, at least, one joyful reunion. When Teddy finally came aboard, he asked first of all after his family, and having found that their names were on the list he refused all offers of blankets, cocoa and medical examinations until he had found them. 'First-class passengers are mostly in the saloon,' he was told. When he came through the door and scanned the huddled bodies within, the first person he saw was Ashley, who was standing and conspicuous by his height. They looked at each other with astonishment, and then clasped hands.

'You're here! You're safe!' Teddy cried. 'How did you manage to get away?'

'The officer in charge – Murdoch – took all the men standing nearby because there were no more women. He just took everybody in sight.'

'The same for me,' Teddy said, tears in his eyes. 'Thank God for Murdoch! On the port side it was women and children *only*. They wouldn't take any men, even when the boat was half empty.'

Ashley shook his head in wonder. 'It was the purest chance, then. If we'd gone out on deck on the port side—'

'Don't. It doesn't bear thinking about. I just thank God you made it. Where's Lizzie?'

Ashley took him to the corner where Lizzie and the children were sitting, and there were cries of joy, and many tears. Brown went completely to pieces when he saw his master safe after all, having believed him dead and himself, Brown, a vile traitor. The old man trembled and wept, and would hardly be comforted. 'I shouldn't have left you, sir.'

'I *wanted* you to go with the boys,' Teddy said. 'I'm damned glad you made it, Brown.'

'When I think of all those poor wretched souls who . . .'

'We can all think that,' Teddy said gravely.

'We mustn't let ourselves feel guilty about it,' Ashley intervened. 'We survived, hundreds didn't. It was just chance.'

And then, inevitably, Lizzie asked about Amalfia: 'Did
you find her? I haven't seen her come in yet.'

She saw the answer in Teddy's face before he spoke. 'I
found her. She was waiting for a lifeboat with a lot of other
people like the Thayers and the Wideners and the Astors.
But when she heard they wouldn't let any men on, she
refused to go.'

'What – you mean—'

'She wanted to stay with her husband. She said – she said
she would sooner die with him than live without him. They
walked away. I hoped they might get another boat later.'

Lizzie bent her head, her face a river of tears. How could
she cry so much when she was so exhausted? Ashley
crouched before her and put his arms round her. He knew
what she was thinking. It was what he had thought himself
only minutes ago. They had turned right at the top of the
stairs and lived. The Penobscots had turned left.

'They might still be safe,' he said gently. 'They might be
on board and we haven't seen them.'

But when he took his turn in the queue that later formed
before the officer with the list of the rescued, there were no
Penobscots on it.

BOOK TWO

At Home

I came into the City and none knew me;
None came forth, none shouted 'He is here!'
Not a hand with laurel would bestrew me,
All the way by which I drew anear –
Night my banner, and my herald Fear.

Francis Bannerman, 'An Upper Chamber'

CHAPTER NINE

Jack was at Brooklands on Tuesday morning, the 16th of April, working in the sheds. At about ten o'clock Miss Ormerod arrived. Because of her fascination with aeroplanes and the mobility it necessitated, her father had recently given her a small motor-car, in which she – rather dashingly, Jack thought – drove herself. When she appeared at the shed door, framed in the sunlight outside, Rug barked and ran to her, tail a blur of welcome. Jack looked up and smiled, wiped his hands and went towards her with a cheerful greeting.

'You're early this morning! Something special on?' Close to, he saw her grave expression. 'Oh! What is it? Bad news?'

'I hardly know,' she said, searching his face. 'Evidently you've heard nothing?'

'Heard what?'

'It's just a rumour – the oddest thing. I don't know if there's anything in it, but I thought you ought to know anyway, given that—' She broke off, evidently ill at ease.

Jack wanted to lay a hand on her arm to reassure her, but neither of his hands was in a fit state for it. Instead he said, 'Come outside and sit on the bench and tell me about it.'

They sat on the bench with their backs to the shed wall, and Rug got up on his hind legs so that he could lay the greater part of his body in Miss Ormerod's lap where she could more easily caress his head and ears. She still seemed hesitant about beginning, and Jack, who could not imagine what she had to tell, said, 'Whatever it is, much better to have it straight out.'

171

'You're right,' she said, briskly. 'Well, the rumour is that something's happened to the *Titanic*.'

'What sort of something?'

'They say that there's been an accident. Daddy heard it this morning from one of his clients, who has a cousin in America. The cousin telegraphed him – the client – very early to say that there are all sorts of stories flying about from people who have intercepted wireless transmissions, saying that the *Titanic* was in trouble. It's very garbled, but they're saying she struck something and was badly damaged.'

'Good God!'

'I don't know if it was another ship or a reef or what – Daddy said his client mentioned an iceberg, but he doesn't think that's likely. After all, they don't move very fast, do they? Any ship would be able to avoid them.'

'One would imagine so. But what of the passengers? Were there any – any injuries?' he completed.

'I don't know,' Miss Ormerod said, evidently upset at not having more information for him. 'Nothing was said about that, only that the *Titanic* was a wreck and another ship has gone to the rescue and is towing her to Halifax, though I don't quite—'

'That would be Halifax in Canada,' Jack helped her.

'Oh, of course. That makes much more sense.' She met Jack's eyes with sympathy. 'I hope I did right by telling you. I don't wish to be a scaremonger, if there is nothing in it, but I know *I* would always rather be told things than have them kept from me.'

'You did quite right,' said Jack, forgetting the state of his hands and laying one warmly on her sleeve. Fortunately the kind of tweed Miss Ormerod wore to the airfield was very forgiving. 'It was the act of a friend. And, after all, it doesn't sound too bad. If they are towing her to port, it could be simply damage to the propellors, or some kind of engine failure. There's no need to think anyone aboard has been hurt.'

'That's what Daddy said. After all, she is unsinkable, and with a ship of that size, it's hard to imagine what she could collide with that would do more than dent a few plates.'

Jack nodded, his mind busy with various imagined scenes. When he came back to himself he noticed that his hand was still on Miss Ormerod's sleeve and that she had laid hers over it. It was a strong, sensible hand, not at all like Miss Fairbrother's tiny fairy-like fingers, but just now it was very comforting. And then he remembered the oil, and snatched his hand away. 'Oh, I'm sorry! My hands are filthy. I do hope I haven't marked your sleeve.'

'It's quite all right,' said Miss Ormerod, standing up with a faint sigh. 'This jacket doesn't show the dirt. Well, I suppose I had better get home. If I hear any more I'll be sure to let you know.'

'Thank you,' Jack said. 'You're so kind. I suppose all one can do now is to wait.'

Late on the Tuesday afternoon, Jessie was at Twelvetrees working with one of the polo ponies. She had set up a line of poles and was bending the young bay in and out of them, up and then down the line, to make him supple and to teach him to turn quickly at the end. She had started slowly, but had now got him up to a canter. Proving that he had grasped the rules of this new game, at the end of the row the pony of his own accord changed leads with a little jump, and dashed back down the poles at speed and with a snort that seemed to indicate enjoyment.

She pulled up and made much of him. 'You beauty! Clever boy.' She leaned forward in the saddle and slipped a carrot chunk under his enquiring nose.

A voice from the fence said, 'He's showing promise.'

Jessie looked up quickly, her heart missing a beat. Bertie, in riding clothes, was leaning against the rails, the late sun shining through his hair and giving him a halo. Brach, who had been lying down waiting for her, was jumping up at him in a very puppyish manner. 'Yes, I'm very pleased with him,' she said. 'You look like a prophet, all outlined in light like that.'

'I hope I'm not a prophet of doom,' he said. 'I've got something to tell you – something not very pleasant.'

She rode over to him, and slipped from the saddle. The

173

bay nuzzled Bertie's hands and, receiving no rewards, instead used his forearm to rub an itch from its eye.

Jessie studied Bertie's expression. 'What is it? Maud isn't ill, is she?'

'No,' he said, noting wryly her immediate choice of subject. 'No, she's fine. It's some news that's come in from America. It will be in the evening papers, but a chap I know in London who knows a fellow who works for *The Times* telephoned me to tell me in advance. It's about the *Titanic*.'

Jessie only looked puzzled. 'What about it?'

'Apparently she struck an iceberg and was wrecked.'

'Wrecked?' The word shocked her. 'How could she be wrecked, a ship of that size?' She stared at him, absently fondling Brach's head as the bitch jabbed her nose into her palm. 'What on earth does that mean?'

'I don't know the details. But it must have been very badly damaged because it's been taken in tow by another ship. They're saying everyone is safe, and they've been taken on board other ships for the rest of the journey to New York.'

'Thank God for that,' Jessie said. 'So Uncle Teddy and Lizzie and everyone are all right?'

'That's what the first report is saying,' Bertie said.

Jessie did not notice his less than wholehearted support for it. She was too puzzled about the collision. 'I just don't understand how a ship that size could be badly damaged. Uncle Teddy told us about the *Olympic* hitting another ship, and even losing a propellor blade, but she still went on under her own steam. How could just hitting an iceberg hurt *Titanic*?'

'Icebergs can be huge,' Bertie said. 'Hundreds of feet high. It would be like hitting an island. But listen, Jessie, there's more.' He closed his hand over hers on the rail, and she felt a jolt, as though he were an electric wire. 'I'm telling you so that you can break it to the family at Morland Place if necessary.'

'Break it? Break what?' Now she was afraid.

'The story that will be in the newspapers this evening is what I've just told you. But this fellow that my chap knows says that more has come in since the paper was put to bed. It's only rumours so far, but the fellow seems inclined to believe there's something in it. They're saying that the towing story isn't true, and that *Titanic* has sunk.'

Jessie stared into his eyes, searchingly. 'But she can't!' she said. 'She's unsinkable, everyone knows that.'

'No ship is unsinkable. Modern liners are made to be very hard to sink, but no-one can claim that.'

'But – but – if she's sunk, what about – about—'

'A lot of other ships went to the rescue. They're saying a large number of people have been saved.' His hand squeezed hers harder. 'It may be all right. But we just don't know yet.'

'I can't believe it. I just can't believe it,' Jessie said.

'No-one will be able to believe it,' said Bertie. 'Your mother—'

'Mother! She was afraid she'd never see Lizzie again, but it wasn't this! She never thought – none of us thought—'

'Let's not get carried away. We don't know that anyone's been harmed. What we must decide is what to tell her now.'

'Should we upset her when there might be no need?'

'It'll be in the papers tonight.'

'Yes,' Jessie mused, 'she'll hear about it then. She doesn't read them, but Robbie does – and the servants' hall has the *Daily Mail*. Someone will tell her. But they'll say that everyone is safe.'

'I think,' Bertie said slowly, 'that she ought to be told that may not be true – to prepare her a little, in case of the worst.'

'You think this story – about *Titanic* being sunk – is true?'

Bertie hesitated, but then said, 'I know the fellow in question. I don't think he'd have passed it to my chap unless it were.'

Jessie sighed. 'Then we'd better tell her. A large number saved, you say?' He nodded. 'I'll go home now, and tell her before someone else does. You must come with me.'

'Oh, but I—'

'Bertie, you know how she dotes on you. She'll believe you if you tell her Uncle Teddy and Lizzie and the others are all right.'

'Very well,' he said, 'I'll come.' He looked at her curiously. 'You really believe it, don't you – that they are all right?'

'I just can't imagine a world without Uncle Teddy,' she said.

Venetia had retired for the night, but had got no further than removing her jewellery when a very embarrassed Burton came to say that there was a caller below who insisted on seeing her.

'At this time of night?'

'It is Mr Culpepper, my lady. He says it is a matter of the greatest urgency.'

Venetia sighed. 'Oh, very well, I'll come. Where have you put him?'

'In the drawing-room, my lady. There was no fire in the library.'

'Very well. Go and tell him I'll be down directly.'

Burton departed as Lord Overton in his shirtsleeves came in through the communicating door from his dressing-room. 'What is it? I heard voices.'

Venetia told him. 'I suppose he's come to tell me what we've already read in the newspapers,' she said. 'Kind of him, but—'

'He may have more details,' Overton said reasonably. 'Consider, he's in the shipping way himself.'

'True,' said Venetia. 'Well, I'd better go and see him. Are you coming with me?'

'Just wait until I've put on my dressing-gown.'

Some years back, Mr Culpepper had married his beloved only daughter Nancy to Venetia's brother, the Duke of Southport. In the six years of the marriage, before Southport's debaucheries brought about his untimely death, he had made Nancy miserable, and she had never felt she was accepted by Society. During that time Venetia had befriended the young duchess and given her both comfort and advice about how to go on in public. Culpepper had never forgotten that kindness, and was always looking for little ways to show his gratitude.

When the Overtons entered the drawing-room, he was standing by the fire, rubbing his hands slowly over and over, and one glance at his face as he looked up told Venetia he had not come here merely to repeat the story that had been in the newspapers. There was shock of no common order in his expression. He looked old and grey with it. 'I apologise for calling so late,' he began, but Venetia waved that away.

'I can see you have something important to tell me. Please sit down, Mr Culpepper. It is very kind of you to call.'

'Can I offer you something?' Overton said. 'A brandy and soda, perhaps. You seem upset.'

'Thank you,' Culpepper said, with an effort. 'I don't usually, but I do believe I would like a glass of brandy. I've had a shock, you see – a very great shock.'

Overton mixed him a large brandy with no more than a dash of soda, and he and Venetia sat on the sofa opposite him and waited in silence for his news.

The brandy seemed to do Culpepper good. After a swallow or two he braced himself and began: 'You have read the reports in the newspapers about *Titanic*?'

'Yes,' said Overton. 'Do you know something more?'

'I do,' he said. 'I wish to God I did not. The first reports were garbled – so many different sources – amateur wireless fellows in America and Canada listening-in to transmissions. There are so many of them these days. But now White Star have a definite report. They sent it by wireless to their office in London, and they, out of courtesy, telephoned me, as head of a fellow shipping line, and also as having some personal interest in the matter. It came in too late for the newspapers. It will be in tomorrow morning's editions, no doubt. But I could not in conscience go to bed without first telling you what I know. *Titanic* has foundered. She has sunk, with great loss of life.'

They stared at him in desperate silence as their minds tried to grapple with the news. At last Overton said, 'Is it true? There is no mistake? You said the reports were garbled.'

'There is no mistake,' Culpepper said heavily. 'I wish with all my heart I could say otherwise. But the report came from

177

the master of the ship that responded to her distress calls, a Cunarder, the *Carpathia* – fellow of the name of Rostron. He wired to the *Olympic* – *Titanic*'s sister ship – that he had reached *Titanic*'s position at daybreak, but found nothing but wreckage and lifeboats. The ship was gone down before he could reach her.'

Venetia grasped at one word. 'Lifeboats, you say? There were survivors, then?'

'Captain Rostron's report said he took on board about seven hundred people, and all lifeboats were accounted for. He's on his way now to New York. The captain of the *Olympic* passed the message to White Star. I know him – a fellow named Haddock. He can be relied on. I'm afraid there is no doubt that this report is true.'

'Seven hundred,' Overton said blankly. 'Is it known how many were on board?'

'The ship was not full, for which I suppose we can thank God,' said Culpepper, 'but White Star says there were about twenty-two hundred souls on board, passengers and crew.'

Venetia could do the arithmetic as well as anyone. '*Fifteen hundred?* Fifteen hundred people lost?'

Culpepper nodded. He looked broken. 'I had an interest aboard that ship, a man I not only esteem but have great affection for. He's like a son to me. It was my idea that he and his family should sail on *Titanic* rather than any other ship. But your connection is much stronger. They were your blood relatives, and Mrs Morland in particular—' He couldn't go on. He passed a hand across his eyes, then took another gulp of the brandy.

Overton got up and went quietly to mix two more drinks, one of which he gave to Venetia. She took it absently, and when he urged her to drink it, she said, from the depths of thought, 'I'm quite all right.' But he insisted, and she drank it off like a man.

Then she said to Culpepper, 'You have no lists yet? No names? I'm sure if you had you would have said so at once.'

'No, no names. I imagine Rostron hasn't managed to get them all collated yet. He will no doubt send a list as soon as he can, and then White Star will publish it. If I hear anything beforehand, I will communicate with you, you may be sure.'

Venetia nodded, but her mind was elsewhere. 'How could it happen?' she said. 'That beautiful ship.' And she thought of Lizzie and the children, Ashley, and dear 'Uncle' Teddy. Two thirds of those on board had not survived. The odds that her own people were among them were horribly bad.

On the Wednesday morning, the news broke in newspapers all over England that the wonderful, unsinkable ship had foundered, with heavy loss of life. The nation was in a state of shock and disbelief. *Titanic* had represented the apogee of technical mastery. The newest, best and most luxurious ship in the world had been a symbol of Britain's dominance of the seas, and of manufacture and trade, and also a sign that mankind had finally conquered his environment. Technology, so everyone had believed, could solve all problems, and would lead humankind inexorably on to ever greater heights of knowledge and prosperity.

Now at a stroke all that was gone. Confidence was shattered. Nature had struck back and punished mankind for its hubris. An *iceberg* – a senseless lump of ice – had done what no-one had believed possible, had sunk the unsinkable, had sent that magnificent, beautiful ship to the bottom of the sea, with appalling loss of life. The scale of the human disaster was beyond anything known before. The sheer number of the dead was a stunning blow. Nothing else was talked of, nothing else was news. The newspapers, with so little actual fact to go on, filled their pages with speculation, with background stories about some of those known to have been on board, and with frankly invented narratives about the sinking from 'eye-witnesses' who were at that moment still incommunicado on the stormy Atlantic.

Crowds gathered outside the White Star offices in Liverpool, Southampton and London, waiting for the casualty lists to come in, a mixture of those desperate for news and the simply curious, all united by a sense of shock and disbelief that was strangely personal even to those with no loved one on board and no connection with shipping. Before the maiden voyage, the advertising had done its work well. There was no-one in the whole country who had not known about *Titanic*, and no-one now who did not mourn with a sense of personal loss. She had been the nation's pride; the nation reeled with shock.

The sweet spring weather and calm waters that had been such a feature of *Titanic*'s maiden voyage disappeared when she went to the bottom, and *Carpathia*'s journey to New York was delayed by much more typical fog, squalls and heavy seas. It only added to the suffering of the seven hundred and five survivors, whose first ship had foundered in calm waters, and who were now aboard a much smaller vessel, which felt the action of the waves. Many clung together in terror at every pitch and roll, and nerves stretched to the limit by their experiences had no opportunity to mend. There was an American Episcopalian monk on board, Father Roger Anderson – one of *Carpathia*'s passengers – who had conducted a service of thanksgiving the first day, and later a burial service for three crewmen and one male passenger who had died after rescue. His services were greatly in demand from the survivors, for spiritual counselling and private prayer. Along with the three doctors and the rest of *Carpathia*'s crew, he got little rest on the four-day passage.

But perhaps the busiest people of all on board were the wireless operators, who were soon close to exhaustion. Captain Rostron kept strict personal control over the wireless and checked every message that was transmitted, to ensure the survivors had priority and that nothing sensational was sent; but he could not control incoming messages. They included scores of offers from American newspapers of money in exchange for stories, for which they were desperate.

Carpathia had not been much more than half full, so most of the survivors were able to have cabins. Ashley, Lizzie and the children were all together in one – a large one by *Carpathia*'s standards, though of a different order altogether from the luxurious suite on *Titanic*. Lizzie was glad. In her state of shock and loss, she wanted to be in a small space, felt the need to draw something closely around herself for safety. The movement of the ship was frightening, and she slept badly, waking every half-hour thinking there was some alarm and that they had to take to the boats again. In the intervals when she did sleep, she dreamed of people drowning. Often it was Amalfia, but sometimes it was the children, being dragged under the water, screaming, holding out hands to her that she could never quite reach.

She had overheard enough to know that those who went into the water with life-jackets on had not drowned. Some of the lifeboats had got close enough to see them, their faces blue-white from the cold, their hair rimed with ice, bobbing a little on the water as though rocked in some ghastly sleep. But how many more had died inside the ship, drowned in their cabins as the water crept up or gushed in? How many drowned in the corridors in belated attempts to escape? It was that trapped death she dreamed of so horribly. She wished she knew what had happened to Amalfia. The Penobscots were not among the survivors, and Lizzie knew that only half a dozen or so people had been rescued from the water. No-one seemed to have seen them once they had left the queue for the lifeboat. Amalfia had turned away from safety to stay with her husband, had chosen almost certain death to be with him. But where had they gone? Had they put on life-jackets, gone on deck in the hope of still escaping, and frozen to death in the black water outside? Or had they gone back to their cabin to lie down and wait for the water to come to them? Lizzie was afraid it was the latter. Ashley gently, and for her own good, pointed out that she had known Amalfia only a few days. She tried to make him understand that in those few days they had become very close, that she had truly loved her; but speaking about her always ended in choking tears.

Teddy's state of mind was turbulent. Added to the shock and disbelief and the after effects of great fear, which all of them were feeling, was a deep and different anguish that his special relationship to the *Titanic* had engendered. He had had a stake in her, in her beauty and perfection; and from the beginning of the disaster he had had a fuller knowledge of what was happening than those who were mere passengers. The horror of the loss of life was the more deeply engraved on his mind. He had seen boats sent off half empty; he had heard people refuse to get into them, not believing the ship could sink; he had struggled to find more women in the flooded below-decks; he had learned about the trick of chance, which had meant that men on the starboard side had lived while those on the port side had died.

And he, Teddy, had lived. He went over and over those last moments in his sleepless, weary hours, and felt all the guilt of being alive when so many others were dead. It was as if those missing hundreds cried out to him accusingly. Where had they all been? He remembered the black wave of them running up the decks as the ship pitched head down into the sea. Where had they come from, when it was too late? But then – he reminded himself every time in a circular, exhausted way – it had always been too late. From the moment the ship struck, they were marked to die.

For the first two days he was as sunk in the lethargy of shock as the others. They lay in their cabins, or sat in a sheltered corner of the deck, staring at nothing, too numb to want to talk. Those who could mostly avoided the public rooms. Once the first frenzy of trying to find out who was aboard subsided, it was as if it hurt too much to be with others who had survived. It reminded one too much of who had not. It was not until the Wednesday that Teddy roused himself to think that he ought to try to get a message to someone. If news of the disaster had reached England, his family would even now be wondering if they were alive or dead, and fearing the worst.

He spoke to Ashley about it, and they agreed that one message would do for all, and that if it were sent to the Culpepper office in New York, the people there would take care to pass it on to everyone concerned. They talked a little about the wording of the message, and then went together to the radio house to see how long the queue was for messages out.

It was while they were there that *Carpathia*'s doctor, McGee, saw them as he was passing, and stopped to talk to them. 'I believe you're a friend of Mr Ismay, Mr Morland? Not just a business associate?'

'That's right,' Teddy said, and realised that he had not seen Ismay since they both reached the deck of the *Carpathia* from the lifeboat.

'I wonder, then, if I could trouble you for a word.'

Ashley said, 'Go ahead. I'll wait here and get the message off.'

So Teddy stepped aside with McGee, and the doctor confided, 'He's distraught, quite beside himself, and I'm worried for him. When he came on board I asked if there was anything he needed and he begged only for a quiet place, so I took him to my cabin. But he hasn't left it since, won't eat, can hardly talk. He blames himself bitterly for surviving when so many have died. Nothing I can say comforts him, and I'm afraid he may lose his reason, or do himself some harm. Won't you come and speak to him, see if you can ease his mind in any way?'

'Gladly,' said Teddy. He understood that guilt. Probably all of them felt it to some extent, but for Ismay it must be worst of all, given that he was the head of White Star. The doctor conducted him along the deck to his tiny cabin, where he knocked at the door. Receiving no answer, he opened it and gestured to Teddy to go in.

Ismay was sitting in the chair at the desk, staring at the wall. His face was drawn with suffering. He did not look round, and only when Teddy addressed him did he give any sign of knowing he was not alone.

'Old fellow,' said Teddy, 'how are you?'

'Alive,' he said. His voice was flat and dark, toneless with grief.

'I know what you're thinking,' Teddy said. He sat on the edge of the bed, there being nowhere else. 'I am too. I keep wondering, should I be?'

'I know the answer to that,' Ismay said. 'I should not be alive when fifteen hundred of my passengers are dead.'

'You couldn't save them,' Teddy said. 'You did your best. I saw you helping to load the boats. I saw you bring women up from below. We both did our best.'

'I've no right to live.'

'You've the same right as everyone else. If you – or I – had stayed on the ship, there would have been two more empty places in the boats and two more deaths on the list. What good would that have done? Anyone would have done the same.'

Ismay only shook his head. Teddy thought involuntarily of First Officer Murdoch, who had sent them off, and had gone down with his ship. The captain, too, and the Chief Officer, Wilde. And Thomas Andrews. Teddy remembered that last sight of Andrews, standing before the clock in the smoking-room, waiting to die. He dragged his thoughts away from them, though he knew they would haunt him for years of nights to come.

'It wasn't your duty to go down with the ship. If nothing else, think of your wife and daughter. They wouldn't have wanted you to die.'

At last there was a reaction. 'Florence,' he said. He turned his head to look at Teddy. 'What must she be thinking? She won't know – she'll think—'

'We've all been slow to come to grips with it. I've only just thought of sending a message to my people myself. Ashley's in the wireless house now, waiting to get one off.'

'I must get word to her,' Ismay said, and his voice was stronger. He looked around him as if he were waking from a long sleep. 'And my office in New York – I must send something to them. They'll be waiting for official information.'

'That's right,' Teddy said, glad to see the revival. He thought, McGee is wrong: Ismay would never have killed himself. Whatever the wounds to his mind, his sense of duty was too strong. 'You are the only person with an overview of events.'

Ismay nodded, his brain obviously working now. 'The crewmen,' he said. 'They must be got home as quickly as possible. What day is it?'

'Wednesday,' said Teddy. 'The seventeenth.'

'*Cedric* was due to leave New York on the eighteenth. I must make sure she waits and takes them. I must get a wire to the office and have her held up.'

'Come along now, then,' Teddy said. 'I'll go with you to the wireless house.'

But Ismay shrank at that, and the brief animation drained out of his face. 'I can't go out there. I can't look at them. It's – it's too soon. You understand.'

'Only too well,' said Teddy.

'If I write out the messages, will you take them for me? I should be –' he swallowed '– most eternally grateful.'

'Yes, I'll do that for you,' Teddy said. And after that, he thought, I must see if I can't find a brandy and soda somewhere. The horrors were coming back, and he could feel his hands beginning to shake.

Wednesday was the longest day any of them at Morland Place had endured. The morning papers reported that *Titanic* had sunk, and that only seven hundred of those on board had survived. Information was evidently still sparse, and the only other factual matter in the newspapers consisted of diagrams of the ship, photographs of *Olympic* (as there were none available of her sister), and general information about icebergs.

Jessie had stayed the night, and remained there all day. Robbie, worried about Ethel, did not go to work. Alice was inconsolable, and wept almost non-stop, which at least gave Henrietta something to do in tending her. Jessie tried to comfort her mother and give her hope, but Henrietta had shut herself away in a place of dread. The servants tiptoed about, bringing cups of tea no-one wanted, and whispering together urgently in corners. An anguished telegram came from Polly at school begging for information, to which Jessie sent what reply she could. It seemed to be up to her to direct things in the house, for Henrietta had become a ghost, and Robbie, when appealed to, only said crossly that he must stay with Ethel and couldn't think about anything else. So Jessie gave orders for luncheon and dinner, answered household questions as best she could, and fielded the steady stream of callers who came with their fears, their condolences, their encouragement and their curiosity, to find out if anything more was known at this focus of tragedy.

185

In the afternoon Bertie came over, and was a source of strength to both Henrietta and Jessie. He urged them to go out and get some fresh air, but neither felt able to leave the house in case of news. Telegrams had come from Jack and Frank, too, and from Venetia and Violet, and from Anne Farraline. A relay of telegraph boys pedalled their bicycles over the long tracks, arriving breathless and red-faced at Morland Place and probably cursing its remoteness.

'If only Uncle Teddy had gone ahead with his plans to install the telephone,' Jessie said. Robbie sent a shocked look across the room at her, and she snapped irritably at him. 'What are you looking at me like that for? Can't I mention his name? You may have consigned him to the past already, but I'm not going to until I have to.' She stalked out of the room to find something that needed doing. It was the helplessness that was the worst of all.

Bertie followed her and caught her up in the staircase hall. She turned a stormy face to him, expecting rebuke, but he only said, 'We're all nervous. Don't mind it.'

'Oh, Bertie!' she cried, and went to his arms. He folded her against his chest and stroked her hair, and this time the embrace was purely cousinly.

Ned came from the mill at half past six, and aside to Bertie and Jessie told some of the bizarre rumours and stories that were circulating. 'I've telephoned the White Star office every couple of hours, but they always say the same – no names yet. They're expecting the *Carpathia* in New York some time on Thursday afternoon – which, of course, will be Thursday evening or night for us. But they must surely wire out the names before that. They can't keep everyone waiting until she docks.'

He came to stay, his own house being empty and cold without his wife in it. Jessie had ordered dinner, and they sat down to it at seven thirty, Ned helping her to force everyone to come to the table – except Alice, who was prostrate in her room – for the good of their spirits. They toyed their way through soup, mutton and pudding, and were staring helplessly at dessert when a muted commotion outside had them all head up and listening. A moment later

Sawry came in, with a telegram that in his agitation he had forgotten to put onto a salver. 'This has just come, madam,' he said, his voice wavering. He handed it to Henrietta. Through the open doorway behind him Jessie could see a huddle of servants who had crept up to hear the news as soon as possible.

Henrietta looked at the envelope, and then passed it to Jessie. 'You read it. I can't seem to make my hands work.'

Jessie tore it open clumsily, and had to force herself to read the words printed there. For a moment she could not make her mind take them in, and then she looked up and cried in a voice lifting with joy, '"All well and unharmed. More news from New York." And it's signed "Ashley."'

Cries of joy and congratulation came from every side. Henrietta burst into tears. Ned flung his arm round Jessie's shoulder and hugged her against him. Robbie thumped the table with his fist. 'All of them? It's a miracle!'

'We're so very glad, madam,' Sawry said, and there were tears in his eyes.

'Thank God, thank God,' Bertie said.

'I knew it!' said Jessie. 'I knew Uncle Teddy couldn't die! Oh, Aunt Alice!' she remembered. 'We must go at once and tell her.'

'I'll go,' Henrietta said, but found she hadn't command of her legs. 'It's foolish,' she said, through her tears, 'to be in such a state when the news is so good.'

'I'll go,' said Ethel. 'I'll stay with her if she doesn't want to come down.'

She disappeared, and Bertie met Ned's eyes across the table. 'It really is a miracle, isn't it?' he said quietly. 'The odds were all the other way.'

'What a story Father will have when he comes home,' said Ned.

Henrietta lifted her face out of her handkerchief with a gasp of shock. 'When he comes home? But he'll have to cross the sea again in another ship! What if it happens again?'

'Oh, Mum, lightning doesn't strike twice in the same place,' Robbie said.

'You know that's a very silly saying,' Henrietta rebuked

him. 'The oak tree up on Bachelor Hill was struck three times one winter.'

'Well, Uncle Teddy's not an oak tree,' Robbie retorted.

'But he's as enduring as one,' Jessie said.

It was not until late on Thursday that *Carpathia* steamed slowly into New York. She passed Battery Park, on the southern tip of Manhattan Island, which was black with the mass of people waiting to see her go past. The weather was stormy and the rain teemed down, but it did not blunt the enthusiasm of the multitude eager for the sensation of the arrival. The steamer was accompanied up the Hudson river by a flotilla of boats, which hampered the movement of the pilot boat and the tugs. Every one of them was crowded with spectators who cheered and shouted questions no-one could possibly have heard through the rain and racket. *Carpathia* sailed first to White Star's pier fifty-nine, where the recovered lifeboats from *Titanic* were swung off, and then returned to dock at Cunard's pier fifty-four.

From the deck it was possible to see the vast multitude that heaved about like a restless sea in the road beyond the terminal building, held in check by a cordon of police and metal barriers. A rolling roar seemed to come from it, like the roar of the sea. There were mounted police, too, the horses moving nervously back and forth on the spot against the pressure. Now and then there was a burst of light as a magnesium flashgun went off: the press was evidently out in force.

At least it was quiet on the quay. The arrangements had been explained by Captain Rostron and his officers during the afternoon: no press was to be allowed on board the ship, and a maximum of two close relatives of each survivor was to be allowed into the Customs shed to meet them. The rest of the public was to be kept outside in the street. Customs and immigration formalities were to be relaxed. Visitors and returning residents would go straight through; for the immigrants from steerage, officials would come on board, examine them briefly, and see what help they needed.

Carpathia's own passengers would disembark first, and

arrangements would be made for their passage to Europe on another ship. The first-class survivors would descend next, also by the forward gangway, then the second-class; third-class survivors would descend by the after gangway, and crew survivors would stay on board until the crowds had dispersed, when they would be taken by tender to the *Lapland*, owned by White Star's parent company IMM, where they would stay on board until she sailed for England.

Most of the first- and second-class survivors were wealthy enough to look after themselves, but for those who were not, and for the third-class, who had lost all they owned in the world, the city of New York had already raised a relief fund of over $100,000, while the same amount again had been added by a newspaper and the Women's Relief Committee.

'What will happen to us?' Lizzie asked Ashley. 'We've lost all our clothes and possessions.'

'Culpeppers will provide,' Ashley said. 'The house in Flagstaff was part furnished anyway, don't you remember? I'm sure the company will pay for the household things – they'll have been insured. And we can buy new clothes.'

'But what will happen right away?' Lizzie asked.

'My brother Nat will be waiting to meet us, and we'll go and stay with him, as we planned. We'll have our two weeks here, then go to Boston to stay with Dan for two weeks, and then on to Flagstaff. Nothing is different.'

'It feels different,' Lizzie said, and there was no argument about that.

Teddy felt different, too. 'I don't think I shall stay here for a holiday, as we planned,' he said. 'I shall get the first ship possible home. I want to see Alice and Polly and James William and everyone at Morland Place. I shan't feel right again until I'm in my own home with my arms round my wife.'

'I don't blame you,' Ashley said, 'but why not wait a day or two? You may feel differently after forty-eight hours on solid land. It would be a shame to miss seeing New York and regret it later.'

Teddy shook his head. 'If I don't get straight back on a

ship I may lose my nerve. I shall be off tomorrow if I can get a passage.'

But a change of plans was even then approaching him without his knowledge. They had already heard that there was to be an official inquiry into the sinking, under the charge of Senator William Alden Smith. He did not waste time, and while the survivors were still waiting to disembark, he came on board with one of his officials. Smith went at once to the doctor's cabin to interview Ismay, who was still distraught and had not emerged since the day of the rescue. The official, meanwhile, handed out subpoenas to various of the passengers.

Teddy was one of them; Ashley was another. They were both required to hold themselves in readiness to appear at the United States Senate hearing whenever they should be summoned, and were forbidden to leave New York until they were released. The hearing would open the following day, the 19th of April, in the Waldorf Astoria Hotel

'Well,' said Ashley, 'it seems you're staying after all.'

CHAPTER TEN

The two close relatives who had come to meet the Morland party were Ashley's two half-brothers: Nat, from New York, who had been expected, and Dan, from Boston, who had not.

While the brothers exchanged silent and heartfelt embraces, Lizzie studied them, and saw a great resemblance between the three, though they only shared the same mother. Younger than Ashley – Dan was forty-six and Nat forty-five – they looked even less than their age; and both were very fair, much more blond than Ashley, and with straight silky hair where his was tougher and tow-coloured. Ashley was the tallest of the three, Dan the most handsome, in a rather quiet, brooding way, and Nat had a wide smile and fine white teeth.

Everyone was greeted with warmth and sympathy, and with an informality of manners that was comforting in the circumstances.

'I wasn't expecting to see you so soon,' Ashley said to Dan.

'I couldn't wait,' Dan said, in his rather deep voice. He spoke more slowly than Nat, and his accent was different – almost English, Lizzie thought. 'As soon as I heard you were among the survivors, I jumped on a train and came straight here. What a fright you gave us! Never do so again, please.'

'Is Madeleine here, and the boys?'

'No, I left them behind, so as to travel light. Well, sister-in-law?' Dan turned to Lizzie and kissed her.

'These must be my nevvies,' Nat said, shaking hands

solemnly with the boys. 'And my little niece?' Rose, in Jenny's arms, was silent, sucking her thumb – a habit to which she had reverted since the sinking. 'And I just know,' Nat said, turning to Teddy, 'that you must be Uncle Teddy. I'm honoured to meet you, sir.'

Teddy shook hands, looked a little bemused. 'I'm not really your uncle, you know,' he said.

'But you must be,' Nat said. 'You're Ashley's uncle now, and we're his brothers, so you must be ours too. I refuse to give up such a distinguished uncle unless I'm forced to. Won't you please be our uncle too, sir?'

Dan intervened, seeing the humour, though well meant, was hard to cope with. 'You must all be so tired,' he said.

'I don't know why,' Ashley said. 'We've done nothing but sit about for three days.'

'Nevertheless, we must get you home. How many taxis do you think we'll need?'

Teddy roused himself. 'We're far too many for you. I and my man will go to an hotel.'

'Oh, no, sir, please,' Nat said. 'My wife will never forgive me if you do that. I assure you we can fit you all in.'

'Nat's house is pretty elastic,' said Dan.

'I shall have to appear at the hearing,' Teddy said. 'It might be easier all round if I stayed at the hotel where they're holding it.'

'I've been served, too,' Ashley mentioned.

'There's no problem about that. We can have you at the Waldorf in no time by taxi, whenever you're needed. Come home with us and be comfortable.'

So all of them emerged together into the evening. The rain had stopped, but it was still windy, the air was damp and the roads and pavements shone wet in the lamplight. There was not much road to be seen immediately outside, however. Behind the barriers and the row of New York policemen in their strange, flat caps, the heaving multitude had not thinned at all, its excitement only pumped up by the long wait. At the front, against the barriers, were the press. As the Morlands stepped out into the street, a scream went up, which made the English contingent jerk back with alarm, but it was only a flood of questions, each yelled at high pitch in an effort to beat the others. Flashguns went off, dazzling them, and the explosions and light reminded Lizzie of the rockets sent up from *Titanic*. She pulled Rupert against her, feeling battered by the relentless howl of questions, and began to cry. Rupert cried because she did; Martial clutched his father's hand very tightly and stared around with wide, frightened eyes; Rose burst into bawling tears at the noise and lights.

Teddy was angry. 'Why are they doing this? Can't it be stopped?'

Nat, beside him, said, 'It's the press, sir. Nothing to be done about the press, I'm afraid. And this is the greatest news story in history.'

'That's a disgusting attitude,' Teddy growled.

'I know, sir. But it's the way they see it. Once we've got you away from here they won't bother us. Just don't look at them, and don't say anything.'

Through the barrage they walked, along the pavement to where a line of taxis was waiting within the barriers, protected by the police. They were ushered in, the doors were slammed, and then the police opened the barrier to let them through. For a frightening moment the crowd pressed up against the vehicles; faces peered into the windows, bawling pointless questions; more flashes went off. Then they picked up speed and were away, leaving the multitude behind them, skimming through the wide, empty streets of the dock area.

Lizzie, sitting by Ashley with Rose on her lap, breathed a shaky sigh of relief and said, 'That was awful. They were like ravening beasts.'

'It's over now,' Ashley said. 'Don't think about it.'

After a moment she said, 'I'm hungry.'

'I'm not surprised,' Ashley said. 'Do you know it's after half past ten, and we haven't had any dinner?'

Lizzie's impressions that first night were hazy. The drive through New York showed streets amazingly straight to one used to London, and buildings so high it was like driving through defiles in the mountains. The roads were filled with motor traffic, the pavements seething with people, and there were lights everywhere. A city of light, she thought, without those quiet dark patches that seemed around every corner in London. There was such a sense of liveliness everywhere, even at this time of night, as if there was a party going on that everyone had been invited to.

Exhaustion was beginning to set in by the time they pulled up outside Nat Flint's house, which seemed tall and rather narrow, part of a terrace in a quiet street lined with trees. It was of red brick with white stone copings, and Lizzie thought it looked rather Londony, which was a comfort. But how would they all fit into it? Inside the front door was a huge hall with a marble floor, and an elegant staircase. Nat must be wealthy, she thought. She wondered how many people they would have to meet. Hungry though she was, she hoped they would not be expected to sit down to dinner and be sociable.

But there was no line of strangers to cope with, just Nat's wife Rosemary, a pleasant, plump woman as fair as himself, who shook hands and said kindly, 'Introductions can wait until tomorrow. I'm just sure all you want now is to get to your rooms. I've had a supper tray sent up for each of you. Go along now, and Mary will show you the way.'

Mary was the servant, round of body and black of face. Lizzie registered it with faint surprise, but not much curiosity. They were led up and on – the house was a great deal bigger than it looked outside, going a long way back from the road – and at last to a large bedroom, which seemed as though it had been freshly decorated. Stumbling with tiredness now, she saw a supper tray on a table, and assuaged her hunger and thirst, though she did not remember afterwards what she had eaten and drunk. And then she dragged off her clothes and without even thinking of washing fell into the large, soft bed. For a moment she wondered why the bed didn't move and why there was no engine noise and vibration beneath her. Then she tumbled into dark, dead sleep, for once untroubled by dreams.

★   ★   ★

'Good morning! You look a great deal better,' said Rosemary, as Lizzie came into the breakfast-room. 'Come and have some breakfast. These are my children, John and Peggy.' They were about seventeen and eighteen years old, tall and well-built, not handsome, but with pleasant faces and nice straight teeth. They seemed very composed and shook hands with her politely. 'My other two, Amy and Nat junior, are in the nursery with your children. They're fine, by the way, slept well and they're eating like horses.'

'Where are the others?' Lizzie asked, sitting down. Supper was a distant memory and she was hungry. There seemed to be the usual breakfast things on the plates around the table, and she could smell coffee, but there was no sideboard. A moment later a maid in a peach-coloured uniform and white apron appeared silently at her side and put a plate of food before her, while a butler filled her cup. Evidently Americans were waited on at breakfast, unlike in England.

'Uncle Teddy had a call to the hearing,' said Rosemary. 'He's wanted this morning, but they couldn't give a time, so he went off right away, and Nat, Dan and Ashley went with him.' She smiled warmly. 'Which is nice for us, because I know the first thing you're going to want is to shop for some clothes for you and the children, so we can have a nice day together without the men bothering us.'

Even now, four days from the disaster, it seemed bizarre to be thinking of anything as ordinary as shopping, but there was no doubt they all needed clothes. All they had were the clothes they had put on in the middle of Sunday night; though Lizzie had found a fresh shirt, stockings and underwear laid out for her this morning, and presumed fresh linen had similarly been donated to the others.

'Thank you for the clean clothes, by the way,' she said. 'I can't tell you how welcome they were.'

'Oh, my dear, that's nothing,' Rosemary said quickly, her eyes filling with tears. 'When I think what you've been through! I can tell you the whole of New York has been in a state of shock, and we've had so many telephone calls from well-wishers who knew we had people aboard. Which reminds me, there's a gaggle of pressmen outside the street door, so there'll be no going out that way. We shall have to sneak out the servants' entrance, to avoid their impertinence. It's a good thing the men went off early or they'd have been caught.'

As the representative of the company that owned the lost ship, Ismay was the first witness to be called at the hearing. It was held in the Waldorf Astoria's East Room, a grand and ornate chamber normally used for banquets. There were several long tables, and the inquiry committee sat at the central one, while other officials, lawyers and witnesses sat at the others, or in close ranks of rout chairs around them. The press and favoured spectators stood in tightly pressed masses all round the room, and there were photographers to take official pictures of each witness as he was examined.

Ismay took his seat at the short end of the main table, neatly dressed in stiff collar, dark suit and waistcoat, but Teddy thought he had never seen a man so pale and haggard. After being asked his personal details, he was invited by Senator Smith to give his account of the voyage.

He began by saying, 'In the first place, I would like to express my sincere grief at this deplorable catastrophe. I understand you gentlemen have been appointed to enquire into the circumstances. So far as we are concerned, we welcome it. We court the fullest inquiry. We have nothing to conceal. The ship was the latest thing in the art of ship-building; absolutely no money was spared in her construction.'

He gave a very brief account of the voyage, mentioning the ship's speed in revolutions and distance travelled each day, and his own actions after the collision. Smith interrupted this to question him about the actions of the officers, and whether they had understood the urgency of the situation. Then he asked if Ismay had consulted with the captain about the working of the ship. He said he had not, except that it had been arranged before they left Queenstown that they must not arrive at the New York lightship before five on Wednesday morning.

He questioned Ismay about the speed, and Ismay said

that they had never gone at full speed, and the rearmost row of boilers had not been fired, though they had hoped to make a full speed trial on the Monday afternoon or Tuesday morning if the weather was favourable. Smith then turned to the question of ice. Ismay said he had known that ice had been reported, but that he personally had not seen any icebergs or large volume of ice.

'Had you ever been on this so-called northern route before?' Smith asked.

'We were on the southern route, sir,' said Ismay.

'On this Newfoundland route?' asked Smith.

'We were on the long southern route,' Ismay explained patiently, 'not on the northern route.'

'You were not on the extreme northern route?' Smith persisted.

'We were on the extreme southern route for the west-bound ships,' said Ismay.

Ashley stirred restively at this and exchanged a look with Teddy. Either Smith was painfully slow, or he was trying to confuse the witness.

Smith asked more questions about ice warnings and the operation of the wireless, to which Ismay could only answer that he had no knowledge of such things. Then he turned to the operation of the lifeboats. Ismay said he could only answer as to what he had seen, having no knowledge of what orders the crew and officers might have had about them. In response to questions he said he had seen three lifeboats lowered, that they had been fairly well filled, that there was no jostling, that women and children were put in first.

'Were these women passengers designated as they went into the lifeboat?' Smith asked.

'No, sir,' said Ismay.

'Those that were nearest the lifeboat were taken in?'

'We simply picked the women out and put them in the boat as fast as we could.'

'You picked them out from among the throng?'

'We took the first ones that were there and put them in the lifeboats. I was there myself and put a lot in.'

Smith asked about crew complements in the boats, then

in a butterfly manner asked how long Ismay had been on the ship after the collision. Ismay said it must have been an hour and a quarter or longer, but it was hard to say, memory of that period being uncertain. Did he see any passengers he knew in that time, asked Smith. Did he know there were Americans and Canadians of prominence on board? Did he see any of them during that time? Ismay said he did not remember recognising any of the people he saw during that time.

Then Smith asked, 'What were the circumstances, Mr Ismay, of your departure from the ship?'

'The boat was there,' Ismay said. 'There was a certain number of men in the boat, and the officer called out asking if there were any more women, and there was no response, and there were no more passengers left on the deck. As the boat was in the act of being lowered away, I got into it.'

Smith asked about the collision itself, about life-preservers, whether Ismay had seen anyone jump into the sea, how long they had been in the boat in the open sea, whether they had seen any other boats, how they got onto the *Carpathia*, whether all the lifeboats were accounted for. Then he asked about the ship's Board of Trade certificate.

'The ship receives a Board of Trade certificate, otherwise she would not be allowed to carry passengers,' said Ismay.

'Do you know whether that was done?' asked Smith.

'You could not sail your ship without it,' said Ismay.

'Do you know whether the ship was equipped with its full complement of lifeboats?'

'If she had not been, she could not have sailed: she would not have received her certificate.'

'Were these lifeboats completed when the ship was completed, or were any of them borrowed from other White Star ships?'

'They would certainly not have been borrowed,' said Ismay.

'Was the lifeboat you were in marked with the name *Titanic*, on the boat or the oars?'

'I did not look to see.'

Smith asked technical questions about the boilers and

engines, which Ismay said he could not answer, then turned to the watertight compartments. Ismay explained that *Titanic* was designed to float with up to four compartments filled with water, and added that if she had struck the berg stem-on she would not have sunk.

Smith repeated questions he had already asked about ice, about women passengers, about lifeboat provision, asked about the wireless on the *Carpathia*, how Ismay was dressed in the lifeboat, how many officers there were aboard *Titanic*, and then said that he had finished for now and asked Ismay to continue to hold himself at the committee's disposal.

Ismay, looking more exhausted than ever, stood to leave, and a buzz of conversation broke out round the room. Nat turned to Ashley. 'This fellow Smith has a very strange way of going about things,' he said. 'He boxes the compass – due north, then south-west, then nor'-nor'-east.'

'I didn't like the tenor of some of his questions,' Ashley said. 'Did you notice how he tried to insist the ship was on the northern route? And his questions about speed? He's looking for someone to blame.'

'Naturally enough,' said Nat. 'If the shipping line can be found at fault, there will be someone to sue for compensation. I'm afraid your Mr Ismay is in the firing line. Smith wants to make him personally responsible for who was and was not in the lifeboats.'

Dan said, 'There's a lot of anti-English feeling beginning to surface in the newspapers. I didn't like the way he asked how long before the sinking Mr Ismay left the ship. He seemed to be hinting at something there.'

The committee had finished conferring, and Senator Smith announced, 'I would like at this time to call on Mr Edward Morland.'

Teddy got up as if he had been stung: his mind had been far away. He walked up to the top of the centre table and sat down amid a flashing of camera-guns, was sworn in, and asked his name, place of residence and age.

'And your occupation?'

'I am a landowner and also have various business interests in the cloth manufacture and retailing way,' Teddy said.

He looked and sounded nervous, Ashley thought, but it was a natural reaction to the occasion and the massed ranks of staring faces.

'Are you an officer of the White Star Line?' Smith asked.

'I am not,' said Teddy.

'You are not? I understood you had some interest in the White Star company.'

'My company provided the linens and some other soft furnishings for the *Titanic*,' said Teddy. 'It was a normal business contract between my company and White Star. I had no other interest in the White Star Line.'

'What was your capacity on the ship?'

'Capacity? I was a passenger, sir,' Teddy said, clearly puzzled.

'You were travelling to New York purely as a passenger?'

Teddy sensed a trap being laid for him. He said, 'I had better explain. Mr Ismay has told you that he always accompanies the maiden voyage of a new ship to see how she works, and to see how she could be improved for the future, and for the next ship. As my company had provided most of the soft furnishing materials he invited me to come on *Titanic*'s maiden trip for the same purpose, to give my observations and advice on any possible improvements. He had asked me,' he added, 'to sail with the *Olympic* on her maiden voyage but I was unable to do so for personal reasons.'

'You say you were invited: did you in fact pay for your own ticket?'

'I did not, sir.'

'You travelled free?'

'Yes.'

Smith then asked Teddy where he had been at the moment of collision and what he had done. Teddy answered to the best of his ability, only adding, 'Memory of that time is not always clear. It was a period of very great strain and anxiety.'

Smith flitted about in his odd way over the topics of ice, speed, wireless messages, ship's officers and other lifeboats, and then asked, 'Please explain the circumstances of your leaving the ship.'

'I was on the starboard side of the ship—'

'Not the port side?' Smith interrupted. He seemed to be looking at some note in front of him. 'That is the left side, is it not?'

'The port side is the left side,' Teddy said.

'Left as you face the front of the ship?'

'Yes, sir.'

'And you were on the left side?'

'I was on the starboard side. I had earlier been on the port side as I have said. At the end I was on the starboard side.'

'Please continue.'

'I helped to load women and children onto the boat. It was the last boat on that side.'

'On the left side?'

'On the right side, the starboard side,' Teddy said. Ashley sighed impatiently at all this left-right confusion and exchanged another glance with Nat.

Teddy continued: 'When all the women and children were in the boat, the officer called to a group of crewmen – firemen, I think they were – to get in. Then there was no-one else left on the deck except Mr Ismay and me, and he asked us to get in as well.'

'Mr Ismay was there?'

'Yes, he had been helping to get the women into the boat, as I had.'

'Mr Ismay is a personal friend, I believe.'

'Yes.'

'You both got into the boat?'

'It was being lowered, and there was no-one else in sight.'

'Which officer was it who asked you to get into the boat?'

'His name was Murdoch.'

'Was he among the survivors?'

'No, sir.'

'Have you any knowledge of any of the officers drinking or being the worse for drink during this time?'

'None at all.'

'How long after the lifeboat was in the water did the *Titanic* sink?'

'It's hard to say. In the circumstances, time does not seem

to pass in the normal manner. But I would think fifteen or twenty minutes.'

Smith asked about the rescue by *Carpathia*, and then one of the other committee members whispered something to him, and he said, 'Thank you for your co-operation, Mr Morland. At this time, the committee wishes to call the captain of the *Carpathia*, for his convenience, as he wishes to return to his ship and set sail as soon as possible. So I would ask you to step down now but to continue to hold yourself in readiness in case we have further questions.'

The shops in New York were a revelation to Lizzie. She had thought that London shops were fine, had marvelled at the size of Whiteley's, but everything here was beyond measure grander, more filled with plenty and, above all, larger. The department stores seemed as vast as cities.

Rosemary trotted her round with brisk efficiency. 'I think we ought just to concentrate on getting a few necessaries. There'll be time later for you to have things made just as you like, but for now ready-mades will do, don't you think?'

Lizzie agreed. She had no heart for shopping, though she acknowledged the necessity. In any case, the ready-made departments of New York's stores were wonderful. There was enormous variety and choice, and a whole army of seamstresses behind the scenes enabled the sales-ladies to promise that any little alterations would be done that day and the things sent home by evening. It was a miracle of efficiency. Lizzie chose, Rosemary charged everything to her account, and the store undertook the rest. They bought underclothes first, then Lizzie picked out some things for the children and a couple of plain dresses for Jenny, then turned to her own needs.

It was while she was trying on an afternoon dress that she began to feel peculiar. Everything suddenly became very strange, the walls were simultaneously too close and too far off; the lights and the surrounding voices seemed alien, as if they came from another world. The assistant was adjusting the lie of the dress and saying, 'Just a tiny alteration, madam, a leetle tuck in the back here, and it will be perfect.' Lizzie met her eyes in the looking-glass, and saw that her own face was white, and there was moisture on her upper lip. The assistant got to her feet hastily and said, 'On second thoughts, madam, I think it will do very well just as it is. I think you can take it right with you.' She helped Lizzie off with the dress, and to a chair. 'Can I get you something, madam? A drink of water?'

'No. No, thank you. I'm quite all right,' Lizzie said, and her voice seemed to come from far away. She got to her feet and was helped into her own clothes, and went out of the changing-room to find her companion.

'I can't see anything else here,' Rosemary said, as soon as she rejoined her, 'but Jenson's next door has a good ready-made department. We'll go and look there.'

She took Lizzie's arm and was leading her towards the exit. The lights were bright; the panelling and gilding, the ornate cornices, the carpet underfoot were luxurious. There was a faint background noise – an air-conditioning machine, she supposed – and the voices above it were bright, American, confident, rich. It was, she realised, very like *Titanic*. New York stores were like great luxury ships floating on the sea of tarmacadam and concrete. She began to shake; sweat trickled cold down her spine. They reached the tall, glazed double doors and pushed out into the vestibule. Opposite them were the gilded elevators, and standing waiting was a young woman in a sable coat and a large black hat. She had her back to them, but in height and build and hair colour she was very like Amalfia. Lizzie's mouth dried; her heart pounded. The young woman turned her head towards them, and Lizzie staggered, clutching Rosemary's arm, and the world went black.

'What a fool I am,' Rosemary castigated herself. 'I started enjoying myself, that's where it went wrong. I should have thought how you must be feeling. I'm *so* sorry, my dear.' Lizzie demurred politely, but she was glad to be out of that place. 'You're still as white as a sheet,' said Rosemary. 'I know what we'll do. Aunt Ruth's is only two short blocks away. We'll go there and you can sit down and rest and have a cup of hot tea.'

Lizzie would sooner have gone home, but she hadn't the energy to resist Rosemary; and in the event, she was glad it had been decided that way. Aunt Ruth, it transpired, lived in an apartment, but it was nothing like any flat she had ever been to. It was big enough to have been called a house, except that it was all on one floor; but it was in a massive, Victorian brick building, and was furnished with heavy, dark old furniture, Turkish carpets and fine, much-polished silver. There was nothing in the least glittery-luxurious about it, nothing *Titanic*. Everything was solidly comfortable, old and well kept. They were admitted by an elderly parlourmaid, and taken straight to the drawing-room where Aunt Ruth rose to meet them.

She was a small, thin old lady with a high-cheekboned, sharp-chinned face, and bright, dark eyes full of merriment. Her white hair was done in a large coil behind, and she wore a plain, high-necked black dress, with a large jet brooch at the throat, and long jet earrings. She advanced at once to shake Lizzie's hand, and used it to guide her to a chair.

'You look plumb worn out, my dear, and no wonder! I know who you are and what you've been through. I'm Ashley's aunt Ruth, his father Fenwick's sister, so I guess I'm your auntie too. Now, don't try to speak. Just sit quiet and get your heart beating regular again.'

'I thought maybe some hot tea, Auntie,' Rosemary suggested.

'Good idea,' said Ruth. She pronounced it 'ideah'. She had a strong accent quite different from any of the others Lizzie had heard so far, and from what little she knew she guessed it was a 'southern' accent. 'Now, don't ring for Ellen, Rosemary. Why make two journeys for her, when she's got enough to do already? Just go to the kitchen and ask. You ain't too proud for that, are you?'

Rosemary departed good-naturedly, and Ruth came back to Lizzie with a mischievous look in her eyes. 'That's got rid of *her*. She's a good creature, but prosy. I'm fond of her, don't take me wrong, but there's not an ounce of brain in her head. The idea of taking you shopping your first day on land!'

'We do desperately need clothes,' Lizzie defended her.

'Of course you do, but Rosemary could have taken your dimensions and sent out for them.'

Lizzie rather liked the idea that she had dimensions rather than measurements. While she was talking, Ruth had gone over to a table in a dark corner and now came back with a glass of something brown.

'Here,' she said. 'Drink this up. Tea is well and good, but from the look of you, you need a heart-stimulant. Don't sniff it, don't sip it, just drink it back. It's medicine.'

Lizzie did as she was told, and the spirits did settle her. She felt less cold and clammy, and her pulse seemed to settle back into its proper place and rhythm. 'It was the store we were in,' she said, as Ruth took the glass away. 'It reminded me so much of – of—'

'I can believe it,' said Ruth. 'From what I hear, it was designed for the same purpose – to part over-wealthy Yankees from their money.'

She sat down in the chair next to Lizzie's and took her hand between both of hers. Her hands were thin and smooth and dry and warm. Lizzie felt she knew her already. Was it her imagination, or had she a faint look of Cousin Venetia about her?

'I lost someone,' she found herself saying. Ruth nodded, her bright eyes waiting. 'I hadn't known her long, but I liked her so much. I loved her, really.'

'Time doesn't come into it,' Ruth said. 'When you love someone, that's it.' Now Lizzie nodded, grateful to be so readily understood. 'My first husband,' Ruth went on, 'we were only married a few months. He died at Manassas, in the Civil War. But I love him still.'

'It must have been terrible,' Lizzie said.

'Losing him, or the war?'

'Both – but especially the first. I don't know how I'd bear it if anything happened to Ashley.' And she thought again of Amalfia, who had died rather than find out.

'But you would, dear,' Ruth said. 'I can see you're a survivor. Life throws all manner of things at us, and we get by somehow. Look at me. I grew up in the South before

205

the war, and there was never a time or place when girls were more cosseted. Even our stockings were put on for us. Afterwards I saw things and did things I could never have imagined – nursed wounded soldiers with half their faces torn off, tilled the soil with my bare hands, near enough starved to death after the war, when the Yankees were doing their best to destroy us all. And look at me now.'

Lizzie did. 'You don't look as though you've done all those things.'

'Well, I take *that* as a compliment. But the hardest thing of all was losing Patrick.' She paused a moment, remembering. 'He left me his son to remember him by – I called him Patrick too, and there never was a better boy. He lives here with me and *his* son, Lenny. His wife died when Lenny was born, so I've been kind of a mother to the boy, as well as his grandmother.' She twinkled. 'There's another thing you'd never believe when you're fourteen – that you could ever be a grandmother. And, come to think of it, life never throws anything worse at you than the stark fact of growing old. There's *no* getting over that one. Are you feeling any better yet?'

'Much,' Lizzie said, and it was true. 'I'd like to hear all about your life, if you could be troubled to tell it.'

'Lord, there's nothing I like better than talking,' Ruth said. 'When I was a girl my aunt used to say my tongue had wheels on both ends, and I've never gotten any better. But at my age, there are few other pleasures left.' She paused and listened. 'Is that Rosemary coming back? No, not yet. Oh, the story of my life is a long one, and I guess it'll have to wait for another time. I'll come over one day while you're still in New York and tell you all about it.'

'I'd like that,' Lizzie said, her hand still warmly held. This person was so full of life and warmth she couldn't help asking, 'Did you never marry again?'

'Oh, yes,' Ruth said. 'You're thinking I dedicated my life to Patrick's memory? I wasn't quite *that* saintly! No, after the war I married Fen's wife's brother, Lennox Mynott, and we were very happy together. He was a good husband, and a good father to Patrick. Indeed, Patrick never knew any other, for he was born posthumously. He called Lennox "Pa", and even named his own son after him.'

'He must have been a good man.'

'He was. The one sadness we had was that we never had any more children. But he loved Patrick like his own.' Her eyes went distant again, and she paused a moment, then said, 'I've had a good life, in spite of everything, and my only regret was that we never got to England. We always meant to go, Lennox and me, but after the war things were so bad, we stayed on to help Ashley's mother Mary – his pa was dead by then. We tried to hold on to the family place, but we were taxed and persecuted and nearly starved to death. Things were terrible in the South after the war. I'll tell you about it some day. Mary married again, to my cousin Martial, and when they went north – Mart had friends among the Yankees – we went too. Lennox was a land agent, and after a few years, when the hatred had died down some, he did pretty well at it. We settled eventually in Connecticut, and saw to it Patrick got a good education. He's an architect,' she said proudly, 'and a right fine one, too! After Lennox died I came to live with him and help bring up little Lenny. And I just never did get to go to England.'

'You still could,' Lizzie said. 'I know my mother would be glad to have you come and stay. She's Ashley's mother's sister – Mary's sister – though she doesn't remember her.'

'There's a lot of marrying of cousins in our family,' Ruth said with a smile. 'But I'm too old to go all that way now. I've resigned myself to never seeing England. Maybe Lenny will go for me one day. He's been dying for it for years, ever since he realised he had relations there.' Rosemary came back in at that point with the maid following, carrying a tray. 'I'm sorry I've been so long,' she said, taking a cup from the tray and handing it tenderly to Lizzie. 'How are you feeling now?'

'Much better,' Lizzie said.

'You look better. Much more colour in your cheeks.'

'She's fine, Rosemary, don't fuss her. It takes more than an appalling catastrophe to break a Morland.' Rosemary handed her a cup of tea and sat down with her own, which she sipped with a flinching expression – evidently, to her, tea was medicine. 'I wonder how they're getting on at the inquiry,' Ruth said, after a moment.

'I don't suppose they will take long with Uncle Teddy,' Rosemary said. 'As a passenger he won't know anything about the working of the ship.'

'He says he wants to go home as soon as they've finished with him,' Lizzie said.

'Oh, I hope not,' Ruth said. 'I want to meet him very much. Rosemary, you'll have to invite us to dinner real soon, in case he does go.'

'Come this evening, if you like,' Rosemary said, with easy hospitality. 'We won't be dressing, of course. It's just family dinner.'

'Please do come,' Lizzie said quickly. 'You've done me so much good, I'm sure you can cheer up poor Uncle Teddy too.'

Ruth patted her hand. 'It's kind of you to say so, child. But what's cheered you up is what's inside you. You just didn't know you had it, or you forgot it for a minute. Life is a great adventure, you know. You never can tell what will be thrown at you. Now, *you*'ve just had a big and terrible experience, but you survived, and it will only make you stronger for the next one. You just have to make sure that precious gift isn't wasted.'

Lizzie thought of Arizona, the next great adventure, and felt the appalling shock of the *Titanic* slip one small but important step into the past. She would not go home or give up, she would go onwards. She would get through the grief and pain, and go on living, as Aunt Ruth had.

Naturally, there was a lot of talk at dinner that night about the hearing.

'The fact of the matter,' said Nat, 'is that a whole lot of very eminent Americans were on that ship, and died or were bereaved, and someone's got to be found to take the blame.'

'The evening papers are full of talk about the lifeboats, demanding to know why there weren't enough of them,' said Dan. 'They don't take the Rostron line.'

Captain Rostron had been asked about lifeboats at the hearing that morning. He said, 'The ships are built nowadays to be practically unsinkable, and each ship is supposed to be a lifeboat in itself. The boats are merely supposed to be put on as a stand-by.'

'Hindsight is a beautiful thing,' said Ashley. 'Who could have thought that *Titanic* would sink, or that she would sink so quickly? In normal circumstances, other ships would have come to the rescue and taken everyone off, and the boats wouldn't have been needed.'

Aunt Ruth spoke up: 'Be that as it may, you're letting English logic rule you, and forgetting Yankee passion. America is angry, and America wants a scapegoat. Every story has to have a hero and a villain, and this is the greatest story ever.'

'And there are the newspapers themselves to think of,' said her son Patrick – a tall man with a face that, while not exactly handsome, was so *nice* it was impossible to look at him without smiling. 'The yellow press will stop at nothing to sell copies, and we have two of the most ferocious proprietors ever – Pulitzer and Hearst – who are locked in battle over their respective circulations. What they don't know they will make up, and their readers won't know the difference, or care if they do know.'

'The newspapers will make capital all right,' Nat said, 'but that doesn't alter the fact that the hearing has started out with an agenda. Haven't you noticed the tendency of some of Senator Smith's questions? He wants to find out that the captain and crew were either drunk or negligent or both, and that the British authorities were careless about safety. Here's a British ship—'

'But White Star is a subsidiary of an American company,' Ashley objected. 'Ultimately, IMM is the owner.'

'I'm guessing you won't hear too much about that,' said Dan's slow, deep voice. 'IMM's owner is John Pierpont Morgan, and he's well known in Washington as a financial backer of politicians – among them Senator Smith. It would not behove Smith to put his benefactor on the spot; and if he was so mad as to do it, the newspapers wouldn't wear it.'

'I agree,' said Patrick. 'A British villain is what's wanted, especially by William Randolph Hearst. He has a violent hatred of all things English and, I'm sorry to say, he has a particular spleen against your friend Mr Ismay.' He nodded politely towards Teddy. 'It dates from when Mr Ismay lived and worked over here. I don't know what's at the bottom of it, but . . .' He hesitated, and then said unwillingly, 'I've heard things already – rumours, stories going round. I'm afraid things may not go so well for him.'

Aunt Ruth looked at her son piercingly. 'Hearst means to black Ismay, does he?'

Patrick shook his head slightly, and did not reply.

'It would be monstrous to blame him.' Teddy spoke up. 'What happened was an accident.'

'There are some people can never bring themselves to believe in accidents,' said Ruth. 'They always think there must be someone at fault. If your Mr Ismay is the target, you should watch your own step. As his friend—'

'I *am* his friend, and I'll stay his friend,' Teddy said firmly.

'I wouldn't expect anything else,' said Ruth; but she sighed as she said it.

CHAPTER ELEVEN

The front page of the newspaper was a horrible shock. In huge, thick, black letters, the headline read 'J. BRUTE ISMAY', and below was a picture of him, ringed by photographs of widows of victims of the *Titanic* disaster. The story that accompanied the headline was that Ismay had pushed aside women and children to scramble into the lifeboat in order to save his own cowardly life.

'But it's not true!' Teddy cried, when he saw it.

Inside pages of the newspaper contrasted the gentlemanly character of those American first-class male passengers who had gone down on the ship with that of the ship's English owner, who had escaped with his life while fifteen hundred souls, many of them women and children, had perished. 'Other men stood aside in accordance with the age-old rule, "women and children first", and would not have dreamed of taking a place in a lifeboat while there were women left on board. Mr Ismay, however, believed himself excepted from this rule. If any life should be saved, it must be his. Mr Ismay is no doubt glad to be an Englishman. He is certainly no gladder than we are.'

'What can we do?' Teddy cried. 'Something must be done. It is a downright lie. I shall telephone the editor of the paper and protest in the strongest terms!'

Nat looked worried. 'It might be unwise, sir. They will not change their story – and it will only bring you unwelcome attention.'

But Teddy was determined. 'I can't see a lie like that published and not refute it.' He wrote a strongly worded letter to the newspaper, saying that there had indeed been no-one else nearby and that First Officer Murdoch had urged them to board.

Ashley was called to the tribunal that afternoon. It was clear from the tenor of the questions that he had been called as a representative of the Culpepper Line, and was assumed to have special technical knowledge. He firmly put paid to that idea.

Smith looked disappointed, but after his deputy, Senator Newlands, had whispered to him, he said, 'You have, however, some experience of sailing?'

'When I lived in Boston I was something of a yachtsman.'

'Have you any experience of ice or icebergs?'

'I have sometimes sailed in ice-field conditions.'

'Were you aware that *Titanic* was sailing into an ice field?'

'Yes, sir. I believed that we would come up to it that night – that is, on Sunday night.'

'Do you think that the lookout kept on the *Titanic* was adequate?'

'I have no knowledge of what lookout was kept. I know nothing about the working of the ship.'

Newlands asked, 'We understand that the lookouts had no binoculars. In your opinion would this make it more difficult for them to see an iceberg?'

'Not necessarily. Binoculars are used to view the detail of something already spotted with the naked eye. You do not constantly scan the field with glasses.'

Smith resumed: 'Would you expect a special lookout to be kept when entering an ice field?'

'I cannot answer that. My experience is in small boats,' said Ashley.

Smith tried a different tack. 'In your opinion, was the *Titanic* sailing too fast on Sunday night when entering the ice field?'

Ashley was under oath, and could only answer, 'Yes. Given the circumstances.'

'I wish you will tell us just what you mean by that,' said Smith. 'What were the special circumstances?'

'There was no moon. An iceberg only shows up white

when light falls on it,' Ashley said. 'Of course, there are many dark nights at sea. When there is no moon, the best way to spot an iceberg is by the white-water – that is, the waves breaking at its foot. But the sea was dead calm that night. I don't mean merely that there was little movement of the water – there was none at all. The sea was as flat and still as glass.' There was a little ripple of reaction along the ranks of the press at this. Ashley went on, doing his best for the dead captain, though he hardly knew why: 'You might sail the North Atlantic a lifetime without seeing such a dead calm. A combination of the two factors, dead calm and dark of the moon, must be exceedingly rare.'

'Have you ever seen such a combination?'

'No, sir. I have never seen a flat calm like that.'

'In your opinion, would Captain Smith have experienced it before?'

'I know nothing of Captain Smith.'

'He was a very experienced sailor, and many years older than you. Ought he not to have anticipated the difficulties?'

'I cannot answer for Captain Smith,' Ashley said firmly.

Senator Smith then asked some questions about the lifeboats, but seemed not much interested in Ashley's answers, for he did not pursue how Ashley, a man, had come to survive at all. He soon changed his line, and asked, 'In your experience as an officer of the Culpepper Line, what instructions would be given to a ship's captain by his employers?'

'General instructions about where and when to sail,' Ashley said, a little uneasily. He could guess where this was going.

'And how to sail? The sea route, the speed?'

'Those things would be decided by custom and experience. The sea routes are very well known and defined. The speed would depend on the ship and the conditions.'

'And who would make that judgement – the judgement as to speed?'

'The captain, sir. He is master of his ship, and all matters concerning the daily management of the ship rest with him.'

'But an owner might order him to drive at maximum speed?'

213

'He might request it, though I cannot imagine in what circumstances. He certainly could not order it.'

There were a few more questions about the rescue from the lifeboats into the *Carpathia*, and then Ashley was released and told he would not be required again. He left with a feeling of relief, and a little of frustration. The senator's hopping, inattentive method of questioning gave him the strong impression that he wanted a particular set of answers, and would get them, one way or another.

The evening papers carried a mention of Ashley's testimony, under the headline of 'Captain was going too fast, says witness'. He could only be glad that his answers were reported verbatim. Unhappily, there were more attacks on Ismay, and Dan reported that a telephone call to his wife in Boston had revealed the story about his pushing women aside to get into the boat was being carried there as well. 'It's going to get worse before it gets better,' he said glumly.

The next day it was worse. Ismay fever seemed to have hit the newspapers. Stories from 'eye-witnesses' abounded, and even when they contradicted each other they all pointed to his selfish cowardice. Everything he had said and done was being re-evaluated to give a bad impression. The fact that he had wired a message from *Carpathia* asking for the *Cedric* to be held back for the crewmen to be taken home was said to prove that he had intended fleeing the country and justice as soon as he arrived. The fact that he had not left the cabin on *Carpathia* proved that his shame and guilt prevented him meeting anyone's eye. He had said in testimony that they were intending to have a full-speed trial on Monday or Tuesday, which was taken to prove that he had ordered Captain Smith to keep up full speed in the ice field. The lack of lifeboats was now solely due to his penny-pinching: he had callously risked passengers' lives to increase his own profits. And the watertight compartments were not really watertight at all – that, too, was Ismay's fault, the result of his 'brutal economy'. Greed and selfishness had atrophied his heart. He was a 'human hog', whose animal desires had swallowed up all finer feelings.

Distressing enough though this was, the Hearst news-paper struck closer to home. Teddy's letter was printed, and Nat had been right to fear it would draw attention to him. There was a whole article about him, under the headline, 'Ismay's friend another survivor'. There was a picture of Teddy, one taken as he left the terminal building at the docks. The lights and noise had startled him, and his natural turning away and narrowing of eyes had been captured, but somehow, out of context, made him look furtive.

J. Brute Ismay was not the only Englishman to save his skin at the expense of others [said the article]. His close friend and business colleague, Mr Edward Morland, also managed to force his way into the lifeboat which carried Mr Ismay to safety, leaving more than fifteen hundred innocent men, women and children to perish. Mr Morland, a gentleman-farmer and mill owner from Yorkshire, England, was travelling as a guest of Mr Ismay. Witnesses say he forced his way through the assembled women to secure his place in the lifeboat. He was fully dressed in suit and overcoat, complete with extra jerseys, proving that, unlike the majority of poor souls on board, he had had ample warning of the ship's impending doom.

Mr Morland had a financial interest in the *Titanic*, and no doubt it was as much to his advantage as to Mr Ismay's that profits were maximised by economising on safety. The multitude of the dead must cry out for justice when they see these two Englishmen parading themselves safe, sound and prosperous through our city. In a letter opposite Mr Morland claims again that there were no other people nearby when he entered the lifeboat. We ask, is this credible? Fifteen hundred people were still on board when Mr Morland and his friend Ismay left the ship. Is it possible, is it remotely likely, that there was *no-one in sight*? Is it not much more likely that Mr Ismay ordered the lowering of the boat to save his own skin and that of his friend, because

215

he feared they might be forced by angry male passengers to give up their seats for the hapless women and children still on deck?

Teddy's head sank into his hands when he read this. Lizzie found herself in tears, Ashley was pale with indignation. With Nat and Dan, and with Patrick Manning when he came round later, they discussed endlessly what might be done, but there seemed to be nothing. 'Once newspapers get hold of a story, they'll run it to death until people lose interest,' said Patrick. 'And I'm afraid interest in the *Titanic* story will last a long time yet.'

The next day was Sunday, and Rosemary was outraged when she came down to breakfast to hear from the servants that there was a crowd of people outside, pressmen and the merely curious, waiting to catch a glimpse of the hateful friend of the hated Brute Ismay. Rosemary ordered the front blinds drawn, and Nat sent for the gardener and his boy to keep guard on the grounds at the back for fear an impertinent newsman would climb over.

The Hearst Sunday paper contained a new story about Teddy: that he had made several attempts to get into a lifeboat before the successful one. Eye-witnesses told how he had pushed through the crowds on the port side to accost Second Officer Lightoller as he was trying to lower a lifeboat. Several of the witnesses, who had been nearby, had heard Lightoller at last threaten to have Teddy clapped in irons if he did not step aside.

Teddy paled. 'I did accost Lightoller, but only to beg him not to send the boats off half empty. I *told* him I was not concerned for myself.' He saw the trap he was in. 'Oh, God, who will believe that now?'

Another witness, Mrs Baxter Benson, wife of the leather-goods manufacturer, said that Mr Morland had told her while she was waiting in the queue at the purser's office that he intended to get into a boat no matter what happened. 'I never said any such thing!' Teddy cried. He tried to remember what he had said to her. He had asked if she'd seen the Penobscots; told her to leave her diamonds and save herself. Vaguely he remembered her saying, 'Well, really!' in an offended tone. Had he called them 'damned diamonds'? Was that all he had done to make her jump into the band-wagon and abuse him?

They spent the day indoors, ignoring the frequent ringing of the telephone bell and the thumpings at the front door. Patrick brought Aunt Ruth and his son, Lennox, to visit, coming in through the back garden, which fortunately had not been discovered yet.

'Well, now,' Ruth said briskly, when all had been discussed again, and a long, gloomy silence had been sat through, 'it's clear we can't go on like this. Your house will be besieged, Nat dear, while this goes on, and it isn't good for poor Miss Lizzie and those children to be witnessing this kind of thing day after day, especially with their nerves already in shreds.'

'But what's to be done?' Rosemary asked. 'I don't much like it for my own children, I might mention. Our name might not be Morland, but it won't be long before everybody knows about the connection, and then only think how Nat junior and Amy will be teased in school. And what about Peggy? This is such an important time of her life, when she's beginning to go into Society, and a thing like this can stick, you know. It could ruin her chances of a good marriage.'

'Rosemary!' Ruth exclaimed. 'I'm ashamed of you.'

Rosemary reddened, but held her ground. 'I don't see what I've said to be ashamed of. *I* don't believe the nasty stories, I never said I did. I only said other people will, and then we'll all be for it. It's the truth, Auntie, and you can't say contrary. I'm entitled to think about my own children's welfare, however sorry I am for Uncle Teddy and Ashley and Lizzie.'

'Rosemary's right,' Ashley said, to prevent Ruth berating her again. 'Just now our name is a handicap. We ought to take ourselves away before things get worse for you.'

Ruth looked impatient. 'That's just what I was going to say. There's no sense in being holed up here with that mob outside.' She made a contemptuous gesture. 'Once the Morlands have gone, you'll be left in peace, Rosemary. What

I suggest is that you go on to Boston. I'm sure Dan is anxious to get back to his family.'

'I certainly am,' said Dan.

'You were going to Boston anyway, as I understand it,' Ruth said to Ashley, 'and there'll be no seeing anything of New York as things are. Boston's a much more sober city, and Dan's house is on the edge of it, quiet and practically rural. It'll be better all round for your health and your nerves. You can forget all this nonsense and concentrate on restoring your spirits before you go on to Arizona.' She looked at Lizzie. 'You are still meaning to go, aren't you? You haven't changed your mind?'

Lizzie managed a smile. 'I had, before I talked to you. Now I think it would be weakness to give up and go home.'

'Good for you, girl!' Ruth said, with a positively youthful grin. 'Never give up. And I tell you what, when you're settled in Arizona I'll come and visit you. I've never been there, and I'm not too old yet for a new adventure, I don't think.'

'I'm sure you're not,' Lizzie said, her smile stronger. She thought it would be wonderful to have Aunt Ruth to stay. She wished she could have had her there when they first arrived, for her advice and spine-stiffening qualities.

Dan said, 'I think it's a good idea, and you're all welcome to come to Boston right away. But what about Uncle Teddy?'

The inquiry was not sitting on the Sunday, of course; and it was moving to the Capitol in Washington on Monday for its third day, where it would remain. All witnesses who had been subpoenaed and had not yet been released were to go with it.

'You know I can't go to Boston,' Teddy said. 'But don't worry about me. Brown and I will be all right. We'll put up in an hotel in Washington until I'm released.'

'I'll come with you,' Ashley said.

'Nonsense. There's no need.'

'But I hate to think of you being all alone in a strange country.'

'I shall do very well. Brown looks after me like a mother, you know,' he said, with a faint smile.

'But when it's over, you'll come then?' Lizzie asked anxiously.

'No, Lizzie dear,' said Uncle Teddy. 'As soon as I'm released, I'm going home. It's all I want now, to get back to Morland Place and see my wife and children. I'm sure you can understand that.'

'Yes, I suppose so,' Lizzie said, though unwillingly.

Ruth looked at her shrewdly. 'Last link with the old country, eh? But there's letters and wires and visits, you know. It's not the end of the world. You can go back and any of your family can come over here.'

'I don't think I could ever bring myself to cross the Atlantic in a ship again,' Lizzie said, with a shudder.

'There's no other way,' Ruth said crisply. 'You'd be surprised what you can do when you really want something.'

'I'd like to go,' said Lennox. 'I wouldn't be afraid. I want to see London and the Houses of Parliament and Windsor Castle and Morland Place. And I'd take lots of photographs to bring back and show you, Grammie.'

'You'll go one day,' Ruth nodded to him, 'if you really want to. Well, is it decided then? You folk's'll all be off to Boston in the morning, Mr Teddy will get the train to Washington, and you, Rosemary, can have your house to yourself again.'

'I didn't mean—' Rosemary began to protest.

'Tush, child,' Ruth dismissed her. 'We all know what you meant.' Her bright gaze went round the group and settled on Lizzie. 'I shall miss you, Miss Lizzie. I was looking forward to some nice long chats, before all this unpleasantness blew up.'

'I shall miss you, too,' Lizzie said, with feeling. 'I haven't heard half your story yet.'

'Not a fraction of it,' Ruth said cheerfully. 'Once you get me started, you know, I can go on for days without drawing breath. Nothing an old Southerner like me more enjoys than talking about the way things were before the war.'

'Why don't you come with us, Auntie?' Dan said. 'I'm sure Patrick and Lennie can spare you.'

Ruth looked pleased. 'Well, if you're sure there's room

for me. I haven't seen Madeleine and the boys in quite a while. And I always did like Boston better than New York. New York's such a Yankee place. Don't know why you settled here, Patrick, my boy. An architect can work anywhere.'

Patrick smiled at her. This was evidently a frequently visited discussion. 'An architect has to go where the work is, like anyone else. And there's no city with more work than New York. It's being pulled down and built up constantly.'

'Yankees always were restless,' Ruth said, with pretended disdain. 'No stickin' power, like us Southerners.'

Teddy finally went home at the end of April, having been called three times to the tribunal. He sailed on the 29th on the White Star's *Attic*, which was on the Liverpool run. By then he felt so utterly exhausted, both physically and mentally, that he had no fear whatever of the crossing, could not whip up the slightest trepidation at finding himself again on a ship on the open ocean. As soon as he was on board he retired to his cabin. Brown had a heavy cold, and was looking grey and old, and Teddy insisted that the man take to his bed and not worry about him. He could look after himself, he said.

He wanted nothing but to go home. He had seen himself traduced and reviled in the newspapers, his name dragged through the mud; he had been stared at and shunned in Washington, to the extent that the waiters in the hotel dining-room sat him away from everyone else at a small table in a sort of alcove. And worse than that, worst of all, was the memory of the tragedy, the agony of the great ship's death, the pitiful wailing across the water as all those people froze to death in the water. He had survived, and the guilt of it ate deeply into him. He remained in his cabin, had his meals brought there (and frequently failed to eat them) and emerged only at night, when the deck was empty, to walk and brood.

By the time they reached Liverpool, he had caught Brown's cold, and at least had an excuse for how wretched he felt. He had not wired anyone to say which ship he was coming on, but someone must have passed the news, because

220

as he and Brown came down the gangway in the sooty drizzle of a wet May day, looking nervously about for pressmen, the first person they saw was Ned. He was huddled in his overcoat against the drifting skeins of rain, and as soon as he saw them he hurried over, his face taut with emotion.

'Father!'

'Ned – my boy.'

They shook hands. Ned looked him over keenly, and thought how ill he looked. The experience must have been terrible beyond imagining. But he was here! 'Thank God you're safe,' he said. 'All of you. It was a miracle.'

'Was it?' Teddy said. He looked around him uneasily. 'Are there any newspaper reporters about?'

'I don't think so,' Ned said. He pressed his father's hand. 'I know what they've been saying about you, Father. We've heard about it over here. It's a damned disgrace. We know it's all lies.'

Teddy gave him an exhausted look. 'I don't want to talk about it. I just want to go home,' he said.

'I have your motor outside. I didn't think you'd want to go on the train. Is this all your luggage? Hello, Brown.'

'Yes, this is everything, Mr Ned,' Brown said.

It brought home to Ned in a very practical way the reality of the sinking, that there were only two small cases to carry. Everything Teddy had taken with him was at the bottom of the sea. It was somehow horribly poignant to think of his shoes and brushes and razors and books deep in the silt in the dark and silence of the sea-bed, never to be seen again. Ned led the way through the Customs shed and out into the street where Teddy's motor-car was waiting with the chauffeur, Simmons, at the wheel; but before they had gone more than a step towards it there was a flash and pop and a press cameraman had taken a photograph, while a reporter presented himself under their dazzled noses and said, 'How does it feel to be back in England, Mr Morland? Have you a comment for our readers?'

Teddy automatically put up his hand to shield his face, and Ned forced himself between his father and the reporter and said, 'Not now. He's very tired. Can't you leave him alone?'

They hurried on, and the reporter scurried behind. 'Just doing my job, sir. Can you tell us how you survived, Mr Morland?'

Simmons had the door open, and Teddy bundled in, turning his face away from the reporter. Ned followed. Brown pushed in the suitcases and shut the door, he and Simmons almost ran for the front seats, and then they were driving away. Once they were clear Brown pulled back the sliding glass to say, 'I beg your pardon, sir, for putting the cases in with you, but I thought we ought to move as soon as possible. When we clear the city, we can stop and put them on the roof.'

'Don't bother,' said Teddy. 'They aren't in the way. Just go straight home, Simmons, as quickly as possible.'

'I'm sorry about that,' Ned said. 'I didn't know there was anyone waiting for you. He wasn't there when I went in – or I didn't see him.'

'No matter,' Teddy said. 'That was nothing compared with the American press. The fellow was positively polite. In New York and Washington—' He shivered. 'Don't let's talk about it. Tell me how they are at home. How's Alice?'

'She's as well as can be expected. Everyone's pretty well, but it's been a hard time. First the shock of the news, and wondering if you were all dead. Then all the terrible stories about the people who didn't survive, and the scandal of there not being enough lifeboats. And now this – these personal attacks on you and Mr Ismay.'

'I suppose there'll be an inquiry over here, too.'

'It began on Thursday – May the second. A full judicial inquiry under Lord Mersey. All the main parties have retained counsel. I understand they are calling officers and crew members first. I don't know,' he added, with a delicate hesitation, 'whether they will be calling any of the passengers later.'

Teddy answered with a grunt and, settling back in his seat, said nothing more. Ned did not press him to conversation. He realised that his father was very low-spirited, and was not in the least surprised. Once they were east and north of Manchester, the rain stopped, the clouds thinned, and eventually there was sunshine. The countryside was looking ravishing in its new spring green, and as they crossed the moors there were lambs everywhere, rushing away, as the motor passed, with high ridiculous leaps, all four feet off the ground at once. But Teddy had no eye for the scenery or heart for its beauty. He was too miserable even to feel the relief of being back in his own country.

Simmons was a leisurely driver, and even though he did his conscientious best to hurry, it was late afternoon by the time they reached Morland Place. As the motor pulled into the yard, the front door opened, and the family came out onto the steps, the dogs streaming past them, ears flattened and tails waving. The afternoon sun glowed on the bricks and gilded the windows, and the house seemed to smile in welcome, but nearly everybody else seemed to be crying. Even Robbie's eyes were moist.

Henrietta reached Teddy first and hugged him, wetting his cheek with her tears. 'Thank God, thank God,' was all she could say.

Jessie kissed him fervently and said, 'It doesn't matter what they say, *we* know the truth. You're here, and that's all that matters.'

But Teddy's eyes and attention were not with her. There was Alice, still at the top of the steps, her emotions too fierce, it seemed, to allow her to move. He detached himself from Jessie, did not even see Ethel's gesture towards him. His eyes locked with Alice's. Tears were running freely down her face, and her mouth was bowed as if with pain. Only now, seeing her in the flesh, did he realise how much she meant to him. He had no knowledge of climbing the steps. He only saw at the last minute her frozen arms found movement and reached out for him with childlike urgency, and then they were together, and he was holding her fiercely against him. They had no words for each other. He closed his eyes, and his helpless tears ran into her hair even as hers wet the shoulder of his coat.

Jack went to the Richardsons' evening party with a firm expectation of enjoying himself. Mrs Richardson was an aunt of Miss Ormerod, which he thought accounted for his invitation; but more importantly the Richardsons knew the Fairbrothers, and he was pining for a sight of his goddess.

A week ago he had been engaged to dine *chez* Fairbrother, but on the day itself, when he went home to change, he found a note from Mrs Fairbrother cancelling the dinner, saying that a relative was ill and she was obliged to go and visit her. He sent back polite regrets and good wishes for the invalid, and a few days later he had called at the house to enquire about her progress, and, of course, to see Myrtle. The parlourmaid had smiled and shown him into the morning-room and gone away, but she was absent what seemed like an unusually long time before she returned, unsmiling and rather red in the face, to tell him she was sorry, she had made a mistake and all the family was out.

Jack was surprised, for it was unlikely that the maid had been unaware of the absence of the whole upstairs contingent, so it must mean they didn't want to see him. He was on such calling terms that, even had it been an inconvenient time, he would have expected one of the family to come and tell him so. But perhaps the illness of the relative was more alarming than he had supposed, and was preoccupying them. 'I'll just leave my card and my compliments, then,' he said, and went away. He expected a note from Mrs Fairbrother saying that she was sorry to have missed him, but none came. Instead there was one from Harry Fairbrother, cancelling his lesson. Either the relative was dearly loved, Jack thought, or there were expectations involved.

So he was very glad of the Richardson invitation and the hope of seeing Miss Fairbrother. Unless the relative was actually at death's door, he was pretty sure she would be there, as the Fairbrothers prized the Richardson connection, and if Mrs F could not go she would arrange some other chaperone to take Myrtle.

He was threading his way through the crowds, exchanging smiles and greetings, when he saw Miss Ormerod, in a claret-coloured silk gown with a deep beaded hem, and her hair done in a large, soft chignon behind. She looked quite different, he thought, from her daytime self in thick tweeds and tightly pinned hair. The high-waisted style suited her, made her look not only more slender but somehow taller, too, and the weight of beads at the hem of the gown emphasised her graceful movements: he was more used to seeing her stumping purposefully through the mud in stout boots.

'Hullo,' he said cheerfully. 'You do look nice! That colour suits you perfectly.'

'Thank you,' she said, a spot of colour in her cheek.

'Is it a new gown?'

'Fairly. I don't think you could have seen it before. We haven't often met at evening parties, have we?'

'No, we haven't,' said Jack. 'That's an odd thing, isn't it? When was the last time?'

'The Alderleys,' she said promptly. 'That was back in January – and I wore my black then.'

'Did you? I don't remember it.'

'No, I don't suppose you would. Black doesn't really suit me, but we were still in mourning for Aunt Fanny.'

'Um,' he said vaguely, his eye scanning the room. 'Is—' he began.

She anticipated him so quickly he only managed the first word. 'Yes, she's here, with her mother. Mrs Fairbrother wouldn't miss a Richardson party.'

The latter sentence was spoken rather harshly, and he glanced at her in surprise to see what she meant by it, but his eyes were almost instantly called away by the sight of a golden head through a parting of the crowd. Miss Fairbrother was there, in sky blue, much beaded and fringed, with a beaded band around her hair, and she was talking animatedly, with many gestures of her delicate little fingers, to a tall young man. Jack knew him slightly – Devereux was his name. The Devereux were a wealthy family, which Jack thought poor recompense to the young man for having already thinning hair and absolutely no chin at all. His face sloped straight into his neck, and an over-large Adam's apple made it look as though his chin had somehow managed to slip down inside his throat.

Despite his physical imperfections Miss Fairbrother

seemed to be finding him good company, and was laughing delightedly at everything he said. Jack felt a rising heat in his blood. 'Excuse me,' he said to Miss Ormerod, and made his way through the company towards her.

The movement evidently caught Miss Fairbrother's eye, for she turned her head and saw him. The gay smile froze a moment on her face and her eyes widened. Jack beamed and was beginning to mouth a greeting when to his astonishment, she put her delicate nose in the air, tossed her head, and turned her back on him. He stopped dead. His natural desire to accost her and ask her what she meant by it was restrained by the unmistakable nature of the snub, and the interested glances of several of those nearby who had witnessed it.

'Cut!' said a voice at his elbow. Miss Ormerod had followed him.

He turned back to her. Her face was full of wry sympathy. 'You expected it?'

She hesitated. 'Not exactly. Let's say I was afraid of it. I've heard rumours.'

Jack re-evaluated the mysteries of the last week – the cancellations and the not-at-home. 'But *why*?' he asked plaintively. Miss Fairbrother had just slipped her hand through the elbow of young Devereux and was walking him away, her slender back still firmly turned to Jack.

Miss Ormerod laid a hand on his forearm – a long-fingered, capable hand, so different from Miss Fairbrother's fairylike little paw – and said gently, 'You know, really, don't you? Your name may be Compton, but everyone knows your connection with the Morlands.'

'Those stories about my uncle Teddy, you mean? But they're lies, damnable lies!'

'Hush! Don't make a fuss. People are looking.'

'In any case—'

'What is it to do with you even if they were true? Which I know they're not, so don't bite my head off! Well, it's more than I can answer. Some people are idiots, that's all that can be said about it.'

Jack could see Mrs Richardson now, over at the far side

of the room, her head together with another matron, both of them talking in low, rapid voices. They looked at him as they spoke. One or two others in the room were looking at him too, in a way he didn't quite like. He felt his face burn, with indignation as much as embarrassment.

'Look here,' said Miss Ormerod, 'come into the other room. Aunt Mary's organising some tables for bridge.' He resisted her urging hand an instant, his mind elsewhere. 'You do *play* bridge, I take it?'

'Eh? Oh, yes.'

'Good. Then you can partner me. I usually get given Colonel Summers, who always thinks spades are trumps no matter what's been bid.'

Jack made an effort. 'Thanks, but I really don't feel much like playing.'

She pushed his arm into the crook'd position and threaded her hand through. 'Nor do I, but we'll still go and play. For heaven's sake, I'm trying to help you, you idiot!'

He looked down at her belligerent expression and a faint smile warmed his troubled features. 'You are?'

'Yes. Giving you a dignified escape from all these eyes,' she said. 'And if I know anything about it, the party will divide into two camps, and the Fairbrotherites will be in this room, so we had better be in the other. Now smile, for heaven's sake, and try to look as though you *like* being with me.'

'Oh, but I do,' Jack said quickly, sensing some under-current in her words.

'Hmph,' she said. 'I know better than that. Your heart is breaking under that noble, manly reserve.'

The following day – a Sunday – Jack was at the airfield, preparing the 70 h.p. Blériot monoplane for a competition cross-country run to Chertsey and back, for the Malcolm Cup. He was in the cockpit listening to the engine when he heard someone calling him and, looking over the side, was surprised to see Harry Fairbrother. The young man was in his usual flannels, his hands stuffed into the shapeless pockets, his shoulders hunched. His fair face was unusually red and he looked extremely uncomfortable. Jack raised an enquiring eyebrow.

'Can I speak to you a moment?' Harry said. It seemed to have taken a good deal of courage, so Jack beckoned him closer. Harry scrambled up onto the wing.

'Well, what is it?' Jack asked coolly, when it was clear that Harry was having difficulty beginning.

Words came out in a burst. 'I came to say I'm sorry. It wasn't my idea. I think it's all nonsense. But – well – you know how I'm placed.'

'What are you sorry about?'

Harry grew redder. '*You* know. Ma and Pa and Myrt cutting you, because of your uncle. They say the whole family's tainted because of what he did, and they don't want to be associated with it. I *hate* it,' he said vehemently. 'I even told Pa it was wrong and – and not *gentlemanly* to cut you without even telling you why. And no matter what your uncle's done, it's not *your* fault, is it? But Pa said I was to do as I was told, and he made me cancel my lesson, and I'm not to have any more.'

'I'm sorry about that,' Jack said. Though he was seething inside, he couldn't help liking this young man, caught up in the whirlpool of someone else's actions. 'You shouldn't lose your flying because of me. Can't someone else teach you? There are lots of schools.'

Harry shook his head miserably. 'Pa thinks flying is tainted too. He's forbidden me even to come here, but I *had* to come, just once, to explain to you and to say it wasn't my idea.'

'Thank you for that,' Jack said. 'Does your sister feel like you?'

He looked more miserable than ever. 'No,' he admitted reluctantly. 'Myrtle agrees with Ma and Pa. She said yesterday she never wanted to see you again and – well – she's going for a drive this afternoon with that idiotic Charles Devereux and his sister.'

'Ah,' said Jack.

'She wanted me to go with them,' said Harry indignantly. 'I told her what I thought of that idea and she slapped me.'

Jack put out a hand. He wanted this conversation to be finished, but he felt for Harry. 'You mustn't quarrel with your sister on my account. I'm very sorry this has happened, and I appreciate your coming here to explain to me. But you mustn't come again, unless your father relents. It wouldn't do to get into trouble with him.'

'No,' said Harry gloomily. 'I'm dependent on him for every penny. I wish I could leave home and get a job and money of my own, but he won't hear of it. But one day, one day,' he squared his jaw, 'I *will* get away, and then the first thing I'll do is come back here and take my ticket.'

'I hope you do,' said Jack. 'But you'd better go now.'

'No hard feelings?' Harry said anxiously.

Jack had plenty, but not for Harry. He held out his hand. 'No hard feelings. Goodbye, old chap. And good luck.'

Harry gave him one fervent squeeze of the hand, then jumped down and walked away. Jack returned his attention to the engine, and signalled to the mechanic to remove the blocks. He was desperate to get into the air as quickly as possible. Up there, everything would seem clear and clean and simple, as he knew from experience. While he was in the air, he could leave all the troubles of life behind him on the ground, where they originally spawned, and find a particular and satisfying peace. If only he could stay aloft permanently, he sometimes thought, he'd be able to avoid all mankind's ills – even age and death. In the sky he could live for ever, and in bliss.

For Venetia, the emotions involved in the aftermath of the *Titanic* disaster – the relief that her own relatives were safe, the horror at the appalling loss of life, the shock and anger at the stories about Teddy, which came back from America to be circulated around London – all faded into comparative insignificance against what had happened a week later.

She and her son Oliver – the only one of her children still at home – had just returned from the Southport hospital. Venetia had had an operating list, and she had invited Oliver, who was training to be a doctor, to observe and assist. As they walked up the stairs towards the drawing-room, still discussing the last operation, the main door down behind them in the hall opened again, and Overton came in. He had been at the House, in a meeting of the Committee of Imperial Defence, discussing the expansion of the armed forces that would be needed if the war with Germany came about. He had been an officer in the Blues in his youth, and Haldane valued his experience and meant to make good use of him.

As Burton stepped forward to relieve him of his overcoat and silk hat, Overton glanced up and saw his wife and son. He shrugged quickly out of his coat, thrust his stick and gloves at the butler, and positively ran up the stairs behind them.

'Come into the drawing-room,' he said. 'Quickly. I have news!'

Venetia and Oliver exchanged a glance, and followed him. 'I've never seen Papa look so excited,' Oliver said. 'Do you suppose war's been declared?'

'Don't be foolish,' said Venetia. 'We'd have heard about that.'

'Well, it's good news, anyway, by the look of it,' Oliver said, as they entered the drawing-room and Overton turned to face them, smiling.

'The most extraordinary thing has happened,' he said. 'I was coming out of the committee room with Haldane when I saw our illustrious son-in-law approaching along the corridor.'

'That stiff-necked ass,' Venetia snorted. 'I suppose he cut you?'

'No, not at all. That's the extraordinary thing,' Overton said. 'He stopped dead when he saw me, and went a little red in the face, but then he came straight towards me with the evident intention of addressing me. I was afraid it might be embarrassing, so I murmured to Haldane that I would speak to him later, at the club, and he trotted off, good fellow. I suppose there can't be many in the House who don't know how things lie. So there I was, bracing myself for the blow—'

'You really do know how to tell a story, Pa,' Oliver said approvingly. 'We're all agog now, absolutely on tenterhooks.'

'Be quiet, you impudent boy!' Overton smiled. 'Well, to

my amazement Holkam was perfectly affable. He said how-d'e-do, asked how I was, and asked after your health, my dear.'

'Mine?' said Venetia in amazement.

'Is that all?' Oliver complained. 'What an anticlimax. I expected the flash of a stiletto at least!'

'Ignore him,' Venetia instructed. 'What did you do?'

'I stammered a bit,' Overton confessed, 'and said you were well, and then had the presence of mind to ask after Violet. He said she was doing very well, but missing her family a great deal, and then – this is the astonishing part – he said that she would love to call on us, but suggested as she was so large with child that you might care instead to call on her.'

'Just like that?' Venetia exploded. 'The impudent wretch! As if I haven't longed and longed to see her, and been forbidden by his stupid spleen against you!'

'Ah, well, it seems that's all over now,' Overton said. 'I was staring at him somewhat in the manner of a codfish – as you can imagine – and he gave an awkward sort of smile and said he was sorry there had been a difference between us but that he hoped it could be put behind us now, and that he would be glad to be on cordial terms with me.'

'No apology?' Venetia demanded.

'No more than what I've just told you. I was tempted to give him a piece of my mind, but I thought of Violet and you and swallowed my pride.'

'I suppose it doesn't do, when one is offered an olive branch, to snap it in two under the bearer's nose,' Oliver said.

'Quite. So the long and short of it, my love,' Overton said, 'is that we now have full visiting privileges restored.'

'Aren't you sorry now you called him a stiff-necked ass, Mum?' said Oliver.

'He apologised that he could not invite us to dine right away,' Overton concluded, 'but he promised that as soon as Violet is out of childbed there will be a dinner party to which we will be invited.'

'Thank God for that!' Venetia said. 'No, Oliver, not for

the dinner party – for being told I can see my daughter again! Is she in London?'

'Yes, he's brought her up to have this one in Town. She hasn't been feeling quite as well as with the first two and, as you know, Brancaster is very remote.'

'Is that what's behind this rapprochement, then?' Venetia asked. 'Is he wanting my medical opinion?'

'I doubt it,' Overton said. 'You know what he thinks of female doctors. No, I think there's something else behind it. When Holkam had left me, I tried to catch up with Haldane, and someone said he had gone into the tea-room, so I went there. I couldn't see Haldane, but Tonbridge was there, and he beckoned me over and said that Holkam had been looking for me. I said yes, he had found me, and Tonbridge gave me an odd look and said, "I think he had something important on his mind."'

'Tonbridge knew?' Venetia asked.

'So it seems. Well, he's such an old friend that I didn't hesitate to say I'd found Holkam a very different person from the last time I'd seen him, and Tonbridge smiled and said, "You can put it down to Abradale. Abradale talked to him yesterday like a dutch uncle." Tonbridge had seen them at the club, stuck away in a corner and such a conversation going on – Abradale talking and Holkam listening rather shame-faced, according to Tonbridge – that no-one dared go near them.'

'But – Abradale? Why him?'

'That's what I asked Tonbridge,' said Overton, 'and it turns out that Abradale is one of the few people Holkam really admires, and whose opinion he values. Holkam's father thought the world of him – they served together on many a committee when the old earl was still active in the House – and he was the only man who could out-shoot him, too! Like the late king, there was nothing Holkam senior admired more than a good shot. So young Holkam, our Holkam, looks up to Abradale as to no-one else. And it seems – so Tonbridge gathered – that Abradale carpeted Holkam and told him it was a disgrace and a scandal for him to be on bad terms with his own wife's family, and that if he didn't patch it up without delay, Abradale would be forced to cut him.'

'Good God!'

'Holkam caved in at once, and promised to seek me out today and mend matters. And he has been as good as his word,' Overton finished.

'What a very odd man my sister has married,' Oliver said. 'Makes everyone miserable by pursuing his opinion against all reason, then gives it up at the simple request of a third party.'

Venetia gave him a sidelong look. 'I don't think he's very bright, you know,' she said. 'You mustn't expect everyone to be as intelligent as you, and not-very-bright people often act in a way that seems odd to thinking people.'

Oliver returned the smile. 'I promise never to tell him what you've just said about him.'

'The thing I can't understand,' said Overton, 'is why Abradale should have intervened in this way; and why he should have done it at this particular moment. If he had so much influence over Holkam, he might have exercised it before now, one would have thought.'

Venetia said thoughtfully, 'I think I know the answer to that. Abradale is Tommy Weston's father-in-law, isn't he?'

Overton's eyebrows went up. 'Bless my soul, so he is. Do you think that's it? Did Weston ask him to intervene on our behalf?'

'I think that must be the answer,' Venetia said. She had told both her menfolk about Tommy's visit and his request that she prepare Emma for her Season. 'He asked me a favour – and a pretty big favour it is, too, given my age and habits – and to sweeten the request he has done me the biggest favour in his power and restored my daughter to me.'

Oliver said, 'You'll have to do what he wants now, won't you, Mum? Sly devil! You're bought and paid for.'

'I'd already decided I'd do it,' Venetia said sternly, 'so it's not a question of being bought, you horrible creature.' Then the irresistible smile broke through. 'Oh, I don't care why anybody did anything! I don't care if I have to take Emma

Weston to parties and I don't care if I have to be nice to Holkam for ever more! All I care about is that I can see Violet again! And be with her when she gives birth. I shall go and see her tomorrow. She hasn't long to go before her time.' She remembered something Overton had said and frowned again. 'I wonder what he meant by saying she wasn't well?'

'I don't think it can be anything serious, or he'd have made more of it,' Overton said. 'He didn't seem particularly concerned.'

'Oh, what would he know about it?' Venetia retorted.

'You'll find out tomorrow,' Oliver said.

And so it was that on Sunday the 5th of May, while Jack was discovering one of the unforeseen consequences of the *Titanic* disaster, Venetia's thoughts were as far from it as possible, for it was on that day that her beloved daughter went into labour. Though Violet had been feeling uncomfortable and unwell in the later stages of pregnancy, she gave birth without difficulty, and with all the comfort of being attended not by strangers but by her own mother. Venetia was ably assisted by Violet's maid Scole, who was a former nurse and had been almost a second mother to her during the time she was estranged from her family.

As the sun was going down and the lamps were being lit around St James's Square, a squalling, red-faced little soul made its first appearance on the world's stage, and it was Venetia who first held it, wrapped it up and laid it in its mother's arms. It was a girl. Her parents named her Charlotte.

CHAPTER TWELVE

The American hearing presented its report to the Senate most promptly on the 28th of May, 1912, and its contents were known soon afterwards in England. The blame for the disaster was laid squarely at English doors: 'We leave to the honour and judgement of England its painstaking chastisement of the British Board of Trade, to whose laxity of regulation and hasty inspection the world is largely indebted for this awful fatality.'

Also to blame was the English Captain Smith for his 'indifference to danger', 'over-confidence', and heedlessness. He had had at least three ice warnings, but the speed was not relaxed nor the lookout increased. Warning signals, messages of danger, seemed to stimulate him to action rather than persuade him to fear.

Third, there had been a British ship nearby, the *Californian*, which had stopped for the night because of the ice, and had not responded to *Titanic*'s signals for help. Her wireless operator had gone to bed, turning off the receiver – customary on small ships with only one operator – but they had seen the rocket signals and not responded. Had they responded at once, said the report, they might have been in time to save many more lives, as they had been closer than *Carpathia*. (The report did not, however, mention several other ships in the area at the time, also closer than *Carpathia*.) For the English master of the *Californian*, Captain Lord, was reserved a unique condemnation for reprehensible negligence, though he had never been called before the hearing.

Ismay was not blamed, though Senator Smith deduced

in his introductory speech that the presence on board of the managing director of White Star, and of Thomas Andrews from Harland and Wolff, might have stimulated Captain Smith to put on speed.

Finally several recommendations were made. In every ship a lifeboat place should be provided for every soul on board; four crew and a specified group of passengers should be assigned to each boat, and drill should be frequent and rigidly enforced. Wireless should be manned twenty-four hours a day. Rockets should only be used as distress signals (shipping lines had been using them for inter-company messages at sea – the *Californian*'s defence). And, lastly, ships should be built with a high double bottom, and watertight bulkheads should go all the way up to a watertight main deck.

It was not mentioned anywhere that the ultimate owner of the *Titanic* was IMM and J. P. Morgan; nor that the guilty *Californian* was also an IMM ship. All those illustrious Americans like Mr Astor and Mr Guggenheim had perished at English hands, and English hands alone.

The British judicial inquiry under Lord Mersey proceeded at a more leisurely pace, and the attorney general, Sir Rufus Isaacs, did not begin his concluding speech until the 29th of June, nor finish it until the 7th of July. He determined that Captain Smith had been going too fast, though he noted that for twenty-five years the custom had been to maintain speed in clear weather regardless of ice warnings: it had been a grievous mistake, in the event, but it had not been negligence.

Isaacs noted that although the seriousness of the damage had been known by the captain at midnight, the first boat had not been launched until forty-five minutes later, which suggested lack of practice. He concluded that many more could have been got into the lifeboats than were actually saved, but noted that many of the passengers had been reluctant to leave the ship, believing that help was on its way.

He noted that the Board of Trade regulations about lifeboats dated from 1894 and were based on the tonnage of the ship, not on the number of people on board; but pointed out that the Atlantic route since that time had been absolutely safe, and that in the two previous collisions with icebergs no-one had been hurt. They had been head-on collisions: no-one had anticipated a glancing, lateral collision with ice at high speed. Experts, he said, believed that *Titanic* could have survived a head-on collision.

His speech finished with a lengthy examination of the role of Captain Lord and the *Californian*. It had been pointed out in evidence that, because of the ice, the *Californian* was two and a half hours' sailing time away, and could not therefore have reached *Titanic* before she sank. Still, it was nevertheless a very serious matter and a deeply reprehensible omission that she did nothing, and Lord was much to be censured.

Mersey's report was published on the 30th of July and ran to seventy-four pages. It followed Isaacs in concluding that the loss of the ship was due to excessive speed, but said that this was not negligence on the captain's part, though it would be considered negligence in any future similar situation. It said that in the light of the disaster Board of Trade regulations should be changed, and made similar recommendations to the American report about ship building and lifeboat provision and drill. And finally it condemned the hapless Captain Lord for not going to the rescue – the only real blame offered in the whole document.

The Overtons read copies of both reports with keen attention.

'It's quite plain the American inquiry was designed to put the blame on the British Government,' Venetia said.

'And equally plain that the British inquiry was designed to avoid it,' said Overton. 'Lord and the *Californian* were distractions, to give the people something to hate, and to take their minds off the Board of Trade's shortcomings.'

Venetia sighed. 'What use trying to apportion blame now? It won't bring any of those poor souls back. In my view it was an accident, pure and simple. With hindsight we can see how it might have been avoided – just as when we make a new discovery in medicine we can see how people might have been saved in the past. It doesn't make past practitioners bad men. What's important is to learn from experience.'

'I think that, at least, is secure,' Overton said. 'The law hasn't been changed yet, but all the shipping lines are putting in more lifeboats. It's the question passengers will be asking now, whenever they book passage on a ship.'

'It's a pity so many had to die to make the point.'

'That's the nature of great disasters,' Overton said. 'They are out of the run of things. Possibly no accident like this will ever happen again. But if it does, everyone will be ready for it.'

Venetia smiled a little. 'Darling, no-one is ever ready for disaster – or even mild accident. How could we go about our daily rounds if we anticipated everything that might happen to us? Life would be impossible if we did not believe ourselves to be more or less invulnerable.'

Teddy had not been called by the British inquiry, and was not mentioned at all in its report. It had nothing to say about Ismay, except that he had had no duty to go down with the ship, and that had he not entered the lifeboat he would merely have added another name, his own, to the list of the dead. But this restraint came too late. The quiet words of a lengthy and unreadable official document could not weigh against the excitable jabberings of the popular press.

York and its surroundings had been as shocked by the disaster as everyone else in the country, and was more interested than many because of the presence on the ship of one of its leading residents. It had been prepared to mourn extravagantly when it was supposed Mr Edward Morland must be dead; but when he turned up alive, and was associated with Mr Ismay in the accusations of cowardice and selfishness, York society split. Those close to the Morlands maintained the stories were all lies, and continued loyally to defend him. Those who did not know him, together with the excitable and the impressionable, seized on the luxury of having someone to hate and gossip about.

They believed that he had made several attempts to get himself into a boat – Officer Lightoller had said so, and Lightoller had come out of the affair as a genuine British hero, so it must be true. And they believed that he had shoved women and children aside to save his own hide, because they'd read it in the paper. In addition, he was undoubtedly a friend of that wicked man Ismay, who had forced gallant Captain Smith to drive too fast through the ice field, and had sent the ship to sea in the first place with too few lifeboats, just to save money and increase his profits. Before long it was being said that Teddy Morland had been asked by Ismay how to save money and had suggested cutting the lifeboats so that White Star could spend more on the soft furnishings he was providing. If a man was to be a villain, then the worse he was the better.

Beside the hot-heads, there were those who, while not depending on extravagant scandal, yet mused that it seemed highly unlikely there was *no-one* else on deck at the time Ismay and Morland got into the lifeboat, considering how many were still on board. And perhaps hardest of all to bear, there were those who, while believing Teddy's story, still thought he should not have got into the boat. It might be understandable, but it was not gentlemanly. Knowing that there were women and children still on board, he should not have saved himself, even if he could not save any of them.

Teddy shut himself away at Morland Place as he had shut himself into his cabin in *Attic*, seeing no-one outside the family, refusing all visitors, and emerging from the house only at night when it was safe from prying eyes, to walk alone around the moat, staring at the black water and trying not to remember. His secretary and his agent tried to get him to concentrate on business, but he was too depressed to give it more than a perfunctory attention. To Henrietta he said more than once that he wished he had not survived. 'What use to save my life when it's ruined? I should never have stepped into that boat. It's true what they say – it was not the action of a gentleman.'

Henrietta refuted this angrily, and said that anyone would have done the same, and that to have refused to get into the boat would have been pointless. 'None of them was there, none of these people so happy to condemn you. They don't know.'

Robbie said, 'You weren't the only man to survive by a long chalk. Why should you be the only one to be blamed?'

Jessie, called by her mother to try to talk to him, was

forthright. 'They're all idiots, Uncle Teddy. Why should you care what they think? You should think about us – how glad we are that you *did* get into that boat, how terrible it would have been for us if you hadn't.'

But Teddy only shook his head. 'I've brought shame on you all. Death would have been better. I *ought* to have died. I can never forget the cries of those people in the water.'

Ned was so worried about his father that he consulted Dr Hasty, who knew all the family very well. 'He has always been such a cheerful man. He never let difficulties get him down. It's not like him to be so low and hopeless.'

Hasty said, 'You must consider that he has been through a most shocking and frightening experience. None of us can imagine what it was like to be on that ship, knowing she was sinking – and, from what I understand, he was one of the few who knew that there were not enough lifeboats for all. Consider the awful burden of that knowledge! His nerves are dreadfully disordered by his experience, and it will take time for them to mend. But mend they will. Let him stay quietly at home, rest, eat well, take gentle exercise in the fresh air, and he will mend.'

Ned did not believe Hasty had understood the seriousness of the situation. 'I'm so afraid he may do something violent.'

'Lay hands on himself, you mean? No, no, I don't believe it. He is not the sort. And he has too much to live for. This is a temporary condition. He will come through.'

But there were practical consequences to the situation that could not be denied. The first was a falling-away of business. Many people boycotted Makepeace's, Teddy's drapery store in York, and the effect was cumulative, for as fewer people went in, it became more conspicuous to shop there. Soon it was only the real Morland adherents who dared to pass its doors, and profits fell sharply. There was a falling-off in Leeds, though not to the same extent, for it was not universally known there that it was Morland owned; and the Manchester shop was not affected. There were cancelled orders at the mills, however; and, more seriously, the Cunard line did not renew its contract. This would be a big loss, especially as the building of the third 'Olympic' looked likely to be delayed, if not cancelled altogether.

Robbie, being a Compton, escaped the worst of it, though some customers asked to have someone else deal with their business, and he was aware of looks and crossings of the street as he walked through York. But he was not of a forceful character and was generally liked, and on the whole people felt sorry for him for his connection, rather than assuming he was made in the same mould.

Ned was not so lucky. He had taken his father's name, and was known to be immensely proud of him. He lost a great deal of business in the aftermath, and noticed the coldness and hostility more than any of them. It was in part a town versus country matter. Old country families, landowners, shooting and hunting acquaintances of the Morlands tended to side with them and to dismiss the scandal as humbug; while business people, town dwellers, commercials, the new rich and middle classes, were much more conscious of anything that affected their status or that of those around them, and dropped the Morlands rather than be contaminated by them.

An invitation for Ned and Jessie to a tennis party at the Surridges was withdrawn, and Jessie had an order for a pair of carriage horses for Mrs Cakebread, of Cakebread's Confectionery, cancelled. She swore the Cakebreads could crawl on their knees all the way to Morland Place before they'd ever be allowed to buy another Twelvetrees horse. But the polo set was loyal, and Colonel Melmoth, who already had a string of four Morland ponies and two Morland hunters, ordered a riding horse for his wife and made sure everyone heard about it.

Much of this might have passed Teddy by in his state of shock and misery, but he could not fail to notice when his daughter Polly wrote from school in Scarborough, begging to be allowed to come home. She had always loved being at school, but since the stories began in the newspaper she had lost all but two of her friends and was now the butt of taunts, insults and practical jokes. She had endured a whole week of detentions for fighting with another girl who had called her father a coward; and being in detention had caused her to miss rehearsals, which had cost her her part in the school play. Someone had filled her gym shoes with wet mud and left a note on them saying it was from the bottom of the sea. The woman in the tuck shop wouldn't serve her. Even the teachers seemed to be looking at her coldly, and Miss Trenchman, her idol, had given her a gamma for her essay, when she'd never before had less than an alpha minus. She was as miserable as could be, and couldn't endure to stay there until the end of term.

The letter was smudged with her tears, and her plea did not fall on deaf ears. The idea of his little girl being taunted and bullied made Teddy mad. He roused himself to write an immediate letter to the headmistress, and sent it by Simmons in the Benz with orders to bring Polly back with him. She arrived looking wan and tearful, and ran into Henrietta's arms and burst into sobs. But after a visit to Emma in the nursery, to tell her troubles and see the babies, followed by an enormous tea, she cheered up a good deal, only asserted very firmly that she wouldn't go back to that *horrid* place.

'This nonsense won't last for ever, you know,' Henrietta said, when Polly sought her out the next day in the linen room. 'People will soon find something else to talk about.'

'They'll still stare at me, and whisper,' Polly said. 'I can't bear it.'

'Well, if they do,' Henrietta said robustly, inspecting pillow cases, 'what then? Are you going to hide in the coal cellar for the rest of your life? You've got to learn to stand up tall when people say unjust things. Be proud of your father and yourself, and don't pay any attention to spiteful gossip.'

Polly looked at her with haunted eyes, leaning against the door and picking unhappily at a splinter on the frame. 'Is it just gossip, Auntie? Sarah Waterman said if it was in the newspapers it must be true.'

Henrietta looked up. 'Polly Morland, I'm ashamed of you! Don't you know your own father better than that? Do you think he would be capable of a selfish or unkind act?'

Polly blushed and looked down. 'No.'

'Well, then. Newspapers say things to make their stories exciting, because that's what makes people buy them. It doesn't make any of it true. Your father's the kindest and best man in the world. And if you're going to stand there talking nonsense, you can help me with the sheets. Idle hands lead to idle minds.'

Polly felt comforted by this. It was what Emma had said in the nursery yesterday. Finding people in the place you expected them – checking the linen was a monthly job of Aunt Henrietta's – and hearing them say things they'd said a hundred times before made you feel that perhaps the world wasn't crumbling away into chaos. She had got home to find her father changed, no longer cheerful and ebullient, but pale and haggard-looking; not busy as always, but sitting in the steward's room staring at nothing, reading in the drawing-room without ever turning a page. But Morland Place was Morland Place, and the women in her life were the same; and Ethel, large with child now, had promised to teach her how to crochet. She helped open and refold the sheets without a murmur, enjoying the stuffy warmth of the linen room and its combined smell of bare wood, starch and lavender.

There was a worse consequence of the *Titanic* disaster to come. Since the first news broke, Alice's feelings had been in a state of wild fluctuation. The shock of the report of the sinking, the terrible waiting and the fear of loss were followed by huge relief that Teddy was safe. Her spirits were on a see-saw while he was kept in America by the inquiry and the first rumours of calumny filtered through, and her delight that he was coming home was tempered by dread of the sea-voyage he must make to reach her. Her joy in seeing him again was countered by worry at how ill and shocked he was. She was grateful to have him back, but raged inwardly at what people were saying about him. And she feared for the future, for his health and the well-being of them all.

Yet outwardly Alice remained serene through it all. She was not a person who showed her feelings, and a burst of tears on receiving the telegram that said he was safe after all, and another on first seeing him in the flesh were the only outward signs of her inward turmoil. In other circum-stances Henrietta might have noticed or at least enquired more, but she had not only a brother but a daughter and grandchildren in jeopardy, and it was all she could do to govern her own feelings.

One day in mid-May Henrietta did notice that Alice looked a littler paler than usual, and asked her if she was feeling quite well. Alice replied only that she had a slight headache, and went away into the drawing-room to lie on the sofa. A little while later Ethel went in there to find a piece of work she had left and, after taking one look at Alice, rushed to the door and shouted at the top of her voice for help.

Alice lost the baby, and with it so much blood that she was very ill afterwards. Dr Hasty said privately to Henrietta that it was a wonder she had survived at all. He would not say as much to Teddy in his present state of mind, but it was one more thing that Teddy blamed himself for. The sight of Alice so white and frail, looking tiny in the great Butts bed, moved him to tears. He slept in the dressing-room so as not to disturb her, but though they had a trained nurse at first, he checked on her hourly during the night, afraid she would slip away from him while he was not looking.

He sat by her most of the day, watching her sleep or trying to entertain her. Conversation did not flourish between them – there were too many painful subjects to avoid – but she liked to be read to, and he read himself hoarse. As she got a little better, he brought up her canary in its cage and put it in the bedchamber window so that she could see it and hear it sing. Ethel brought her white cat, Snowdrop, who enjoyed sleeping on the counterpane on the big, soft bed, something usually forbidden him. Polly brought her step-mother flowers every day, and looked at her tremulously, remembering that her own mother had died in childbed and realising how much quiet Alice had come to mean to her. Emma brought James William, two years old and as lively as a cricket, and understood when the sight of her son reduced Alice to tears that this was not necessarily a bad thing.

She was a long time recovering. When she was able to sit up, Henrietta brought her her embroidery, thinking it would do her good to have a little occupation. She made an attempt when anyone was watching, but left alone, her fingers would slow, the needle would fall idle, and she would stare for hours at the patch of sunlight making its way round the room and across the ceiling. Snowdrop, curled up and purring under her stroking hand, was her favourite companion; her second choice was Ethel, who would sit by the bed and do her own work without feeling the need to converse or ask how she felt. Alice loved Teddy, but she was too weak to cope with the tumult of feelings he aroused in her; and Henrietta, kind though she was, always brought with her an invisible aura of busyness that Alice found exhausting.

She always felt weary now. The least effort tired her. She did not even want to think, though as she gained a little strength, thoughts came to her unbidden. So many things brought her to tears – the sound of her canary's singing, the smell of the gillyflowers Polly had put by her bed, James William's chuckling laugh, the distant sound of baby Roberta crying . . . especially that.

All the world seemed fecund, except only her. At the beginning of May, a letter had come with the news of Violet's baby, and at the end of the month, Maud was safely delivered of a son, whom they called Richard after Maud's father. Then in June, in a muted disturbance that everyone tried to keep from her, Ethel went into labour and, in a short time and with apparently little effort, produced a baby boy.

Alice kept up a brave and cheerful face. She sent her good wishes to Ethel, congratulated Robbie on a son and Henrietta on another grandchild. She was politely interested when it was explained that Robbie wanted to call the child Jeremy as a nod to his own late father, Jerome. But she was firm – or as firm as she ever was – in her refusal when Henrietta offered to bring her the baby to hold. She longed for night time so that she could be alone and weep. She was forty years old. She knew Dr Hasty believed she should never have been allowed to get pregnant again, and thought it was probably a blessing in disguise that she had miscarried at an early stage. He feared going to term might have killed her, and she was sure he had advised Teddy never to put her in that danger again.

She would see and hold little Jeremy one day, and even grow fond of him, she was sure. One day – but not now.

Towards the end of June a letter came from Lizzie in Flagstaff, telling about their journey and arrival, describing the town and their new house. It had been supplied partly furnished by the company, and Mr Culpepper had not been slow in providing the wherewithal to replace their lost household goods and furniture.

It's not the same as having one's own bits and pieces [Lizzie said], though it's fun, in a way, to have a completely fresh start. But it does make being here seem much more final, and England farther away than ever. Our house couldn't be more different from Endsleigh Gardens. It is enormous by London standards, and stands splendidly detached in the middle of a wide lawn in a pleasant, quiet, tree-lined street just a few minutes' walk from the centre of the town. Though the lawn is very large and very green, it has no fence around it but is open to the street, like everyone else's, which seems a trusting and friendly sort of way to live. People 'pop in' a great deal more here, and all the early visitors brought food, which was kind but struck me as rather odd, as though we had just been washed up from a shipwreck (as I suppose in a way we were). Pies and cakes and whole hams and bottles of home-made cordials were the favoured gifts, though one nice old lady brought a real live lemon tree in a pot. There should be no difficulty about growing it. It is very hot here, and we're told will be hotter still soon. The trees everywhere make pleasant shade, and the verandah all round the house keeps it cool, though I have had to learn to keep the shades drawn and not be tempted to let in every scrap of light as we do at home. It's as different as can be from smoky, drizzly London. The strong sunshine makes everything seem brilliantly coloured and sharp-edged. I feel as though we have been living in chiaroscuro all these years!

She wrote about Ashley's job and the town and surrounding countryside, and then went on,

Titanic is still very much talked of, but we have been kindly received on the whole. The people here are what we might think of as 'pioneers', and therefore take things much more as they find them. I have had one or two odd looks and questions when I have given my name as Morland, in shops, for instance, but on the whole they seem to ask what they want to know and then drop the subject. No-one has shunned us, and one of our neighbours came over specifically to tell us that 'newspapers are full of lies and only a fool takes heed of 'em'. The boys are enjoying the freedom and space here, and seem to have made friends already. For them the *Titanic* episode is now a source of pride. The other boys ask them to tell their story again and again, and regard them with admiration and awe for having experienced such an adventure. I fear the basic story has been embroidered with each telling: any day now I expect there to be pirates, whales and sea monsters in it.

Henrietta was so comforted by the letter that she had her little phaeton harnessed and drove out to Twelvetrees to show it to Jessie. She found her working on Mrs Melmoth's riding horse. Jessie dismounted, tied up the horse, and climbed up into the phaeton to sit beside her mother while she read the letter.

'Well, that is all good news,' she said, when she finished it. 'I'm glad they're happy – though I suppose you'll think it makes it less likely that they'll come back,' she added, looking sidelong at her mother.

'I've resigned myself to that already,' Henrietta said.

'You might go over there and visit them,' Jessie said.

Henrietta shuddered. 'Not until they invent a way of flying over the sea. Nothing will ever persuade me to get on a ship after this.'

Jessie sighed. 'I might be persuaded. Anything to get away from the gossip and the stares.'

'You look a bit out of sorts,' Henrietta noted. 'Are you feeling well?'

'Oh, yes, quite well, only glum. People are so hateful. Ned said Uncle Teddy's been asked to resign from his club.'

'Yes, the letter came yesterday.'

'How can they be so mean, with poor Aunt Alice still bedridden?'

'I don't suppose they even think of that,' Henrietta said. 'It hardly matters – I can't see him wanting to use a club for a long time to come.'

'But it must hurt him to be thrown out like that. And after all he's done for York and for everybody.'

'It will all die down one day. They used to shake their heads at your father and me. I was a scandal and a talking for marrying a divorcé.'

'That was why you went to London, wasn't it? To get away?'

'Partly. But it was mostly to protect your uncle Perry – Bertie's father.'

Jessie's eyes darkened at the mention of Bertie's name. Maud had given him a son. She had managed to get her thoughts into good order over the past few months, but Maud's baby had brought back all the things she didn't want to think about.

It was the action of Providence that the following day a letter arrived for Jessie from Violet, inviting her to come and stay.

We shall be in London a few weeks longer, and though the Season is near its end there is still plenty to do. I so long to see you, and show you my new baby. I never had a daughter before and I'm so thrilled with her. Come and visit, and stay for a month if you can. I want you to be little Charlotte's godmother. She is absolutely a treasure – and, best of all, she can be all mine, not like the boys, who will belong to tutors and schools and other such manly institutions and only pay the occasional polite visit to their mama.

The thought of Violet being a three-times mama – she

was actually five months *younger* than Jessie! – tickled her so much that, added to the desire to get away from the nastiness of York and the sadness of Morland Place, it made her determined to accept the invitation.

'Shouldn't you like to go?' she coaxed Ned. 'We only had one night in London on our honeymoon. There are still plays and concerts and all sorts of things going on, and no-one in London has seen my Paris gowns.'

Ned smiled. 'A very important consideration. But I can't possibly go away at the moment, with all this trouble.'

'I should have thought it was the very time *to* go away.'

'How can you think that? I'm losing business at the mill. Orders are being cancelled and fewer new orders are coming in. People cross the street to avoid me and leave the room when I go into the club. I can't go away now and let them think they've won, or that I've something to be ashamed of.'

'I'm so tired of it all,' Jessie said.

'So am I,' said Ned, 'but running away isn't the answer. Besides, I couldn't leave Father when he's so miserable.'

'He wouldn't even notice you were gone,' Jessie said. 'He's shut himself away from everyone. When I went over the other day I'm sure he didn't know I was there. He didn't even look at me when I spoke to him. And Aunt Alice doesn't like to be visited because she feels she has to talk, and she'd much rather not.'

Ned inspected her face. 'Would you like to go?'

'Well, you've just said we can't.'

'You could go without me. Violet's your friend. The two of you wouldn't really want me around anyway, when you're exchanging secrets.'

Jessie's face lit up. 'Wouldn't you really mind?'

'Not if it would make you happy,' Ned said, but he didn't get the answer he was hoping for.

'Oh, I should like it of all things! To have a change from all this gloom. I'm sure it isn't good for me. Mother said yesterday I was looking peaky.'

Ned tried again. 'What about the stables? Can you leave them? Haven't you got work in hand?'

'Only the Melmoth hack, which she doesn't want until

September, and the polo ponies for next season. Nothing that can't wait a month.'

'A month?'

'Violet wants me to stay a month. It's hardly worth going for less than that. Well, three weeks at the least.'

'No,' said Ned, 'I suppose it isn't.'

Belatedly Jessie noticed something, but she longed too much to flee to say more than, 'Oh, you won't even notice I'm gone, you spend such long hours at the mill.'

Violet herself met Jessie at the station, and Jessie almost didn't recognise her. She looked so smart and rich and, most of all, grown-up. Jessie was used to thinking of her as the junior partner in their friendship. But this little woman in the smart costume, fox cape and gigantic hat, with the ropes of pearls round her neck and the glint of diamonds on the one ungloved hand, was very much a young matron. Violet had just had her twenty-first birthday, but in her affluence and confidence she looked several years older.

But the smile was just the same, and there was no doubting Violet's delight in seeing her, though she greeted her with a grasp of the hands and a restrained kiss on the cheek, rather than a girlish hug. Belatedly Jessie noticed a tall, good-looking man in footman's uniform standing behind her. 'Frederick will see to your luggage,' Violet said. Jessie began fumbling for a coin to give to the porter who had brought her traps this far, but Violet caught her hand and drew it through her arm. 'Oh, Frederick will see to that, too. Let's go and wait in the motor. It's so noisy here.'

The motor was enormous and with such a high roof it was more like a building than a vehicle. The uniformed chauffeur stood beside it and held the door for them with the ceremony of an usher at church. Inside, Jessie did feel rather as though she was in a leather-scented cathedral, and that talking aloud or laughing would be sacrilege. Violet was obviously used to it, however, for she settled herself, loosened her fur, letting out a little gust of expensive scent, and said, 'Now, let me look at you. Oh dear, you do look pale and thin! Is it this awful *Titanic* business? Mama said unkind things are being said about your uncle Teddy.'

'It has been dreadful, but don't let's talk about that now,' Jessie said. 'I really want to forget about it all for a while. Your invitation was just what I needed.'

Violet looked pleased. 'I think we shall have fun. My new baby is an angel, and now I'm allowed to see Mama again, I haven't a care in the world.'

'Then you're just what I need to cheer me up,' Jessie said. She noticed something and leaned forward to look at Violet's jacket, where her fur had fallen back and exposed it. 'Oh, Vi, you aren't still wearing that silly brooch I gave you for your wedding?'

'It isn't silly at all,' Violet said, putting a protective hand to it. It was a little coral hand holding a mother-of-pearl rose – all Jessie could afford back then out of her allowance. 'I wear it nearly all the time. I love it, because it reminds me of you.'

'Don't people stare?' Jessie said, wrinkling her nose to hide how much she was touched.

'I don't care if they do,' Violet said magnificently.

'What it is to be a countess!' Jessie laughed.

The servants arrived. Frederick loaded the luggage onto the roof, helped Tomlinson into the back where she took the drop seat, and got into the front. Violet took up the speaking tube and said, 'Straight home, Dawson.' Then, to Jessie, 'I thought you'd sooner have a quiet day at home today, so we can talk. But tomorrow we're having luncheon with Mama, and then there's a ball at the Prestons' in the evening. I've asked Oliver to escort you. What a pity Ned couldn't come.'

She said it in a very nice way, but Jessie couldn't help feeling she was just being polite. It was not that there was anything wrong with Ned, but now she was here, Jessie felt he was very much a York and Morland Place sort of person, that he would not really have enjoyed London high society. Jessie had had a taste of it at her come-out, and though she would not have liked it for a permanency, she thought that dipping into it from time to time under Violet's patronage would be delightful – the perfect compromise.

They arrived at Fitzjames House in St James's Square, and as soon as they stepped into the entrance hall two little dogs came running up, barking shrilly. They had long blond fur and sooty faces, and they jumped up on their short hind legs and reached up to Violet like children wanting to be picked up.

'They're Pekingese,' Violet said, in answer to Jessie's question. 'They were Holkam's Christmas present to me. Aren't they sweet? This one's Lapsang and that's Souchong. They're brothers.' She scooped up Lapsang and caressed him, and Souchong, left behind, appealed to Jessie, pawing at her leg. 'Do pick him up, and we'll go straight to your room,' Violet said.

Jessie picked up the little dog, which came lightly, evidently used to the soaring ascent, and settled into the crook of her arm. She was used to big dogs, and didn't care for all this jumping and yapping, but she had to admit that they were attractive little beasts. Their fawn-blond coats were luxuriously silky, their ears velvet-soft and delicately feathered, and close to, with his rather bulging, round eyes, Souchong looked like one of those Chinese dragons one saw on firescreens and vases.

As they walked up the stairs Violet told her about some of the things that had been done to the house in the past two years. 'We haven't finished yet, of course. All the state rooms are in a dreadful condition and the dining saloon needs refurbishing, but we've done the rooms we use most.' She smiled back at Jessie. 'Besides, it's rather nice to have something still to do. Don't you think?'

'I suppose it's different when you have a house like this,' Jessie said. 'I must say, if my house is warm and comfortable, that's all I care about.'

Violet looked a bit taken aback. 'Oh! Well, I do like refurbishing my houses. Holkam and I have great plans for Brancaster Hall. It's something we spend a lot of time talking about.'

At the top of the stairs she put down Lapsang, and

Souchong struggled in Jessie's arms so she followed suit. The little dogs ran ahead, their feathery tails waving gaily. Violet showed Jessie into a fine room with a twenty-foot-high ceiling and the long windows, elaborate cornice and fireplace of its period. The bed was modern, however, and the carpet new, and though most of the furniture was from a mixture of past periods, there was a large modern wardrobe and a new mahogany washstand with a marble basin.

'It's lovely,' Jessie said. A quick glance round the room noted the little touches she remembered from country-house weekends: fresh paper laid out on the writing desk, books and periodicals on a table, a biscuit tin on the overmantel. Violet had learned in a good school.

'I'll just leave you while I take off my hat,' Violet said, 'but I must take you to see Baby before tea, so I won't be more than a quarter of an hour. I can't wait for you to see her.'

Left alone, Jessie did no more than take off her coat and hat and wash her face and hands. There was a jug of warm water ready on the washstand, and a fresh cake of soap still in its wrapper, which smelt deliciously of lily-of-the-valley. She wondered how the marble basin, which was large and solid, could be lifted for emptying, but then realised it was permanently fixed, and had a hole in the bottom with a plug in it. Investigation showed that in the cupboard underneath was a bucket into which the water drained for removal. A very good idea, she thought. But in the corner of the room behind a Chinese screen was a grand mahogany commode. For all the luxury, they didn't have water closets yet, as Maystone did.

She tidied her hair – she could not have done any more anyway, as Tomlinson and her luggage had not arrived – and then looked out of the window until Violet arrived to take her upstairs.

'No dogs?' Jessie asked, as they climbed the stairs.

'They're not allowed in the nursery,' Violet said. 'The new nanny doesn't approve.'

'Good heavens,' said Jessie. 'Think of Morland Place! It never did us any harm.'

'I know. But she's very good in every other way, and very modern.'

'Who's looking after the boys? You don't have them here with you, do you?'

'No, they're at Brancaster with the old nanny. But she's much too old, and we're going to retire her, and then Nanny Cadogan will take over all three children. Here we are. Isn't it a nice room? So light and sunny. And this is Nanny Cadogan. Good afternoon, Nanny. And *this*,' she concluded, with verbal flourish, 'is Charlotte.'

Jessie was not so antipathetic to babies as she had been, and she had to admit that little Charlotte was quite a beguiling specimen, tiny and smooth and pearly of skin, and much less ugly than most infants. Indeed, she was really quite pretty, for a baby. Violet was evidently besotted with her; and having held and cuddled and cooed for a while she handed the baby to Jessie with an air of bestowing a great honour. Jessie took her and made the right comments, then settled her in her arm while Violet conducted a long and technical conversation with the nurse. And oddly, as she sat looking down at the tiny face, and the baby looked up at her, she felt an unexpected stirring. There really was something about this creature, small and helpless and fresh-smelling, that plucked at some thread inside her. What would it be like, she wondered, to have one of one's own? She thought of Ned, and a small, hot pang started up in the middle of her. Ned would love to have children, she knew; but she had always avoided discussing it with him, thinking of the discomfort and inconvenience, not having any particular urge on her own behalf and not willing to sacrifice herself on his. But Violet's baby was such a dear little thing, perhaps it wouldn't be so bad after all . . .

'Well,' said Violet, coming to an end of her catechism of the nurse, 'isn't she just the loveliest little thing?'

'Yes,' said Jessie, with more sincerity that she could have expected, 'I really think she is.'

Violet looked pleased. 'I knew you'd love her.' She leaned over and touched the baby's cheek; and at that moment Lady Charlotte Augusta Mary Fitzjames Howard let out a yell that made Jessie start violently and was quite out of keeping with her delicate face and aristocratic name. The yell was followed by another as piercing, and as she settled down to a steady rhythm, Jessie thrust her hastily at her mother.

'Here, you'd better take her.'

'She's hungry,' said the nurse. 'It's time for her feed. If you'll allow me, my lady.' She took the baby away firmly, and gave the two women the sort of look that said their presence was no longer required.

Jessie was afraid, despite this, that Violet might want to stay and observe or even take part in the feeding, and was glad when her friend said, 'Let's go and have some tea.'

'Yes, please,' Jessie said. It had been a long journey and she was very hungry.

Tea was waiting for them in a small parlour, which Violet said she used as her private sitting room – though 'small' was a relative term. It was larger than the drawing-room at Maystone. It was a splendid tea, beautifully laid out, with bread-and-butter and sandwiches, and strawberry tarts as well as cakes. Also waiting for them were the two dogs, who frisked about them madly as though they hadn't seen them for hours. Violet took her tea sitting on the sofa, and both the dogs got up with her, to rest their forepaws on her lap and accept morsels of sandwich and cake from her fingers. Jessie disapproved of this, but she supposed in fairness it was very different with these little house-pets from the big, hairy and usually muddy – or worse – animals at home.

And having seen Violet firmly dismissed from her own nursery, Jessie could see the particular attraction of the little dragon-dogs: Violet was allowed to hold and pet them as much as she liked. There were disadvantages, after all, to being a countess.

CHAPTER THIRTEEN

The Conciliation Bill – an all-party Bill to give the vote to women property owners – had twice been passed in the Commons, but each time the Government had refused to give it the time needed to make it law. At the end of March 1912 it had been brought before Parliament again, but this time it had been fatally weakened by the prospect of the Manhood Suffrage Bill, which the Government intended to introduce in June, and at the end of March it had been defeated in the Commons by fourteen votes.

It was this defeat that had provoked the mass window-breaking demonstration in London. So many women had been arrested that Holloway was full and many of the women had been sent to Winson Green and Aylesbury gaols. The period since then had been quiet as far as the Suffragettes were concerned, because almost all the active women were behind bars.

Mrs Pankhurst and Mr and Mrs Pethick Lawrence were out. They had been released on bail, pending their trial for conspiracy to incite WSPU members to commit damage, injury and spoil certain glass windows. This charge was a new departure by the Government, intended to destroy the movement by making it impossible for the leaders to lead: the maximum sentence for conspiracy was two years, which would take them out of circulation long enough for all momentum to be lost.

At the trial in May, the three had offered no defence in law, only stating the reason and justification for their actions. The judge, summing up, had said that it was no answer to say that the attacks had been made for political reasons, not for private gain: criminal law dealt with intentions, not motives, so the fact that the crime was political was irrelevant. The jury quickly returned a guilty verdict, but had entered a recommendation for clemency because the motives of the accused were 'undoubtedly pure'. All three had been sentenced to nine months in the second division.

Political prisioners – those who had broken no moral law – were traditionally put into the first division, where treatment was lenient, and visitors and letters were permitted. The second and third divisions were for common felons. The regimes there were much harsher, and prisoners were treated as moral delinquents.

Though the sentence was much less than the maximum allowed, it was generally regarded as extremely severe. Some of the jurors had raised a petition, and one of them wrote in protest to the Home Secretary, calling for the prisoners at least to be allowed to serve their sentences in the first division. Reginald McKenna wrote back to say that there were no grounds for leniency, as the defendants had not shown any contrition and furthermore were determined to repeat their offences.

But the protests had continued, not only in the national press but in newspapers abroad, notably in France, India (where English-trained women doctors were much prized) and America. Letters, telegrams and an international memorial signed by sixty eminent thinkers had been sent to the Prime Minister. There were further memorials from universities and learned societies in Britain, and Keir Hardie led a protest in the lower House.

Under this pressure McKenna transferred Mrs Pankhurst and the Pethick Lawrences to the first division on the 10th of June, but the other eighty-one suffragettes who had not finished their sentences were still in the second division.

Matters were made worse by the introduction of the Manhood Suffrage Bill on the 17th of June, because it was made clear from the first speech that it contained no provision for women's suffrage. A hundred MPs signed a protest on behalf of the women, and a number of eminent men spoke out in public.

Lord Overton, at a dinner in the Middle Temple that evening, said that women's suffrage was not just an issue for women but for the good of the whole country. 'I have never believed in the possibility of a sex war, but during the last year there has been sown the seed of hatred between women as women and men as men. If such a seed should ever germinate, it would be an unparalleled curse on the nation. It is only thanks to the men who have stood beside the women in this battle that a sex war has not come to pass.'

'But I might as well have saved my breath,' he told his wife afterwards. 'They listened, of course, out of courtesy, but I doubt if one of them was really moved. They don't view women, you see, as a uniformity, as a mass or a class: they think of their own mothers, wives and daughters, and they shrug and say, "They're perfectly happy. They are comfortable, well fed and protected. What more do they need?"'

Venetia said thoughtfully, 'It is an intellectual conundrum, isn't it? What we want is to have women regarded as individuals with rights, as men are. The last thing we want is for women to be viewed as a class apart; yet to get the vote that is precisely what we have to make happen.'

'Yes,' said Overton. 'It's the most difficult of struggles. I can't see that anything the Suffragettes are capable of doing will change minds – if anything, their actions only harden resistance.'

'The Manhood Suffrage Bill proves that.'

'Only if they took up arms and conducted an all-out war – a *coup d'état*, in effect – could they prevail, and God forbid women should ever turn to violence of that sort! A real war of women against men would mean the end of civilisation – perhaps the end of mankind.'

'No,' said Venetia soberly, 'I don't think women would ever do that. What they are more likely to do is to turn violence on themselves.'

'Which will only convince the diehards that all women are mentally deranged by their physical differences.'

'Men already believe that,' Venetia said. 'It's no chance that the word "hysteria" derives from the Greek for "womb".' She sighed. 'You know what comes next, don't you? With

McKenna refusing to move the Suffragette prisoners into the first division, there'll be a mass hunger-strike.'

'Do you think so?' asked Overton.

'I know so. I had a note from Evelyn Sharp at WSPU headquarters – she's running things while the leaders are all absent – to say that the prisoners will refuse to eat from the nineteenth. She let me know out of courtesy – a kindness prompted, no doubt, by your speech – because of Anne.'

Her cousin Anne Farraline, one of the best-known WSPU activists and a member of a sub-group called the 'hot-bloods', was in Holloway gaol. Though she had escaped arrest after the March mass window-breaking, she had taken part in another demonstration in April and was serving three months.

'The nineteenth? That's tomorrow,' said Overton.

Venetia nodded. 'There's no doubt Anne will join the hunger strike,' she said. 'And then there'll be forcible feeding.'

'It's an abomination,' said Overton.

'Asquith and McKenna should be made to stand and witness it,' Venetia said savagely. 'They would never condone it if they knew what it meant.'

For Anne in Holloway, the time since April had been strangely peaceful. There were so many of them in there that the prison authorities had been obliged to relax the rules. During yard exercise they were allowed to walk together and to talk – a luxury always forbidden before – and though they were not permitted to send letters, it was easy enough to slip them to anyone who was leaving prison. One woman, on the day before her release, walked round the yard wearing a red dressing-gown over her shoulders, saying she was a pillar-box. The sleeves had been turned inside out and sewn up at the cuff, and the women 'posted' letters down them for her to deliver when she got out.

The terrible solitude of previous prison sentences was absent. The women were put to 'associated labour': all together in a large hall they were given knitting and sewing to do, and though Anne had never been fond of, or good at, needlework, it was almost pleasant to sit with the other like-minded women and chat quietly as they worked. Anne made up dozens of pair of knickers for convict women as her task, and since there was little close supervision of the work, she exercised her artistic urges by embroidering a small WSPU on each.

'If any of the staff should ask,' said her friend Vera Polk, 'you can say it stands for Women's Standard Prison Uniform.'

Anne laughed, but said, 'I should do nothing of the sort. I never conceal anything.'

'Only stones,' said Vera, with a grin, 'before a smash-up.'

Having Vera nearby was another difference for Anne this time. They had been given cells next to each other, and the matron even allowed Anne to visit Vera in hers, something usually strictly forbidden. It meant that, along with yard exercise and daily work, they were together almost as much of the time as they were outside. Lying on her plank bed unsleeping one night, Anne realised that she felt, oddly, quite content. In here, there was nothing she had to decide, no dilemmas, no responsibilities. It was comfortless and the food was meagre and unappetising, but she had grown used to that, and being confined in a cell was not so hard when there was so much time spent out of it in company. She was admired by many of the women, especially the younger girls, who liked to sit near her during associated labour and persuade her to talk about the Cause. Some of their hero-worship was foolish – they copied the way she did her hair and adopted her mannerisms – but she could not deny it was agreeable to be so looked up to. She had always been a somewhat solitary person – losing her mother at birth, much younger than her only brother, always at odds with authority as she grew up – and cleaving a lone path through stormy seas had been her life. This spell in Holloway was like a holiday to her.

But all that changed as soon as the hunger strike began. There was no more associated labour or yard exercise: the women were locked in their cells day and night. Anne was no longer allowed to visit Vera's cell, though as they were next door to each other they were still able to converse by climbing up to the window and calling to each other. On the first and second days of the strike these conversations kept up their spirits, but on the morning of the third day Vera confessed herself to be feeling very weak and sick. 'I don't think I can come to the window any more,' she said.

'It's all right,' Anne said. 'I understand. Stay in bed if you like. Preserve your strength.'

'I wish I could see you,' Vera said. 'Oh, Anne! I wish I was with you.'

'I know. I wish it too. But it won't be for ever.'

After a pause, Vera said, in a subdued voice, 'When will they start – you know? Forcing us?'

'I don't know. Today, tomorrow perhaps.'

'I'm afraid.'

'Don't let them break your spirit, darling,' Anne urged. 'I'm going to barricade my door, and fight them with every weapon that comes to hand. You must do the same.'

'But I feel so weak,' Vera said faintly.

'You won't, when the time comes. Your anger will carry you along. Think of the Cause. Tell yourself we will never give in. We will *never* give in.'

A sigh came from the other window. 'I must get down now,' Vera said. 'I'm dizzy.'

That was the last Anne heard from her that day. She went to the window several times, but calling elicited no response; and by the evening she felt almost too weak herself to make the effort. Her hands trembled when she tried to pull herself up, and a fit of uncontrolled shivering sent her back to her bed.

Forcible feeding began on the 22nd of June. The screams of the first victim alerted the women to what was happening, and those who could took the warning and barricaded their doors. Anne hoped that Vera had done so, but she heard nothing from the next cell, and though she called to her through the window, she heard no response.

All through the day, the sickening sounds told the story. The prison authorities broke through barricaded doors with crowbars, or with wedges and sledgehammers; and the crash of the door finally being forced open was always followed by the sounds of violent struggle and by the cries of the victim being forced down and held. Afterwards came the moans and the weeping. Women still had to be taken to the water closet, and on the way there and back they did their best to tell the news as they passed the cell doors. The harrowing stories made the stronger among them the more determined to resist.

In the afternoon of the 22nd, Anne heard the multiple footsteps approaching her cell, and dragged herself out of bed to man the barricade. The door was tried, and a male voice – one of the doctors, she supposed – shouted, 'Open this door!'

'I won't!' Anne shouted back, bracing herself for the hideous fight.

There was muttered conversation outside, and to her surprise the door was locked again and the footsteps moved away. The easy victory unnerved her. In her state of famine her nerves were on edge and she imagined some fiendish trick being planned. Later she needed to go to the lavatory and was afraid to ask, fearing that as soon as she moved the barricade they would burst in on her. When she did finally go, she shouted, 'Votes for women!' at each cell door on the way out and the way back. Most of the women called back, and it did her good to hear Vera's voice, even though she couldn't hear what she said. She asked the wardress who took her how Miss Polk was, but the woman was one of the most unfriendly and wouldn't answer her. When Anne tried to linger at Vera's door the wardress took her arm in a grip that hurt and hurried her along. Some of the prison staff hated her more because she was an earl's daughter. It was an odd philosophy, she thought, that said someone with privilege had no right to fight on behalf of those without.

Through the night she drifted in and out of nightmares. Light-headedness made it difficult to know when she was awake and when asleep, and the bad dreams overlapped with reality in a particularly unpleasant way. In the morning there was a foul taste in her mouth and she had a constant, grinding headache. The twitching began – an irregular but frequent involuntary tic of one group of muscles or another – and the strange pulses, as though her heart were moving about her body and knocking to try to get out. Sometimes she felt she could not catch her breath, and the walls of the cell would seem to be closing in on her to suffocate her and crush her out of life.

But soon these troubles were forgotten in contemplation of the hideous sounds from outside, as forcible feeding was resumed. Anne lay on her bed, preserving her strength: after over a hundred hours without food the least effort made her tremble. She drifted a little from time to time, though she tried not to, fearing they would come for her while she was unaware. At one time she was brought back with a start and a frightened knock of her heart by voices outside her door; but as she struggled to rise she realised it was only two wardresses conversing. She shook her head to clear it, and then dragged herself over to the door to hear what they were saying. Much of it she could not catch – they were talking in low voices – but she gathered there had been a serious incident. Straining her ears, she understood at last that Emily Davison had thrown herself over the prison stair-case. She was seriously hurt and had been taken to the prison hospital. Why had she done it? Anne wondered. Had she tried to kill herself, hoping that the tragedy would stop the ghastly process for the others? Emily was utterly reck-less of her own safety.

Anne had heard some of the younger of her hot-bloods talk about martyrdom. She had even sometimes dallied with the thought of her own death, and it had not been wholly repulsive. She had imagined her name going down in history as the one whose ultimate sacrifice finally secured women the vote: it would, she had thought, be something worth dying for. But that had been before she met Vera. She realised, even as she thought about it now, that she didn't want to die. Having one's name in the history books was not to be set against the reality of warm, active life when there was companionship and love in it. Death was no longer a matter of indifference to her. She would still fight, but she would fight to live.

It was hard to be sure about the passage of time when one was locked up and fasting, and it seemed almost on the heels of that thought that she heard a piercing scream

263

nearby. It jerked her out of her state of semi-consciousness, for she recognised the voice as Vera's. They had come for her! There came the sounds of violent struggle, the thumps and bangs and scuffings, the blurred and angry voices, Vera's shrill cries, which stabbed Anne to the quick. She was out of bed almost without noticing, and found herself pressed against the dividing wall, as if she might force herself through the solid brick to her friend's aid. Vera fell silent as the disgusting business was carried through, but there were other sounds that made Anne tremble with rage and hatred for the tormentors.

It did not take many minutes to finish with Vera. Anne guessed they would come for her next. She pushed against her barricade, making sure it was as firm as possible, and then leaned her weight against it. Yes, here were the footsteps and the voices, then the rattle of the key in the lock. The door was pushed but gave only an inch.

'Take down this barricade, Farraline!' came a shout from outside. It was one of the wardresses, Anne recognised – Scully, the one who had taken her to the lavatory.

'I will not!' she shouted back, and was shocked to hear how weak and wavering her voice sounded. Because she was dehydrated her mouth and throat were dry.

'We'll break it down if you don't, and it'll be the worse for you!' Scully shouted.

'It will be the worse for *you*!' Anne cried, and her voice was stronger now.

Someone said, 'This is wasting time. Break it down.' It was a male voice – she thought it might be the governor. If so, it was proof that they recognised she was an important prisoner. There were noises outside, and the barricade trembled. They were inserting some kind of wedge into the door. Then there came a series of fearful thuds, which she felt through her body as she leaned against the barrier, and a creaking, groaning noise, and then the furniture started to slide and the door to open. Anne heard herself shouting – she had no idea what she was saying, perhaps simply, 'No!' And then suddenly the whole thing gave, there was a sound of splintering wood, and she was flung full-length on the floor as the elements of the barrier broke or scattered and the door slammed back.

Scully was the first into the doorway. She was a big woman with huge arms, and an expression of permanent disdain for her charges. 'Now we'll settle with you!' she sneered.

Fury filled Anne, gave her strength she could not have imagined was still in her. She scrambled to her feet. One of her hands, thrusting at the floor to help her up, found something solid and gripped it as she rose. It was the broken-off leg of the chair that had been part of the barricade. She backed a step or two and raised it up as the group of wardresses and two doctors came in at the door. She had time to see that the governor wasn't there – if he ever had been, he had gone now rather than witness what was to come next. She saw one doctor holding the enamel tray containing the red rubber tube, the other the gag and funnel; a wardress was holding a large jug. There was time to see all these things, to remember they had just been used on Vera, to remember her cries. She raised the chair leg with a hand that miraculously no longer trembled, and said, 'Stand back!'

They stopped. A strange thrill of power swept through her as she abandoned everything to the purity of violence. She cared for nothing any more. She would kill if necessary. They might kill her, but she would never submit.

'Stand back!' she said again – almost snarled. 'If any of you dares to come any closer I shall defend myself! I will not submit to your vile torture. I will die rather than submit. Be warned!'

There were eight wardresses and the matron, as well as the two doctors, but she saw they were afraid of her. She had stepped beyond the bounds of civilisation, which still contained and controlled them. Scully began to say something. 'We could—' Was she about to say, 'We could rush her'? But the matron put a hand on her arm in a restraining gesture and cut her off.

'Now, Farraline,' the matron began in a reasoning tone, 'just be calm.'

Anne made a gesture with the chair leg. 'I warn you!' she said. 'I will not hesitate.'

265

The foremost doctor shrank back a little, looked at his colleague, who shrugged, and then muttered, 'Tomorrow will do as well.'

His colleague replied in an undertone, 'She'll be weaker by then. She won't be able to resist.'

'Oh, yes, I will,' she said. 'You had better not come tomorrow. I will fight. And if you kill me, you will suffer. I have friends outside. You know who I am.'

They were all backing away, the wardresses, the doctors. The matron was the last to remain in the doorway. She had the key in her hand, and she looked more troubled than afraid. Perhaps she was contemplating for the first time what it would really mean to have a death on her hands. She was about to pull the door closed when Anne cried out, 'Wait!' The matron stopped. 'I heard,' Anne said. 'Next door – Miss Polk. I want to see her.'

'Impossible,' said the matron.

'I must see her. I demand you let me see her,' Anne cried. She reached into her mind for arguments, but it was so hard to think clearly. 'Come,' she said, trying to sound reasonable, 'you let me go in before. What harm can it do now? Let me go to her, for God's sake.'

The matron hesitated a moment longer, then shrugged and said, 'Very well. Come along.'

Vera was lying on her plank bed, seemingly unconscious. Her face was dead white, her hair and clothes disordered. There was vomited milk on the floor, and a smear of it on her chin and cheek; her nose looked swollen, and there was blood on one nostril.

Anne ran to her, crouched down, took her hand and patted it. It was icy cold; there was a greenish tint to the whiteness of her skin. 'Vera, Vera,' she cried in distress. 'What have they done to you?'

'She fought like a mad thing,' the matron said dispassionately. 'She's stronger than she looks.'

Anne gave her one look of searing hatred, then her attention was all for her friend. She kissed the cold forehead. 'Don't die, please don't die,' she whispered.

'She's not dying,' the matron said. 'She just fainted.'

Anne paid her no attention. She rubbed the cold hands, smoothed the hair back from Vera's brow. Then the eyelids flickered, Vera moaned, the eyes opened, and she looked up at Anne with a puzzled frown, like a hurt child.

'It's me, it's Anne. Are you all right?'

Vera moaned again. 'It hurts,' she said feebly. 'Oh, it hurts.'

'It's over now, darling,' Anne said, stroking her brow.

Vera whimpered, closing her eyes again. 'Why do they torture us?'

Anne squeezed her hand. 'They'll never defeat us. Never. Oh, Vera, Vera!'

The eyes opened again. 'It took all of them to hold me down,' she said, with faint pride. 'I fought. Oh, it hurts! My head. My chest. Such cramps in my stomach.'

'Don't try to talk,' Anne said. 'I'm here, I'll stay with you. Hush, now, hush. I won't leave you.'

The matron backed out of the cell and locked the door, leaving them together. Anne dampened her handkerchief at the water-jug and gently cleaned Vera's face, then remained crouched at her side, murmuring to her, stroking her head, while she drifted in and out of consciousness, moaning, trying to hunch herself to ease the pain. Already the bruises were beginning to come out on the exposed areas of her skin. Anne wanted to cry, but there were no tears in her at this stage of fast.

The door opened again and a bucket of water and a cloth were dumped inside with the curt command, 'Clean up the floor, Polk.' Anne pressed Vera's shoulder reassuringly, and got up herself to do it. As she knelt on the stone floor and wiped and rinsed she contemplated the bitter irony of an earl's daughter reduced to such a condition; yet she was glad to do it for Vera, to save her pain. There was no-one else in the world, now or in the past, for whom she would ever voluntarily have done such a thing. When the floor was clean, she returned to Vera's side and held her hand while she slept fitfully.

After some time – she had no idea how long it was – the matron came back with a wardress and took Anne back to her own cell, where she passed a restless night, worried about Vera, dreading the resumption of the battle the next day. Vera would be subjected to torture again, and Anne knew that it grew progressively worse with repetition, as the nasal passages and throat became inflamed and raw, and the spirits failed under the weight of dread and pain and humiliation.

And the doctors had said they would come for her tomorrow, too. Determined and angry though she was, she flinched at the prospect. They had taken away her broken chair, and she had no idea what she could use as a weapon. The water jug perhaps? But she would be weaker, and they would know it. If they rushed her, what chance would she have?

Before eight in the morning of the 24th the matron came back accompanied by a single doctor, who said he wanted to examine her. There was no sign of the beastly apparatus, so Anne did not resist. She asked how Vera was, but neither of them would answer her. The doctor felt her pulse, listened to her heart and lungs, and asked her how she felt.

'How do you think I feel?' she answered angrily.

The doctor made no answer, and the two of them left. A short while later the matron returned alone to say that Anne was to be released on medical grounds.

Anne was astonished. Then she realised it was an excuse to get rid of her without losing face. She was an important person with powerful friends, and she was an embarrassment to them, as well as a nuisance. It was a hideous injustice to the others who had no such influence, who were 'nobodies'. But still she felt a surge of relief wash through her. She longed to be out. She didn't want another trial of strength, when her own strength was waning fast. Oh, God, she didn't want to be forcibly fed!

But she said, with all the determination she could muster, 'I won't go without Miss Polk.'

The matron nodded, as though she had expected that. 'She's being released too. On grounds of ill-health.'

Anne's heart contracted with fear. 'Is she ill? What's wrong with her? Is it her heart?'

The matron looked at her sturdily and said, 'My orders

are that she's to be released, and that's all I know. Do you want to go together, in the one taxi? Or is there someone you want to come and fetch you?'

'My chauffeur – Mary Taylor,' Anne said, from the depths of her distraction. 'She can fetch us in my motor.' She searched the matron's impassive face. 'Please tell me, is Vera really ill?'

'I'm just passing on the governor's orders,' the matron said, and went away.

Less than two hours later Anne and Vera were being driven home in the Wolseley by Mary Taylor, whose exultant grin was a comfort to Anne, suggesting this was a triumph and not a betrayal. She knew they were leaving their friends behind, and that they were getting special treatment because of her rank. But Vera looked both shocked and ill, and Anne wanted to get a doctor to examine her. For once in her life personal considerations were outweighing the political in Anne's mind.

Jessie was surprised to learn that Holkam would not be taking them to the Marchioness of Preston's ball. But Violet only said, 'He's otherwise engaged,' in such a matter-of-fact way that Jessie assumed it was nothing out of the ordinary. She was not sorry that they would not be spending the evening in his company. There was an element of embarrassment to any meeting she might have with the earl. In her come-out year she had been madly in love with him. She and Violet had both thought he fancied her, but in the event it was Violet he had offered for. Things he had said and done later suggested to Jessie that he had regarded her not only as far beneath him, but also as something of a lightskirt whom he might have at will; and the implied insult had helped kill any feelings she had for him.

On the day of Jessie's arrival Lord Holkam had come in when they had just finished tea. He greeted her civilly, shook her hand, said he was glad she had come to stay and hoped she would be comfortable, and then left them. Jessie did not see him again that day. She and Violet dined alone in the small dining-room, and when she asked after Holkam,

Violet said, 'Oh, he's dining at his club.' She looked at Jessie enquiringly. 'Isn't this cosy, just the two of us? I could have invited people but I thought you probably wouldn't want company the first evening.'

Holkam did not appear at breakfast – 'He never does,' said Violet – and in fact Jessie did not see him at all that day, though she presumed Violet had, for she mentioned something he had said to her. But Violet seemed happy – happier than ever – and the fact that she did not see much of her husband did not appear to trouble her in the least. She spoke of him calmly and with affection.

On that second day they drove to Manchester Square to have luncheon with Cousin Venetia. Jessie was warmly received, and embraced like a second daughter. 'You are looking very well,' Venetia said. 'Marriage evidently suits you. And I'm glad to see you are not too cast down by this business about your uncle.'

'I try not to be,' Jessie said, 'but it is so horrible. People won't shop in his store, and they've asked him to resign from his club. Ned's losing business too, and I've had horses cancelled. It's so beastly to have people say Uncle's a coward and a villain when the truth is he helped save lots of women. And other men got into the boats, lots of them – why don't they say things about them? But it's only him and Mr Ismay they abuse.'

'The opinion of fools isn't worth worrying about,' said Venetia.

'I know,' Jessie sighed, 'but it's hard to keep thinking that when you're surrounded by them. And, of course, everything's been made worse for Uncle Teddy by Aunt Alice losing the baby and being so ill.'

'He must be suffering from the after-effects of shock, too,' Venetia said.

'That's what Dr Hasty said. Poor Uncle is very low.'

'It will pass. He has loving family about him, and I'm sure he will come through. Now, come into the drawing-room. I have a surprise for you.'

The surprise was her brother Frank, who had been invited to luncheon. He kissed her fondly, and asked after the family.

Jessie asked if he had suffered any *Titanic* after-effects, but he said he hadn't.

'I don't think anyone associates Frank Compton with Edward Morland. There's no reason for them to do so. In any case, academics live in their own world. Planck's constant is much more exciting to them than a mere disaster at sea. Has anything been heard from Lizzie yet?'

'Yes, I've brought her letter to Mother to show you. Have you heard from Jack lately?'

Frank gave a rueful smile. 'His lady-love has turned him off.'

'Oh dear, not another one!' Jessie said. 'How can all these women treat my poor Jackie so badly?'

'Because he picks the wrong women, of course,' said Frank. 'But it's such a difficult business anyway, I'm sure those dons at Oxford have the right idea. I shall steer well clear of any romantic entanglements myself, I promise you!'

'Such a waste!' Jessie said. 'You're so handsome and nice.'

'Thank you. But I shall still be handsome and nice whether I marry or not,' he pointed out.

Oliver was there too: Venetia thought he and Jessie ought to renew their acquaintance before the evening engagement. During their come-out year, Jessie and Violet had spent two weeks in a cottage on the Isle of Wight, and Oliver had joined them for a while. He and Jessie had had long, frank talks and they had become quite close. Jessie found she still liked him very much – more, in fact, than she remembered – and thought having him for an escort that evening a good bargain. He was good-looking, he enjoyed conversation, and the self-assurance that came from his birth and upbringing had been enhanced by a new maturity, which she supposed had come from the discipline of medicine.

Oliver asked his sister where Holkam would be engaged.

'Some learned society dinner or other,' Violet said. 'I can't remember for the moment which one.'

'I'm sure he'll be very sorry to be kept from us,' Oliver said – Jessie wondered if she had detected a touch of irony there. 'Where do we dine first?'

'At the de Veres',' said Violet.

'Well,' said Oliver to Jessie, 'I propose that we have a dazzlingly erudite conversation at the de Vere table, and hope it gets back to Holkam so that he'll know what he missed.'

'I'm not sure I could be dazzlingly erudite,' Jessie said. 'I only had a few years at school, you know. And I think I ought to warn you that I sometimes forget myself and say the wrong things. I got terribly stared at, at a dinner party at home, for talking about the benefits of late gelding for racehorses.'

Oliver gave a shout of laughter. 'Now I know I shall enjoy myself! I must thank you, Mama, for engaging me to the perfect partner.'

'I hope you won't encourage him to misbehave, Jessie,' Venetia said.

'A hard-working medical student must have some relaxation – as *you* know very well,' Oliver replied.

'I didn't have the luxury of misbehaving,' Venetia said. 'Women medical students were barely tolerated, if at all. Any misbehaviour would have provided the perfect excuse to get rid of us.'

Oliver turned to his sister. 'So, Vi, am I escorting both of you, in Holkam's absence?'

'Goodness, no,' Violet said. 'That would have a very off appearance, besides putting Agnes de Vere's table out. No, Billy Copthall is partnering me.'

'Oh, good. I like old Billy,' Oliver said. To Jessie he explained, 'Sir William Copthall, Bart, is one of Vi's tame . . .' He paused. 'Well, what are they, Vi? Ciceroni?'

'I don't like that word,' Violet said.

'It doesn't mean anything indecent, love,' Oliver assured her. And to Jessie, 'I'm surprised you haven't come across any of them yet – but perhaps it's early days. Her house is always full of handsome young men longing to be of service. Men who like female company but don't want to get trapped into marriage – like your brother Frank.'

'Only much wealthier,' Frank suggested.

'Oh, certainly,' Oliver agreed. 'For them, a beautiful young *married* woman is the perfect companion. She enhances their standing but is no threat to them.'

'You needn't suggest there's something regular about it,' Venetia scolded him.

'Why not? The whole arrangement is elegant in its simplicity, and serves all concerned very well.'

'I look forward to meeting some of them,' Jessie said.

'You might even borrow some,' Oliver said. 'I'm sure Vi has enough for two.'

'You're such a fool,' Violet said, but her cheeks were a little pink and she looked as though she didn't much like the teasing. 'They're just friends.'

'Of course they are,' Oliver said soothingly, but his eyes were twinkling with amusement. 'How are we travelling to the de Veres' tonight?'

'We had better go in my motor-car,' Violet said. 'I'll send it for you and Billy and it can come back for us. The de Veres live in Eaton Place.'

Oliver winked at Jessie and whispered, 'I wonder if that's why Holkam is otherwise engaged. Quite the wrong side of the park, you know.'

Venetia heard, as she was meant to, and gave her unruly son a stern look. Now that Holkam had renewed the relationship between the families, she did not want anything to disturb the situation again.

Jessie enjoyed the evening very much. She and Oliver got on like a house afire, and Billy Copthall turned out to be a pleasant-looking man of about thirty whose well-bred manners made him very easy company – though afterwards Jessie could not remember anything in particular that he had said, even though she had danced with him several times at the ball. He and Violet seemed to be on comfortable terms, and Jessie found herself thinking that he was just the sort of person Violet ought, perhaps, to have married, and very well might have, had not Holkam made the running.

But while she was dancing with Oliver, he told her that Copthall was not only a confirmed bachelor, but that his fortune was not large enough for him to maintain the kind of establishment to which Violet was entitled, as the daughter of an earl and granddaughter of a duke.

273

'Lord Holkam didn't have any money either,' Jessie pointed out. 'All the money was Violet's.'

'Ah, but he had the title and the estates, even if they were run down. Copthall lives in good style in Albany, but he doesn't own anything except his name. He would never have done for Violet, but he makes a safe companion.'

They did not stay to the end of the ball: one had to be in love, Jessie thought, to want to dance until dawn. Violet said there was no need for either of the men to see them home, and Oliver said that in that case, as the night was still young, he would go off to a little place he knew, and invited Copthall to go with him. Copthall hesitated, but Violet said, 'Yes, do go, Billy. I shall be quite all right in my own motor with my own chauffeur.'

The traffic down Regent Street was heavy, and towards the southern end it seized up altogether. There seemed to be some sort of unusual excitement in the streets, and Violet used the speaking-tube to ask Dawson what was going on. He lowered his side window and enquired of a passer-by, and then reported, 'It seems, my lady, there is some trouble with the Suffragettes. They've been breaking windows in Piccadilly.'

'Can you go another way?' Violet asked.

'I can make a diversion, my lady, once the traffic starts to move.'

As he spoke they were stationary between side-streets. The traffic crawled a few yards at a time, stopping and starting, and they were still short of Glasshouse Street when two people, a woman and a boy, who had emerged from Vigo Street, ran across the road, hurried up to the motor, opened the door and climbed in. Violet and Jessie were much startled, and Dawson jerked his head round in alarm and was moving to get out of the car when the taller of the two said, 'No, no! Don't scream! It's me, Anne.'

She sat down hastily between Violet and Jessie and her companion took the drop seat.

'We're being pursued,' she went on urgently. 'Don't give us up, *please*! Tell your chauffeur to drive on.'

Violet caught her breath, made a negating sort of wave

to Dawson, and picked up the speaking-tube to say, 'It's all right, Dawson. Please drive on. I know these people. Take the quickest way home and don't stop for anything.'

He gave her a doubtful look, but it was a direct order. A gap opened up in the traffic ahead, and he moved on and turned down Brewer Street.

'Thank God for you!' Anne said to Violet. 'I can't tell you how relieved I felt when I saw your motor-car. You've saved our skins. We got clean away but two detectives who spotted us turning into Stafford Street decided we were their quarry and came after us. They'd have taken us for sure if we'd stayed on the street.' She noted Jessie's presence. 'Good evening, Jessie. You're looking well.'

'Good evening,' Jessie managed to reply. She would hardly have recognised Lady Anne Farraline, whom she remembered as being golden-haired, imperious and beautiful. This woman, dressed in the garb of the respectable middle classes, with a rather cheap fur piece round her neck that matched the large muff she carried, looked old and haggard. Her face was not just thin, but seemed marked with suffering, the eyes shadowed and the skin sallow and unhealthy, and she had rather coarse brown hair under her hat.

Anne noted the examination and said calmly, 'You think me changed?'

'I – was wondering if you had been ill,' Jessie managed to say.

'I'm not long out of prison,' Anne replied. 'We were on hunger-strike.'

Jessie could not think of anything to say to that. It was all too startling, and too far removed from the evening she and Violet had just spent.

'But, Cousin Anne, your hair,' Violet protested. 'What have you done to it?'

'It's a wig,' Anne said impatiently, as though they should have known. 'May I introduce?' she went on. 'My friend Miss Polk – Vera, you know of Lady Holkam, and this is an even more distant cousin of mine, Mrs – oh dear, what is your married name?'

'Morland,' said Jessie.

'Of course it is,' Anne said. 'How could I forget?'

'How d'you do?' Miss Polk said, in an ungracious sort of mutter.

Jessie tried not to stare, but on Anne's introduction, and further inspection, she saw that what she had taken to be a youth of about fourteen, dressed in a knickerbocker suit and a tweed cap, was in fact a young woman. How young was hard to tell, for her face was gaunt and her expression grim, and she seemed not to like her present company. What shocked Jessie most was the short hair – a proper, short, boy's haircut. Though she herself had always been something of a tomboy and even now had little patience with the sillier, frillier end of womanhood, she would never, never have done that to herself. She recollected her manners and said faintly, 'How do you do?'

'You needn't stare as if I was something out of a freak show,' Vera said sharply.

'Vera, don't,' Anne said, a little wearily; and to Jessie, 'We've had a wearing evening, and Vera's a little overwrought.'

'I'm not overwrought. I just don't like them looking down their noses at me.'

Violet felt the duty of the hostess, to avoid awkwardness, thrust upon her and said, 'Wh-what sort of evening have you had? Were you—' And she stopped, unable to think of any way to end the question.

'We've been breaking windows, of course,' Anne said cheerfully. 'Did you think we were at a masquerade? It was a protest: Miss Polk and I were released from Holloway, but there are seventy women still in gaol, in the second division, being tortured by this foul government. There's to be a debate in the Commons on forcible feeding tomorrow and we are making sure the Home Office has its mind firmly on the subject.'

Violet looked dismayed, but Jessie thought it interesting and asked, 'How many windows did you break?'

'Half a dozen, I suppose. We had the stones ready in my muff, with a note wrapped round each, saying, "A woman's protest against the government that tortures women." I'd like to have done more, but I'm still not very strong after the hunger strike, and Vera is even weaker than me, so we were rather slow, which was why we almost got caught. We didn't dare run, because someone would have been sure to collar us, so we had to walk quickly and dodge up this street and down that. We thought we were free and clear when I spotted the two detectives, and I suppose they saw me looking at them and became suspicious. I'm so glad I recognised your motor-car. I simply couldn't bear another spell in prison just yet.'

Violet looked aghast. 'How can you do such things? I'm glad we were able to help you, of course, but if Holkam should find out . . .'

'Ah, yes, the egregious Lord Holkam,' Anne said lightly. Jessie wasn't sure what egregious meant, but she was sure from Anne's voice that it was not complimentary. 'Well,' Anne went on, in a kinder tone, 'I have no wish to make difficulties for you, Violet dear, so when we're just a little further away from the scene of the crime, we'll get out and walk.'

'Scene of the crime?' Violet said. 'Oh, I wish you wouldn't say such things!'

'Well, I'm afraid Reggie McKenna regards it as a crime, whatever we think.'

'Why do you *talk* to them?' Miss Polk said abruptly. 'Talking does no good with women like them. They side with the enemy. They'd sooner fawn like lap-dogs than fight and be free.'

'Vera, dear,' said Anne, trying to make a joke of it, 'these nice ladies have just saved our necks. It would behove you to be a little grateful.'

Vera snorted and seemed about to say something even more unforgivable when the motor slowed sharply, and looking ahead the women saw a policeman standing in the middle of the road with his hand up. Violet, in a panic, grabbed for the speaking-tube but dropped it. 'Don't stop!' she cried, though Dawson could not have heard her.

Anne put a hand on her wrist and said calmly, 'The poor man can't run him over. Now, Violet, I don't want to get you into trouble. Do you want us to jump out and run for it? Say quickly before he stops.'

'No,' Violet said. 'I'll protect you. But what shall I say?'

'We're friends of yours and you know nothing of the window-breaking. I don't know that constable, so with luck he won't recognise me. Bless you, darling! Be calm.'

Then the motor stopped, and the policeman made his way round to the side window. Violet lowered it, and the policeman touched his helmet and looked in.

'I beg your pardon, ladies, but we're looking for some fugitives. Might I ask who you are?'

Violet said, 'I am the Countess of Holkam. Do I look like a fugitive?'

'No, your ladyship, of course not,' he said hastily. 'I beg your pardon, but we were given a description of a motor-car the fugitives were thought to have got into. A woman and a boy.' He directed a keen look at Vera. Fortunately the street lighting in Rupert Street was not very bright, and her cap threw a shadow over her face, or he might have been roused to more suspicion by the glare she gave him.

Violet spoke: 'This is my cousin Mrs Morland, and my friend Mrs – Copthall, and her son.' The hesitation as she tried to think of a name was minute, but to Jessie's charged nerves it sounded horribly obvious. Yet Violet's voice was amazingly calm. Jessie wondered at how well she did it.

The police officer looked the other three over once more, but Violet's name, or her manner, or both, seemed to have done the trick. 'Thank you, your ladyship. I'm sorry to have troubled you,' he said, saluting her again and stepping back. 'Goodnight.'

He seemed to be staring at them thoughtfully, but Violet put up the window and said, 'Drive on,' to Dawson and the motor moved off and left him behind.

Anne laughed in relief. 'Well done, Violet! You did it beautifully. You are a great loss to the stage.'

'The Holkam name got him,' Vera said sneeringly. 'He must know Holkam hates us worse than Asquith and McKenna put together.'

Violet's head jerked round. 'You are riding in my husband's car and under the protection of his name!'

Jessie was startled. She had never heard Violet speak so sharply.

'Quite right,' Anne said. 'Vera apologises. She didn't mean anything uncivil. We're both very grateful to you.' They all travelled in silence until the car turned into Pall Mall, when Anne said gently, 'If you would ask your man to stop at Waterloo Place, we will relieve you of our presence. We'll be safe enough now.'

Violet gave Dawson the instruction and the motor glided to a halt. Anne got up, and said, 'Thank you, Violet dear. We shall not mention this to a soul, I promise you. No-one will ever know who helped us.'

She gave Vera a sharp look, and she said, a little sulkily, 'I won't tell anyone.'

'Goodnight, Violet. Goodnight, Jessie. Thank you again,' Anne said, and they were out and gone and the motor moved on.

Violet drew a long, wavering sigh of relief. 'That was terrible,' she said. 'If Holkam ever finds out, it will ruin everything.'

'I won't tell,' Jessie said. 'Not a word to a soul.'

'I just hope that horrid Miss Polk doesn't,' Violet said crossly. 'It would be a fine joke for her to tell everyone that the Earl of Holkam saved her from the police. I don't understand why Anne likes her so much.'

There was only one more thing to do. When they arrived at Fitzjames House, and Dawson opened the door for them, Violet stopped and looked up at him, straight into his eyes. 'Dawson, about what happened this evening...'

Jessie, standing behind her, saw a softening of the normally rigid expression of a good servant, and realised that Dawson had a warm feeling for his beautiful mistress.

'Nothing at all happened, my lady,' he said. 'You can rely on me.'

Jessie thought of Lord Holkam, and hoped desperately that Violet really could.

CHAPTER FOURTEEN

When Venetia called at Anne's house in Bedford Square, the door was opened to her not by a butler or even a footman, but by a maid in a crumpled uniform and with untidy hair. Venetia gave her a severe look and asked for Lady Anne Farraline.

'I think she's still having her brekfuss,' the girl said, staring openly at Venetia's clothes.

'Will you please ask if she will see me?' Venetia said firmly.

But before she could give her name, the girl stepped back and said, 'Oh, you can go up if you want,' and, to Venetia's utter astonishment, she turned away and walked off, leaving Venetia and the open door to look after themselves.

On her way upstairs, Venetia saw further signs of servant dereliction: the carpet appeared not to have been swept, there were fingermarks on the looking-glass at the bottom of the stairs, and dead flowers in a vase on the mid-way window-sill. At the top of the stairs she hesitated, feeling uncomfortable; but the door to the morning-room was open and she heard voices from within, so she crossed to it and tapped as she presented herself in the doorway.

At the small table in the window two people were sitting facing each other, and despite its being past eleven o'clock, they did indeed appear to be having breakfast. The sideboard was empty, but on the table was a loaf of bread in cut, a coffee-pot and an empty serving-dish, while before the two people were plates that plainly had recently accommodated bacon and eggs. Anne, in a dressing-gown of foaming frilliness, with her hair hanging loose down her back, was opening letters. Her companion across the table

280

was flicking through a newspaper. Venetia did not immediately recognise the companion, and was thrown into a shock of embarrassment by the initial impression that it was a man. She thought she had walked in on Anne and a lover at a moment of intimacy.

Then the other person looked up and she recognised Miss Polk. She was wearing a suit of striped pyjamas under a beige felt dressing-gown, secured with a cord round the waist, and her hair was cut as short as a boy's. On seeing Venetia her brows drew down into a scowl.

Anne was saying, 'And after that I think we ought to —' when, glancing up, she caught the scowl and turned her head to see what Vera was staring at. The sight of Venetia made her start so violently that she knocked over her cup and spilled the dregs of the coffee on to the tablecloth. She struggled to her feet, scattering letters to the floor around her. 'How did you get here?' she asked.

'In the usual way, through your street door and up the stairs,' Venetia said drily. 'I'm sorry to arrive with so little ceremony, but your maid told me to come up.'

Anne read Venetia's disapproval easily enough in her face and voice. She seemed embarrassed, and looked across at Vera. 'It's that girl again – Sarah. She really will have to go.' And to Venetia, 'It's so hard to get good servants nowadays.'

Venetia had never suffered from bad servants. Servants were only as good as their employers in her experience, but she didn't say so. 'What happened to your butler?' she asked. She hadn't thought much of him, but he had been better than nothing.

Vera answered before Anne could. 'He's gone. We don't have any male servants in this house.'

Venetia addressed herself to Anne. 'No butler?'

'Not even a footman,' Anne said. Where Vera had spoken boldly, she sounded apologetic, though she smiled as she said it.

Venetia spoke gently, not wanting to stir things up, but it had to be said: 'Anne, it really isn't suitable for you not to have a male servant to keep order below stairs and receive your guests.'

But Miss Polk jumped in again: 'Not suitable? Not suitable? Who says? We don't want men around. This is an all-woman house and that's all there is to it. I don't see what business it is of *yours* anyway.'

'Vera, dear, don't be rude,' Anne said.

Vera turned on her passionately. 'She doesn't like me. You know she doesn't. See the way she looks at me! She just comes here to cause trouble and turn you against me. You shouldn't listen to her. It isn't fair!'

Venetia's patience with bad manners had never been great, and she itched to slap the girl. But she kept her countenance and said politely, 'I wonder if I might have a word with you alone, Anne?'

'No!' said Miss Polk. 'I know what you're up to. You want me out of the way so you can talk about me. Well, I won't go! Anything you want to say to Anne you can say in front of me. I'm staying, and that's my last word.' She folded her arms across her chest to emphasise her immovability.

Venetia waited for Anne to speak and, when she did not, said, still politely, 'You are mistaken, Miss Polk. I have family matters I wish to discuss with Lady Anne.'

'*Lady* Anne!' Miss Polk sneered. 'You think I'm not good enough for her. Well, *I'm* her family now, so if it's family matters, I'm staying!'

'You are not, however, a member of *my* family,' Venetia said.

Anne roused herself and said, 'Vera, dear, would you mind leaving us alone? Please. I promise we're not going to talk about you. Why don't you run along and get dressed, and we'll go out in the motor as soon as I'm done here?' Vera stared at her, sulky and defiant, and Anne said again, 'Please. I won't be long.'

'Oh, all right!' Vera said, with the greatest unwillingness. She got up, threw the newspaper down on the floor, and flounced out, only pausing in the door to say to Venetia, 'Don't think what you're saying to her will be a secret. She tells me *everything*!' And then she was gone.

Anne sat down again and drew a shaky breath. 'I'm sorry,' she said. 'She's so passionate. She doesn't mean half what she says.' She reached out and righted her coffee cup with an automatic hand, then recollected herself and gestured to the chair beside her. 'Won't you sit down? I'd offer you some coffee but I'm afraid it's all gone.'

Venetia didn't know why that should deter her. She could ring for more, couldn't she? But then she thought of the slatternly girl downstairs. She sat down and said, 'Anne, what is happening in your house? The girl who opened the door to me just left me there and walked off. And your breakfast table!' She waved a hand round it. 'Nothing set properly, no sideboard – is this always how you are served?'

Anne sighed. 'Things have got a little out of hand, I admit. It was Vera's idea that we shouldn't have any male servants in the house – to show loyalty to the Cause, you see.'

'But that's foolishness,' Venetia interrupted.

'Is it? The women's hospital you operate in doesn't have any male doctors. That was a fundamental principle, wasn't it, established by Elizabeth Garrett Anderson?'

'That's a very different matter. She didn't want anyone to say that the achievements of the hospital were due to male intervention – as people would have if there were any male staff. But not to have a butler and footman? Come, you can't think it's the same thing!'

'I suppose not,' Anne admitted unwillingly. 'But Vera was so set on it, and it seemed a small enough thing just to please her.' She gave an embarrassed laugh. 'It made perfect sense when she said it.'

'It isn't suitable for someone of your rank not to have proper service, especially when you're living alone. And a house this size can't be run properly without either a butler or a very good housekeeper.'

'It isn't run properly – I think you can see that. Things have got worse and worse since I dismissed the last butler. Nobody in their right place and nothing done as it should be. Vera isn't good with servants. Well, she didn't grow up with them, so she doesn't know how to handle them. She's too friendly and lax, and then when they get lazy and impertinent she tells them off in the wrong way and they either give their notice or sulk.'

Venetia was sorry to see Anne, who had always been so effortlessly commanding, reduced to this apologetic, helpless creature, no longer mistress in her own house, seemingly unable to get to grips with the situation. 'For goodness' sake,' she said impatiently, 'take charge yourself. Why leave things to Miss Polk if she can't manage?'

But Anne only said, 'Well, it's all a nonsense anyway, isn't it? We shouldn't mind if our breakfast is served one way rather than another, as long as there's food on the table. Bad servants, good servants, what does it matter in the end? Why should we have servants at all, if it comes to that? We ought to clean our own houses and cook our own meals.'

'I can't bear to hear you talking such socialistic nonsense,' Venetia said angrily. 'Bad servants are bad for everyone, including themselves. People need to take a pride in their work for the good of their own characters; and the whole fabric of society will crumble if we allow laziness and impertinence to flourish. As to cleaning your own house – words fail me! Who will give the servant classes employment if people like us do not? Do you want them to starve? I suppose you want to grow your own corn and weave your own cloth rather than pay farmers and mill-hands?'

Anne smiled, and it was a little like her old smile. 'That's good. Give me more of that, if you please. It's like a dash of cold water in the face.'

'I haven't come here to re-educate you,' Venetia said.

'Ah, yes, I was forgetting you came with a purpose in mind. Family matters, you said?'

'I came to protest at your involving Violet in your business. How could you, Anne? Don't you know we've only just got back on terms with Holkam? If he hears about Violet rescuing you – in *his* motor-car – we shall be ruined. He'll cut us off again, and I shan't be able to see my daughter or my grandchildren. I don't understand how you could be so thoughtless and inconsiderate.'

Anne's cheeks coloured a little, and she said, 'I didn't plan to do it. It was the action of the moment. But Holkam will never find out, I'm sure.'

'*I* found out.'

'Did Violet tell you?'

'No, she didn't. An obliging person in the Movement told me. So much for your secret!'

Anne drew breath to speak, and then stopped. She had told no-one, and she would have staked her reputation that neither Violet nor Jessie had, which only left – Vera. It was horrible to have to admit to herself but, little as she wanted to, she could imagine Vera talking about it. It had been an exciting incident, and she would want to share it with her friends in the Movement. She wouldn't mean any harm. No, Anne was forced to be honest with herself: she might well mean harm. She was jealous of Anne's aristocratic relations, and convinced that they looked down on her. Despite Violet's having saved them from arrest that night, she might still want Violet to suffer – or, at least, would not care whether she suffered or not. To keep a secret, when the only reason was not to embarrass and upset Violet, would seem pointless to her. And such a delicious secret! Of all motor-cars in the world for them to have escaped in, that it should belong to Holkam, the implacable anti-suffragist!

Venetia had been studying Anne's face while this thought process was going on, and she was pretty sure it was Vera Polk who had let the secret out. She saw the conflict in Anne's expression, as she tried not to think ill of her friend. The marks of her latest imprisonment were still on her. There were dark stains under her eyes; her face was drawn and pale, and there was suffering in its lines. Venetia was used to thinking of her as a young woman, but she was young no longer. Despite her anger on Violet's behalf, and her indignation, she felt sorry for Anne, and spoke more gently than she otherwise might have.

'I can't understand what's got into you, Anne. You used to be so strong – too strong, I sometimes thought – but lately you seem to have turned into a jellyfish. It's not like you to be ruled by events, pushed about by the currents. You don't control your own household, you wantonly endanger Violet's happiness . . .' She didn't say, 'ever since Miss Polk came on the scene', but the words hung in the air between them.

Anne said, 'I'm very sorry about Violet, and I promise I shall never do anything like that again. I should have thought about the possible consequences, but I was so anxious not to get caught. Not for myself so much, but for Vera. I was afraid another spell in gaol so soon would do her real harm. She was very ill after being forcibly fed, you know.'

'You have been ill, too,' Venetia said. 'I can see it in your face.'

Anne sighed. 'This last hunger strike seems to have taken the strength out of me. I expected to bounce back, but I haven't.'

'You shouldn't be doing it at your age. You could seriously damage your heart.'

Anne shrugged that away. 'The Cause is too important to consider things like that. If my health – or my life – is demanded, then so be it.'

'I wish you wouldn't talk like that,' Venetia said.

'I should have thought you of all people would understand. You had your own fight for women's rights.'

'I would not have died to become a doctor, far less for anything as intangible as the vote.' She put out a hand and rested it on Anne's, and tried not to notice the initial and instinctive flinch away from being touched. 'I think you are a little depressed at the moment. It's a natural reaction to the physical strain you have been under. Don't make any serious decisions while you are feeling like this, will you?' She stood up and Anne stood too. 'I suppose I shall have to see myself out,' she said.

'I could ring,' Anne said, with a faint smile, 'but I don't know if anyone would come. I'll see you out myself.'

'Not in your dressing-gown. I'll manage.' At the door they paused, and Venetia said, 'Anne – Miss Polk's hair!'

Anne grinned with a hint of the old mischief. 'It was necessary for the masquerade, but Vera says she likes it so much she may keep it that way.'

'It looks so shocking.'

'Oh, don't worry. We're off to the countryside at the end of the week, and no-one who matters will see us for several months – long enough to grow it back.'

'You're going down to the country? That's an excellent idea. Peace and quiet, plenty of fresh air and good food will set you up again. You might,' she added, 'take the opportunity to sack your servants and start again when you come back to Town.'

Anne laughed. 'That's my dear, dogged Venetia. Never give up a point!'

'How else could I have become a doctor?' said Venetia.

Holkam did not get to hear about the incident involving his motor. It seemed like a miracle, but Venetia considered that, unlike her, he had no contact with the Suffragette world; and hating the very idea of women's rights he was the last person who would be likely to take part in a conversation about the militants and their concerns.

Jessie thoroughly enjoyed her visit. Though the Season was nearly at an end there were still dinners, evening parties and a few balls, along with plays, concerts and exhibitions to attend; and there were all the wealthy and titled people in the Holkams' circle on whom to make 'morning' calls, and to take tea with. Jessie missed riding – Violet no longer rode, and since Holkam had gone over entirely to motorcars she did not even take a carriage drive in the park. She seemed almost to have given up outdoor exercise, though she spoke fondly of her garden at Brancaster Hall, for which she had plans stretching forward many years.

'But it will be some time before I can do anything more to it,' she said. 'We have a full round of country-house visits as soon as we leave London, and we won't be at Brancaster until September.'

'Won't you see your children until then?' Jessie asked.

'Oh, I shall have Wednesdays and Thursdays with them most weeks,' Violet said. 'Then we're home for nearly three weeks in September before we go to the South of France, and another week in October before the shooting starts.'

After the shooting came the hunting, as Jessie very well knew, which both involved more country-house visits since Brancaster Hall supported no hunting, and no shooting except for duck. The primary estate at Holkam could have

287

supported shooting, but the house was virtually a ruin, and Violet's dowry was only slowly effecting repairs. For the hunting season, the Holkams of yore had kept a small house in Leicestershire, but it had been sold when the old earl had become too infirm to hunt. The present earl and countess would have to rent a house for a week in order to repay the hospitality of the rest of the season.

It charmed Jessie to think of the story-book life Violet led, and to see her so absolutely in her element with it. She was the gracious hostess and the perfect guest, able to make small-talk, patient with dullards and bores, a fine dancer, an adequate card-player, a competent performer on the pianoforte – and beautiful and elegant to boot. From the time they were children, Violet had only ever wanted a home, husband and children. She had inherited not her mother's restless intelligence, but her father's good looks and charm. Overton had never been a scholar, and had been sent into the army as a young man to keep him busy until he should inherit. He had always been, above all, a social creature, and Violet seemed to have the same bent.

That she was happy with Holkam was beyond doubt. It seemed an odd relationship to Jessie, and she said to Violet one day, when they were breakfasting together, 'Your life is so very different from mine at home. You hardly ever seem to see your husband.'

Violet laughed. 'But I see him every day,' she said.

'Yes, but it isn't like Ned and me. In our little home, we're always together in the evenings unless he has a meeting or something of the sort. But you and Holkam seem to have quite separate lives.'

'That's quite usual for people of our rank,' Violet said. 'My mother and father have separate interests. Papa is at the House a lot, and he goes to his club and so on, and Mama has hospital meetings.'

Jessie found it hard to express the difference, though she felt it clearly enough. Cousin Venetia and Lord Overton, despite their different interests, maintained a level of intimacy that made it clear they were married and loved each other. But Holkam and Violet were like polite friends who shared an address. It was almost as if they had to make an appointment to be together.

Violet always seemed delighted to have her hand on her husband's arm when they were out together, and he behaved attentively towards her. When they met at home, they would discuss future engagements, the children, and plans for the two houses in a way that showed Jessie these conversations were carried on on other occasions when she was not present to witness them. But though they seemed perfectly comfortable together, she could not see any signs of deep love. Violet had been mad for him before their marriage, she knew. Was it simply marriage that had reduced her passion to this politeness?

This puzzle was the background to an enjoyable visit. Jessie loved Violet, and she savoured the brief taste of high living, the glittering occasions and gorgeous clothes. She liked the people Violet had around her, other wealthy young married women, and the seemingly endless supply of handsome and charming young men who hung around the house dying for the honour of escorting the countess.

Oliver was often Jessie's escort, and the more they saw of each other, the better they got on. One day he drove her and Violet down to Brooklands to watch Jack taking a test flight in a new tractor biplane he and Fred Sigrist had built, a hybrid of Tom Sopwith's Burgess Wright. They were intending to enter it for the Michelin duration prize in the autumn.

Jessie was delighted to see Jack again. She did manage a brief private word with him, and when she asked him about his lost love he answered her lightly, though his face darkened. 'Ah, you heard about it, then?'

'Frank told me. Poor Jackie, are you very cut up?'

'Yes, but I'll get over it.'

'Why did she drop you?'

'This *Titanic* business,' he said tersely. 'Miss Fairbrother didn't want to be associated with the nephew of the evil Edward Morland.'

'Oh, darling! But if she thinks like that, she isn't worthy of you.'

'I'm learning to believe so, but it's a slow and painful process. Miss Ormerod does her best to educate me.'

Jessie had met Miss Ormerod. 'She's very nice.'

'Yes, you can always rely on her for good advice,' said Jack fondly. 'Rug thinks the world of her.'

'Rug is a sensible dog,' said Jessie.

Another day, Oliver took her to dine with the Darroways. Mark Darroway was a physician who had helped Venetia when she was a medical student, and later had 'crammed' Oliver before he joined medical school. Darroway had a practice in Soho, and lived in a tall, shabby house in Soho Square. Many of his patients were poor people and he had never made much money, but he and his wife had been very happy in their tumbledown home with their large family. The children were all grown-up and had flown the nest, but many of them lived nearby and, as Oliver had told Jessie, there always seemed to be some around, to say nothing of the grandchildren, neighbours and friends, to fill the house with noise and movement.

Oliver thought so highly of Darroway that Jessie understood it was an honour for him to arrange the invitation for her; Violet and Holkam were dining at the Palace that evening, so it was just the two of them. It was a very different sort of dinner-party, and Jessie could not imagine Holkam feeling at ease there. The house was so very dilapidated, and full of undistinguished people, and the table was laid with cutlery that did not match and serving dishes that had lost their lids; but the food, though simple, was ample and good, and the company was cheerful, noisy and interesting.

Dr Darroway was thin and grey and a little stooped – like a heron, Jessie thought – but his eyes were bright with intelligence, and within minutes of his cordial greeting Jessie was discussing the diseases of horses with him as if they had known each other all their lives. Mrs Darroway was as round as her husband was straight, and moved at astonishing speed on her little plump feet, helping the lone servant fetch dishes from the kitchen, greeting newcomers, chatting nineteen to the dozen. But she was no empty gossip. Talking to her, Jessie discovered a fierce intelligence allied to a strong will, both of which she had evidently bent to the service of her husband when she married.

It was a wonderfully noisy dinner for fourteen, crammed around a table that would have been adequate for ten, everyone helping to pass dishes and clear away. There were always at least three conversations going on at once, elbows planted on the table, fingers wagging to emphasise points against the hurricane of words. No verbal quarter was given. Jessie argued along with everyone else, and felt as though her brains were being stirred up from long idleness with a big stick. It was as different as could be, she thought rather wistfully, from the dull, polite dinner she and Ned had given for his business connections, or the glittering, stately affair Violet and Holkam had hosted a few nights before.

When the dessert was finished there was no thought of the women having to withdraw. Eventually everyone went together into the drawing-room, except for the two or three who went to the kitchen to help carry in the coffee. Other friends dropped in then, on their way home from engagements, and brought fresh blood to the conversations.

At one point a fierce July rainstorm broke, and Mrs Darroway had to rush upstairs to supervise the placing of vessels under the leaks in the roof.

'We'll have it mended one day,' Darroway said.

'When your ship comes in, Dad,' said one of his grown sons, and everyone laughed. The ship had obviously been long delayed.

When eventually Jessie and Oliver rose to go, the Darroways themselves fetched their coats and helped them into them.

'I hope you've had a pleasant evening,' Dr Darroway said to Jessie.

'Oh, I have!' Jessie said. 'I can't remember when I've talked so much. I shall be hoarse tomorrow.'

'We do have a contentious lot of friends,' Darroway said, smiling.

'I wish our friends at home were as interesting,' Jessie said, and then realised it sounded rather disloyal. She hurried on, 'I've enjoyed everything very much, and I'm so glad Oliver brought me.'

'We're very fond of Oliver, you know,' he said, glancing across to where his wife was now brushing down Oliver's lapels like a mother with a schoolboy. 'He's like an extra son to Katherine and me. He helps me with my poorest patients every summer, you know, the ones who can't pay even if they want to. He's going to make a very fine doctor one day. When this war comes, we're going to need all the doctors we can get.'

'When do you think it will come?'

'Two, three – five years at the most,' he said gravely. 'It's coming, no doubt about it. Germany will attack France, and then we'll have to go in.' He stared past Jessie a moment, looking at something in his thoughts, and the reflection of it in his face made her shiver suddenly. He came back to himself, and smiled at her warmly. 'We have so very much enjoyed your company this evening, my dear. I hope you will come and see us whenever you're in London. You will be welcome at any time, I hope you know that.'

'I do – and I will,' said Jessie, and she meant it. There was something about this house that reminded her of Morland Place – nothing physical, of course, but in its spirit. It was like Morland Place used to be, crammed with people and movement and talk.

In the taxi-cab on the way home, Oliver said, 'You enjoyed it?'

'Very much.'

'You didn't mind the shabbiness and the lack of form?'

'Not at all.'

'I didn't think you would.'

'I had a delightful evening.'

'They liked you very much.' Oliver laughed suddenly. 'Katherine was asking me all sort of questions about you. She looked so wistful, poor dear, when she heard you were married. But even though you can't be my bride and redeem me from frozen bachelorhood, they still want to see you again.'

'Dr Darroway invited me to come any time I was in London,' Jessie said.

'Then I shall engage you now for the next time you visit Violet. It's fun, isn't it, being able to keep one foot in each camp? I love luxury as much as the next man, but I couldn't live Vi's life for anything. Variety, that's the stuff! I suppose I'm my mother's son.'

During her stay with Violet, Jessie was often calling on Cousin Venetia, and several times met Emma Weston. She took a great fancy to her. Emma was a lively and remarkably pretty girl, small and slender with a wild-rose sort of beauty, curly dark hair, large dark eyes and a high colour in her cheeks. Venetia said she was the image of her mother. Jessie saw she didn't at all resemble her father: when he called to take Emma home one time, she thought him a grim-looking and very unprepossessing man, though he spoke pleasantly to everyone.

Emma took a fancy to Jessie too. Venetia treated her with kindness, but was too many generations separated for Emma to regard her with anything other than respect; and Emma was in plain awe of Violet. But in Jessie she felt she had found someone who might stand in the position of older sister, young enough to be accessible and sympathetic but old enough to give her advice when she wanted it.

Venetia watched the rapid advance of friendship with interest, and one day at the beginning of August she called at Fitzjames House. She found Jessie and Violet at breakfast, but there the similarity with her visit to Bedford Square ended. She was admitted with the greatest formality by a well-trained butler, the two young women were fully dressed, and there was a properly laid table and a laden sideboard. The dogs sat on cushions on chairs pulled up to the table, their little black faces turning from person to person, smiling engagingly.

Venetia accepted a seat at the table, but refused refreshment. 'I breakfasted hours ago.'

'Won't you at least take some coffee?' Violet said. 'Let me ring for fresh.'

'No, darling, thank you,' Venetia said, remembering Anne again. 'I hope you don't feed those dogs at the table. It's a very bad habit to get into, and it does them no good.'

'I wouldn't dare while Jessie's here,' Violet said. 'She's terribly strict about dogs. Was there something in particular you wanted, Mama?'

'Yes, I want to talk to Jessie. You like Emma Weston, don't you, Jessie dear?'

'I like her very much,' said Jessie.

'Has Violet told you of her circumstances?'

'That her father's ill?'

'Dying, poor man,' Venetia corrected. 'But Emma doesn't know it, and he doesn't want her to know yet.'

'Yes, Vi told me. I won't say anything.'

'I'm sure you won't. But the reason I want to talk to you is this. Emma's father was looking forward to spending the summer with her in the country, but his physician wants him to undergo a treatment that he thinks might prolong his life, and for various reasons it has to be done next week. Of course, he can't tell Emma about it, so he came to me and asked if I would invite her to stay. But Overton and I are engaged already for Cowes Week. We're staying with the Sandowns on the *Tutamen*, which is a very comfortable yacht but simply not big enough to accommodate an extra person. So, as I know you're going home next week, I wondered whether you would consider inviting Emma to stay with you in Yorkshire.'

'I'd be very happy to have her,' said Jessie. 'But won't she think it odd?'

'Wouldn't it be better for her to go to one of her sisters?' Violet put in.

'She doesn't like staying with them, and Tommy Weston thinks she'd be suspicious if he packed her off to them when she knows they were supposed to be going to Brighton together. That's why he asked me: an invitation issued from outside the family would be something he would naturally give priority to. He would tell her they'd have their Brighton trip later, and if necessary insist on her accepting. But of course,' Venetia added, 'she's taken such a liking to you, there'd be no need to insist.'

'Well, I'd be glad to have her to stay, if she wouldn't find Yorkshire too dull,' Jessie said.

'From what she's said to me, I think you'll find she regards your life up there as the very pattern of romance,' Venetia said, with a dry smile. 'She pictures you riding wildly about the countryside like a Cossack; and as she's never been anywhere further north than Oxford, Yorkshire might as well be the Ural mountains as far as she's concerned.'

And so it was that when Violet and Holkam closed up their house to go down to the country, and Jessie was taken to the station to catch the train home, she was accompanied by a very excited Emma Weston, invited initially for a fortnight, but with possible extensions, depending on what news came privately to Jessie about Mr Weston's health. As they settled down together in the first-class compartment – which they had, fortunately, to themselves – Emma seemed very excited, and chattered about Yorkshire and what they might see and do there. Jessie was amused to find that Cousin Venetia had been quite right, and that Emma thought of Yorkshire as some wild and craggy place of adventure, probably seething with corsairs, mountain lions, bears, robber bands and the odd chest of buried treasure. As she tried to let her protégée down gently and paint a more faithful picture of Maystone Villa and its surroundings, she found herself feeling unexpectedly old by comparison to this youthful exuberance.

It was strange not to have Uncle Teddy waiting to meet them as they pulled in to York station. Ned was there instead, and he looked so handsome and familiar that Jessie felt a pang in the pit of her stomach. He waved as they passed him – he hadn't his father's knack of positioning himself just where their compartment would stop – and Emma, who was pressed against the window like a puppy, said, 'Is that your husband? He looks nice.'

'He is nice,' Jessie said. 'He's my cousin and I've known him all my life.'

He caught up with them as the train stopped and opened the compartment door. He handed Jessie out, beaming with delight at seeing her again, and they exchanged a chaste matrimonial kiss. 'This is a pleasant surprise,' she said. 'I wasn't expecting you to meet us.'

'I came from the mill. I shall have to go back for a little while but I thought I'd see you comfortably home first.' He put out his hand to help Emma down. 'Miss Weston, welcome to York. I hope you'll be happy staying with us. You and I are cousins of a sort, you know. Your great-grandmother and my great-grandfather were brother and sister.'

Emma, her feet now on the platform but her hand still in Ned's, gazed up at him as though stunned, in a way that must have been gratifying for him, Jessie thought. She was amused: Ned was handsome enough, but he was no Greek god, and it would not have occurred to her that anyone could ever hero-worship him.

Their trunks were in the luggage car, and Ned looked round for a porter. It seemed curiously hard to catch the eye of any of them, as they hurried past, heads averted, to attend to other passengers. A red spot of annoyance appeared in Ned's cheeks, and Jessie's mouth grew grim as she realised they were being ostracised by the station staff. During her London visit she had almost been able to forget the troubles of Yorkshire, but here they were again, making themselves felt. She felt angry and hurt.

But then one of the older men, coming back in through the barrier from the previous job, saw them and hurried over, looking indignant. 'Any bags, Mrs Morland, Mr Morland?' he said, touching his cap.

'Thank you, Field,' Jessie said. She had known him since she was a small girl. 'I thought we'd have to carry them ourselves.'

'It's a disgrace,' he confided, whirling trunks onto his trolley as if they weighed nothing, 'the way them others are be'aving. Ah've never seen the like of it. After all the family's done for t' railways, *and* for York, and your uncle the kindest and best of gentlemen, ma'am – why, you could search the world and never find a better. So generous as he's always been to all of us! I'd 'ave them newspapers burned and the fellers 'at write 'em flogged, I would that, for the scurvy lies they've told!'

'Never mind it, Field,' Jessie said. 'People who believe that sort of thing are not worth bothering about.'

'Aye, ma'am, you're right,' he sniffed. 'They're fools, an' that's all about it! But there's plenty of us older folk 'at know the truth of it, and you'll find us loyal, beggin' your pardon, ma'am.'

Emma was attending to all this wide-eyed, not under-standing what was going on but too polite to ask. Ned offered her his arm and engaged her in conversation as they walked out to the motor-car, and on the drive home took pains to point out anything of interest and enquire about her likes and dislikes in order to keep her amused.

At the house he saw them received by the servants and the luggage taken in, then excused himself to go back to the mill. 'I'll see you at dinner,' he said, bowing over Emma's hand and completing her rout.

When he had gone, Jessie took her up to the room she had telegraphed ahead to have prepared. 'You're the very first guest to stay in our guest room,' she said.

'I think it's lovely!' Emma cried. She could hardly wait to remove her hat and jacket to be shown over the rest of the house, and she exclaimed satisfactorily over every corner and contrivance. 'It's the loveliest place, so neat and nice and comfortable. To think it's all yours, and you're not very much older than me! Don't you find it odd to think of owning a whole house to yourself?'

'Not quite to myself,' Jessie said, amused. 'There is Ned to consider.'

'Oh, you are *lucky* to be married to him!' Emma said. 'I *wish* I were married, too, and had a dear little house of my own, like you. But I'm not even out yet, and it'll be years and *years* before I'm allowed to get married.'

'Is that what you want most, to be married?' Jessie asked. Her own young life had been so full of things it had never seemed of the highest importance.

'Oh, yes! I want to marry and have lots of children. You haven't any yet, have you? Don't you long for them?'

'Oh, yes, of course,' Jessie said automatically. She was a little surprised that such a spirited girl should have such conventional ambitions; but she soon learned that Emma's enthusiasm had many different directions. It tended to spurt

297

out as a mechanism to relieve the inward pressure of her young energy. As the visit progressed Jessie heard about a lot of other ambitions, born of what they were seeing, doing or discussing at the time – to be a concert pianist, a great sculptress, an actress; to write a novel; to breed dogs; to be the first woman Member of Parliament; to be an explorer; to be a famous aviatrix.

'I'd like my name to go down in the history books,' she said at one time.

'Well, if you do all the things you've talked about, it will,' Jessie said.

Emma certainly brought life to the house, and when Jessie took her over to Morland Place, she seemed to cheer up the inhabitants so much that Henrietta talked wistfully about having her to stay there, if only Jessie could spare her. Emma thought Morland Place wonderfully romantic, and begged so to see the drawbridge raised and lowered that Teddy roused himself from his sad inertia and went out to see about it. The mechanism, however, had rusted with long disuse and couldn't be moved. He apologised profusely to Emma and promised her that he would have it fixed for 'your next visit'.

Jessie was shocked to discover that Emma couldn't ride – 'There was never any need for it in London. I don't think Daddy can ride either' – and set about giving her lessons right away. Emma took to it readily, and was off the leading-rein in the second lesson. By the end of the first week she was able to keep up with Jessie, and the two young women rode every day, going further afield as Jessie showed her the Morland estate and something of the countryside. She couldn't play tennis, either, and having been introduced to the Cornleighs, who had a tennis lawn behind their house, she was taught by one of Ethel's younger sisters, and was soon knocking the ball about with almost as much accuracy as gusto.

The visit passed quickly. Jessie divided Emma's time between Maystone, Morland Place and the Cornleighs' house; and with riding, tennis, family dinners, and the sort of cheerful evenings of games and music that the Cornleighs always seemed to generate, there was no need to risk the hostility of York at all. For Emma, everything was so different from her life at home in London that she was perpetually in a whirl of excitement. Jessie taught her how to groom and saddle her own horse, and in an empty field gave her a driving lesson in Uncle Teddy's small Renault. At Morland Place she fell in love with the dogs, cooed over the babies in the nursery, and played for hours with James William. She helped with the plum-picking and, at her own request, learned to milk a cow.

Polly thought her both beautiful and exciting and soon had quite a 'crush' for her. One day when she rode over to Maystone to visit, Emma took her up to her room and let her try on her finest clothes, turned up her hair for her, and won Polly's heart for ever by saying that she looked 'nineteen at least'.

The most remarkable thing to Jessie was Uncle Teddy's teaching Emma to shoot. She had no idea how it came about, whether Emma asked or Uncle Teddy offered, but either way it was a wonder, when he had barely left the house since he came back from America. First he had her shooting at a cardboard target on the Long Walk; then, after a few lessons, he took her out after pigeons in Acomb Wood. She didn't get anything, but Jessie told her it was no disgrace. 'Pigeons are very difficult to hit.'

'Have you ever got any?'

'One or two.'

'Oh, you do have such an exciting life in Yorkshire!' Emma sighed. 'I can't think why you wanted to come to London when there's so much to do here.'

'Variety is nice,' Jessie said, remembering Oliver's words. 'I love Yorkshire, but London was a change for me.'

'And your mother is just the most perfect mother in the world,' Emma went on. 'If I had a mother I'd want her to be just like that.'

'I think she's very nice too,' Jessie said, smiling. 'I can't give her up to you entirely, but I'll share her with you, if you like.'

She meant it as a joke, but Emma took it quite seriously. 'Would you really?' she asked. 'Do you think she'd mind?'

Henrietta was perfectly happy to be surrogate mother to Emma, and gave her a hug and said she must come and stay any time she liked. 'You've cheered us all up wonderfully,' she said.

'I'd like to stay here for ever,' Emma said.

But in her third week Ned had a telephone call from Tommy Weston one evening to say that he had recovered from his treatment and was eager to have Emma back. He did not want to waste any of the time they had left together.

She took the whole of the next day to say goodbye to everyone and everything, and on the day after that she was put on the train for London, with Tomlinson to escort her. As well as her luggage she had a basket containing several pounds of plums, a Morland Place cheese and a bottle of Henrietta's own cherry brandy for her father; and she took with her a permanent invitation to Morland Place and the promise of a puppy next time. She left behind a small part of her heart, and for several weeks at Brighton she dreamed at night of Ned's face; until, in the normal way for sixteen-year-olds, she fell in love with the riding-master Tommy hired to indulge her new-found passion for horses.

CHAPTER FIFTEEN

Emma Weston's visit marked a stage in Teddy's recovery from the shock and horror of the *Titanic* tragedy. She seemed to have broken through his terrible lethargy, and he began to come out of himself a little and take an interest in things again.

Alice was out of bed and had resumed her normal domestic round, though she was still weak and tired easily. A gentle walk out of doors was all the daily exercise she took, and Teddy liked to take it with her. Arm in arm they would stroll around the moat or through the gardens for an hour, stopping to sit when Alice grew tired, chatting comfortably about the flowers or the weather or the house. But now that Emma had broken the ice with the shooting expedition to Acomb Woods, he began to go further afield.

He still would not go into York, or into public. He would not even go out walking anywhere that took him close to other habitations, but there was plenty of his own land where he could roam safely without meeting anyone. He took a gun and his dogs out after rabbits or pigeons, went riding, walked up to look at Jessie's horses or examine a crop, and the gentle hand of nature laid a balm over his wounds.

He began to conduct business again, though only at home, and through his secretary, agent and steward. There was no entertaining at Morland Place, and Teddy and Alice did not accept any invitations, though there were a few from friends loyal to them, who wanted to show their confidence in him. But it was all too painful for him even to consider going into company: the subject might be raised, there might be

301

looks, comments – and even kindly ones would hurt. He did not even go to the Cornleighs, and when Mr and Mrs Cornleigh called he always managed to slip out of the house without seeing them.

The horror of the sinking, the pitiful cries of the hundreds dying in the black water, still haunted him; the terrible, unjust things that had been said about him rankled in the most bitter way. But the worst thing of all was the deep conviction, which he could hardly bear to acknowledge to himself, that he should not have survived. The guilt ate at his soul. He remembered all those other men from the first class who had put their wives and children into the boats and then gone back down to the saloon to die like gentlemen. What people said about him – that he had forced his way onto a boat at the expense of others – was not true; but there was a seed of truth in it. He was ashamed.

So he cut himself off from all except his family. But he was a man still in the vigour of his years, and as his body recovered from the physical effects of the shock, he found a need to be doing, and the estate gave him the outlet. The land was forgiving; the earth, the trees, the crops would not judge him; the cattle and sheep, horses, pigs and fowl would not shun him. He began to make plans for the working and improvement. He had a son, now, and one day James William would inherit all this. He must make sure he passed it on in good heart.

He was coming home one day with his gun under his arm, and Digby and Danby, his pointers, trotting on either side of him. He had not got anything today, and they remained hopeful, looking up every few steps to see if he was going to swing the gun to his shoulder. The spaniel Muffy still coursed about from one side of the path to the other, nose deep in the odours of the grass; Bell, who had met them half a mile from home, frisked foolishly, trying to entice someone into a game.

It was a fine late September day, with all of summer's stored heat in it, a golden, ripe heat that spoke of harvests and apples and the good laziness of lying in the long grass staring up at the sky. The events of a bitter black night five months ago seemed far away. The walk had pleasantly tired him and the sweetness of the natural world had relaxed him, so his mind for once was not tormenting him.

As he approached the drawbridge, he saw a man coming towards him along the track from the village direction. All three of his own dogs stopped at the sight and began growling; Bell, who had been frisking in the hedgerow, had not seen or smelt him yet. Teddy slipped the gun down into his grip and closed the breech. It was not loaded, of course, but would serve as a club if necessary. The man was not someone he knew, and there was something odd about him. His clothes were poor and dirty, though not ragged. He had a greasy cap on his head, and walked with his hands stuffed into his pockets, with a curious, rolling gait. He had a full beard, which was unusual enough in these days, and it was grizzled, though he did not look old. His skin was very tanned, and perhaps dirty too – dark enough, at any rate, to make him look almost foreign.

He reached the drawbridge before Teddy, and stopped there, watching him. Bell had seen him now, and approached with his head lowered and his hackles up, growling. The man did not seem to notice the hound at all. He had taken his hands from his pockets and was looking at Teddy eagerly, clenching and unclenching his fists in an odd, snatching movement. When Teddy was still a few paces off, and wondering what was going to happen, the man called out to him: 'Mr Morland! Mr Morland, sir. It is you. I know you. I seen you before.' He had a country accent, but not from these parts. The south or south-west country, Teddy thought.

'What do you want?' Teddy said. He stopped, the dogs making a bristling hedge round him. The man was between him and the house, but he seemed to have no weapon, and what could he do against a man and four dogs, except be a nuisance? 'I don't know you.'

'No, sir, no, sir. You don't know me, rightly speaking, but I know you,' said the man. He moved about on the spot, as well as making that strange hand movement, and his eyes were not constant, but flitted about.

Teddy came to the thought that he was mad – a madman. That would account for the dogs' hostility. But was he a dangerous madman? 'What do you want?' he asked again.

'I've been looking for you, Mr Morland, sir. Walked all this way from Leeds, where I got dropped off. Carrier gave me a ride from Liverpool. Walking's not natural to me, as you might say. I don't like walking. But I had to see you. Was going to call at the house when I seed you coming. I know you, sir. Don't remember me, do you?'

'I've never seen you before in my life,' Teddy said impatiently. If this man had come begging, he was going the wrong way about it. This was the first stranger he had spoken to for weeks, and he didn't like it a bit.

'On the *Titanic*, sir. Barrett's my name – Fred Barrett. Fireman on the *Titanic* – transferred from the *Olympic*, like a lot of us was. I was in the lifeboat with you, sir. A hull lot of us firemen got in afore you, don't you remember? Soaked and wore out and half mad, we was, be the time we got topsides. But I watched you and Mr Ismay come over the side into the ole lifeboat, got a good look at you, sir, so I never forgot your face.'

The man had fidgeted closer, and Teddy could see that the darkness of his face was in part due to ingrained coal dust. His eyes were pale blue, and the contrast with his dark skin gave them a mad look. When he licked his lips his tongue looked pale, too, and much too pink.

'Get away from me,' Teddy said, and the dogs, who had quietened, began growling again.

The man seemed to see them at last, looked from them to the gun, held defensively before Teddy, and he looked a little dazed. He opened his clenched hands in a universal gesture. 'I don't mean no harm, sir. No, sir. I just want to talk to you. *Got* to talk to you.'

'Well, I don't want to talk to you. I don't talk about that ship, not to anyone. Get on your way, Barrett, and don't come here again.'

The man was unmoved by the command, or the gesture Teddy made with the gun. 'No more don't I want to talk about her,' he said, with calm urgency, 'but I got to, and

you got to hear me, sir, because there's no-one else. I tried
and tried, but no-one won't listen. They all think I'm mad,
but I'm not, sir. And the newspaper fellers, and the lawyers,
and Board o' Trade – I don't know any more who was in
on it and who wasn't. But I know you're straight, sir, a
honest man, and they've treated you shabby, like they done
to me. You'll hear me out, I know you will, because you
want to know the truth, don't you, sir?'

Despite himself, Teddy was caught. Mad, perhaps – even
probably – and who wouldn't be mad, having gone through
what this man must have gone through? But a rogue, no,
he didn't think so. And the truth? Didn't everyone always
want the truth? Was there something about that ship he
needed to know? She stood out in his mind ringed in a
doomed light, always there in the background of his
thoughts, something he tried not to look at, was aware of
but would not turn to face.

'What—' he said, and had to stop and begin again because
his mouth was dry. 'What do you want to tell me?'

The man took a half-step nearer, his eyes burning into
Teddy's, and lowered his voice as though someone might over-
hear them. 'It warn't her, sir,' he said. 'No, sir, not her at all.'

'What are you talking about? Who wasn't her?'

Barrett shook his head. 'They looked the same, you see,
sir,' he went on confidentially. 'Well, you know that.
Identicule, they was. No-one couldn't tell 'em apart. And
no-one hadn't never seen the *Titanic* anyway, only them in
the dockyard. So it was easy.'

Teddy began to have an inkling of what the man was
talking about, and he felt the hair rise on the back of his
neck. The postcard Lizzie had sent from Queenstown –
Henrietta still had it. She had shown it to Teddy once, some
time after he had come home. It purported to be a picture
of *Titanic*, but in fact it was *Olympic*. All the photographs
that had been used by way of advertisement had been of
Olympic because there had not been time to take new ones
of *Titanic*, and in any case the ships were the same. Near
enough identical, as this man said. Near enough so that a
layman wouldn't tell them apart.

'What was easy?' he heard himself asking, though his voice seemed far away – as did the man Barrett and, indeed, everything around him on this sunny afternoon. The real world had become unreal; his thoughts were all that seemed convincing.

'Easy to swap 'em, sir,' Barrett said. 'In and out o' the graving dock, was the *Olympic*, all that year, turn and turn about with her sister. Nothing to tell 'em apart but the name plates, three on each of 'em, and easy enough to take them plates off and swap 'em. She was an unlucky ship, sir, the *Olympic*, that I do know. Some ships just are, you know it when you first goo aboard. You can feel it. I was near a year on the *Olympic*, and she had a bad feel about her, sir. I'm not the only one as felt it. Lots of us had the creeps about her – officers too. Mr Wilde, he fair hated her. An' I got that same feeling when I went aboard the *Titanic*, for to take her down to So'thampton. I said to Beecham, sir, a mate o' mine, this 'ere ain't the new ship at all, an' he agreed with me.'

'This is all you have – a feeling?'

'No, sir. There was little things you could reckernise, too. The place on her starboard quarter, f'rinstance, where the hull had been repaired – you could see it from inside, down below. One o' the bunkers caught on fire, sir, on the way down to So'thampton, and we was told to leave it burn, sir. Five days it burned, sir, 'fore they let us put it out, so as to hide where she'd been repaired. Oh, yes, we knew, sir, down the ingine-room. We knew.'

Teddy shook his head to clear it. 'If I understand what you're saying, why on earth would anyone want to swap the two ships?'

'She was bad damaged, sir,' Barrett said earnestly, pushing his face closer so that Teddy had to take a step back. 'Wuss 'n anyone reckoned. She wasn't never going to be no good after all them accidents. So they swapped her over with the new ship, for to take her out to sea and scuttle her. The new ship, see, she was insured, but old *Olympic* wasn't.'

'You're mad!' Teddy said, aghast.

'No, sir, no, sir.'

'Fifteen hundred people lost their lives!'

'They didn't mean for that to happen, sir, no, sir, only she sank so quick! Everyone'd've got off, normally. No, sir, I don't say they meant it to happen the way it did. But scuttle her, or damage her so bad she had to be scrapped, and get the insurance money – that was the plan. The way it worked out – well, that was the worst luck of all, and she always was an unlucky ship. But it's the *Olympic* that's at the bottom of the sea, sir, not the *Titanic*, and that's the truth of it.'

He stopped talking, and seemed exhausted now he had said his piece. His pale eyes wandered again, having been fixed and burning while he spoke. He looked tired. Under his worn black suit he was thin; his big hands were all knuckles. Teddy guessed he had not eaten for some time. Hunger was probably making him light-headed, to add to the madness brought on by the shock of the sinking. 'Very well,' he said. 'I've heard you out, and now I want you to go away.'

'But it's true, sir, every word!' Barrett protested.

'Even if it were true, what would you expect me to do about it?' Teddy said impatiently.

'Tell people,' said Barrett faintly. 'Tell everyone. Bring 'em to justice.'

'Bring who to justice?'

'I dunno, sir,' Barrett said. He seemed dazed. 'I thought you'd know. You're a gentleman, and you knew all o' them high-ups in Harland's and White Star.'

Teddy shook his head. 'Even if your story were true, it could never be proved. And it's not. It's a fairy-tale. Look here, here's money for you. You probably haven't eaten. Go away and get yourself something to eat, and then go home – wherever home is.' Barrett was staring at him despairingly, and Teddy hardened his face against him. 'Go away now. Go on! I want nothing to do with you, or your story. If you ever come here again I shall have you put in charge.'

'Sir!' Barrett protested, but weakly.

'If you take my advice, you won't talk about this again to anyone. There's such a thing as the law of slander, you know. You could find yourself in prison. Now be off with you! Go right away from here, or I'll set the dogs on you. Go!'

Barrett began clenching and unclenching his hands again, and the action made him look down at what he was holding – the money Teddy had thrust at him. He stared at it for a moment, then closed his hand round it and pushed it into his pocket. But he gave Teddy a long, steady look before he turned away, a look of hurt and reproach, which was more effective than any bluster could have been. Teddy stood his ground and watched until he was sure that the man was well away, walking slowly but steadily with that slight roll of the lifelong sailor. Then he called the dogs, who had sat down towards the end of this long conversation, and went in over the drawbridge. He took the time to tell Sawry that if the man Barrett ever showed his face again he was to be turned away at once and if necessary put in charge, then went to the steward's room where he could be alone.

He cleaned his Purdy, put it back into the gun cupboard and locked it, then poured himself a glass of sherry from the decanter that always lived on the side table and sat in the big old leather chair by the fireplace. He thought of Barrett's story – utter fantasy, the wild imaginings of a deranged mind. The poor fellow was crazy, and who could wonder? For those firemen deep under the waterline it must have been more dreadful than anything Teddy had experienced. He remembered his own sick fear when he had forced himself to go below to look for survivors. No, the man was mad, no doubt about it, and presumably he hadn't worked since, so poverty and hunger had affected him too, to make things worse.

And yet, he thought, and yet . . . Lord Pirrie, the owner of Harland and Wolff, and J. P. Morgan, the owner of the line, had both cancelled their passages on the *Titanic* at the last moment – as had a number of Morgan's friends. And there was the question of why the brand-new ship should have had a persistent list to port all the way across, in calm seas. Ashley and Penobscot had both noticed it.

He remembered the shocked, almost dazed look on the

captain's face: of course, Smith knew that he was doomed to go down with his ship, but then first Officer Murdoch also knew he was doomed, and had not looked like that. A man who had meant to scuttle his ship, only to have it happen too soon, with disastrous consequences, might look like that, perhaps.

But, no, it was nonsense, utter nonsense. He finished his sherry and stood up, ready to go upstairs, see Alice, and change. And then something came to him that stopped him in his tracks. He stared blankly at the wall, seeing not what was before him, but a bright window opened in memory. He saw Thomas Andrews standing before the fireplace in the smoking room – the last time he had seen him. What was it he had muttered? Hadn't it been 'Can't tell them apart'?

And then he had said, he had said – Teddy squeezed out the memory. The picture was as clear as a lighted room, but the words wouldn't come just at first. Then he got it. Andrews had said, 'Did you ever notice, on the *Olympic*, the tiny flaw in the enamel of the clock face? Just here.'

What had he meant by that? Teddy stared at the memory, still now, with Andrews frozen in time as Teddy had last seen him, his hand up to adjust the clock. Had there been a flaw in the clock face? Teddy had not gone close enough to look. He had barely heeded the words in any case, having had other things on his mind at the time. He had turned away and left and never gone back, never seen Andrews again; Andrews, whose body was presumably at the bottom of the sea with the ship he had loved, surrounded by the debris of the most fabulous artefact man's ingenuity had ever created. Gone, wasted, lost for ever.

If there had been a flaw in the clock face, the one person who would have known about it, who would have noticed, was Thomas Andrews.

He shook himself out of his thoughts and turned for the door. It was impossible. It was nonsense. It was madness. He stamped out determinedly and went up the chapel stairs to find his wife.

★   ★   ★

'Will you be wearing your Paris gown to the mayor's banquet?' Ned asked. 'The pink silk?'

On the other side of the breakfast table, Jessie looked up in surprise. 'Surely we aren't going?'

Ned waited until Daltry had put down the coffee-pot and gone out before replying. 'Of course we are,' he said.

'But Uncle Teddy isn't going,' Jessie said. 'They didn't invite him. Mother told me yesterday.'

'I know.'

'You *know*? Then – I don't understand.' She became indignant. 'You can't mean to make up to people who snub him?'

'It's not a question of making up to people.'

'Oh? Then what is it?'

'It's a matter of being seen, keeping contact with the right people, making oneself agreeable. I don't care for these things, but it's important for me to be there – important for my business,' he said.

'Your precious business,' she said witheringly.

'It's what keeps a roof over our heads and puts food on the table. You know perfectly well that things have been bad, first with the coal strike and then this terrible business with the newspapers. Everyone in the Chamber of Commerce will be at the Mansion House, along with all the influential people of York and the county.'

'All except Uncle Teddy,' said Jessie, staring at him angrily. 'Well, you may do as you please, but I'm not having anything to do with people who treat my uncle that way. I should have thought you'd have more loyalty, after all he's done for you.'

'Don't you think I care for him every bit as much as you do?'

'I begin to wonder,' Jessie said. She saw how her words had hurt him, and was both glad and afraid. That they should be at odds on this of all subjects made him seem suddenly like a stranger, rather than the man she had slept beside last night. 'Poor Uncle Teddy is cut from the guest list, when he's been invited every single year until now, and you want to go and pretend that nothing has happened, and smile and be agreeable, as you put it, to the very people who are breaking his heart!'

'Lower your voice,' Ned said. 'Do you want the servants to hear?'

'I don't care who hears me,' she said, but she did lower her voice. She didn't want to quarrel with him, but everything about the way her uncle had been calumnised sickened her, and her helplessness to change the situation was unbearably frustrating. 'I'm not going, and that's that!' she declared.

'You *will* go,' he said. He was angry too, for many of the same reasons.

'You can't make me,' she snapped.

'Yes, I can, and I will,' he said, in a low, intense voice. 'You are my wife, and you will do as I tell you. Understand me, Jessie, I *will* be master in my own house.'

She was so surprised by the words that they silenced her, and she looked at him with her eyes wide.

He took advantage of her silence to say, 'I've always let you run on a pretty free rein, because I know it's what you're used to and I like to see you happy. But you married me of your own free will, and marriage involves some sacrifices and obligations. There are times when you must obey me, even when you don't like it. We have been invited together to the Mansion House, and you will appear there on my arm, because that is what's expected. Your absence would cause unpleasant speculation. I won't be made a fool of, especially by my own wife.'

She opened her mouth to answer, but at that moment Daltry came back in with a rack of toast, and she snapped it shut again. She was dumbfounded by what Ned had said. They had grown up together, played together, and in her mind he was still, to a large extent, her dear old cousin Ned. There was a sense in which the Ned she slept with, the lord of her bed, was a different person, someone who existed only in the dark. That exciting stranger, who did such secret and wonderful things to her, was additional to, rather than the successor of, the Ned who had always admired and flattered and tried to please her. She had always had the upper hand in their relationship, and she had never thought that that might be changed by marriage. The idea of his telling

311

her what she should and should not do was astonishing to her.

While Daltry's presence prevented them speaking, she studied the face of the man opposite her, and noticed that he looked tired and a little drawn. There were frown lines in his forehead and the creases beside his mouth seemed to have deepened. The worry of the situation had marked him. He looked, she realised with an inward shiver, older – and more than that, suddenly very much a grown-up. She did not feel like a grown-up, not in that way. Inside her, she was still at heart her mother's daughter, Uncle Teddy's niece, the young lady of Morland Place. Maystone Villa was a play-house; but now Ned had suddenly shown himself a real husband.

Daltry left them again – so very much *not* noticing the prevailing atmosphere that, despite Jessie's inner turbulence, one part of her mind wanted to laugh. When they were alone, she determined to get her word in first, but kept her voice down and tried to speak reasonably, though it quivered with the force of her emotions.

'I really, really can't go to the Mansion House. It isn't that I don't want to be a good wife to you, but you must see that people – one's own people – are far more important than any old business.'

'It's not—'

'I'd sooner starve than hurt my family, and I'd have thought you'd feel the same.' Under the table Brach whined softly and licked her hand, disturbed by the heat in her voice. 'I don't understand how you can *want* to go when they've cut Uncle Teddy like that.'

'Jessie, will you listen to me?' he said. He spoke with such urgency that she subsided, and looked at him in silence. He was a little pale. He said, '*I* don't understand how you can believe that I care nothing about my father. How can you not know me after all this time?' She saw then that she had hurt him more than she realised. 'If we stayed away, people would think we were ashamed, or afraid to face them. They'd think there must be something in the talk after all. But if we go, and behave normally, they'll understand that we don't mean to be intimidated. It may not be pleasant, but we'll face them down. We can't spend the rest of our lives skulking in the shadows and not meeting people's eyes. We have to go into the world with our heads held high, and show everybody that we are proud to bear the Morland name, because *we* know that nothing has been done to tarnish it.'

He stopped then, and she waited a moment to be sure he had finished. And then she said passionately, 'But you're wrong! People won't think what you just said. If we go, they'll think that we're just currying favour at any cost. We have to stay away and show that we side with our own people, and that they can't buy us with trifles.'

He shook his head slowly. 'I understand your argument, but you must trust me to know best about this.' He tried a faint smile. 'Don't you believe I want to do what's right, for Father as well as for us? For all the Morlands? Don't you believe that?'

'Well – yes – I suppose so.'

'You suppose so?' The smile was gone.

'Oh – yes, of course I know you love Uncle Teddy. But I do too, and that's how I *know* we must stay away. You're wrong, Ned, you're wrong! And I won't go!'

'Jessie—'

'No!' She pushed her chair back violently and jumped up. 'I won't talk about it any more!' she cried, and ran from the room. Brach got up, extricated herself from the table and chair legs and tried to follow, but the door swung shut before she could get to it. She stood looking at it hopefully, her tail swinging, then gave a plaintive whine and raised a paw to rattle the doorknob.

Ned got up and walked across the room to open it for her. She wriggled out as soon as the crack was wide enough and trotted off across the hall with a clattering of her nails, looking for her mistress. Ned returned to his seat, poured himself some more coffee, and opened the newspaper, but though he stared at the print he was unable to read a single word. He felt scraped out inside by the quarrel, but worst of all was the thought that he had it all to do again. He had not convinced her. He racked his brain for more and better arguments, for the worst thing of all would be to force her to go against her judgement, which was what he would have to do in the last event.

Brach found Jessie out in the stables, tacking up Hotspur. She had been already dressed for riding, but in her anger had not stopped to collect either jacket or hat, and sent Gladding, the stableman, away with a sharp word when he came to see what she wanted. He gave her a queer look and left her alone, but he hovered nearby, obviously intrigued by the situation, which only made her angrier, so that she fumbled the straps and pinched poor Hotspur's mouth with the bit.

But she had him ready at last, led him out and scrambled up from the mounting block, half afraid Ned would followed her out to continue the argument. He didn't, of course; and she rode out of the gate with Brach at her heels and Gladding wandering into the middle of the yard for a good stare and a scratch of the head.

She had to ride along Water End to begin with, because it was the only way to cross the river. It was so *stupid* to live in Clifton, she thought, with the river between her and Morland Place, forgetting that it had never bothered her before. People stared at her as she passed, and when a neighbour, Mrs Warne, gave her a very severe look she began to wish she had stopped long enough to get her jacket and hat before storming out. But after the bridge there were no more houses, and as soon as she had crossed the railway and the Roman road she was on Morland land and safe.

She did not ride towards Morland Place, however. She wanted to be alone with her turmoil, and turned away through the North Field and out onto Low Moor. There she had a good gallop until Hotspur began to flag, then turned back and let him walk on a loose rein towards the far side of the Whin. She had a favourite spot there, where the little wandering Smawith Dike met the trees, and a fallen trunk made a good seat from which to view the wide moor and the distant roofs of Hessay. Brach soon found her – she had got left behind in the gallop. Having greeted Jessie with the enthusiasm of one who has been parted for months rather than minutes, she flopped down on her side on the cool turf and was soon snoring and twitching her big paws in dream.

It was a lovely day, more like August than October in the warmth and softness of the air. The trees still had a base of green against which to display their reds and gold. The sky was a high, intense blue, and large, achingly white clouds sailed slowly across it with the grandeur and glamour of great ships. But the thought of ships brought her straight back to Uncle Teddy and the happiness that riding always engendered evaporated.

Uncle Teddy had been involved in what would become part of history. The loss of the *Titanic* was a public event, as were the hearings and everything that had been written in the newspapers. The calumny heaped on him was public property, and she knew that no matter what was said or done, no matter what evidence anyone brought forward to the contrary, there would always be people who believed that Uncle Teddy and Mr Ismay were villains. It was there in black and white, preserved for ever. In years to come, when she and her family were all dead and gone, people would read what had been said and believe it.

She clenched her fists in frustration. There was nothing she could do, *nothing*, to change any of that. But here in York, in their own circle, they could at least show what they thought of the accusation – and the accusers.

And that thought brought her straight to Ned. He was wrong, she was sure of it; and yet he was prepared to make her go against her will and her conscience. The thing that shocked her was the notion that he should feel he had the right to tell her what to do.

At home, before she married, she had occupied a privileged position. She had been the daughter of the house, and her father's particular pet, and few things were absolutely forbidden her. In the years immediately before her marriage she had enjoyed a freedom of movement and decision not known to many unmarried girls. Her late father had left her his share in the horse-breeding business, which she had been running for him during his illness, so she regarded herself as an independent businesswoman.

She had had many admirers, a coterie of nice young men who flattered her, hung on her every word, and seemed to ask nothing greater of life than to be allowed to ride beside her at the hunt, partner her at tennis, fetch her ice-cream at a ball. She had not wanted to marry any of them, which she realised in retrospect had given her a certain power over them.

To acknowledge the authority of any man who had been a supplicant for her favour would have gone against the grain, but somehow it was especially hard with Ned. She supposed that might be the penalty of marrying a cousin she had grown up with, and who therefore did not come wrapped in a package of glamour and mystery.

She felt that if making her own decisions was not to be allowed in marriage, she should have been warned. Why were girls not told that the man who solicited a smile from you as if he were the lowest mendicant on earth would turn into a sultan once you married him? She remembered Ned's words: *I will be master in my own house.* Why didn't her mother tell her beforehand that that was what marriage meant?

She sighed, coming to no conclusion, except that it was all very hard. She stood up, and Brach woke with a grunt from a deep dream, lifted her head and looked about her with such obvious bewilderment that it made Jessie laugh.

She stirred the hound with the toe of her boot. 'Come on, foolish. It was a dream, that's all.' For a moment Brach looked at her with unfathomable yellow eyes, and her lips lifted from her savage white teeth so that she looked like an untamed wolf. But it was only the precursor to a tremendous yawn, one of those that made the ears touch behind, and then Brach clambered to her feet, tail swinging, and banged her head against Jessie's knee as a suggestion that they move on.

Jessie laughed and rubbed the rough head and said, 'Yes, we're going now. You're just a dog, aren't you? Just a big old dog.'

Brach smiled in agreement. Jessie unhitched Hotspur's reins from the bush she had been using, tightened the girth and used the tree trunk to mount. Yes, Brach was just a dog, but she had a wolf's heritage, and the teeth were real teeth. A creature that seemed tame and gentle could still have hidden powers, which they chose not to exercise. Chose not to.

By evening, Jessie's mind was if possible even more unsettled. The activities of her day, both domestic and at the stable, had done nothing to distract her from the feelings of confusion, frustration, indignation and worry. Ned was late back from the mill again – he had telephoned while she was out and left a message that he would be – so she had set back dinner by half an hour: they were dining alone that evening, fortunately. But still he did not arrive home until she was already dressed and, sitting before the dressing-table with nothing more to do, wondering whether she ought to put dinner back yet further.

But she heard the sound of the motor below and calculated that if he changed quickly and they did not take sherry beforehand the meat would not be ruined. Her heart began to beat faster as she heard his footsteps on the stairs, and she hoped he would go straight to the dressing-room, and put off the impending argument until later. After a good dinner and a bottle of claret he might be more amenable to reason.

But the steps paused outside the bedroom door, and then he came in quickly, closed the door behind him and leaned against it. His sudden appearance and her taut feelings made her jump to her feet in a movement that looked guilty.

'You're very late,' she said, in the desire to say something, anything, rather than endure a silence.

'Yes,' he said. 'I'm sorry. There were things to do.'

He looked tired to death, she thought, and a surge of pity and affection went through her. If only they could put this business behind them – if only he would agree with her – she would enjoy being kind to him again. Better, perhaps, not to postpone it. 'Ned, about the mayor's banquet—'

'Yes,' he said. 'We have to talk about that.'

'I've been thinking about it all day,' she said.

'I hope you've been thinking to good purpose,' he said, and he looked so grim that it rankled.

Her brows snapped together. 'If by that you mean giving in to you—'

He sighed and pushed a hand over his forehead and into his hair. 'Jessie, don't try to make a quarrel out of this. Can't you just accept that I am older than you, and wiser in the ways of the world, and that I must know better than you what's right to do?'

'Not if it means truckling to the people who are hurting my uncle,' she said defiantly.

'It would be truckling to them to stay away,' he said in exasperation. 'Don't you understand? That's what they want us to do, the people who are cutting him. It would be a triumph for them if we went into exile too. Why should we give them an easy victory?'

'If they wanted us to stay away, why did they invite us?'

'It's a struggle between two factions, the pros and the antis. The antis got my father cut, but the pros got us invited. If we don't go, we've let the antis win.'

This new perspective silenced her. He pressed his advantage. 'I know you think that a Morland bows the neck to no-one. Well, I've exactly the same amount of Morland blood in me as you have. Why won't you trust me?'

She opened her mouth to retort, then closed it again, shocked with herself at what she had been about to say. She had been going to remind him what his mother had been; to remind him of his illegitimacy. In her desire – no, her *need* – to get her own way, she had been ready to hurt him with the deadliest weapon in her arsenal. She looked at him, and for once saw him as a person outside her; not her cousin or her husband or *her* anything, but an individual quite separate, with his own set of feelings, desires and fears, his own inner landscape as individual and undeniable as hers. He was a man, and she was suddenly, powerfully aware of the fact. He had a man's tall, hard body, a man's smell, a man's mind, a man's power; extraordinarily, physical desire suddenly thrust up in her, hard and imperative. Their eyes met, and she saw the recognition in his of what she was feeling. A light flush coloured his work-pale cheeks, and his eyes seemed to spark. She looked at his lips, and then at his hands, those male hands that could be so gentle when they were alone together in the darkness.

'Jessie,' he said, and his voice was husky. 'I love you. I would never lead you wrong. Don't you know that?'

Somehow she had crossed the room to him. Her body took her, without her mind's authority. She was in his arms, those male hands touched her waist, pressed against her back, he was kissing her neck, her ear, his breath coming shorter.

'I love you, I love you,' he whispered.

A desire so fierce it was making her legs weak, a desire like something molten in the pit of her stomach, overwhelmed everything in her, all thought, and she lifted her face, nudging his round so that she could find his mouth. They kissed, and there was both relief and imperative in it for her.

It was he who stopped – she had gone beyond caring about time, servants, dinner, anything in the worldly world. He said, 'Later. My darling, later. Oh, God. I must change, we must go to dinner.' And he kissed her again, and dragged himself loose from her. His face was flushed, his hair ruffled, his eyes bright. He smiled at her and said, 'You're so beautiful. Go down – I'll change like lightning.'

And he went away. She remained in the bedroom a moment longer, feeling weak and sick with unsatisfied desire. Yes, he was wolf as well as domestic dog; he was her husband as well as her cousin Ned. And she knew something else about him too, now – that he needed her to love him, to agree with him, to esteem him, far more than she needed that of him. She went slowly downstairs, her thoughts a tumble: dinner, their quarrel, the banquet, the evening to come, the night after that. He did change very quickly, joined her before she had begun to think clearly again, just as Daltry – no doubt at the urging of Mrs Peck – stepped through to announce that dinner was ready.

She did not notice what she ate, though she had perhaps more wine than she usually did, which warmed and relaxed her and set her thoughts running faster but less turbulently, like a stream that had got past the rocky narrows and into a deep bed. Ned set himself to entertain her, as he had used to when he was courting her. She had forgotten how amusing he could be, how well he talked – knowing intimately, as he did, what would interest her. He did not mention the banquet again, and she allowed herself to be charmed: laughing, sparkling, accepting the tribute of his attention as if he were still supplicant and she the capricious mistress who might grant or withhold favour. But the brightness of his eyes said that he anticipated no rebuff.

For the sake of the servants they moved to the drawing room and took coffee, but it was the merest gesture. Soon they were walking up the stairs, to part at the bedroom door for the brief period that only enhanced anticipation. Then he came through from the dressing-room, locked the door, and took her in his arms.

At some point during the night that followed she realised that she had tacitly allowed him to win over the mayor's banquet; but she found she did not much care. He would have insisted she go, so it was as well to let him have his way with a good grace, rather than continue the quarrel. And she supposed he might be right about it after all: perhaps as a man of affairs he understood the public perception of such actions better than her. In the languor of sated passion she felt it hardly mattered, and wondered that she had been so agitated about it. Uncle Teddy and everyone important to her knew how she felt and would not misjudge her motives. What mattered was this power she had over Ned. He might order her to do things in the outside world, but here in bed he came to her trembling with desire and need. She turned over on her side to look at him sleeping, and found that his eyes were open. She smiled and reached out to touch his face, stroke it with the tips of her fingers. He caught her hand and kissed it, and then, almost with a groan, drew her to him again.

BOOK THREE

At Hazard

Let thy young wanderer dream on:
Call him not home.
A door opens, a breath, a voice
From the ancient room,
Speaks to him now. Be it dark or bright
He is knit with his doom.

George William Russell, 'Germinal'

CHAPTER SIXTEEN

Things had moved quickly in the world of flying in 1912. Following the foundation of the Royal Flying Corps in April, a Royal Aircraft Factory had been built at Farnborough. A Central Flying School, on the training gallops near Upavon village, had opened to train flyers – or 'pilots', as they were beginning to be called, a term borrowed from ballooning – for the coming war. A mark of the government's new interest in the military application of flying was the Military Aeroplane Competition held in July on Salisbury Plain, for which both Jack and Tom Sopwith had been asked to test machines.

In July the Sopwith school had taken on a new pupil whose name was familiar to Jack. Major Hugh Trenchard chose Sopwith's establishment on the recommendation of Miss Ormerod's father, an old friend. The major, thirty-nine years old and well over six feet tall, was hardly ideal material to make a flyer. He explained to Tom Sopwith his predicament: he wanted to take a course at the Central Flying School, but had to get his ticket first – and within four weeks, or he would be over-age for the course. He took his first lesson on the 18th of July. Jack discovered that, although the major was not what he would have called a natural flyer, he was intelligent, disciplined, and utterly determined to succeed. By the last day of the month he had passed his test and was awarded his ticket, no. 270.

Another pupil to pass during that month was Jack's former employer, Howard Wright, who was now designing aeroplanes for the Coventry Ordnance Works. In between lessons he and Jack had many an interesting conversation about aeroplane design, and especially about the machine Jack and the Sopwith team were building – a new tractor biplane. Jack also taught a young Australian, Harry Hawker, who was a natural, talented flyer and a genial, amusing young man. He had soon joined the school to help Jack test new machines.

The school had some success that summer in competitions. In August, while Tom Sopwith was on another visit to America, Jack spent time down in Southampton in discussion with another former employer, the owner of Rankin Marine, over the possibility of building a flying boat. The advantages of landing on the water rather than the land were obvious, and Mr Rankin was very interested in the project. Carrying mail, he suggested to Jack, would be revolutionised by a reliable flying-boat service.

When Sopwith returned from America, he and Jack concentrated on readying the tractor biplane. Jack flew it to Farnborough in October to demonstrate it to the Royal Aircraft Factory, with such success that an order was placed for one for the naval wing of the Corps. Work was also completed on the Burgess Wright hybrid in time to enter it for the Michelin endurance prize, but this time it was young Harry Hawker who flew it. Three attempts failed through minor technical faults or bad weather, but on the 24th of October Hawker managed to stay up for eight hours twenty-three minutes, a new British record. During the attempt, Jack and Sopwith both took aeroplanes up and flew round with Hawker to keep him company. On the ground, Miss Ormerod helped Fred Sigrist to keep score, looked after Rug, and was ready with hot tea when any of the flyers came down.

Jack was so used to Miss Ormerod's presence and company that he felt a little odd when she was not around. Her father had put in the telephone, and Jack was accustomed to call and ask if she would care to accompany him to exhibitions, competitions and displays – had even telephoned to ask if she could pick him up in her little motor when he came down in a ditch one time after engine failure.

She nearly always seemed to be available. In reciprocation, he had been invited several times to play tennis at the Ormerods' large, comfortable house, Fairoaks; and once to make up a theatre party with Miss Ormerod's parents and her married older brother Freddie and his wife.

One day in August, when Jack motored down to Southampton to watch a demonstration of the Compton 5, the latest version of a speed-boat he had designed while at Rankin Marine, he had bethought himself to ask Miss Ormerod if she would like to come too, for the outing. For decency's sake, her sister Mary accompanied them: though Miss Ormerod was no chit of a girl, a long day out in the country in a motor, alone with a man and unaccountable, was not considered the thing for an unmarried young woman, and Miss Ormerod's father was particular.

It was a fine day, and they motored along in great good humour. In recognition both of the amount of motoring he was doing, and his increasing salary, he had recently exchanged his little Peugeot 10 h.p. two-seater for a four-year-old 18 h.p. Armstrong-Whitworth. It had a landaulette body, and was a very smart dark green with black mouldings, and green leather upholstery. It was in some style, therefore, that he drove the Ormerod sisters, and he was pleased to note that Miss Ormerod had honoured the occasion with a new outfit of pale blue and buff and a hat almost large enough to be called foolish – large enough, anyway, to require a veil to be tied over it.

Miss Mary – Molly – sat in the back with Rug for company. Rug loved to motor almost as much as to fly, and hung over the side, facing into the wind, ears blown backwards, with his mouth wide and his eyes screwed almost shut in bliss. Every now and then some flying insect would be blown into his mouth, and he would have a coughing fit, which always brought on monumental sneezes. Molly was enchanted by him and went into fits of laughter.

'When you take him up with you in an aeroplane, does he have his own goggles?' she asked. 'He ought to be wearing them now, so that he can see the scenery.'

Miss Ormerod, sitting beside Jack in the front, enjoyed

the speed at which Jack liked to drive, enjoyed the fat, green country of England reeling past her beyond the dusty hedges, and reflected that with Molly along, this was likely to be the most privacy she would have that day for communicating something delicate to Jack. She glanced sideways at him, at his strong profile, his lean, tanned cheeks, the sun freckles across his nose, his brown, capable hands on the steering-wheel, and sighed inwardly, wishing she might be talking to him about herself instead.

But she said bravely, 'I have something to tell you – something I think you ought to know.'

Jack smiled – how she loved his smile! 'That sounds ominous.'

'Does it?'

'If you have to tell me you want to tell me something, rather than simply telling me, it must mean you think it's something I had rather not know.'

'Well, I suppose it is,' she said. 'Or I think it may be. I don't know precisely.'

Now Jack laughed. 'Coiling yourself in toils! Come, out with it. I can't think of anything you might say to me that you need be afraid of.'

'All right. You asked for it,' she said. 'Miss Fairbrother is getting married.'

'Oh,' said Jack.

Stealing glances at him, Miss Ormerod could not tell how the news had affected him. His smile faded, but it was replaced only with a slight, thoughtful frown, which could have meant anything. He didn't *look* heartbroken – but, then, he might well wish to conceal his feelings if they were deep.

He continued looking ahead at the road, and in the absence of anything further from him after the 'Oh', she went on: 'It's to be next Saturday, and a pretty grand affair, as far as I can gather. A hundred and fifty guests. Addlestone church is really quite handsome, and Mr Fairbrother will spare no expense, of course, so it should be a good show. Miss Fairbrother is to have eight bridesmaids and her gown has been made in London. She will,' Miss Ormerod went on, faltering a little as she got no response, 'make a beautiful bride.'

'Yes,' said Jack, and seemed to rouse himself a little, to say, 'It's that fellow I saw her with at the Richardsons', is it?'

'Charles Devereux,' Miss Ormerod confirmed.

'The man with no chin,' Jack mused.

'He's very well-to-do,' Miss Ormerod said, and then, thinking that sounded rather unkind, she added, 'He's a very decent sort, from what I hear of him.'

'This Saturday?' Jack said. 'Well, I hope it stays fine for them.'

For the life of her, Miss Ormerod could not tell if this was sarcasm or not; and after a moment's reflection, saw no reason why she should not be told. 'I hope you're not very upset,' she said.

Jack considered, and then said, 'I think I'm over the worst of my disappointment.'

'She wouldn't have done for you, you know,' Miss Ormerod said, greatly daring. 'I know she was very pretty, but she wouldn't have shared your interests.'

'Does a man generally expect a wife to? Females have their own interests, inhabit their own world. One can't expect them to think like a man, or be interested in men's things. That's the charm of them, that they're different from us.'

Miss Ormerod felt depressed. 'Well,' she said glumly, 'I'm glad you're not heartbroken about it.'

Jack glanced at her. 'I shan't be sobbing into my pillow tonight, if that's what you mean,' he said. 'I suppose it was the realisation that she didn't love me any more that upset me most. That she could love the Devereux fellow instead.'

Miss Ormerod closed her mouth tightly to stop herself telling him that, in her opinion, Miss Fairbrother did not love Charles Devereux, and had never loved him, Jack, either. It was not easy for her to speak about Myrtle Fairbrother – or even to think about her – without sounding catty.

And while she was controlling herself, Jack exclaimed, 'I say, look at that place – the Fox and Geese! Doesn't it look jolly? It's got a garden, too. What say we stop, see if we can get some bread and cheese and beer? I don't suppose we'll find anything prettier between here and Southampton. What do you think?'

'I'd love it,' Miss Ormerod said sincerely. He sounded so cheerful and normal, that she hoped Miss Fairbrother might soon be forgotten.

'Oh, yes, please,' said Molly promptly from the back, leaving Miss Ormerod to consider that her private conversation with Jack might not have been quite as drowned by motor noises as she had supposed.

The prize money from the Michelin competition in October was five hundred pounds, a considerable sum, and with that behind him, Tom Sopwith came to a decision, which he conveyed to Jack one evening as they sat smoking outside the sheds at Brooklands.

'There doesn't seem to be much point in continuing with the flying school,' he said. 'After all, there are four schools here now, besides ours, and there's Graham-White's at Hendon, as well as the Blériot and Deperdussin schools—'

'Not to mention Blackburn's and Ewen's,' Jack said. 'But there seem to be enough people wanting to fly to keep us all going.'

'Yes, but flying instruction is just a routine matter now, and I think our talents could be better used elsewhere. You don't really want to be nothing but an instructor for the rest of your days, do you?'

'It depends what else is offered,' Jack said. 'I was afraid just then you were going to turn me off.'

Sopwith grinned. 'Nonsense. You didn't think any such thing. Look here, between us you and I and Fred Sigrist have all the skills we need, and there's so much to be accomplished in the field of aircraft design. We ought to be concentrating on that. What do you say? Give up the school and start a factory?'

'Nothing would please me better,' Jack said. 'I'm flattered you've asked me.'

'Couldn't go ahead without you, old chap, you know that,'

said Sopwith. 'Well, we've sold our first aeroplane to the Admiralty Air Department, and they've already ordered a second—'

'And I've plenty of things I'd like to be working on,' Jack said eagerly. 'The flying boat for one thing, and an idea for a new biplane that ought to be faster than the first. But in the long term, the main difficulty, as I see it, is that for military use we've got to find a way to design something bigger and heavier, which would seem to require more than one engine. And with two engines—'

'All in good time,' Sopwith interrupted him, laughing. 'Let's get ourselves set up first. Look here, there's the Aero Exhibition at Olympia coming on in February. If we let the teaching wind down – don't take on any more pupils, just finish the ones we have – and put everything into design and manufacture, we ought to be able to get a flying boat and a biplane ready in time to exhibit, don't you think?'

'We can do anything we set our minds to,' Jack said. 'Of course, the sheds here have their limitations, but—'

'Oh, I've thought of that. We'll have to have a proper factory, of course. As soon as we've delivered the biplane to the Admiralty and they've paid me, I can look about for suitable premises, and we can keep the sheds just for testing purposes. With any luck at all we can be up and running by the beginning of December.'

'Assuming,' Jack said, 'that the Admiralty pays up promptly.'

Sopwith's enthusiasm wasn't dampened. 'Oh, they will, I'm sure. I'm going to go ahead and book a stand at Olympia anyway. We'll be there, by hook or crook.'

Luck was with him. The navy paid up promptly, and with cash in hand he was able to take on a recently closed skating rink in Kingston-upon-Thames, close to the railway station, which had the floor space and roof height necessary. A draughtsman was employed, and fitters and carpenters were hired, and in early December the Sopwith Aviation Company was registered.

'I suppose this means we won't be seeing much of you down here,' Miss Ormerod said to Jack.

329

'Oh, I shall still be here for test flights and experimentation,' he said.

'But you'll be at Kingston most of the time, I imagine,' she said, with elaborate unconcern. 'You'll be here much less often.'

'Yes, I suppose that's true,' Jack said, and wondered why the thought of that made him feel a slight damper on the occasion.

Jessie was at Morland Place one day in December getting help from her mother with her household accounts, which she complained, crossly, would not add up.

'I was never very good at them myself,' Henrietta said.

'You? But you've been doing the accounts here for years and years,' said Jessie in amazement.

'Practice makes perfect, they say. Or, at least, not perfect, in my case, but I get by because I have to. But I'll have a look for you, if you like.' She sat down with the book at the round table in the drawing-room, and Jessie took up position behind her, looking over her shoulder. 'Here,' Henrietta said at last. 'You've put this amount in twice – the butcher's bill, look.'

'Oh, yes,' said Jessie.

'Let me see, now, that makes it – hm – hm – hm. Still a shilling out.'

'Oh, as long as it's only a shilling, I don't care,' Jessie said.

Henrietta was shocked. 'You must have it right, dear. Even it if it were only a penny, I would go over and over until I found it.' She ran down the column again. 'Ah, here it is. You didn't carry over the one.' She looked up in triumph, tapping the page with her finger, but it was evident that Jessie's attention had strayed. Henrietta said, 'You look a little peaky, my love. Are you well?'

Jessie sighed heavily, and abruptly pulled out the chair beside her mother and sat down. 'I haven't been feeling quite the thing lately,' she admitted.

Henrietta's thoughts leaped, as mothers' thoughts do, in one direction. 'In what way?'

'Oh, just cross and out of sorts,' Jessie said.

'Any little dizzy spells?'

'One or two,' Jessie said. 'But they only last a moment. And,' she added, with increasing reluctance, because she saw where this was tending, 'I've been sick once or twice. I expect it was something I ate, though.'

Henrietta's worried look cleared and she smiled. 'Jessie, darling, don't you think you might perhaps be going to have a baby?'

Jessie met her eyes. 'You don't think so, do you?'

'Well, my love, it's likely enough. You *are* married. When did you last see anything?'

'I can't remember,' Jessie said. 'But – a while.'

'Don't you keep a record?'

'No,' said Jessie. 'I've never bothered.'

'You are a funny girl! But if you can't remember, then it's likely some time ago. Oh, I've been hoping and hoping for this! It's a year since your wedding, and I've wondered every month when it would happen. You had better see Dr Hasty about it as soon as possible.'

'Oh, I couldn't,' Jessie said. 'Not Dr Hasty! I've known him all my life.'

'That's precisely why. Dear child, there's nothing to be embarrassed about. It's the most natural thing in the world.' She studied her daughter's face. 'Aren't you pleased? You must *want* to have a baby.'

'Ned will be very happy,' Jessie answered, which was no answer. 'But if it is a baby – I feel bad enough now. What will it be like later on?'

'Oh, darling, it gets better, I promise you!' Henrietta laughed. 'The sickness and dizziness goes away after a while, and then you feel wonderful.'

'Hmm,' said Jessie. 'Well, I suppose I shall have to ask old Hasty. But, Mother, don't say anything to anyone, will you? Not until I tell you.'

'Of course not, my love. You'll want to tell yourself – I understand.'

That was not quite it, but Jessie let it stand. She sent for Dr Hasty the next day, waiting until Ned had gone to work,

331

and Daltry – whom she didn't feel she could trust not to tell Ned – had gone out on an errand. Hasty was growing a little grizzled now, and what Jessie thought of as 'comfortable' around the middle, but he still had the same twinkle in his eye, and treated her much as he had since she was nine. It didn't make it any less embarrassing for Jessie, who would sooner have had a broken leg than have to discuss something so awkward.

When he had quizzed her and – oh, worse still! – examined her, he said, 'Well, young lady, I think it's safe to say that you are going to have a baby. Congratulations.'

'When will it be coming?' Jessie asked, with a sinking of her stomach. It was a frightening thought, and she wasn't ready for it. She'd had her suspicions, but had hoped that if she didn't acknowledge them to herself, the thing might go away and not have to be faced.

'Well, let me see now – without the date of your last menstruation it's difficult to be precise, but I should say some time in July.'

'Oh,' said Jessie. It seemed at once far off, and horribly close. In July she would have a baby. She would be a mother – oh dear! She didn't feel at all ready. Mother was a mother; she, Jessie, was a daughter. That, she had assumed, was the immutable way of things.

But worse was to come. 'You're a healthy young woman,' Hasty said, 'and you should make nothing of it. But you must be sensible, not overtax yourself – and you must give up riding.'

'No riding?' Jessie said, aghast. 'But – for how long?'

'For the rest of your pregnancy,' said Hasty. 'And for some time afterwards. Riding is far too violent an exercise for ladies in your condition. I'm perfectly serious about this, now,' he added sternly, meeting her eye, for he knew her very well. 'No riding at all. Do you hear me?'

Jessie heard. When he had gone, she rushed out, saddled Hotspur, and rode straight over to Morland Place. Henrietta was in the kitchen with Mrs Stark pickling walnuts. 'It's been such a wonderful harvest this year,' she greeted her daughter, 'and although everyone likes them fresh for

Christmas, your uncle does so like a pickled walnut with his cold goose and turkey. Robbie, too. And your father always said . . .'

Jessie had no time for this. She grabbed her mother's arm and hustled her out of the kitchen for 'a private word', leaving Mrs Stark, who had pretty much guessed which way the wind blew, to smile to herself as she packed the finished walnuts into jars.

Jessie pulled Henrietta into the dining-room, the nearest empty place, and told her the news.

'Oh, Jessie, darling, I'm so pleased! When did Dr Hasty say it would be coming?'

'In July, he said – but, Mother, he said no more riding. He said I mustn't ride at all until afterwards.'

Henrietta said, 'Well, of course – oh, Jessie, you didn't ride over here?'

'I had to come and see you. What else was I to do? But, Mother, it's not right, is it? You didn't stop riding, did you?'

'I had all of you in London,' she said. 'I never rode in London.'

'But if you'd been here?'

'Well, my love, I can't really say. Some ladies ride for the first few weeks, but after that it becomes dangerous, especially with the first baby – and very soon, now, you'd find it too uncomfortable even if you tried.'

'But, Mother,' Jessie wailed, 'what am I supposed to do? How am I to get about?'

'You're not supposed to do a great deal of getting about,' Henrietta said gently.

'But I have the stables to run. And I can't stay indoors for eight months – you know I can't. I'd go mad!'

'Well, darling, can't you have the motor? Ned doesn't use it during the day, does he?'

'He does sometimes. And he wouldn't want me to drive it anyway. It's not like Uncle Teddy's Renault – he thinks the Arno is too heavy for a female to drive, so I'd be dependent on Purvis, and I'd hate that.'

'I suppose you would,' Henrietta said, knowing her independent daughter. It was a shame Teddy had sold the

Renault recently. He hardly ever went out now, and saw no point in keeping two motors. No-one else at Morland Place could drive, anyway, so if they went out, they went with Simmons in the Benz. 'Well, let me think. I know – there's my old phaeton. You could have that. I know it's not like riding, but it's better than nothing.'

Jessie hardly wanted to be comforted. 'But what will I do with Hotspur?' she said. 'He's not broken to harness.'

'Well, darling, you'll just have to turn him out,' Henrietta said.

'He'll hate it, poor boy. I'd have to take his shoes off. And practically rebreak him afterwards.'

'Oh, Jessie, you're just making troubles for yourself. Hotspur's a sensible horse. He won't revert to the wild in a few months. Or, I tell you what, I could ride him now and then for you. And Polly could take him out at weekends.' Polly had not been sent back to the school in Scarborough, but was attending a school in Thirsk as a weekly boarder. 'She's a good enough rider now, isn't she?'

'I suppose so,' Jessie sighed. She didn't want anyone to ride her darling Hotspur. And the months without riding stretched ahead like a desert.

'Have you told Ned yet?' Henrietta asked, hoping to get away from the subject of horses.

'Not yet. I suppose I'll have to tell him tonight.'

'Well, do try to be a bit more cheerful about it, or he'll think you don't want the baby at all,' Henrietta said.

Whether it was because her own feelings were equivocal, or from the physical modesty girls were brought up with, Jessie felt strangely shy about broaching the subject with Ned. At first she planned to tell him as soon as he came home; then before they went down to dinner; but she had still not told him when they sat down at the table. It was impossible during the meal, for Daltry was in the room the whole time, and the maids were in and out, removing dirty plates and bringing the dishes for him to serve. Ned was obviously tired, and soup and fish passed with little conversation; but as Daltry was serving the beefsteak pie, he suddenly roused himself and said, 'By the way, Seb Cornleigh said he might call this evening. He has a book he is going to lend to me.'

Seb was a pleasant young man of twenty, probably the brightest one of the family, and studying to be a solicitor.

'What book is that?' Jessie asked, to keep the conversation going.

'It's called *Spies of the Kaiser*. It's by that fellow Le Queux, who wrote *The Invasion of 1910*.'

'There seem to be so many of them these days – books like that, I mean,' Jessie said. 'I wonder if German people are reading books about English spies landing in Germany?'

'No, they'll be reading about how they conquered us almost without a fight,' Ned said. 'The book's probably something of a penny dreadful, but Seb said it was a good yarn, and there's no harm in having one's eyes opened to how the thing *might* be done.'

Jessie didn't reply, picking at her beefsteak pie with a sudden loss of appetite. If Seb did come, he would probably stay all evening. He might even bring his sister Ada, who at sixteen was always longing to exchange her home fire for someone else's – anyone else's – and was the chatterbox of the family. She must take her chance and tell Ned the news as soon as they left the table.

It wasn't easy. Ned seemed inclined to linger over dessert, though Jessie had an empty plate – the smell of the cheese had nauseated her, and she could not even fancy an apple from the bowl – and then the telephone rang and he was summoned to the hall to take the call. Jessie took the opportunity of leaving the table and told Daltry that he could clear, despite the remains on Ned's plate. 'And bring the coffee right away, will you?'

Ned joined her in the drawing-room, and did not comment on his abbreviated dinner. 'That was Turner from the mill,' he said, taking his usual fireside seat. 'Hobbs, the night-watchman, reported an intruder in the yard. Someone climbed over the gate, apparently, but he ran off as soon as he was challenged, and there was no damage done. Just a footpad or an idler, Hobbs said, probably hoping to pick something up. Turner's told him to keep a special watch, and he's informed the police. They said they'd send a constable by later, which ought to frighten the man away if he's still hanging around. I can't think what a footpad would hope to steal from a paper mill. He must have been desperate, or mad. What times we live in! Aunt Alice says in the old days Mr Meynell's father didn't even lock the gate, only closed it at night.'

He noticed at last that Jessie was not responding and, looking at her more closely, said, 'Are you quite all right? You didn't eat very much at dinner.'

It was now or never, Jessie thought. Seb might arrive at any moment. She left her chair and went to sit closer to him, on the edge of the sofa, and said, 'There's something I have to talk to you about. Something important.'

Before Ned could respond, the door opened and Daltry came in with the coffee. Jessie could have screamed. He put the tray down on the table and she said quickly, 'I'll pour it out. Thank you, Daltry.'

Daltry left without a murmur, sensitive to atmosphere as always. When he was gone, Ned said, 'What is it, then? You aren't looking very well. Perhaps you ought to see Dr Hasty.'

'I've seen him. I saw him today,' Jessie said. She swallowed, and then, afraid of more interruptions, blurted it out: 'I'm going to have a baby.'

She wasn't sure what reaction she had expected from him, but hard on the heels of astonishment came delight. His face lit with joy, and for a moment he looked more than handsome, he looked beautiful. He jumped out of his chair and knelt down in front of her, took both her hands and kissed them, gazed into her face as his broken words tumbled from him. 'Oh, my darling! At last! So happy! Wonderful, wonderful news. I can hardly believe – a baby! But how are you feeling? Are you comfortable? When did Hasty say? Are you well? Oh, darling, a baby!' He laid her hands against his cheek in a gesture that disarmed her, and murmured foolishly to them, 'I'm going to be a papa!'

Jessie told him what little she knew, answered his questions as best she could, and felt herself warming to the idea by the powerful glow of his happiness. She had known it had meant a lot to him, but had been unable to anticipate exactly how much. Ned got up from his knees, sat on the sofa beside her and took her into his arms, kissed her tenderly and held her against him, her cheek on his shoulder, his resting on her hair. 'A baby,' he said, over and over. 'A baby.'

They had been married almost a year, and he had been afraid that it was not going to happen. He had worried about all sorts of things, from the fact that they were cousins, and many people said cousins shouldn't marry, to his own obscure origins. Unspoken and superstitious fear that he was unworthy haunted him. Jessie was a gentleman's daughter, with armigerous families on both sides, going back into history. He was the bastard child of a servant girl – was it possible that such things affected one's ability to engender a family? If one had no right to the normal, good things of life, perhaps one would be denied also the ability. Gratitude and humility were a heady mixture for a man to swallow and remain level-headed.

But it had happened at last, and his loved, his adored wife – who looked more beautiful to him just then than she had ever done before – was with child. A son! he thought. A son to carry on his name, to inherit his estate, one day to give him grandsons and secure his place in the world. Uncle Teddy had given him a home, a family, a name, unstinted love, and a fortune – but Jessie's child would stitch him into the fabric of time and space in a pattern that could not be undone.

'I'm so happy,' he murmured, and felt a tear run sideways down his cheek and into her hair. 'I love you so much.'

A few moments later they had to part because both of them needed to blow their noses. Daltry came in, to announce Mr Seb and Miss Ada Cornleigh. Ned jumped to his feet and even before the visitors had passed Daltry in the doorway, he cried out, 'I have news! Daltry, you must hear this, too. Ada, Seb, you come most timely. Jessie has just told me that we are going to have a baby!'

Seb and Ada were probably not the best audience he could have hoped for. One of the older Cornleighs – David,

Ethel or Angela, who were all married – would have had a more exact understanding of the importance of the news. But they were genuinely pleased, and said all the right things; and Daltry, who had been with Ned for some time now, was delighted. Jessie found she did not need to say anything, which suited her, for she felt very tired. She sat and smiled, while the rejoicing went on around her, and felt that, after all, it was something rather wonderful, and that it was worth facing the loss of horses for eight months to see Ned so very, very happy.

Having a pregnancy announced, Jessie discovered, meant one was visited. All sorts of people came, and she was obliged to be 'at home' day after day to receive them. Mrs Cornleigh senior came with good advice and calm cheer. 'Don't fret or fuss yourself, my dear. Remember that having a baby is perfectly natural, and what we're made for.' Angela Cornleigh, who had been Jessie's particular friend, called to congratulate and swap symptoms: she was Mrs John Fulbright now, and was expecting her first, though she was further along than Jessie. Ethel had herself driven over from Morland Place as soon as she heard, with the offer of little Jeremy's first clothes and binders. 'They grow out of them so quickly, it's hardly worth having new.' She brought with her Alice's hearty congratulations, and a basket of flowers she had arranged for Jessie. It was lined with moss and the flower stems were pushed through it. 'She says if you keep the moss damp, they'll last for ages.'

Robbie bicycled over on his way home from the bank, and was rather lordly about it, as a father of two himself. Uncle Teddy sent a brace of pheasants and a letter with an invitation to a family dinner of celebration, and an urgent request that she have the child christened in the chapel at Morland Place when the time came.

Mrs Wycherley called, and sympathised in a heartfelt way, though with a twinkle in her eye, about how the news would curtail Jessie's activities. Mrs Melmoth called, and asked if it meant Jessie would not be hunting that season. Mrs Hamlyn brought congratulations and flowers. Mrs

Micklethwaite brought an enormous box of chocolates and warned Jessie not to stint herself with food. 'There's nothing worse when you're in an interesting condition than a low diet, my dear.'

Maud called, and seemed rather distant, though she said all the right things. There were letters from Venetia and Violet, a hasty but loving note from Jack, with an oily thumbmark on the envelope, and a charming one from Frank with a short poem about the delights of being made an uncle again.

The day came when the stream of visitors had tailed off, since everyone close to them had made their calls, and Jessie decided it was safe to go out. She told the servants she was not at home. She had just gone up to her room to change when Peggy knocked at the door and told her that there was a visitor below.

'This early?' Jessie said, with a frown. It was not the hour of calling.

'It's Sir Percival Parke, madam,' Peggy said, with round eyes. Jessie's heart gave an unruly thud at the sound of his name.

'And Lady Parke?' she asked.

'No, madam, just the gentleman. I did say you weren't at home, but he said he thought you might see him, as he's family.'

'Yes, of course,' she said absently. 'I'll come.' Peggy went away. Jessie turned to look at Tomlinson, who had come up with her to dress her. Was there a hint of sympathy in her eyes? But no-one knew about Jessie's former feelings for Bertie, no-one. 'I expect he has some business to discuss,' she said.

'Yes, madam,' Tomlinson said. 'I'll see you're not disturbed.'

Jessie hurried away from any further revealing looks. She found Bertie in the morning-room, and although someone had laid the paper on the table for him, he was standing by the window staring out, slapping his riding boot with his crop in a way that did not suggest complete ease. He turned his head at the exact moment she entered, as though he had eyes in the back of his head; but probably, she told herself

339

firmly, he had heard Brach's nails clicking across the hall.

He didn't speak, only turned fully and stood with his hands down at his sides as she came in, closed the door, and then, nervously, stood with her back to it. Brach trotted across, tail swinging, to nudge Bertie's hands, but he did not seem to notice her. She sniffed interestedly at his boots, and then went circling, nose down, around and under the table in case anyone had dropped anything at breakfast.

'You look – different,' Bertie said at last.

'Do I?' she said. A beam of sun came in at the window, lighting his hair into a nimbus. 'You look pale,' she said, after a moment.

'I feel pale,' he said. The sunbeam cut off abruptly as a large, watery cloud chased by outside, and beyond the window Jessie saw the cherry tree wave its arms from side to side like someone signalling. She heard the wind in the morning-room chimney. Another few of the last leaves detached themselves, and one hit the window high up and stuck there for a moment, before peeling off and disappearing in another gust.

'Won't you sit down?' she said, feeling that she had to say something.

He sat, without looking, on the windowseat; sat abruptly, as if someone had knocked him across the back of the knees. She walked across the room and sat down on it too – it ran right round the bay window, so she was half facing him, their knees almost touching. Close to, his face suddenly returned to all its old familiarity, the way it had always seemed to her, before she married Ned, as the face she knew best in the world beside her own, something so much a part of her mind's landscape that it hardly seemed separate from her. It was disturbing, it made her feel hollow, to be so close to him and seeing him in the old way. She wanted to look away from him, but it would have been too revealing. She prayed he would not try to touch her.

'Jessie,' he said.

How it shook her, his voice, the way he said her name! She had to say something, to interrupt him. 'I don't think you've ever been in this house before, have you?' she said brightly.

340

'No,' he said.

'Somehow or other, you were never here when we were entertaining. And then, of course, there was that awful business, and we didn't entertain for ages.'

'I've tried to avoid coming here,' he said.

She didn't want to think about the implications of that. She blundered on: 'Maud was here last week. She came to call to – to congratulate—'

He had held out his hand, to stop her, and she shrank a little away from it. 'Jessie,' he said again.

'Bertie, don't,' she said in a faint voice.

'I have to know,' he said, and his face was urgent, his eyes searching her. 'I have to know if – if it's what you wanted.'

She felt the pressure of tears at the back of her throat, and resisted them. She shook her head a little – not a negative, but a denial of any answer.

'I know we swore we would be nothing more than cousins to each other, and since you married Ned I've felt that you had accepted that, that it was all right with you. I only came here today to congratulate you, but then, when I saw inside this house – when I saw where you live, everything so complete – so real—'

'It is real,' she said, without any clear idea of what she meant by it.

Now he shook his head. 'I'm lying,' he said. 'I didn't come here to congratulate you. Did you know I've passed this house a score of times – not on the way to anywhere, but just to look at it? If it weren't such a public road,' he added, with a faint, deprecating smile, 'I might have hung about outside, somewhere out of sight, just so I could stare at it.'

Brach left her investigation of the carpet and came back to Bertie, nudged his hands again; and this time he responded, though he did not look at her, and stroked her head and ears with hands that knew their business without his attention. She stood with her head tilted and her eyes shut in pleasure, her tail slowly swinging.

'And now you're having a baby,' Bertie said. He managed at the last moment not to say 'his baby'.

'Yes,' said Jessie. She knew she ought to say something

341

conventional about how happy she was, but the moment seemed too fragile for many words.

'I remember,' he said, 'when I came to tell you about Maud being in the family way. You were so . . .' He couldn't think of the right word to describe the strength of her then, the dignity. 'I said I was sorry, and you said, no, I had to be glad about it, poor baby.'

She bent her head in acknowledgement, unable to think of anything to say.

'I do love him, my little son,' Bertie went on. 'I think I shall love him more and more all the time.'

'It's natural,' she said.

'Yes,' he said, as if she had answered something else, something he hadn't asked. 'Yes, it's natural.'

He put his fist up to his mouth and coughed, and then passed the hand before his eyes and over his forehead, as though pushing his hair back; it served to cover his face for a moment. Then he sat up straighter and said, in a conversational voice, 'I have something to tell you, something I wanted you to know first. We're going to give up the Red House.'

She was startled out of her dream state. 'No!'

'Maud has never liked it,' he said. 'It's old and uncomfortable, in spite of everything we've done to it. Most of all, it's too far from London for Maud and Richard. So we're going to take a place in Hertfordshire or Northampton, something within easy reach of London for their sake, but where the grazing is good.'

'You won't sell the Red House?' she asked.

He gave a rueful smile. 'It's not such an ancestral place, you know. My great-grandfather bought it. But, no, I shan't sell it. I shall rent it out. It may be foolish of me, but there's a corner of me that hopes one day I might come back, or my son might, if not me.'

His son – there was that small word, which separated her from him so completely. And now she was to have a child, too – a double barrier. 'When?' she asked. 'When will you go?'

'Maud and Richard were going to go to London in

February anyway, so I shall aim to have everything done by then and go with them – then or soon after. I shall have Christmas here, and the rest of the hunting.' Something occurred to him. 'But you won't be hunting, will you?'

'It seems not,' she said. 'I'm told I can't ride any more, not until – afterwards.'

'Poor Jessie,' he said, and it was warm, affectionate, cousinly, slightly teasing, just as if nothing had ever come between them.

'It's a woman's lot,' she said lightly.

He stood up. 'I'd better go.' She stood too. He held out his hand, as though automatically, and automatically she gave hers into it. It was the hand she remembered, large and hard of palm, and he folded his other round, engulfing hers. 'Dearest,' he said, 'I have to ask you, just once and then never again. Are you happy with him? Are you happy, my Jess?'

She lifted her face, but she could not see him; he seemed hidden in a bright mist. It was just the light from the window, she told herself. 'Yes,' she said. 'I am happy.'

He blinked once, twice, and then he nodded, and pressed her hands, and released them. When he spoke again, it was cheerily. 'It's a great shame you won't be able to hunt any more, but I hope we'll still see you at the meets. We'll be having a lawn meet at the Red House in January – you must come to that, at least. What will you do with that nice hunter of yours? It would be a great shame to have to turn him out.'

'I suppose I could try to find someone to hunt him for me.'

'I'd offer to hunt him myself, but he wouldn't be up to my weight.'

'Mrs Wycherley might take him. It would have to be someone I could trust not to spoil his mouth.'

Talking easily about horses, they left the room. She showed him out herself.

CHAPTER SEVENTEEN

'It's much too cold,' said Ned.

'A bit of cold never hurt anyone,' Jessie said.

He changed tack slightly. 'It's too cold for there to be any scent, anyway. Look at the frost out there.'

'That will melt away as soon as the sun gets on it. There's no bone to the ground. You're just making excuses.'

He was. He wanted to forbid her to go, but he was afraid of provoking her. Everyone knew pregnant women had to be humoured – and he was less sure of Jessie in late weeks than before. 'I just don't want you to go racketing about the country like a tomboy. It isn't seemly.'

She put down her eggspoon in exasperation. 'I don't know why you're making such a fuss. You knew what I was like before you married me.'

Ned sighed. 'But didn't you expect to change *anything* about your behaviour when you married? Did you think you would go on exactly as before?'

'Yes,' she said, putting up her chin. 'I thought it was *me* you wanted to marry, not some mimsy, prim and proper—'

'*That* you'll never be. But I didn't say I wanted it. A married woman can't behave like an unmarried girl, that's all. I'm entitled to expect *some* restraint from you, some dignity, some – propriety.'

'*Propriety?*'

'What you do reflects on me. You are my wife.'

'Yes, your wife and your property, it seems. You've certainly changed since we married. You used to admire me

344

just as I was. Now it seems I'm not good enough for you.'

'Yes, I have changed,' he said gravely, trying to hide how her words stung him. 'I've had to. I'm a householder, a husband, and I'll soon be a father. I have responsibilities. I have to keep a roof over our heads and food on our table. I have to get on in the world so that I can support my family. I don't have any choice about that. I can't go out riding whenever I feel like it, or spend evenings at the club getting drunk and playing cards until all hours.'

An unwilling smile tugged at her lips. 'You never did that anyway. You were always an old sobersides.'

'You just said I'd changed.'

'I meant – oh, never mind! This is such a stupid argument. All I want to do is to go to the meet, and perhaps follow a little way. I don't understand what's so objectionable about that.'

'A pregnant woman, alone, driving herself? It isn't proper and it isn't safe.'

'I have to drive because Hasty said I wasn't to ride. Now you don't want me to drive either. I don't know why you don't tie me up in a kennel like a dog!'

He had done what he had not meant to do, and agitated her. He bit back the next words that had flown up into his mouth. It had been hard on her, not to hunt. The only meet she had attended was the one on Boxing Day – a great social occasion – which he had taken her to in the motor. She had not even been to the Red House lawn meet, because he had been needed at the mill that day. He said quietly, 'I don't want to curtail all your pleasure. Let Purvis drive you in the Arno.'

Jessie was silent. She didn't want to be driven by the chauffeur, who would be Ned's eyes and ears and whose presence would nag her like a conscience. And she couldn't follow the hunt in a motor-car, not even as far as the first draw.

Ned studied her face, and hoped the silence meant a softening on her part. 'Promise me you won't go in the phaeton.'

She looked up, her eyes veiled. 'All right,' she said at last. 'I promise.'

345

She had had a better idea. The phaeton was not a good vehicle to drive other than on the road. But Hackett at Prospect Farm had a little two-wheeled tub cart that would dash through gates and over rough ground much better, and she was sure he would lend it to her. He might lend her his smart little bay pony, too. Dunnock, whom Henrietta had lent her with the phaeton, was getting old.

'Thank you,' said Ned. He eyed her cautiously. But she didn't seem to be angry any more. 'I know you feel cooped up because you can't ride. Would you like to go out somewhere on Sunday? We could motor over to Scarborough, perhaps, and have a look at the sea.'

'Mm, yes, that would be nice,' she said demurely.

The answer seemed to lack something, but he couldn't put his finger on what it might be.

Jessie hadn't meant to do more than potter along with the foot-followers, but other influences came into play. For one thing, the first person she saw at the meet was Mrs Wycherley, mounted on her own darling Bay Rum, who was curvetting about with his neck arched and his tail held as high as an Arab's, so that she longed and longed to be in the saddle and feel his eager power under her.

Mrs Wycherley rode him over to her and said, 'How does he look? I hope you don't think I'm spoiling him.'

'Of course not,' said Jessie. 'I'm just green with envy. He looks wonderful. How has he been going?'

'Very well. I had him out last Thursday and he didn't put a foot wrong.'

'Dear old boy,' she said, as Rum slobbered over her sleeve, trying to get to the pocket where she kept the titbits.

'He hasn't forgotten you, you see,' said Mrs Wycherley. 'I talk to him about you every night while I'm cleaning his teeth and tucking him into bed.'

Jessie laughed. 'You should have a good run today. The frost has all gone, and the ground's warm enough to give plenty of scent.'

The second person she saw was Bertie. She was glad not to have missed him. This might be the last time he hunted here. The season was almost over, and next month he would be moving to London. As soon as he saw her, he swung down from the saddle and handed Barnabas's reins to his groom, who was riding his second horse, a big black called Nightshade, which he had got from Ireland in the summer. He walked across to her, and leaned on the front of the tub cart, taking hold of the rein as the bay pony fretted a little.

'What's this?' he said. 'Is it yours?'

'No, I borrowed it. It belongs to one of Uncle Teddy's tenants. The pony too. His name's Firecracker.'

'That sounds ominous,' Bertie said, smiling.

'He's very sweet,' Jessie said. 'The farmer's wife dotes on him.'

'I'm so glad you came. I always look out for you, but you haven't been to anything, have you? I looked for you inside today, but I didn't see you.'

'I've only just got here. The loan of the trap took time to arrange.'

'What a pity. Hounds will be here any moment. It's a long way to drive for five minutes of a meet.'

'Oh, I mean to follow, as long as I can keep up.'

'Ah. Well, then, I hope for your sake we won't find at the first draw.'

'I wouldn't be such a dog-in-the-manger as to wish that.' She laughed. It was so pleasant, so comfortable to be near him again, talking, as they always did, with the intimacy that nothing could ever destroy. However long they were apart, it felt to Jessie always as if they were two halves of something that fitted neatly together whenever reunited. But the comfort was not to last long. There was a cry of 'Hounds, please,' and she had to say, 'Here comes the pack. You'd better go and mount.'

The other element was the keenness of Firecracker himself. As soon as hounds appeared, his ears shot forward and he began to snort softly; as Jessie checked him he raked at the ground with a forefoot. In a few moments the hunt moved off, and Jessie had difficulty in keeping back, for Firecracker wanted to be up with the leaders. Several people smiled down at her as they passed, some made comments about the pony's eagerness. Peter Firmstone, a former beau, lifted his topper and said, 'Not quite in your usual style, Mrs Morland, but he looks like a goer.'

Jessie laughed up at him, acknowledging the jest, but it was hard to see everyone going past her, the big, handsome horses, the men in pink, the women in fine black habits, her own Bay Rum sidling by, his shoes slipping on the damp cobbles as he tried to jog. The sun was as high now as it would be this short winter day, and there was warmth in it: the more highly strung horses were steaming a little already. The frost was gone, except for a few pockets at the foot of walls and under hedges, or in shadows where the sun couldn't reach. The bare trees poked at a pale, clear sky; everything was brown and green, with a touch of colour here and there where a few scarlet berries and hips still clung to the hedgerows. It would be a good day, she knew in her heart. There would be scent and a good run, and she could have been up there, galloping in the first flight with Bertie.

As soon as the last ponies had passed, Jessie let the fretting Firecracker go, and he set off after them, leaning into his collar, snorting like a small steam engine as if that would get him on faster. He spanked along after the field, and when it turned off the road through a gate and onto a grazing meadow, she followed, smiling thanks at the labourer who held the gate for her. If she wasn't the first in the field, at least she was the first of the foot-followers.

The tub cart worked out very well, being small, stout and handy, and Firecracker was so keen to follow hounds she hardly had to guide him at all. The only difficulty was in preventing him trying to jump the hedges. They dashed across fields, bounced across plough, shot through gateways and barnyards, took short-cuts along lanes, and managed to keep the hunt in sight for a good hour, with the aid of two checks just when they were needed, when the distance of the line from any gate looked like thwarting her. But at the end of an hour Firecracker was blowing like a porpoise from the unaccustomed exercise, and Jessie's conscience pricked her on Farmer Hackett's behalf; so she was not too disappointed when she found herself separated from both the field and the foot-followers by a stile, which the former had jumped and the latter scrambled over.

She was not sure where she was, and drove on down the road at a walk until she reached a crossroads with a sign-post and got her bearings. The sun was sliding down now, and the spurious warmth had gone from it. She was quite a way from home; and she had to take this rig back first and pick up the phaeton, which she had left at Prospect, before she could drive back to Maystone. Firecracker clipped along quietly now, tired after his exertions. The lanes seemed very quiet. She saw no-one about, and there wasn't a sound on the clear air except the occasional yark of a distant crow. It began to get cold quite quickly as the sun declined, and Jessie wished she had remembered to transfer the rug from the phaeton, for her legs were cold and her feet quite numb.

The moon rose before dusk, enormous and almost full. It hung romantically in the pale afternoon sky, lemon-yellow and growing luminous as the sky gradually darkened to slate-blue behind it. There was mist across the fields now, milky in the hollows, making like a flood until the trees and hedges rose out of it as though drowned. Looking away from the moon, Jessie saw Venus rise, fat and luscious. She shook Firecracker into a trot, and he responded, wanting to be home as much as she did.

It was dusk when she got back to Prospect, and Hackett's son Jim was looking out for her. He had the phaeton harnessed and ready, and she had only to climb stiffly out of one vehicle and into the other. Firecracker was too tired to need holding, and Jim let him go so that he could spread the rug over Jessie's knees.

''Aven't you got a lamp, then, Miss Jessie?' he asked

'No, but don't worry, I shall be home before dark. I shall trot all the way.' Dunnock was fresh from being in the stable all day, and the track was good.

There was still a last glow in the sky when she got home, though the lights in various windows made it seem darker than it was; and it was bitingly cold. There'll be another frost tonight, she thought. Her hands and feet were aching

349

with cold, and she felt as tired as she ever had after a day's hunting. A bit 'saddle sore', too, from bouncing on the tub cart's seat when it went over bumps. Dunnock whinnied loudly as she turned him into the gate, and the horses in the stable answered. Gladding emerged, wiping his mouth, and came to Dunnock's head, grumbling routinely.

'Just this moment set down to a cup o' tea. Ah knowed summat 'ud come oop, soon as Ah set down. It allus doos.' He caught Dunnock's head as though he were a mettlesome steed. 'Ah were gettin' reet worried about you, Mrs Morland. Out all day and never a word where you were goin'. The maister telephoned a bit sin', and Ah couldn't tell 'im where you'd gone or when you'd be back. Fair framin', he were.'

A faint gloom settled over Jessie, but she was too desperate to get indoors and warm her extremities to think about much else just then. The lighted house looked so welcoming; and she was hungry too, having had nothing since breakfast. She climbed down, abandoning the pony to Gladding's tender care, and hurried inside, calling for tea and hot toast.

She had just finished the last of it, and was licking gooseberry jam from her fingers and contemplating a hot bath to complete her restoration, when she heard the motor coming in at the gate, and a few moments later Ned appeared – early for him. He looked pale with anger, and telepathically she knew he already knew she had been at the meet. Someone must have seen her and passed it on.

'Where on earth have you been all day?' he demanded, without preamble.

This annoyed her. If he knew where she had been, why was he asking? Was he expecting to trap her in a lie? She stuck her chin up and said, 'I went to the meet. Why do you ask?'

'You went to the meet, after you promised me you wouldn't?'

'I promised nothing of the sort,' she said. 'I only said I wouldn't go in the phaeton, and I didn't.'

'Gladding said you went out in the phaeton this morning, and that you came back in it not long since.'

'Are you calling me a liar?'

This was unanswerable, and it stopped him. He stared at her, breathing hard, and then said, 'I've been told by someone that you followed the field, driving yourself.'

'Someone was very obliging,' she said sarcastically. 'They didn't happen to tell you *what* I was driving? Or what I was wearing, or how much I tipped the boy who held the gate?'

'What were you driving?' he asked, gritting his teeth.

'I borrowed Hackett's tub trap and pony. Hackett of Prospect,' she added, since the name did not seem to mean anything to him.

He passed his hand over his eyes and brow in a gesture of weariness and helplessness. 'You drove yourself in a borrowed farm trap? And you think that makes it all right?'

It seemed to be a rule of domestic quarrels that they were always interrupted by servants just as they reached a crucial point. Daltry came in with a polite cough to ask about dinner, and to bring a letter that had been delivered by hand and was marked urgent.

Jessie saw that this would occupy Ned for some minutes, and took the opportunity to stand up and say, 'I must go and have a bath. My hands and feet are still cold. Daltry, is the water hot?'

'Yes, madam.'

'Very well. And I shall dress afterwards, tell Tomlinson.'

She thought that would put paid to the matter until after dinner, when Ned might be in a softer mood, but he came into the bedroom when she was dressing and, with a sharp look and jerk of the head at Tomlinson, sent the maid away.

Jessie turned to face him, matching him frown for frown, though hers was angry and his was – what? Hurt? Disappointed? Worried? All of those, perhaps.

'Jessie, you haven't been honest with me,' he said.

'I've told you the exact truth,' she retorted.

'Yes, I know. But what you said was intended to deceive. You knew when I asked you not to drive yourself in the phaeton that I didn't mean any other rig would be quite all right. You knew I didn't want you to drive yourself at all.'

Jessie felt a twinge of shame, but she resisted it. What was the old saying? *Tyrants make liars*. If he had not been so

351

unreasonable, she would not have had to resort to subterfuge. 'I went to a meet, just as I have thousands of times before. I don't see what business it is of yours to forbid me to do something I've always done.'

'I have your best interests at heart – as well as mine.'

'Well, I just don't agree, so we might as well leave it at that,' she said, and turned away again, pretending to search for something on the dressing-table.

He watched her in silence for a moment, and then said very quietly, 'Do you regret marrying me?'

She looked up, startled, and met his eyes in the looking-glass. He looked unhappy, and there was a droop to his head that reminded her of a miserable dog. Her protective crossness fell away from her on the instant, and she felt only miserable too, and tired – and lonely. It was lonely not to be friends with him. 'No,' she said at last. 'Of course not.'

'It just seems that ever since – well, for a couple of months now – you've been—' He sought the right word. 'Discontented. Is it the baby? Are you worried about having the baby, or – or afraid?'

He was trying so hard to understand that her conscience twinged again. It came to her that, as a man, his expectations had been very clear, and were completely conventional and understandable. A man married, he then had a wife and a home, and he expected children. She had thought Ned was different because he was her cousin and she knew him very well, and because, since he also knew her better than men generally knew their wives beforehand, he had seemed more sympathetic to her as an individual. But Ned was a man as well – or perhaps first and foremost. Perhaps that was the only way of being a man? He had expected what men expected, and it was not really his fault that things had turned out awkwardly. She had not adapted; and there was that in her – her Morland blood, perhaps – that didn't think she should have to.

But the baby – ah, the baby made everything different! She remembered her words to Bertie, and felt guilty not only towards Ned, but towards the unborn thing in her womb. No-one should come unwanted into the world. She might have conceived at once, the moment she was married, and the fact that she had had a year off had given her a false expectation. But now she was in for it, and there was no way out, so it was foolish to rail against it. Foolish and undignified. And wrong.

She drew a deep breath, with something of a sigh in it, and turned to face him again. 'I've been feeling a bit cross and out of sorts,' she said. And, with an effort, 'I'm sorry.' She raised her eyes to his. 'I'll try to do better in future. I expect it's something to do with being pregnant.'

His face cleared instantly, and he fell on his knees in front of her, all contrition. 'Oh, Jess, I'm sorry too. I should have thought. It's monstrous of me to be so cross and short with you at a time like this. I should have been patient and tried to understand. How are you feeling now? You look tired. You must say at once if ever you feel unwell, or—'

She caught his face in both her hands and kissed him hard to stop him. 'I'm fine, don't worry. I was cross and naughty but I'll try not to be again. So are we friends now?'

'Friends?' he exclaimed. And he put his hands round her face, too, and kissed her – and kissed her. Their arms went round each other, and Jessie felt the stirring of the familiar, pleasant desire. She felt it in him, too. She liked his mouth and the clean male smell of him and his strong arms holding her. Folly to be at outs, she thought vaguely, sliding down a delicious slope to passion.

But he pulled back, remembering, as she did a moment later, that it was nearly dinner time. 'Friends,' he said, smiling at her. He was handsome, her dear old Ned, she thought. A tap on the door made him leap to his feet. Jessie called, 'Come in,' and the door opened to admit a squirm of Brach, who ran from one of them to the other, jabbing with her cold nose and whacking with her tail as if she had not seen either of them for a week, and an apologetic Tomlinson to remind them of the time.

Two days later, in the middle of the morning, when Jessie was getting ready to go out, intending to drive over to Morland Place, she was stopped by a sharp pain that seemed to lance through her middle, and was instantly gone. She paused thoughtfully for a moment, frowning into the hall glass at which she had been putting on her hat. Brach, sitting on her tail just behind, intent on not being left, smiled encouragingly at her reflection. Jessie shrugged and continued to push in the hat pins. And then she felt as though one of those long, sharp pins had been driven into her groin – and this time the pain did not stop.

Her reflected eyes widened, and she gasped. Brach stood up, waving her tail uncertainly. Now, down below, Jessie was aware of wetness and discomfort, and as the pain deepened to a grinding horror, her mind caught up with her. Her hand flew to her mouth, and she whirled in panic, almost stepped on the dog, cried out inside herself for her mother, and then ran towards the kitchen, for Tomlinson, for anyone – for help.

In February 1913, the country was again shocked by a national tragedy: Captain R. F. Scott, the explorer, who had been expected back in New Zealand in April from his expedition to reach the South Pole, had perished with all his companions on the return journey. The news had only just reached London from Antarctica that a search party sent out from the base camp in November 1912 had discovered his tent. In it lay the bodies of the last three members of the expedition – Scott, Dr Edward Wilson and Henry Bowers. They had died from starvation and cold, only eleven miles from a food depot. Scott's diary, discovered on his body, revealed that they had been prevented by eight days of continuous blizzards from making the attempt to reach it.

The public was deeply moved by the pity of that lonely death, so close to salvation; by the valour of Captain Lawrence 'Titus' Oates who, crippled by frostbite, had walked out to his death in the blizzard rather than slow down his companions; by the stark yet quiet courage with which Scott and his companions had faced the certainty of death.

The last entry in Captain Scott's diary was much quoted, and never failed to move.

Every day we have been ready to start for our depot eleven miles away, but outside the door of the tent it remains a scene of whirling drift. I do not think we can hope for better things now. We shall stick it out to the end, but we are getting weaker, of course, and the end cannot be far. It seems a pity, but I do not think I can write more.

The diary also revealed that Scott and his party had reached the South Pole on the 18th of January 1912, only to find that the Norwegian explorer, Roald Amundsen, had been there five weeks earlier, so Scott and his companions had not even had the distinction of being the first men to reach the Pole to comfort their last days.

Yet the expedition was by no means a failure. The story of how five men had battled their way across eight hundred miles of the highest and coldest plain on earth, in the most unimaginably harsh conditions, to reach their goal was an inspiration to all, and seemed to exemplify all the qualities that were most valued and most British: courage, modesty, loyalty, selflessness, hardiness and persistence. While the nation mourned, it also celebrated. There was to be a memorial service in St Paul's with the King in attendance, honours for Scott's widow Kathleen, a statue to the hero at public expense. While Scott's papers had been sent back to England, the bodies of the three men had been left where they were. The tent was collapsed, an ice cairn built over it and a pair of crossed skis driven into the top. Here they would lie until the majestic ice drift would one day carry them to a last resting-place in the sea. The bodies of Oates and Evans, who had died earlier on the march, were not found.

'So,' Venetia said to her husband, 'twice in two years we've been forced to acknowledge that nature is mightier than man.'

Overton looked up from the newspaper. 'I do not think we should underestimate man's potential to hurt us. I heard news today that makes war with Germany a certainty.'

'Everyone keeps saying it must come,' said Venetia, 'but I've always taken that as so much talk. Those stories in the sensational press, the dreadful novels and serials—'

'I don't know whether they somehow guessed the truth, or whether it's that they've spun a story for so long everyone now feels obliged to act it out,' said Overton. 'But Germany is about to announce a massive increase in conscription. All the previously exempt classes are to be called, with the corresponding increase in officers, horses, guns and equipment.'

'But Germany has been building up arms for years,' Venetia said reasonably. 'It doesn't necessarily mean they have to use them, does it?'

'I think it is different this time,' said Overton, and he looked unexpectedly grim, giving Venetia pause. 'Along with this new conscription, they are going to raise a capital levy for military use of a thousand million marks. That's equivalent to about fifty million pounds.'

'*Fifty— !*'Venetia exclaimed. It was an unimaginable sum. Lloyd George's budget of 1909, which had convulsed British politics and practically caused a revolution, had only aimed at raising fifteen million.

'Germany is not a rich country,' Overton went on, 'and she's already suffering severe taxation. To raise such an enormous extra sum in one year, in peacetime – well, when such a supreme sacrifice is demanded of the people, it cannot possibly be wasted.'

Venetia said thoughtfully, 'Yes, I see. You mean they wouldn't do it if they weren't intending to go to war –'

'– and having done it, they *must* go to war,' Overton concluded.

'You're sure about this?'

'Oh, yes. It will be officially announced in a week or two.'

'And what will we do about it?'

'Well, you know that we are already doing something,' said Overton.

'You mean the War Book?' said Venetia.

Lord Overton had been appointed by Haldane to the sub-committee of the Committee of Imperial Defence charged with producing the War Book. The sub-committee had been in existence since January 1911 – proof of how long the shadow of war had been looming over Europe. The War Book was in fact an encyclopaedia of instructions to be followed in case of the declaration of hostilities. Every possible eventuality was imagined, and orders laid out to meet it; all the proclamations, orders in council and necessary forms were kept ready in type. It was the duty of the sub-committee to try to foresee every situation that might arise, and to plot the response step by step, so that no question could ever be asked in an emergency that the War Book had not already answered.

Men like Overton, with practical experience in the Colours, and others with administrative expertise, went through everything in painstaking detail, so that when the order came to mobilise, there should be no delay, no muddle, no excuse for anyone not to be in the right place at the right time. Every post office, police station, town hall, shipping line and railway station in the land would have its close-printed sheaves of instructions. Every government department and military command in every region of Britain, the Dominions and the Colonies would know exactly what to do.

How would the reservist get to his unit? He would present his identity document at any post office and receive five shillings for travelling expenses; present it at the railway station and receive a travel warrant to his destination. How would a battalion that had suddenly doubled in strength acquire the necessary stores and equipment? It was in the War Book. Billets for the extra men? Transport to move them? Horses for reservist officers? Fodder for the same? All in the War Book. How would the soldier get his letters and parcels from home? The War Book said how. What would the police do if someone brought them a suspected spy? The War Book gave instructions.

All that would be needed when the moment came would be to fill in the blank on the ready-printed War Telegrams:

357

IN THE CIRCUMSTANCE THAT GREAT BRITAIN IS AT WAR WITH—, ACT UPON INSTRUCTIONS. The blank space had been left because the War Book was intended to be a permanent fixture, to be constantly updated so that it could be used at any time in the near or far future; but rubber stamps had already been made of the word GERMANY.

'The War Book is very well,' Venetia said, 'but is anything being done about increasing our army?'

'There's no stomach for it in cabinet,' Overton said, with a sigh. 'Churchill and Grey are both determined appeasers, Lloyd George actually wants to *cut* military expenditure so as to leave more money for his socialistic plans, and Asquith doesn't believe it will ever come to war. Lichnowsky tells him so, and since he doesn't *want* a war, it's convenient to believe everything Lichnowsky says.' Prince Lichnowsky was the German ambassador in London.

'I suppose one can't blame him,' Venetia said. 'No-one wants a war, do they?'

'I'm not so sure. I think we have got into one of those intermittent periods of restlessness that overcome mankind. Look at this country, the strikes and riots we've been suffering; and now all Ireland is in a ferment with them. Look at the willingness of people to use violent action as a first resort instead of the last. Look at the new ideas coming in, none of them peaceful. The new movements in art – futurism, fauvism and the rest of it – modern music, that fellow Stravinsky, for instance, the yellow press, socialism, rag music, jazz: everything tends towards jittery activity and constant change. Things may look calm on the surface, but underneath there's a restless sea of desire for newness. It's a craze for something, anything, that's *different*.'

'But why should that lead to war?'

'Belligerence is the easiest outlet for restlessness. It takes a very cultured mind to use it creatively. Can you imagine the man in the street saying, "I feel restless, I want a change, I think I'll go and cultivate my chrysanthemums"?'

Venetia laughed. 'No, I see what you mean. All the same, don't countries have to have reasons to go to war with each other?'

Overton stared into the fire. 'At the bottom of it, we have two empires wanting to expand – Russia in search of warm-water ports, Germany in search of territory. They are bound to clash.'

Venetia imagined a map of Europe. 'In the Balkans, perhaps?' she queried.

He nodded. 'There has always been trouble in the Balkans and I suppose there always will be. But in particular there's the trouble between Serbia and Austria. The Serbs think they ought to rule the whole of the Balkans, and Austria thinks pretty much the same. Russia will always support the Serbs because they are Slavs, and the Austrian Empire is already little more than a semi-detached part of the German Empire. Add to that the old rivalry between France and Germany, still unsettled, take into account that Russia and France are allies, so if Germany attacks France, Russia will have to go to her aid –'

'– and *we* are in alliance with France and Russia,' Venetia completed for him.

'Not only that,' said Overton, 'but we depend on the Channel ports and the Rhine delta for our trade access to the mainland. Between Germany and France is the little triangle of Belgium. The first thing Germany will do in a war with France is to take Belgium. Another fifty miles of coast, and they have Calais and Boulogne as well. We can't let that happen. A German Empire that engulfed Belgium and France would leave us shut out from Europe altogether – especially as they now have the second largest navy in the world, so they could defend the coast against us.'

She met his eyes and saw the gravity in them. 'When, do you think?'

'This year. Next year.'

'But – we will win?'

He did not immediately say yes, and her heart turned cold. At last he said, 'It's unthinkable that we should not. But at what cost?'

In January 1913 the Government's Manhood Suffrage Bill went into its committee stage, and the Suffragettes' supporters among the MPs intended to propose an amendment to extend the vote to married women. Asquith, Churchill and Harcourt had threatened to resign if any women's amendment were adopted; but Lloyd George and Sir Edward Grey had spoken, before the session began, cautiously in favour of some extension of the vote, and they now agreed to receive a deputation of working women.

The Movement became very excited about it, and extensive and careful arrangements were made to bring together three hundred women from all over the country, to be led by Mrs Drummond and Annie Kenney, with twenty of them, carefully selected, to speak to the ministers on behalf of various professions and trades.

The deputation took place on the 23rd of January, at the Treasury. Nurses, teachers, shop assistants, factory hands, domestic servants, agricultural workers were all represented. A Mrs Cohen spoke on behalf of tailoresses, paid at half the hourly rate as men for the same job, and always the first to be laid off at slack time, because without the vote they did not have equal status with men. Mrs Bigwood represented the workers of the East End sweat shops. 'I earn six shillings a week, that's all, for making pinafores – and out of that I have to buy my own thread and pay for my own fire and gaslight to work by.' A laundress spoke of the labour of handling a seven-pound hot iron all day. 'They've tried out men, Mr Lloyd George, but the men can't do it. We women ought to have the vote, and it's a disgrace we've not got it by now.' A fisherwoman had come down from Edinburgh, a pit-brow lass from Yorkshire. A housemaid told of her day that began with laying fires before her employers were awake, and often ended after they had gone to bed, banishing dirt and disorder. 'The country would come to a standstill without women's work, Mr Lloyd George. Why haven't we the vote?' Mrs Drummond, in her clear, strong voice, spoke wittily; Annie Kenney was fierce.

The ministers listened, but they would not commit themselves. And then, on the same day, came the news that the Speaker, James Lowther, had ruled that amendments to create a new franchise would so alter the nature of the Bill that it would have to be withdrawn. Suffragists believed it was a deliberate ploy to wreck the women's chances again: probably Asquith was at the bottom of it. It was taken by the Suffragettes to prove that constitutional means were useless and that there was no alternative to direct and militant action. In a last attempt to salvage something from the situation, Mrs Drummond led a deputation of twenty to the House on the 28th of January, but they were treated with great brutality by the police and finally, bruised, battered and mud-covered, they were arrested.

A prolonged period of violence broke out, beginning with window-smashing and going on to arson. Pillar-boxes were set on fire, and letters containing materials that burst into flames when opened were sent to Asquith and Lloyd George. One woman broke the glass cases containing the Crown Jewels in the Tower. Telegraph wires were cut. Golf was a favourite pastime of cabinet ministers, and there was a concerted attack on golf courses, with greens being damaged by trowels, and by having slogans burnt into the turf: 'No Votes, No Golf', 'Justice Before Sport', 'Votes or War'. On the 8th of February the greenhouses at Kew Gardens were attacked and plants destroyed. On the 12th a refreshment kiosk in Regent's Park was burnt down. And on the 19th a bomb exploded in a house that was being built for Lloyd George at Walton-on-the-Hill in Surrey. A letter was sent to the press to explain that measures had been taken to avoid any harm to the workmen; and Mrs Pankhurst made a public speech claiming responsibility for the bomb. As a result, she was arrested on the 24th of February, and committed for trial in the Old Bailey on the 1st of April.

It was anticipated that she would be given a long sentence, and as she had already sworn to starve herself if imprisoned, there was much speculation as to how the Government would deal with her. She was an elderly woman, and forcible feeding might well kill her: it was likely she would have to be released. Many Suffragettes had been released before finishing their sentences because of hunger striking, and the situation, where flagrant law-breakers could not be punished, was making a mockery of the police and of government policy. There was also growing public concern about forcible feeding. Harrowing accounts had been smuggled out to the press; one woman, Lilian Lenton, had tried to thwart attempts to feed her by continually coughing as the tube was pushed down. Food had got into her lungs and she had developed double pneumonia and pleurisy.

Bernard Shaw, in a speech, said, 'If you take a woman and torture her, you torture me. These denials of fundamental rights are a violation of the soul. They are an attack on that sacred part of life that is common to all of us, that has no individuality. I say that the denial of these fundamental rights to ourselves in the persons of women is a denial of the life everlasting.'

Suggestions were made in the press for ways around the forcible-feeding dilemma: that the women should be given food and allowed to choose whether to eat or die; that they should be transported to St Helena; that they should be given fines without the option of imprisonment. The cabinet discussed these and other possible measures, and finally came up with a ticket-of-leave system, which was rushed through Parliament as the Prisoners (Temporary Discharge for Ill-Health) Bill, with the intention of having it in place before Mrs Pankhurst came up for trial. This new measure allowed the authorities to release prisoners judged to be seriously weakened by hunger striking under a licence that specified the date they must return to prison, usually a week later. While out on licence prisoners had to notify the police of their address; they must not change their address without giving written notice, nor be absent from that address for more than twelve hours. Failure to comply or to re-present themselves to continue their sentences rendered them liable to immediate arrest.

The militant disturbances continued through March, with arson attacks and vandalism carried out on empty buildings: sports pavilions, boathouses, two schools, a railway station, a grandstand, a disused church. Some large unoccupied houses were set on fire, as was an empty railway train in a siding, and more pillar-boxes. Golf greens all over the country were attacked, and Walton Heath, where Lloyd

George played, was guarded day and night by fifty caddies. Some of the royal palaces – Kensington, Kew, Hampton and Holyroodhouse – were closed to the public, and there was talk of closing museums and art galleries.

In this atmosphere there was no difficulty in getting the Prisoners Bill through Parliament in time to trap Mrs Pankhurst. She offered no defence at her trial, merely making a political statement, describing the condition of her daughter Sylvia, who had just been released from Holloway after being forcibly fed for two months, following her conviction for breaking a small pane of glass.

'This is the kind of punishment you are inflicting on me or on any other woman who may be brought before you. I ask you if you are prepared to send an incalculable number of women to prison.' She said that she would refuse food in prison, and that as soon as she was released she would take up the fight again. 'Life is very dear to us all. I am not seeking, as was said by the Home Secretary, to commit suicide. I want to see the women of this country enfranchised, and I want to live to see it done.'

Under determined direction by the judge, the jury found her guilty, but entered a 'strong recommendation to mercy'. Nevertheless, she was sentenced to three years' penal servitude, a very heavy sentence.

In Holloway, she went at once on hunger strike, while outside prison Suffragettes mounted renewed attacks on empty houses, railway stations and racecourses. The Home Secretary issued a statement that Mrs Pankhurst was being supplied constantly with fresh and appetising food, and the governor of Holloway listed what was offered her – boiled egg and thin bread-and-butter for breakfast, filleted plaice, roast chicken or beefsteak for dinner, buttered toast for supper. Outside, Suffragettes laughed at the list, remembering the usual prison fare. On the 11th of April the prison doctor saw her and said she was too ill for forcible feeding, and so on the 12th she was released. The prison authorities gave her a licence, requiring her return to Holloway in fifteen days' time, and in defiance she tore it up under their noses.

She was taken home, desperately ill. She was nursed with great care by friends and supporters, but at the end of the fifteen days a police doctor pronounced her still unfit to return to Holloway. She remained where she was, and the house was guarded by two detectives at the front, two at the back, and another on a nearby roof, while a taxi waited in the street outside to give chase if she tried to escape. She was eventually returned to prison on the 26th of May, but this time was released, ill, after only three days of fasting, with a licence to return on the 7th of June.

Pethick Lawrence dubbed this new legislation 'The Cat and Mouse Act'.

In the late spring of 1913, Lizzie was feeling restless. She had got over the terrible events of the previous April, had settled in to her new life in Arizona, and with the children at school, and Ashley away a good deal in the course of his business, she was finding herself with too little to do. So it was a great boon to her to receive a visit from Aunt Ruth.

She brought with her her grandson Lennox Manning, who was seventeen. He ought to have been in school, but was convalescent from an attack of the whooping cough, for which the doctor had recommended the dry air of just such a place as Flagstaff. Martial and Rupert were wild with envy every day when they went off to school leaving Lenny behind to enjoy his freedom, but the three boys enjoyed one another's company during their leisure hours.

Lizzie was very glad of Aunt Ruth's company. She was missing her mother, and while there was nothing very motherly about Ruth, she was at least of an older generation, and interested in how Lizzie felt and thought. She found herself able to talk to Ruth about the tragedy, and Amalfia's death, and the difficulties and pleasures of settling in to a foreign country, with a depth and intimacy impossible with anyone else – even with Ashley, who was too preoccupied with work and too often absent to be a good confidant. Ruth had gone through sufferings herself, of an order to make Lizzie's trivial by comparison, which made her sympathetic in the true sense of the word. While she was always bracing and unsentimental, she *understood*.

It was too hot to be out and about much in the middle of the day, but the house, like all those in the neighbourhood, had a deep verandah, and Lizzie, who had always been an active housewife, learned to enjoy sitting in the shade through the heat of the day, rocking gently and talking. She discovered that when led on with suitable questions, Ruth would lose her habitual terseness and describe the old world of her childhood and early womanhood with a breadth and lyricism not to be suspected from her usual utterances. Lizzie listened, entranced, to the account of life in the South before the war, saw vividly the Twelvetrees plantation, Charleston, Washington, Richmond – the balls and parties and barbecues, the hunts and horseracing and yachting expeditions.

Lizzie asked her, tentatively, about slavery. 'Wasn't it horrible?'

'Pretty much, I guess,' Ruth said. 'House slaves had a pretty good life on the whole, and field hands – well, they were fed and housed, the work wasn't hard, and they didn't know any better. I was hardly more than a child, so I didn't appreciate fully, but having slaves was no bed of roses. Mary – your Ashley's mother – told me once the burden of it fell mostly on the women, like her, and that if it was up to them, there'd *be* no slavery. You could never get slaves to work properly, you couldn't leave them to do anything unsupervised. You spent your life chasing after them, scolding them, trying to sort out their petty arguments with each other, listening to their complaints, taking care of them when they were sick. You never got away from them for a minute. Someone like Mary, living out on a plantation, was a slave to them near as much as they were to her. You couldn't dismiss 'em, no matter how stupid and lazy and useless they were; you couldn't do the work yourself, because there they were, and they had to be kept occupied; and you couldn't get any other kind of servant, because slavery meant no-one else would be a servant. That's all there was.'

Lizzie thought this was rather missing the point. 'But don't you think slavery was a bad thing in itself?'

'Oh, yes, dear, of course. All the thinking people in the South hated it, and my cousin Martial – Mary's second husband – said that the South would have done away with it pretty soon anyway, war or no war. In any case, the North didn't start the war to end slavery. They only claimed that afterwards so's people would think they were the angels and we were the devils. They attacked us without good cause, that's the truth of it, and all the thousands that died and all the starvation and misery afterwards were down to their account. It was all the Yankees' fault.'

She spoke with the vehemence of old resentment, which years had not dimmed, and Lizzie asked her, 'But you live in the north now. How do you manage that?'

'Same as you,' Ruth said. 'It's a foreign country, and you have to adapt. I wouldn't have chosen to come here any more than I suspect you would, but you have to go where your husband goes.'

Under Lizzie's questioning she told her whole story; but it was plain that it was her childhood in ante-bellum Carolina that was the most vivid to her. She remembered horses and dogs, servants and friends, every corner, field, wood and 'crick' of her childhood home, in loving detail, described them so well that Lizzie could really see it all in her mind's eye.

The thing Ruth questioned Lizzie most about was Morland Place. It held a fascination for her, and again Lizzie urged her to visit and see it for herself. 'Mother and Uncle Teddy would be glad to have you,' she said. 'You could see everything you've heard about – the house and moat and the horses and the original Twelvetrees.'

But Ruth only laughed, and said, 'No, no, puss, I'm too old now. I can't go all that way, especially not on a ship. Lenny must see it for me. Lenny will go one day.'

And during the course of the visit, when the subject came up in general conversation, it became clear that Lenny's intention to go to England was even stronger than Ruth's on his behalf, for while she said, 'One day,' he began to say, 'Next year.'

'Next summer,' he said, one evening when they were

sitting on the porch with the sound of the crickets like a symphony orchestra in the background. 'Do you think they'd really have me, Cousin Lizzie? I could go over as soon as I finish school. Gran'ma's put money aside to pay for it – haven't you, Granny?'

'How d'you know that, boy?' Ruth said, drawing her brows together sternly.

'Oh, I hear things,' he said lightly. 'And I know you, besides. You want me to be your eyes and ears.' He grinned at her affectionately and went on, 'I could have two or three months there, before I have to come back and go to college, if they'd have me. What do you think? Could I stay at Morland Place? I could make myself useful.'

'I'm sure you could,' Lizzie said. 'If you're serious about it, I'll write to Uncle Teddy and ask him, if you like.'

'Would you really? Gee Christmas, that's swell of you!' Lenny cried.

'Watch your language, young man,' Ruth admonished him.

And Martial, listening as he swung idly back and forth on a rope hung from the shade tree, said, 'Fancy wanting to go to England! It's much better here.'

CHAPTER EIGHTEEN

It was evident through the spring of 1913 that Tommy Weston was failing fast. At Emma's seventeenth birthday in January he was still himself, though thin and a bad colour; but by the end of February it was plain that a change had come over him. The fight to stay alive was wearing him out.

Venetia was only surprised that Emma did not seem to notice it: in March she felt sufficiently secure of her father to complain that her coming-out ball was being held so early.

'The Season doesn't properly start until Easter,' she said. 'A lot of people won't even be in London.'

'Only the landed and titled families,' Venetia said. 'There'll be enough people in London for you, young lady. Where did you get such high ideas?'

She had agreed to present Emma, though privately she thought this an unnecessary refinement. Emma's sphere, she thought, would lie outside the Court. Her maternal grandfather might be a baron, but her father's background would not stand looking into. He had made his way in Society through politics, and it was more likely Emma would marry into that world. She would be a considerable heiress – Tommy had set money aside for her, and she would inherit a large sum from her mother – but in Tommy's place Venetia would not have sought a title for her.

But by the time Emma was trying on her finished presentation gown, the change in Tommy had become so marked that even she had noticed it – or perhaps it was that she had been denying it to herself, and now could do so no longer. At all events, she was very quiet at the fitting, and silent in the motor-car afterwards. Venetia was taking her to Gatti's for ices, expecting to meet Violet there, and Emma ought to have been bubbling over in anticipation of the treat.

Guessing what was wrong, Venetia thought she should use the privacy of the short drive to allow Emma to ask anything she had to ask. So she said, 'What's the matter, Emma? You're very quiet.' Emma looked up at her, chewed her lip, evidently needing more encouragement to get past the barrier she had erected. 'Is it your father?' Venetia asked quietly.

Emma struggled, but the opening was enough. 'I don't think he's well,' she said at last. She surveyed Venetia's face in the shadow of her hat and her heart grew heavy at what she read there. 'You know what's wrong with him, don't you?'

'Yes,' said Venetia. 'He confided in me long ago – last year, in fact.'

'Last year? But he was all right last year,' Emma said, much puzzled. 'It's only just the last few weeks . . .' She stopped, thinking things through. Then she said, in a small voice, 'He's been ill all that time? Is he – is he going to die?'

Venetia reached out a hand and took hold of Emma's; Emma gripped it tightly, knowing that pain was to come. 'Yes, I'm afraid so,' she said. She waited a while, as Emma stared into mid-air, trying to adjust to the knowledge, and then went on, 'That's why he's bringing you out so young. Because he wanted so much to be there.'

'But – but why didn't he tell me?' she asked. 'If I'd known—' She thought of all the wasted time, when she could have been with him, and had chosen to be elsewhere. The weeks at Morland Place last summer. The week in autumn with her sister Ada. The time over Christmas when she had stayed with sister Fanny. 'Why didn't he tell me?'

'He wanted to keep it from you because he wanted you to be happy. This is a special time of your life and he didn't want it to be blighted,' said Venetia. 'And, Emma, I think it would be kind of you not to let him know that you know.'

'Not?'

'He wants to do his best for you. Let him be happy

369

thinking he has done that.' She looked down into the tear-filled eyes. 'It will be hard,' she said gently.

Emma nodded, unable to speak. They drove on in silence, and it was as they were pulling up before Gatti's that she finally managed to ask, in a sort of gasp, 'Does it hurt?'

The true answer and the tactful were at variance. But Venetia looked into the pale face, saw the determined teeth that were preventing the lips trembling, the effort not to cry, and felt that such courage deserved respect. 'Yes,' she said. Emma nodded and closed her eyes a moment, and then as the door was opened was ready to climb out and face the world.

Emma's ball was a success. Venetia did not know how he had managed it, but Tommy had persuaded Lord and Lady Abradale to abandon the habits of a lifetime and come down for the Season, so that Lady Abradale could act as his hostess. He rented a house with a ballroom, and Betty Abradale seemed somewhat surprised to find herself there, but she knew well enough what was to be done, having had her own come-out and attended those of her four sisters.

By the night of the ball Tommy could only stand for short periods, and had to sit down between receiving each few guests. Emma managed to be almost feverishly gay, though the looks she cast across the ballroom at her father would have alerted the least noticing in Society that something was wrong. But the news had already spread by a kind of osmosis, and as it was plain that the Westons did not wish to acknowledge the truth, everyone joined in a benign conspiracy to pretend they didn't know.

Violet brought plenty of her young men along and Tommy raided the worlds of politics and public office, so the ball avoided the one fatal failing, of having too many girls and not enough men. Emma was so pretty and lively that she was never without a partner. Sitting beside Tommy at one point, Venetia asked him, 'Well, was it worth it?'

'Yes,' he said. It was such a short answer that she looked at him for enlightenment, and then looked away quickly. Such feelings as those were too private to be acknowledged.

The following week Venetia presented Emma, relieved to have made it to Court in time – Tommy's death would put

Emma into mourning for a year, and a girl in mourning could not be presented. Emma went through the ceremony with a smile fixed on her lips and an air of being in a dream. Violet had agreed to share the chaperonage of Emma for the rest of the Season, taking on the more energetic functions and late-night dances that Lady Abradale felt too old and very much too disinclined for. But it seemed that Tommy had worn out his last reserve of strength with the effort of the opening ball. By the time Venetia was presenting Emma, he had taken helplessly to his bed; at the end of another fortnight he was dead, and Emma's Season was at an end.

It was good that the Abradales were there to cope with things, since they were Emma's nearest relatives. They arranged both the small private funeral and the much larger memorial service in St Margaret's, which was attended by many notables from the Prime Minister downwards, showing how wide Tommy's circle of influence had been. Venetia shared a pew at the service with her daughter and Lord Holkam, which made her reflect on what she, personally, owed him. Black suited Violet, and she looked staggeringly beautiful, and hardly any older than poor little Emma, sobbing helplessly in the pew in front. And Holkam was a handsome man, Venetia thought, glancing at him beyond her daughter. They made an impressive couple, and if Venetia found her son-in-law dull, it seemed that Violet was content, which was what mattered.

A few days later Emma came to see Venetia to say goodbye.

'I'm going to Scotland with Aunt Betty,' she explained. 'Uncle Bruce is staying here to sell everything and deal with the lawyers, but he says there's no need for me to be here.'

Her face was pale and her eyes and nose were red-rimmed. Black did not suit her colouring, and with her mournful expression she looked, as she must be feeling, quite bereft – a lost child.

Venetia was stirred to pity. She thought of worthy but taciturn Betty Abradale, and of what little she knew about the Abradales' life in their chilly Scottish castle. Such isolation was not, perhaps, the best way to help Emma recover:

371

without some activity and variety, she would have all too much time to brood. 'It's very kind of your aunt,' she said carefully, 'but I wonder if you won't find Aberlarich too quiet and dull.'

'I want it quiet and dull,' Emma said starkly. 'I *hate* London, with all the noise and dashing about and people dancing and *laughing* and everything, just as if, as if—' Her eyes filled with tears again and she had to stop.

Venetia nodded. 'I quite understand. And it's natural you should feel like that at the moment. I just want you to remember that if at some time you would like to come back – for any reason – you may always come here.'

Emma nodded, and then in a little broken flurry of movement ran against Venetia and put her arms tightly round her. Venetia was surprised, but recovered quickly and put her arms round the child in response. It lasted only an instant. Emma quickly recovered herself and backed off, blushing at the enormity of the *faux pas*. To ease her embarrassment Venetia smiled and said kindly, 'I hope you will always feel that you have a friend here, two friends, in Lord Overton and me.'

'Thank you, ma'am,' Emma said; and there was just a watery suggestion of a smile in response.

A few days later again, Abradale himself came to call on Venetia. He seemed ill at ease, though he began by exchanging the usual words of any formal visit, enquiring after her health, commenting on the weather, mentioning some matters in the House of Lords in which he knew Overton had an interest. In fact, these ponderous formalities went on so long Venetia began to feel restless, for she had a great deal to do. Abradale was actually younger than her by some ten years, but with his old-fashioned ways and face lined by Scottish weather he seemed much her senior. There had been an enormous gap of years between him and Emma's mother Beatrice, which Venetia suspected must have been accounted for by a string of miscarriages or infant deaths.

At last, to help him along, she took advantage of a pause to ask him how the business of winding up Tommy's estate was faring. Abradale seemed almost relieved to have the cue tossed to him. 'Quite well, quite well,' he said. 'As smoothly as can be expected of anything which has the involvement of lawyers to obfuscate matters.'

'Emma will be a wealthy young woman, I imagine,' said Venetia.

'Indeed she will.' He seemed to want to say more, and she had to guess what it might be or they would be here all day.

'I assume that you are her legal guardian?'

'Ah, well, now,' said Abradale slowly. 'Indeed, it is natural that you should assume that, Lady Overton. From the time that we learned the nature of Weston's illness, we assumed the same ourselves, given that we are Emma's only kin apart from her half-brothers and -sisters. While I cannot say that it was a duty we relished, being, as we are, somewhat advanced in years and perhaps a little elderly in habit, her ladyship and I were fully prepared to discharge that duty with every care and energy it might require. But the preliminary reading of the will, which I attended yesterday, revealed that Weston has introduced another, one might say an unusual, element.'

Venetia was well ahead of his stately periods, and had guessed now what he had come to tell her. 'Surely you cannot mean that you are *not* her guardian?'

'I am her guardian, but not her sole guardian. It is an honour – and a duty – I am to share with you, ma'am.' He managed to bow from the waist quite gracefully, even though he was sitting down.

'Tommy Weston named me joint guardian with you?'

Abradale nodded. 'He has given me sole trusteeship of her fortune, but you are named with me as having custody of her further upbringing.'

Venetia felt a certain exasperation. It was one thing for her to invite Emma to stay if Aberlarich got too dull, another to have legal responsibility for the girl thrust on her! She knew Tommy had had ambitions for his girl, and had wanted Venetia's social influence and London house to be put at Emma's service, but it was too bad of him to have done it without asking her.

'I suppose,' Abradale said, in more direct language than he had employed so far, 'he thought me too old to have sole charge of such a lively young girl.'

She assembled her words with care. 'I am sure it was nothing of the sort. He and I were childhood friends, and I dare say he only meant it as a compliment to me. He gave you trusteeship of her fortune so he plainly meant you to have care of her. I assure you that nothing could be further from my thoughts than to challenge your authority.'

She could see she had not entirely satisfied him, but when he spoke again, it emerged that he had not been suffering from hurt feelings.

'Thank you for those words; but I fear you mistake me.' He became almost agitated. 'Far from wishing – my life and her ladyship's, you see, are conducted in such a way – indeed, Emma is so very . . . Lady Overton, may I be blunt?'

'Please do,' said Venetia fervently.

'Aberlarich is not the place for a young girl, and when I come to London, it is always alone. I live at my club. Her ladyship does not care for Town life. Though we love Emma dearly, we have dreaded the charge laid upon us, and when I heard you named yesterday with me, my heart was considerably lightened. I am hoping – we are both hoping – that once the first mourning is over you will take charge of her.'

That was blunt enough, at any rate. Venetia saw the trap closing, but she said, 'I am, in fact, older than you, Lord Abradale.'

He was too eager to compliment her. 'Oh, but you live in London, ma'am. You move in Society. You have children of your own – her ladyship and I, being childless, would be quite bewildered by the charge. And your daughter, Lady Holkam – I am sure she would share the physical burden of chaperonage with you. She expressed herself most kindly prepared to help her ladyship in that way before the Unhappy Event.'

Venetia saw that there was no way out – and in fairness to poor Emma she could not think of her being exiled to the far reaches of Perthshire for the rest of her life, condemned, no doubt, to marry some unpolished Scottish laird with a draughty castle and large debts. She would have to have the girl to stay, and take charge of her matrimonial campaign, little as she wanted to. Violet would help her, and she supposed that from time to time she would be able to pack Emma off to one of her half-siblings – Fanny, the eldest, loved her and was a friendly and motherly woman, even though she lived in suburban Surrey. But it was monstrous of Tommy to have forced it on her, all the same – and the fact that he had not consulted her first showed that he had known it.

This conclusion was further confirmed when the will was settled, and a package arrived by courier for Venetia, which contained a sapphire pendant that Tommy had left to her. It came with a note in his hand, which said that it had belonged to his grandmother Lucy, Lady Theakston, who had been Venetia's great-grandmother – their common ancestress. He might have been expected to leave it to one of his daughters, but he had left it to her with the thought that 'it was appropriate that one great lady should wear the jewel of another', especially as it matched her eyes.

'A handsome compliment,' Overton said, when she showed him the note.

'It makes me want to say, "Bah! Humbug!"' Venetia complained. 'My eyes aren't even blue.'

'But you are a great lady,' Overton said, with a smile.

'Hm,' said Venetia. Bright blue sapphires were not as valuable as the dark ones, as she knew very well, though the size of the stone alone made up for that. She laid the pendant across her palm, and the light sparked deeply in the heart of the jewel. 'It is a very pretty thing, though,' she said, grudgingly, at last.

Jessie's body recovered quickly from the loss of the baby, but her mind was more deeply hurt. She had not thought much about the child while it was there, but when it was gone, she found herself mourning it. Dr Hasty was comforting. He told her that there was no reason why she should not have another – plenty more, in fact. As to why she had lost it – these things were a mystery. 'It happens a great deal, much more than you would think. It's what I would call a natural thing – very sad for the parents, but just part of the way things are.'

Jessie had pressed him to say what caused it, but he told her it was impossible to be sure. Any one of a thousand little things could have gone wrong, he said. But in Jessie's mind was the knowledge that she had lost the child soon after following the hunt in Hackett's cart. She asked Hasty straight out whether that was the cause, and he looked straight back at her and said, no, he didn't think so.

'Then why did you tell me not to ride?' Jessie demanded bluntly.

'Riding is a different matter from sitting in a carriage – or even a cart. And it's not unknown for ladies to fall off horses.'

'Carriages overturn,' she said.

'Much less often. It's a matter of striking a balance, you see. It would be foolish to tell a pregnant woman to stay in bed for nine months. Some risks are better avoided, others don't matter so much. No, I don't think you lost the baby because of that. My advice to you is to put it out of your mind, and in a few months' time you can be starting another one. This time next year you'll be well on the way to being a mother.'

Jessie knew that Hasty had had a long talk with Ned. She supposed he had told him the same things. At all events, Ned never suggested by so much as a look that he thought her guilty of killing their child; but Jessie could not get it out of her head that that was really what had happened, and that Ned knew it. It created a distance between them.

On the surface, all went on as usual. As soon as she was well again – much sooner than Ned really liked – Jessie was out of bed and resuming her normal activities. Hasty had told her not to ride for six weeks, but she was soon driving the phaeton over to Twelvetrees to supervise the work that had been neglected. Ned tried each evening to ask her what she had been doing that day as if it were a normal conversational ploy, but Jessie felt he was checking on her, and it made her replies stilted.

Hasty had told Ned there should be no marital activity

for three months, and so the thing that had always gone well between them, and which brought them together, was forbidden him. To avoid temptation, Ned continued to sleep in the dressing-room, as he had begun doing during the immediate aftermath. Once she was well, Jessie would have liked him in bed with her, just for the company; and perhaps being close at night would have helped them cross the gap between them. As it was, his physical absence seemed to set the new order in stone. They behaved towards each other in a friendly way, talked together much as they always had as cousins, but they were no longer touching, either physically or emotionally.

Jessie threw herself into her work. When the six weeks were up she was back in the saddle at once, for there was a backlog of orders to see to. Businesses were picking up after the troubles of the previous year, and people were buying horses again. In addition, she had an order from the army procurer, Mr Forrester, for ten remounts, and the horses needed to be brought up and finished off. She did not do the rough breaking herself, but the men who did were taken off other duties, like schooling, which she then had to take over. Constant activity helped to blunt her emotions, and made her tired enough at night to sleep, but it did not stop her feeling lonely.

With Ned away all day, there was nothing at Maystone to comfort her, and she began to spend more time that spring at Morland Place. Uncle Teddy no longer wanted to go into public or interest himself in his businesses, so he was turning all his energies to his land. Jessie gave him someone to talk to about it, someone quick of apprehension who was as interested as he was.

'Planning, that's the thing,' he said to her. 'Planning and efficient use of everything. There's a lot of new thinking these days about land management. I've been reading a great deal, and it's all a matter of thinking the process through and not wasting anything.'

'What do you mean by that?' Jessie asked, leaning her elbows on the table and her face in her hands.

Teddy was only too pleased to explain. 'Well, you see, to

begin with, you have to look at what people want to buy. Here we are, right beside a big city – and with others not far away. And what do city people want? They want meat, milk, fruit and vegetables.'

'Market gardening,' Jessie agreed. 'That's what Dad said years ago – go into market gardening.'

'Yes, and we have, but not enough. I was reading an article in the farming magazine about tomatoes.'

'Tomatoes?' Jessie wrinkled her nose.

'Easy crop, tomatoes – big yields, few diseases – and there's a growing market for them. But you've got to get them to ripen quickly and that means glass.'

'Greenhouses?'

'Exactly. But it said in that article that you can't grow only tomatoes in your greenhouses, because when they're done, there's all that glass standing empty, doing nothing. So you have to grow a succession of things.'

'That makes sense,' Jessie said. 'What other things go with tomatoes?'

'Cucumbers,' said Teddy, 'and then chrysanthemums for cutting. That takes you through a cycle. But there's more. What do you need to grow tomatoes on this scale, apart from glass?'

Jessie was amused at his schoolroom delivery, and keeping her face straight obliged him by saying, 'I don't know. Earth?'

'Manure,' said Teddy triumphantly. 'And where does manure come from?'

'Horses,' she hazarded.

'Quite right. Towns are full of manure, and they're so anxious to get rid of it, they'll even pay to have it taken away. So we get it for nothing, and turn it into tomatoes, which we sell back to the towns at a large profit.'

'Very clever,' Jessie said. 'Are you going to build lots and lots of greenhouses, then?'

'I was thinking of it. They need to be on level ground that's not overshadowed by trees. There's that big field beyond the stables that might serve. Of course, it would involve a certain capital outlay, but they'd soon pay for themselves. We've the best railway connections in the country

378

here in York, and I don't see why we shouldn't send our tomatoes all over the place – Leeds, Manchester, even London. They're mad for tomatoes in London, so I read.'

They talked about this idea for a while, and then Jessie asked, 'What about the tenants? Are you going to make them into market gardeners as well?'

'Not yet,' said Teddy. 'Perhaps in the future – but this is a new venture, and I must see how it works out first. But there is one thing I want to try, and I'm going to talk to the Pikes about it, and see if we can try it out at Eastfield – milk. I don't mean just a few cows producing for your table and your neighbours', but going in for it in a much bigger way.'

'Like the tomatoes.'

'Yes. And if you're going in for it seriously, you have to pay attention to milk yields. I've been reading about a new breed, the Holstein, that gives much more milk than other breeds. I'm going to talk to Pike about it, and see what he thinks about buying some of 'em.'

Jessie laughed. 'You really have been reading up! I never thought to hear words like "milk yield" on your lips.'

He smiled unwillingly. 'I know, I know. Jumping on a hobby-horse, ain't I? But it's dashed interesting, all the same. I never realised. When I was a young man, farming bored me stiff, and all I wanted was to live in the city and poddle from home to the club and back. But there's so much going on now, so many new ideas – and there's little James William to think about.'

Over the weeks, Teddy unfolded his ideas to her. Woodhouse Farm had always made a certain amount of cheese, some of which was quite prized locally, though it was sold only to friends and neighbours. Teddy's idea was to expand the cheese-making into a regular business. Eastfield could provide the milk required.

'And there's something else,' Teddy said. 'You know I was talking about efficiency and using everything? Well, it seems that when you make cheese, you get a lot of skimmed milk left over.'

'Yes, I know,' Jessie said. 'The Waltons give it to their pigs. Everyone says they have the best bacon in the country.'

'But making a lot of cheese will leave far too much skimmed milk just for the Waltons' pigs. What it says in the magazine is that you should use it for calf rearing. You buy them at a few weeks old, feed them all your skimmed milk, and when they're big you sell them for beef. Nothing wasted, you see.'

'Cattle make manure, too,' Jessie thought aloud suddenly.

'That's right. Now you're getting the idea.'

'It's a different way of thinking about farming, isn't it?' she said.

'It's more businesslike,' Teddy said. 'Farming's been through a bad time, and if we're ever going to get back to the good times, we've got to change. Of course, we've never suffered up here the way they have down south. But the land should be able to support itself, *and* make a profit. Now that a lot of the old generation of farmers have gone, the younger ones are more ready to try new things.'

'You talk like a young thing yourself,' Jessie said, amused.

'Oh, I'm not so mossy yet. I've a kick or two left in me,' he said, more cheerfully than she'd heard him say anything in a year.

Losing a baby herself gave her common cause with Aunt Alice, and she had a new admiration for her aunt's courage and serenity. Her mother, who had also lost a child, was a comfort and a fortress. Morland Place was always so full of warmth and life that Maystone seemed cold and empty by comparison.

Perhaps Ned felt it too, for he began to issue and accept invitations with increasing frequency. York was forgetting the events of the previous spring, and though there were still people who condemned and cut Uncle Teddy, there were others who welcomed the Ned Morlands at their gatherings. So began a very busy period of social life, which saw them engaged, one way or another, most evenings. Often they would find themselves hurrying home from their work – Ned from the mill and Jessie from the stables – with only just enough time to change before the motor was brought round or the first guests arrived. Given that Ned continued to sleep in the dressing-room, it meant that they hardly had to spend any time alone together. When they were alone, it always seemed that the lost baby made an invisible third, and with the baby always came the unspoken and unspeakable memory of Hackett's tub cart, so it was better that way.

'What do you think of this new situation?' Anne asked Venetia. Venetia had asked her to sit down, but she did not seem able to keep still, had immediately jumped up and was walking – prowling – up and down the room. Outside it was a bright May day, and the intruding bars of sunshine illuminated her as she moved in and out of them. She looked far from well. She was very thin, her skin was a bad colour, and the lines had deepened in her face. She was almost fifty, Venetia reflected, and the periods of imprisonment and starvation had left their mark on her. It was hard to remember that she had been an acclaimed beauty.

'What situation do you mean?'

Anne stopped on a turn. 'The Cat and Mouse Act, of course,' she said. 'Only this despicable government could have thought of it.'

'It is very bad,' Venetia said.

'It's worse than bad. It's the most tyrannical, unjust, illiberal—' Words failed her for a moment. She resumed, 'Consider the case of Mrs Pankhurst. She's been given three years, and if she serves the sentence a few days at a time, broken by time out on licence, she may spend the rest of her life serving it. Is she to die still under sentence? And when she *is* out, she's watched night and day by detectives. Is she never to be free again? What sort of man could order something like that? Ha!' she answered herself. 'The sort of man who tries to suppress a newspaper, of course: Mr Home Secretary McKenna.'

She was referring to an incident at the beginning of May, when the Lincoln's Inn premises had been raided, and the public prosecutor had ordered publication of the *Suffragette* to be stopped. The staff, and WSPU leaders, including Mrs Drummond, Annie Kenney and Anne herself, had been arrested and all were awaiting trial for conspiracy. Even the printer of the paper had been arrested.

There had been a public outcry, led by the *Manchester*

Guardian, for freedom of the press was a cornerstone of British democracy. On the Sunday after the raid a rally had been held at Hyde Park, where the Suffragette speakers had been very well received by the public. A massive attendance of thirty thousand had cheered them, and saved them from arrest by forming protective crowds round them, shouting, 'Free speech! Free speech!' and 'Shame!' when the police tried to break through. Anne had been one of the speakers, each of whom was equipped with a flag and a folding camp stool. They spread out over the park, and when a suitable moment came, each climbed on her stool, waved her flag, and began speaking. The crowds at once rushed to surround them, and when the police tried to break through, the speaker packed up, shielded by the crowd, and fled to another spot. They made a game of evading the police all day, and almost all of them managed to escape arrest and continued the rally until sundown.

'When does your trial come on?' Venetia asked.

'June the fifteenth,' Anne said, with magnificent indifference. 'I'm only glad they didn't arrest Vera this time. Ironic, really. I've never had much to do with the *Suffragette*, but Vera's often at Lincoln's Inn and she's helped with both writing and editing. But I suppose they were more eager to get me, and overlooked Vera as a small fish.'

'Supposing they do find you guilty—' Venetia began hesitantly.

Anne anticipated the question. 'Oh, yes, I shall go on hunger strike. What else can I do?'

'You're not a young woman any more,' Venetia warned. 'You know the damage you do to your body. It could kill you.'

'It would kill me to bow down to McKenna,' Anne said grimly. 'But let's not talk about that now. I came, in fact, to take my *congé*.'

'You're leaving Town?' Venetia was surprised. 'In the middle of the campaigning season?'

'I'm leaving Bedford Square,' Anne corrected. 'Frankly, my dear cousin, I can't afford it any more. The Union and the Cause take up so much of my income – and it's foolish for me to keep up a big house when I no longer belong to

Society. Also,' she added, with a twinkle, 'it's quite hard to get in and out of when one is being watched or chased by a detective.'

'Have you been, recently?' Venetia asked. She was glad at least that the restless pacing had stopped. Anne seemed rather pleased with herself now, which made her more relaxed and expansive.

'Haven't you noticed the latest outbreaks?' Anne said. Since the raid on the WSPU offices there had been renewed arson and other attacks on property. A bomb had even been found in St Paul's. 'Vera and I have been pretty busy, one way and another, and mean to be busier still, especially as I have to anticipate being out of circulation after the middle of June.'

'Arson?' Venetia asked shortly, for she still found it shocking.

'The house of Mr Arthur Fernleigh, MP, at Barnet – that was one of ours,' Anne said. 'I was very tempted to burn down Brancaster Hall, given that Lord Holkam is such a dedicated opponent of the Cause, but I refrained for your sake – though I dare say Violet would be glad to be relieved of the draughty old pile. But, however, it was occupied, so it fell outside our remit.'

'Oh, Anne, I wish you wouldn't joke.'

'What else is there to do? We are engaged in a life-or-death struggle now, and it's the only way to relieve the tension. We cut the turf at the Oval, too,' she went on quickly, before Venetia could speak. 'We wanted to do Lord's, but there were too many policemen around it, and since I'm out on bail it would not do to be arrested. But we mean to try and cut the turf at Epsom next week. Will you be there?'

'On Derby Day? Yes,' Venetia said absently. 'We're going with Violet and Holkam and a small party.'

'Well, I can't promise to see you there. I don't suppose I shall be in the same company as you.'

Venetia sought to change the subject. 'So you are giving up Bedford Square? Where are you going to live – have you decided?'

'Yes, I am taking a small house in Chelsea, just off the King's Road, in Paulton's Square. Quite the wrong part of

London for you to visit me, I know,' she added, 'but Vera and I will be snug there. There are quite a few other Suffragettes in the area, and there's a community of artists and, shall we say, more *liberal* thinkers, so we shan't lack for friends.'

'I hope you will be happy there,' Venetia said doubtfully – not because she had any particular prejudice against Chelsea, but because Anne's career seemed to have been carrying her steadily downhill towards disaster for years.

At the beginning of June, the WSPU held its summer fair at the Empress Rooms. Given that a campaign of arson and destruction was going on at the time, the hall gave an odd appearance of dainty femininity. There were flowers everywhere, and hosts of children flitted about dressed gauzily as fairies, elves and butterflies, in pretty, soft colours – the fact that they were selling copies of the *Suffragette* striking the only false note. There was a representation of a seventeenth-century knot garden; the ice-cream stall, always a favourite, was a bower of greenery with red and white toadstools to sit on. The produce stall was constructed in the form of an old barn, and featured real live hens roosting up in its beams. Suffragettes dressed in white muslin with pink sashes walked about with trays selling dishes of strawberries and cream.

The only thing at all militant about the exhibition was the statue at the end of the hall, which was of Joan of Arc. On the 3rd of June, the opening day, Anne and Vera were standing looking at it when Emily Davison and her friend Mary Leigh came up beside them. '"Fight on and God will give the Victory",' Emily read out the inscription. 'Do you remember, Anne, when you dressed as Joan of Arc and rode that white horse to Holloway in the release procession?'

'I certainly do. My brother came all the way down from Manchester to remonstrate with me for riding astride in public.' Anne smiled at her. Emily was a striking figure, tall and slender, with red hair and sparkling green eyes. Full of fun and very intelligent – she had taken a first-class degree – she always had about her an air of suppressed excitement. Anne thought of it as a kind of brightness, like the brightness of the air that tells you the sea is just over the next horizon. It gave her the same feeling, that there was something wonderful just waiting to be discovered. They had been in prison together more than once, including the occasion when Emily had thrown herself over the railings into the stairwell and had been quite badly hurt. She had always felt a sort of kinship with Emily, as being one of the few in the Movement who really understood the final implications of what they were doing. Vera was no less passionate about the Cause, but it was a blind passion; Anne and Emily saw all the consequences, and carried on under that burden of knowledge.

But today Emily seemed happy without shadow. She turned from the statue and surveyed the room. 'It all looks splendid, don't you think? The essence of summer.'

'If only Mrs P could be here,' said Mary Leigh. 'Have you heard how she is?'

'I spoke to Sylvia this morning,' Anne answered, 'and she said she was better than expected. Weak, of course, but she said she was ready to go back to prison next Monday, and didn't mean to ask for an extension of the licence.'

The background sounds of cheerfulness seemed suddenly distant and hollow. Anne met Emily's eyes. 'It will kill her eventually,' Anne said. 'She is not young any more, and the fasting has weakened her, more than she lets anyone know.'

Emily nodded. 'It will be murder,' she said. 'They know what they are doing. They will keep on arresting her and releasing her until she dies. The only thing they care about is that she shan't die in prison. They'll release her just in time to prevent that.'

The four women were silent a moment in contemplation of the hopelessness of the situation; and then Emily seemed to brace herself, and smiled round at them. 'Well, let's not think about that now. The fair looks to be the best one yet, and we should enjoy it. It's what she would want.'

'Quite right,' said Anne. 'I've come prepared to empty my purse and sample everything.'

'Oh, leave something for another day!' Emily laughed. 'You can't mean only to come once? I shall come every day – except tomorrow. I'm going to Epsom tomorrow.'

'For the Derby?' Anne said. 'So are we.'

'To watch the race?' Mary Leigh asked. 'Or do you mean to do something?'

'Oh, we have a little something planned,' Anne said. 'What about you, Emily? What are you going for?'

'Look in the paper tomorrow and you'll see.'

'Oh, Emily, do tell,' Mary urged.

'No, no, it's a secret,' Emily said, laughing. 'Look in the paper – I promise you won't miss it!'

Anne and Vera went to Epsom in the motor. Anne had offered Emily Davison a seat, but she had refused it, saying half the fun was in going down on the train with the crowds. Motoring down made it easier to get past the police, with their trowels hidden in their clothing; but though they had gone early, it was not early enough. The Epsom crowds were already so great, and there were so many policemen on duty, that there was no chance of doing anything without being instantly arrested. With a certain prison sentence already ahead of her, Anne was not eager to lose her last days of freedom.

'Don't let's, then,' Vera said. 'Can't we just enjoy ourselves for once?'

'Enjoy this?' Anne said, pretending to be shocked. 'The sport of kings? The pastime of the aristocrat? And it's a man's world, don't forget. Where are the women jockeys? Why, even most of the horses are male!'

Vera missed the joke. 'Oh, but everybody knows Derby Day is the people's day. Look at them all having fun! It won't hurt for once.'

'No, it won't,' Anne agreed. 'All right, let's go and see if we can get ourselves a good position, down by Tattenham Corner. If you try to look frail and feminine, we might get ourselves passed down to the front row.'

They managed to get themselves into position before the start of the big race. A kindly coal porter, his face ingrained with dust though he had evidently scrubbed himself for the occasion, passed them forward, bellowing with gusts of beer breath for those in front of him to 'Let a coupla girls through, mates!' He gave Anne a broad wink as he parted the crowd in front of her, though whether it was to share with her the joke of calling her a girl, or an invitation to some other intimacy she didn't know.

There was nothing but the railings between them and the turf, and Anne thought briefly of slipping through now and doing a bit of digging. But the sun was shining and she felt relaxed and there were so many policemen around she was sure if she ran onto the course they would get to her before she so much as pulled out her trowel. So instead she stood enjoying the moment, looking about her at the seething, eager, holidaying crowds.

'This is the best spot,' she told Vera. 'You see the horses come thundering round the bend – most exciting.'

'Oh, look,' said Vera, 'there's Emily Davison.'

Anne looked across a sea of boaters and caps to where Emily was standing, rather unseasonable in dark coat, skirt and hat when so many of the female spectators were in pastel cottons or white muslin.

'She's got herself into the front row, too,' Vera said.

'It just goes to show that some men are kind,' Anne said teasingly, to which Vera only sniffed and tossed her head. Anne caught Emily's eye, and she grinned back and mouthed something. Anne made a questioning face, and Emily shook her hand in a 'never mind' gesture, then pointed at her midriff and mimed undoing her buttons. She had something hidden under there, then. Probably a Votes for Women banner, Anne thought. It was customary to hide a banner by winding it around the waist.

Venetia and Overton, though on the other side of the course, had also gone down to the railings for the big race, leaving the rest of their party so as to have a moment of pleasure together. Venetia was not a gambler, but she liked horses, and enjoyed pitting her knowledge of equine conformation against the bookmakers. Overton had brought his field glasses, and when the race had begun he proffered them to her, but she shook her head. Against the solid wall of noise there was no sense in trying to explain that she preferred to watch them with her own eyes. You got more of a sense of the field and the endeavour that way than by scanning details through binoculars.

The crowd's yelling rose to a deafening pitch as the horses came into sight in a tight bunch, thundering round the bend, a mass of flashing legs, stretched nostrils, flying manes, divots of turf and flecks of foam. Venetia recognised the King's colours, and saw that the horse she had backed, Anmer, was in the lead. Overton had just lowered the glasses; she heard him say, 'What the—!' and at the same instant the horrible thing happened.

There was a little flurry of movement from the crowd on the other side of the course as a dark figure ducked under the rails and ran out in front of the horses, waving something white. Venetia's mind, lagging fractionally behind the power of sight, told her it must be a woman from the size of her before she recognised the silhouette shape of skirt and woman's hat. By then the little dark shape had jumped up at the King's horse, presumably trying to grab the rein. The horse shied violently, the jockey went flying off sideways making a little starfish shape against the sky, and the horse slipped and turned a somersault, crashing down on its back and rolling over.

The little dark doll of the perpetrator had disappeared, first under the falling horse, but as the rest of the field thundered by Venetia thought she saw it being tumbled among the legs like a stone in a waterfall's eddy. Then the horses were gone and past, galloping on, and all that was left was the King's horse, beginning to struggle to its feet, the sprawled, white-breeched shape of the jockey, and the dark tumble of the woman.

It had all happened so quickly that Venetia could see the jockey's round cap still bowling along with the last of its momentum as she ducked under the rail and ran onto the course. Instantly there was a policeman in front of her, his hand out to seize her, his bulk blocking her. 'Now then, none of that,' he said sternly.

'Let me through,' she cried. 'I'm a doctor.'

'Ho, yuss?' he said derisively, but with an uncertain look, obviously confused by her clothes. Was she a lady, or – as once so tellingly phrased by a newspaper – 'a Suffragette disguised as a lady'?

'I am!' she cried. 'For God's sake . . . !'

And then Beauty was there right behind her, blessed Beauty, so obviously a gentleman in his silk hat and frock-coat with a rosebud in the buttonhole, saying with calm authority, 'I am Lord Overton and I assure you that this lady is indeed a doctor. Let her through, Sergeant.'

Before the policeman could speak again, Venetia had taken the chance to dodge past him and run across the course. Out of the periphery of her attention she saw that the horse was on its feet and apparently unhurt, and that the jockey was sitting up and moaning; but the woman was lying horribly still, a mere bundle of dark rags. Already several policemen had gathered round her, while others had run to the spot and were keeping the crowds back behind the rails. Venetia flung herself down beside the injured woman, warding off the officers who would have stopped her with her breathless mantra, 'I'm a doctor.' The woman's head was bare and bloody, her face a sheet of red. One of the constables was kneeling by her, hopelessly trying to staunch the flow with a crumpled page of a racing newspaper.

She pushed him gently away and made a careful examination of the skull. Her enquiring fingers encountered an area of horrible squashiness where hoofs had shattered the bony vault.

The policeman with the newspaper – quite a young man – seemed close to tears. 'It was the other 'orses,' he said, in a country accent. 'They kicked her as they went over.' He looked up at Venetia. 'They didn't mean to. They'da tried to jump her, Miss. They don't like to step on a hooman being, don't 'orses.'

'I know,' she said kindly, still searching for other injuries. The woman was unconscious – no wonder, with a head injury like that. Amazingly, the limbs seemed to have escaped. The white thing she had waved was lying nearby, shredded and trampled by the field, but clearly a Suffragette flag.

'Is she dead, Miss?' the policeman asked her. All around her were strong serge legs, and their owners all seemed to bend towards her for the answer. It was almost frightening, like a forest bowing.

'No,' she said. 'But she's badly hurt.' She had pulled out her handkerchief – not the dainty lace one, but a large, stout cotton square she always carried in case of emergency. She folded it and placed it over the wound, where it instantly blotted to scarlet. Other handkerchiefs were passed to her, from the police or the crowds, she didn't know which. 'Someone must go for a stretcher,' she said, 'or a hurdle if there's none available. As quickly as possible.'

Now a voice could be heard saying loudly, 'Let me through, please. I'm a doctor. Let me through!' It was a male voice, and the human barriers parted magically before it. A man in summer flannels and boater thrust into view. He seized Venetia by the shoulder and roughly wrenched her away so that she fell back on the grass, and took her place. 'Stand back, all of you,' he commanded. 'Give her air.'

Too late for that, Venetia thought. She got slowly to her feet and straightened her hat. There was blood on her hands and the front of her dress, and she looked at it helplessly, having nothing, now she had parted with her handkerchief, with which to wipe it off. She looked up, and saw, past the police cordon, among the people who had come onto the course for a closer look, her cousin Anne. It seemed part of the lunatic logic of the situation that Anne should be there. Her eyes were stretched wide and her face white with shock.

'It's Emily Davison,' Anne said. Belatedly, with this information, Venetia remembered her, from the days when she had marched for the Cause, before the violence began. 'I didn't know this was what she was going to do,' Anne went on. 'Is she dead?'

'Not yet,' Venetia said. She felt Beauty come up behind her, and was comforted by his warm presence. She had been feeling cold with shock.

Anne still stared at her, reaching into her with her eyes, desperate to communicate something. But all she said was, 'I couldn't have stopped her.'

'No,' said Venetia. 'I don't suppose you could have.'

CHAPTER NINETEEN

Emily Davison died four days later, without ever regaining consciousness. It was a terrible blow to the Cause, for she had been universally admired, and had long been one of the most visible of Union members, always so bright, so clever, with a wide-ranging intellect and a fine sense of humour. Since earliest youth she had been passionate for the Cause. As Anne said to Vera, she would never have the vote now.

Her funeral was to be held on Saturday the 14th of June. Mrs Pankhurst, who should have gone back to Holloway on the 7th, had evaded the detectives and remained at large, but as she could not show her face in public the arrangements were undertaken by Grace Roe, with Anne's help. It was hard to find a clergyman prepared to conduct the service. Many had been alienated by the recent campaign of wrecking and burning churches; others were afraid of the public disturbances that might attend the funeral. Others still objected on the grounds that, though the inquest verdict was death by misadventure, Emily had in fact committed suicide.

Anne was infuriated by this, and argued vehemently. 'She didn't want to die. She loved life! I spoke to her the day before, I even saw her on the day itself. She was laughing and happy, only determined to do what she thought right. It was a frightful risk and she knew it, but she didn't *intend* to get herself killed.'

The truth was, as Anne knew, that though Emily had loved life, she had not feared death, and had always been ready to give her life if that were the price demanded. While she had not intended to die at the Derby, she had accepted that that might be the outcome. Did that count as suicide? It was a theological debate she did not want to have. Emily had flung herself at the King's horse to make news, in the hope that newspaper attention would force the Government to abandon the Cat and Mouse Act and let Mrs Pankhurst live.

'What about Captain Oates?' Anne demanded hotly. 'There's nothing more certain than that he committed suicide, but because he did it to save his friends, he's considered a hero, and the Church practically canonises him. How is Emily's case different?'

She knew the answer to that, of course. Emily was a woman, and the cause she had died for was the Women's Cause. But at last, through a combination of her influence and Grace Roe's steady determination, they found a church for the service – St George's, Bloomsbury – whose vicar, the Reverend Mr Baumgarten, held more advanced views than some of his confrères, perhaps because of the proximity of the university.

The funeral procession was enormous, and all the newspapers agreed it was deeply moving. In front of the coffin walked the standard bearer – Charlotte Marsh had been chosen for this duty – but instead of the Suffragette banner she carried a huge wooden cross. Behind the bier walked the women awaiting trial for conspiracy – Annie Kenney, Rachel Barrett and the office staff, Anne among them – and behind them came Mrs Pankhurst's carriage, empty: she had been arrested on her way to the funeral and taken back to Holloway. Behind the carriage came thirty leading Suffragettes, dressed all in white, and carrying white lilies; behind them came rank after rank of women dressed in black and purple, carrying irises and peonies.

The women walked in grave silence, accompanied by bands playing solemn music, from Victoria station to Bloomsbury, past the crowds lining the route who seemed awed to silence by the spectacle. Many of the women wept, and there were tears on the faces even of some of the men.

After the service the procession formed again and walked to King's Cross, where the coffin was put on a train on its way to Morpeth, the Davison family home in Northumberland, for interment.

On the following day, the trial of the conspirators opened in the High Court. There was no direct evidence against Anne, or against the office staff, who were simply employees, but all were found guilty under the direction of Mr Justice Phillimore. They were sentenced on the 17th of June to periods of between six months and two years. Anne's sentence was six months. All were to be sent to the third division, and the judge directed that none of them should be released early in any circumstances. They were sent to different gaols widely separated – Anne was sent to Maidstone, others as far afield as Bristol and Warwick – but all went immediately on hunger strike and, despite the judge's prohibition, all of them were out on licence and back in London by the end of ten days.

Venetia went to see Anne in her new house, worried by what the ordeal would do to her at her age, and found her weak and emaciated, but flushed of cheek and with eyes burning brightly. She was in bed, but sitting up; in the room there was a strange, sweetish odour, reminiscent of ketones, which always pervaded the room of a hunger striker.

Anne allowed herself to be examined, and heard without interest the recommendations of milk and beef tea. 'So it begins,' she said. 'Cat and mouse.'

'How long is your licence?' Venetia asked. 'I saw what looked like a detective leaning on the lamp-post opposite the house.'

'Five days,' Anne said. 'But I shan't have recovered enough by then for them to keep me long. It's cumulative, you see.'

'I know,' said Venetia. Mrs Pankhurst, arrested on the 14th of June, had only been kept two days before being released in a seriously ill condition.

'If you refuse water as well, you get ill very quickly,' Anne said.

Venetia hated to hear her speak like that. 'It's so self-destructive. Is this what your life is to be, serving your sentence two days at a time, making yourself more ill with every repetition? Where does it end, Anne? With your death?'

'No, with the vote. We are making progress,' Anne insisted. 'Emily's death brought the debate back to life in the papers. The press was very scathing about the Government's spitefulness in arresting Mrs Pankhurst on the way to the funeral rather than after it. And the Cat and Mouse Act will bring the Liberals into disrepute. McKenna is not respected – hardly even inside his own party.'

Venetia left soon afterwards, hastened on her way by the black looks of Miss Polk, who wanted to keep all the nursing to herself.

Anne was right that there had been renewed debate about the Question. Asquith, in the House, had shocked many people by opposing the franchise for women on the grounds that woman was not the female of the human species but a distinct and inferior species of her own, and disqualified from voting in the same way that a rabbit was disqualified. When it was reported there were angry letters and much protest in the press, together with several satirical cartoons about the lapine origins of various public figures. Someone commented that Asquith's 'rabbit theory' made it difficult to vote Liberal and then look the women of one's household in the face.

There was also much debate over the treatment of Mrs Pankhurst, and whether it should be continued until she died. The Cat and Mouse Act had been successful in making her serve her sentence without the authorities' having to forcibly feed her, but at her age it was doubtful how long she could stand the strain, and there were growing rumblings from ordinary people who, while not feeling particularly favourable towards the Suffragettes, felt that this form of harrying was inhumane and degrading. As June became July, letters appeared in the press condemning the Act, there were protests and demonstrations; one day a man in the Strangers' Gallery threw a dozen mousetraps down onto the floor of the House.

Bernard Shaw wrote, 'The women who want the vote say in effect that we must either kill them or give it to them.

In spite of lawyers' logic, our conscience will not let us kill them. In the name of common sense let us give them the vote and have done with it.'

But McKenna, pressed by Sir Edward Busk at the Home Office, smiled and said there was no prospect of repealing the Act. Under pressure, however, from all sides except the parliamentary, he ruled that the Home Secretary could not prevent women under licence going abroad. By then Mrs Pankhurst and the conspirators had all been released and rearrested several times, and Mrs Pankhurst and Anne, the eldest of them, and Annie Kenney, who had a weak heart, were all showing severe signs of strain. They took advantage of McKenna's ruling, and went abroad. Mrs Pankhurst and Annie Kenney went to stay with Christabel in the South of France, as guests of some wealthy American supporters. Anne and Vera, together with Mary Taylor, Anne's chauffeur, packed everything into the Wolseley, crossed to Calais and motored slowly down through France, stopping wherever the fancy took them. Venetia indulged an inward sigh of relief that at least she would not have to worry about her cousin for the next few weeks.

The Aero Exhibition at Olympia back in February had been a success for the Sopwith Company. They had exhibited both the new tractor biplane, and a flying boat they had called the Bat Boat, both made at the factory in Kingston. The Bat Boat had caused a headache when it came to transporting it to Olympia, for it was found to be too big to pass through the old rink doorway. A local builder had to be summoned in haste to dismantle part of the brick wall so that it could be got out and loaded onto the waiting lorry. But both machines were well received at the exhibition, and the aeronautical press praised the attention to detail and superb finish of the Sopwith products.

The Bat Boat was still a prototype, and it was not until the week after the exhibition that it went for trials down at Cowes. Jack, Sopwith and Hawker all took turns at trying to fly it, with an interested audience that included Mr Rankin and his senior designer, but the Bat Boat would not rise off the water. One evening Tom Sopwith managed to coax it up a few feet, but it fell back immediately, damaging the hull, and after beaching it the three men retired, discouraged and weary, to the hotel. During the night a strong wind got up, and when they returned in the morning they found the Bat Boat had been blown over and wrecked.

But they were all young and enthusiastic, and setbacks were to be expected in a new science. Even as they picked over the wreckage, they were talking about the next Bat Boat, with Jack suggesting that what was needed was ailerons, rather than relying on wing-warping.

During the spring they worked on producing two more biplanes for the Admiralty, and the summer brought the usual aviation meetings and competitions. On the Saturday of the Whit weekend Harry Hawker won a height contest in the new biplane at Hendon; on Whit Sunday Jack had it at Brooklands where he gave passenger flights in it, and on Whit Monday he won a cross-country race in it.

It was good to be back at Brooklands, especially as Miss Ormerod's father had invited him to stay for the two nights at Fairoaks, rather than motor back to London each evening. Jack felt very much at home there, and enjoyed Miss Ormerod's company, realising perhaps only then how much he had missed her friendship since he had been seeing less of her. On the Sunday, when he was doing the passenger trips, it suddenly occurred to him that he had never taken her up, and he asked her if she would like a turn.

'You always said you wouldn't be scared,' he said.

'Scared? No, of course not,' she said. She at once tied a scarf over her hat with an air of determination, and said, 'Can Rug come with us?'

The biplane was a three-seater, so there was plenty of room for the dog too. It had a covered-in body with celluloid windows, so was much more comfortable to ride in than the first machines Jack had flown, where the pilot had been completely exposed to the wind. It also had small outrigged front wheels in addition to the main wheels, which made landing more comfortable. Jack had taken many female passengers up by now, and he was prepared for Miss

Ormerod to squeal as the aeroplane left the ground, as most ladies did, but she did not so much as gasp.

'Are you all right?' he shouted to her.

'Oh, yes!' she called back, but that was the only thing she did say. There were no comments about the height from the ground or how frightening it was, or whether it was safe, or what would happen if the engines failed. He supposed he ought to have known that she would not say anything silly – she was not only extremely sensible, but knew a great deal about aeroplanes from all the time she had spent around them; but he found it rather flat not to hear any comment from her at all. On returning to the ground, he had frequently been clutched about the neck by shaken young ladies whom it had been his pleasure to comfort, and he was used to hearing himself called wonderfully brave, and being gazed at as a hero. But Miss Ormerod did none of those things, though as he helped her down he noted that her cheeks were pink and her eyes very bright, which he thought suited her.

'Well?' he said at last, when she had seen Rug down, removed the scarf and straightened her hat and jacket. He could not wait any longer to hear what she thought about it. 'Well, how was flying?'

She turned to him then with her face alight. 'Wonderful!' she said. 'I understand now why you flyers can't have enough of it. Every moment on the ground must seem like a wasted eternity to you.'

'Well, perhaps not quite that. I do love to design and make aeroplanes as well. But in essence – yes. Flying is—'

'Very heaven!' she finished for him.

'Would you like to go up again some time?' he offered.

'More than that,' she said. 'I want to learn to fly myself.'

'Really?'

'Yes – why not? I don't see anything about it that a woman couldn't master. It doesn't take great physical strength.'

'No, of course not. I only meant – well, would your father approve?'

She smiled gently. 'You know Daddy can't deny me anything. He bought me my own motor-car, after all.'

'True.'

'And I'm sure a motor-car is harder to handle than an aeroplane.'

'It's heavier,' Jack conceded. 'Well, if your father doesn't mind—'

'Will you teach me?' she asked hurriedly. Her cheeks were very pink and she did not quite meet his eyes.

'But you know we've closed the school.'

'I know,' she said, 'but that needn't be a difficulty. I'm sure my cousin would let us use one of her school machines, if you don't want to risk yours.'

'Wouldn't you rather have one of her instructors teach you?' Jack asked.

'No, I want to learn from you,' Miss Ormerod said. 'But if you would rather not teach me . . .'

'Oh, it isn't that,' Jack said hastily. 'But you'd have more regular lessons at a proper school. I may not be able to get down here every weekend.'

'I can take a lesson whenever you can get away,' she said. 'And I don't mind how long it takes.'

'Not long, I'm sure,' he said gallantly. 'You'll get the hang of it in no time.'

'I don't know about that,' Miss Ormerod said, with a small smile.

So in addition to working on the new Bat Boat, and modifying the tractor-biplane design so that it could be fitted with floats to make a 'sea-plane', and entering for competitions and exhibitions, Jack took whatever time he could to go down to Brooklands and teach Miss Ormerod to fly. He was generally asked to stay at Fairoaks, which often involved dinner or luncheon parties, games of tennis, picnics, or other entertainments to make it 'worth your while coming down', as Molly said one day. Rug enjoyed visiting Fairoaks, where he was soon close friends with Mrs Ormerod's two dachshunds, and lived a life of bliss between riotous games in the garden, basking in the conservatory and expeditions to the kitchen where the cook, who had taken a fancy to him, would fill a special bowl with delicious scraps for his delectation. Molly drew a picture of him one day, lying full-bellied in his favourite sunny corner, and entitled it 'Dog In Heaven'.

Meanwhile, orders were coming in to the Sopwith factory, not only from private buyers but from the navy and the military authorities. The Admiralty had ordered a Bat Boat and three float-plane versions of the tractor biplane. The latter had been adapted with ailerons replacing the wing-warping control, and the army now ordered four of them, but with wheels rather than floats – the first army contract for the Sopwith company, and much prized in consequence. In July Hawker flew a Bat Boat, which had had wheels added to make it amphibious, down at Cowes to win the Mortimer Singer prize of £500 for a machine that could take off from either land or sea, and the subsequent good publicity meant that extra staff had to be taken on to handle the orders that were coming in.

The *Daily Mail* had offered a new prize – an enormous one of £5000 – for a 'Circuit of Britain Race'. This prescribed a course around Great Britain, which had to be completed within seventy-two hours, the contest opening on the 16th of August. Owner and flyer had both to be British and the aeroplane completely manufactured in Britain – with war expected by almost everyone at some not too distant date, patriotism was very much the order of the day. In July the Sopwith Aviation Company entered the new biplane with floats for the competition, where it was one of only four entrants, so win or lose it would be good publicity. Jack worked on a new 100 h.p. engine for the floatplane for the attempt. Though it was decided that young Hawker should actually fly in the competition, his name and face were often in the newspapers on the run-up to the event.

Perhaps as a consequence, Jack found himself frequently invited to parties and dinners, and at one, in July, he met a young woman called Christina Monkton, who showed an immediate interest in him, and whom he very soon thought the most beautiful girl he had ever met. With some friends, Miss Monkton went to watch Jack flying in an exhibition at Hendon, and they met again in a party at the Kingsway roller-skating rink, and the following week at a tennis party in north London. On his next visit to Brooklands to give Miss Ormerod her lesson, Jack told her about this new goddess, and was quite disappointed that his friend evinced so little interest, and even cut him off once or twice quite tersely by changing the subject when he tried to talk about her.

In July, Jessie was again invited to go and stay with Violet, and when she put the suggestion rather tentatively to Ned, he made no objection. She had hardly expected him to, but perhaps she had hoped that he might at least seem reluctant to let her go or say that he would miss her. But he only looked up from the newspaper, said, 'Yes, by all means,' and went on reading again.

As she composed her letter of reply to Violet, she glanced across at her husband and thought he was looking tired and worn. She said on an impulse, 'Why don't you come too? You haven't had a holiday since our honeymoon.'

'A man in my position doesn't take holidays,' he said, still reading.

'But things are going better now, aren't they?'

'Hm,' he said; and then, looking up, 'Orders coming in mean more work, and more work means I can't be away. Besides, I don't think it's the kind of holiday I'd enjoy. I wouldn't fit in there. You go, with my blessing, and enjoy it.'

She had to be content with that; and, secretly, she thought he was probably right. He would have made an awkward third between the intimacy of her and Violet, and she could not see Holkam paying him much attention.

Violet met her at the station as before, looking, she thought, even more beautiful, and dazzlingly smart. The new style was for soft, uncorseted bodices and skirts draped over the hips and narrowing to the ankle, which called for a slender figure and good carriage; even more so with the new colours, for the soft pastels of the recent past were being augmented with brighter 'Japanese' or 'Oriental' colours. Violet's gown was of sea-green and gold silk in a swirling pattern, with a loose, scooped neck worn over a soft lace underblouse. It was short-sleeved and Violet had kid gloves that reached all the way over her elbow – Jessie did not like to imagine what those gloves alone had cost. Hats were smaller this year, but Violet's was big enough still, and decorated with a great waterfall of black marabou. Jessie, in her travelling suit of fawn linen, and a modest turban-shaped hat with a white cockade, had set off from York feeling unusually smart, and was quite cast in the shade. But then Violet enfolded her in a surprisingly unrestrained embrace, and was just Violet again.

'Darling Jessie!' she cried. She examined her face closely and said, with great feeling, 'I'm so very sorry about the poor little baby. Are you terribly upset still?'

'Oh, no, I've got over it now,' Jessie said. 'You mustn't worry. Dr Hasty says these things happen and there's no reason why I shouldn't have another any time.'

'But it must have been so terrible for you,' Violet said, gazing into her eyes. 'When I think of my own three . . .'

'Don't let's talk about it,' Jessie said, linking arms with her and turning to walk towards the exit. 'I've been so looking forward to this visit. Tell me all the news.'

Violet's most exciting news was the visit to London of her elder brother Thomas, Lord Hazelmere, who was a military attaché to the Court of St Petersburg. He had just been reappointed for a further term, and had come home on a month's furlough. 'He's so very glamorous,' Violet said, 'I can hardly believe he *is* my brother. Mama's so thrilled – except that he's going back again. She'd hoped he would have an appointment here, or at least closer to home than Russia. But he loves it there. He says the society in St Petersburg is wonderful. You'll see him tonight – they're all coming to dine at our house.'

Jessie had not seen Thomas for years, though they had met often as children. He had always been kind to her, exercising a softening influence when the other boys – her brothers, Oliver, Ned and their cousin Eddie Vibart – had teased her. He was twenty-six now, and Jessie was almost nervous of him just at first – he was, as Violet had said, *very* glamorous, not only extremely handsome and well dressed, but with a certain air about him that came, she supposed, from his exalted post and his title as well as his wider experience of the world. But he smiled very kindly at her, and once he had reminded her of some little incident from their childhood and laughed at an old joke, the awe rubbed off and she got on very well with him.

The evening's conversation rightly belonged to him. Everyone wanted to know about his life in Russia.

'Petersburg is a fabulous place,' he said. 'It's hard to find words to describe it to someone who's never been there. The size of everything, to begin with: vast palaces – a façade can stretch for a quarter of a mile. Standing at the middle of one, the effect is rather like that game we used to play – do you remember? Standing between two mirrors? The streets are so wide and the public squares so huge, the sense of space around one is astonishing. Then there's the river – far, far bigger than the Thames – and all the canals, so that in spring and autumn the air is full of dancing light, and the water is full of reflections, all the golds and blues and wonderful colours of the buildings. And in the winter all the water freezes, and there's a great winter fair held on the river, with a huge toboggan slope. People skate along the canals, and everyone puts runners on their carriages when the first snow settles, so there's no sound but the jingling harness bells.'

'You've mentioned spring, autumn and winter – what about summer?' Overton asked.

'Peter's not nice in the summer – the dust and mosquitoes are terrible – so everyone goes out into the country. The Emperor and his family go to the Crimea, or to the hunting lodge in Poland, or on the yacht.'

'What are they like, really?' Venetia asked. 'I've only met them on a few formal occasions, though my sister says the Empress was sweet as a girl.'

'They're very affable and kind to me,' Thomas said. 'Devoted to each other. And you couldn't want nicer, more unassuming girls than the grand duchesses. They've been brought up very plainly, so there's no arrogance in them – they're just four pretty sisters, full of fun and chatter, looking forward to growing up and going to dances. It's a terrible pity that the Tsarevich is so sickly. The sadness of it touches everything. It changes people,' he concluded, with a slight, involuntary frown.

Venetia asked him then about his social activities, and the frown disappeared. 'Oh, Peter is a Mecca for the arts. There's ballet and theatre. All the new waves in painting started there, long before they went to Paris. Music – you know that Russian music is the most exciting in the world. Literature, philosophy – salon life is thriving.'

'It all sounds exhausting,' Overton said, making everyone laugh.

'But what about *you*, Thomas?' Venetia insisted. 'Do you get to sample all these wonders?'

'Yes, of course. Because of my position, I'm invited every-where – to all the best balls and parties, Mama, so you needn't worry.'

'And are the Russian young ladies beautiful?' Violet asked.

'In other words,' Jessie translated, 'is there a particular Russian young lady?'

Thomas smiled indulgently at his sister. 'Oh, is that what she means? Well, then, Lady Holkam, let me see. There is a certain princess . . .'

'I knew it!' Violet cried. 'A princess?'

Oliver laughed at her. 'Don't be too impressed, Vi. Princesses are two-for-a-penny out there – isn't that so?'

'Not quite that,' Thomas said, 'but it's not the same as a princess in England.'

'And who is your particular one?' Venetia asked.

'Princess Olga Narishkina. She's a lady-in-waiting to the Tsaritsa.'

'What a pretty name,' Violet said. 'Is she beautiful?'

'Of course she's beautiful,' Overton answered for his son. 'The real question is, how serious is it?'

'Yes, are you going to bring her to see us?' Venetia asked.

Thomas laughed. 'It's early days yet. But I think I may, some time in the future.'

Later, in the drawing-room, Jessie found herself between the two brothers and listening to a very different conversation.

Oliver had asked Thomas about the conditions for the working classes, and he replied, with a shake of the head, 'There's terrible poverty. The sort of slums you hardly see any more over here are widespread, and there's a feeling – I don't know how to describe it – that everything's balancing on a knife-edge, that it could tip over into starvation, riot and slaughter.'

'Slaughter?' Oliver asked, with a frown.

'Any kind of violent public demonstration would be put down harshly. The army would be called out and they wouldn't hesitate to fire. It isn't like here, you know.'

'But I thought you liked the Emperor,' Oliver said. 'Why would he allow that to happen? Isn't he the autocrat?'

'Yes,' said Thomas, staring into the depths of his coffee-cup as though seeking the right words there. 'The Tsar is the ultimate authority. But Russia is so huge that a message can take weeks to get to Petersburg from the outlying parts, and an answer, if one was sent at all, would probably take months. So it's the local men who have power over their own little fiefdoms, and they are so far from any chance of retribution, they are virtually dictators. Orders may go out from the centre, but there are so many levels of administration, and there's corruption at every level – no-one does anything without a bribe – so the end result is that no-one is really in control. Until you get to the very bottom, that is, and there's some poor illiterate peasant smarting under an injustice inflicted by a local jack-in-office – who's probably an illiterate peasant himself, and got his preferment by bribing or possibly murdering his predecessor.'

'You paint a pretty picture,' Oliver said. 'Does the Emperor know all this?'

'I suppose he must do, since he's lived in Russia all his life,' Thomas said. 'Though sometimes it's the outsider who sees most of the game. He doesn't exactly have his nose rubbed in the situation.'

'Is he a good man?' Jessie asked. 'Does he care?'

Thomas looked at her sharply, in a way that told her he had forgotten her presence for a moment. 'He's a well-meaning man, and very devout, and I think he does care

404

about the sufferings of his people. But I don't think he has much imagination. In any case, there's actually little that he can do. The problem is just too big, and corruption in office is too much a way of life.'

'It all sounds very grim,' said Oliver. 'What will the end be?'

Thomas seemed to shake himself. 'Oh, it has trundled along like that for centuries, and I suppose it will trundle on for a few more.' He paused in thought.

Oliver prompted him. 'Yes? What did you just think of?'

'There's a new element which disturbs me, and I'm afraid may bring trouble. I told you that the salons were seething with new ideas. One of the least savoury of them is a passion for spiritualism.'

'Oh, yes,' Oliver said. 'I'm afraid we are seeing something of that over here. It's most unhealthy – and the practitioners are utter charlatans, of course.'

'Yes,' said Thomas, 'and one of the worst of them has become a darling of Petersburg society. He's a *staritz* – a wandering priest. In reality he's nothing more than a dirty, ignorant peasant who knows a few parlour tricks; but for reasons I can't fathom, he seems to be irresistible to some of the more impressionable females. They fawn over him, and allow him liberties they would hardly grant to their own husbands.'

'Perhaps it's because he *is* dirty and ignorant,' Oliver suggested. 'If they are bored enough, it may give them an unwholesome thrill.'

'Unwholesome, that's the word,' said Thomas. 'Some of the things he gets up to with them – well, I won't go into it. And outside the salons he's constantly drunk, goes in for all sorts of debaucheries.'

'But why should you be so worried about this fellow – what's his name?'

'Grigori Rasputin – Father Grigori, he likes to be called.'

'He may be a bad hat, but what danger is he, except to a few silly women?'

'One of the females who finds him irresistible is the Empress herself,' said Thomas.

'Good heavens!' Oliver said. 'I'd have thought she was too well brought up for that.'

'He does have a particular hold over her,' Thomas said. 'I've mentioned that the Tsarevich is a sickly boy. I don't know what his illness is, but he has attacks of some kind. The Empress is afraid he will die during one of them – and I have to say from what little I've heard it seems quite likely he may. But this Rasputin fellow seems to be able to ease him, and even bring him out of his fits. So the Empress is now convinced that the boy's life depends on Father Grigori. She showers rewards on him, and listens to his advice, not only about the boy, but about everything else, too. Naturally Rasputin wants to advance those people he likes and confound those he doesn't, so now he's starting to interfere in politics.'

'Can't the Emperor put his foot down?'

'He believes in Rasputin's powers too – and, of course, the old rogue behaves better in front of them than he does elsewhere: cleans himself up, talks respectfully, behaves like a real priest. So when people tell them about his drinking and debauching, they think it's just a jealous attempt to poison their minds against him. Worst of all, the Tsarevich's illness is a closely kept secret, so outside the Court the people don't know the real reason the Empress values Rasputin. They think she is favouring a filthy reprobate for her own degenerate pleasure. A lot of people think they practise witchcraft together, and that the Emperor is their victim and dupe. It's bringing the Court into disrepute, and with a volatile people like the Russians, I don't know what the end of it will be.'

During the time Thomas was in London, the Ballets Russes were performing for a short season at the Theatre Royal, Drury Lane. He knew them from St Petersburg, explaining that the ballet was central to Petersburg social life. 'We go to the Maryinski every week, sometimes several times a week. The names of the leading dancers are household words, and they're received everywhere.'

'Even at Court?' Violet asked. Actors, musicians and dancers could not be presented to the King and Queen.

'Especially at Court,' Thomas said. 'I must take you all to see them while they're here.'

He took a box and organised a party for it, though Holkam excused himself, and Lord Overton had to be absent because of an important debate and division in the House. Oliver and Thomas escorted Venetia and Jessie, and one of Violet's young men, Lord Hollister, made up the party. In the event, Jessie was rather disappointed. Though she had never been to the ballet before, she had seen pictures, and *Le Sacré du Printemps* was nothing like them. She had expected sumptuousness, gorgeous costumes, romantic sets. Where were the tutus, the gauze, the spangles?

Violet was frankly bored, but fixed a pleasant smile on her face and settled to observing the clothes and jewels of her nearest neighbours. Venetia was absorbed. She thought the dancing, though probably very skilled, most ungainly and awkward, and not at all attractive to watch. But the music, though difficult to listen to, she did not absolutely hate. There was something there, she thought. If she had the opportunity to listen to it several times without distraction, she thought she might come to understand it. It certainly generated an exciting atmosphere – perhaps a little too heating, given the antics of the dancers and some of the costumes. No wonder its first performance had been greeted with a near riot in Paris.

After the ballet, Violet had a reception at her house for the company. It became clear that Thomas must have spent a good deal of time at the Maryinski, for all the cast seemed to know him very well. Jessie was fascinated to meet them close up. Some of them still had their makeup on; their clothes were strange and colourful, their movements fluid. They talked and laughed loudly, using their supple arms and hands to accompany everything with extravagant gestures. Jessie was quite glad that Lord Holkam did not return while they were there, as she was sure he would have disapproved. But Lord Overton looked in, and seemed at once to settle in and enjoy himself very much, with a laughing look in his eyes as he watched these exotic creatures flit and lounge about Violet's rather stiff drawing-room.

Violet had provided a lavish buffet supper, and the company fell on it, and on the champagne, like starvelings. Violet's little dogs were much admired by the Russians, were petted and passed about among them, cooed over, and fed more scraps than was good for them. Conversation was loud, and the air grew hazy with the smoke from strange dark Russian cigarettes. Many of them spoke a little English, and all of them spoke French to some degree, so the hosts' lack of Russian was not a difficulty.

One thing that interested Jessie particularly was to observe Thomas with one of the *danseuses*, a very pretty dark girl called Tatiana. He spent a long time in conversation with her, over in a corner of the room, where she leaned against a column in that curiously disjointed fashion of ballet dancers. The bend of his head, the lift of her face, the low tone and feeling of ease between them suggested to Jessie that this was no new acquaintance, and that perhaps his arranging this occasion had not only been for Violet's sake.

While she was watching them, Oliver came up to her with a fresh glass of champagne, saw the direction of her eyes, and said, 'I hope you are not seething with disapproval?'

She looked up, startled out of her thoughts, and said, 'Why should I disapprove?'

'You shouldn't,' he said. 'It's a tradition as old as the hills, and confers benefits on both sides. A man is regarded as a lucky dog who wins the favour of a leading ballerina. Thomas tells me that the Emperor himself had a mistress from the ballet – before he married, I hasten to add.'

Jessie sipped her champagne and said, 'I'm not so ignorant of the ways of the world that I don't know it happens. In certain circles. I was just thinking about Princess Olga.'

'I gather from Thomas that that affair is in the very early stages. But no doubt when things progress the little ballet girl will step back and become just a pleasant memory.' He caught Jessie's eye and said, 'Now what is that question I see lurking there? You have a dangerous look about you, Mrs Morland. You aren't going to ask me whether I have any pleasant memories, I hope?'

'Goodness, no,' she said. 'That would be most improper.'

Oliver laughed. 'Improper! That serves me right! I like you, Cousin Jessie, more than I can say. Bring your champagne and come and meet the star of the company, Mr Nijinsky. I don't know much about these things, but I understand he is the most extraordinary and talented dancer in the world.'

'Oh, I've met him already,' Jessie said. 'Thomas introduced him. He seemed a nice enough boy, but he has very bad teeth.'

Oliver laughed so much at that, she began to think he must have had too much champagne.

CHAPTER TWENTY

One of the pleasures of her London visit for Jessie was catching up with her brothers. Jack was very busy, but came over to visit several times and again invited Jessie and Violet to an air display. Oliver accompanied them, as before, enjoying this brush with a radically different world from his own. Since Jack was still living in lodgings and therefore could not entertain at home, he repaid Violet's hospitality by inviting her and Jessie to dine with him at Claridges, and asked Oliver to make the fourth. Eating in restaurants was not something respectable ladies did, but hotels, especially Claridges, were different, and since Violet and Jessie were both married and would be accompanied by their brothers, it was unexceptionable.

On another day Jack took Jessie roller-skating, something she enjoyed, though not as much as ice-skating. Roller-skating had become the craze a few years earlier and showed no sign of waning in popularity; new rinks opened up wherever a suitable space could be found. Jessie thought that much of its popularity must come from its offering somewhere respectable for young people to meet each other.

This latter idea was confirmed when after only a few circuits she and Jack met up with a party of young people among whom was a Miss Monkton, whom Jack introduced with such an air that Jessie sighed inwardly, realising her susceptible brother had fallen victim again. Miss Monkton was very pretty, small and dainty with golden curls and blue eyes. She seemed almost in awe of Jack – all the group was impressed with him, but Miss Monkton most of all. It made

Jessie regard her brother in a new light. She had always loved Jackie best, and thought him a nice-looking man; but to an outsider a presentable, charming, intelligent fellow who was also a flyer – a Hero of the Air – was something very special.

Miss Monkton seemed hardly to believe her luck that such a godlike creature was paying attention to her, which Jessie thought spoke well of her modesty. Despite being very pretty indeed, Miss Monkton did not preen or flounce or seem to regard herself as in any way above her plainer companions. Jessie absolved her of any tendency to pride or conceit, spite or capriciousness – the traits that so often seemed to attach to acknowledged beauties. Indeed, she seemed a very nice, good-natured girl – only very *dull*.

After going around with her for a few circuits, Jessie came to the conclusion that Miss Monkton was not very bright, had little education, and had no deep interest in anything. Because she was good-natured she listened happily to whatever was said to her, but she contributed nothing herself but the occasional 'Indeed?' and 'I see,' and 'My goodness!' With patient questioning Jessie managed to elicit that she lived at home in Surrey with her parents, a younger brother called William, who plagued her by taking her things and spoiling them, and a dear little doggie called Bobby, who really belonged to her mother. Apart from home and family, the only subject she had anything to say about was Jack, and her contribution there was limited by her blushes. Jessie gathered she thought him 'splendid' and 'terribly brave' and, pressed further, thought it was 'terribly nice' of him to bother with her – an opinion in which Jessie concurred.

She was pleased that the new goddess seemed unlikely to prove as nasty as Miss Fairbrother. The disadvantage was that she was so inoffensive it might prove difficult for Jack to untangle himself. He would not like to hurt someone so harmless. Jessie was afraid that he might end by marrying Miss Monkton, either because he genuinely thought her the right person, or because he couldn't get out of it. Either way, Jessie thought it would not be good for her darling Jack.

Oliver, however, when she put it to him tentatively on another occasion, said there were plenty of men who liked stupid women and were perfectly happy with them. 'In fact, I think it's the rule rather than the exception. What could be nicer than coming home from a day's grappling with the world to find a sweet, pretty creature waiting to hang on one's every word and think one perfect?'

'Almost anything would be nicer than that,' Jessie said robustly. 'You might as well buy a dog.'

Oliver laughed, and said she overestimated the male sex. 'We like to have our conceit bolstered, and we dislike being argued with and proved wrong by those nearest us. If Miss What's-her-name is genuinely good-tempered and modest as well as pretty, your brother ought to make sure of her before someone else cuts him out.'

Jessie gave him a baleful look. 'I wish you'd be serious!'

'I am.'

'*You* wouldn't marry someone like that.'

'I might,' he persisted. 'I can see the attraction of the idea.'

'But you couldn't fall in love with someone like that.'

'You think being in love is essential to marrying? Even if it is, falling in love often has no reason to it. It can happen with the most unsuitable person. Everyone else says, "How can you?" and you can't answer, but you just know that person is for you, all appearances to the contrary.'

Jessie considered this, and for a fleeting moment her mind glanced at Bertie, and she made it look away again. Then she said, 'You may be right, but I still think that for a comfortable marriage you ought to have someone you can talk to – and who understands what you are saying, not just a lap-dog who licks your hand at the sound of your voice. I'm sure Jack wouldn't be happy with Miss Monkton. I'm not sure who he would be happy with, though.'

'Perhaps he hasn't met her yet,' Oliver said.

'Perhaps. But if he marries a pretty fool, he never will.'

Jessie's other brother, Frank, presented no problems of that sort. He called on her at Violet's house, and on another day took her out to tea at the British Museum. He, too, was still living in lodgings and so couldn't entertain her at home. She told him about Jack's new infatuation, and he listened but did not seem either much interested or at all worried. 'Oh, these flyers are the men of the moment and it's natural for women to throw themselves at them. But Jack has his head screwed on the right way. He won't come to any harm. It's my belief,' he went on, surprising Jessie, 'that he's still carrying a torch for Maud. It protects him from other women. He may flirt, but he's never really serious about any of them. In fact, I think he chooses impossible women precisely so that he *can't* fall in love again.'

Jessie thought this even worse. She hated to think of poor Jackie still heart-lorn for Maud after all this time. She eyed her brother keenly. 'What about you? You aren't in love with a pretty fool, I hope?'

Frank raised an eyebrow at her. 'Me? I haven't time for that sort of thing. Actually, I'm not sure I'd tell you about it if I were – exposure rather tends to take the bloom off a delicate sentiment, don't you think? But there are no women in my life, I assure you, apart from my landlady and the assistants at the library. And in fact there will soon be even fewer.'

'What do you mean?'

A gleam of enthusiasm came into his eyes, now that he was turning to a subject that interested him. 'I don't suppose you will have heard, hidden away from the world as you are down in Yorkshire, but I had a paper published last month that received a great deal of favourable attention.'

'A paper?' For just a moment, her mind still being half on Jack's problems, she thought he meant a newspaper, and was puzzled; and then she shook herself and realised he meant an academic paper. 'Congratulations,' she said warmly, understanding that this was something important to him. 'What does it mean? Will you be paid a lot of money, or receive an honour, or anything like that?'

'No, nothing like that,' he said, with a look of patient amusement, 'but the praise and regard of the academic world is worth far more than either. I've had letters from leading men in the field expressing an interest in my ideas, even

413

one –' the tone of his voice here told her this was a signal honour '– from Hilbert in Göttingen.'

'Göttingen!' Jessie said, trying to sound impressed.

'That's where the best work is being done on electron theory and mathematical physics, which is what I'm interested in,' he said. 'A letter from Hilbert – well, that's like a letter from—' He struggled for a comparison.

'God?' Jessie supplied, and it made him laugh and come down to earth.

'But aside from that, the exciting news is that, on the strength of my paper, I've been offered a readership at University College. It means I can continue my work and develop my ideas.'

'That was what you always wanted, wasn't it, to study?' Jessie said. 'Except when you were a very little boy, and you wanted to be a soldier.'

'I hadn't discovered mathematics then,' Frank said, offering the cake plate again. He took a bun for himself with the air of not knowing he had done it. His appetite was healthy though, as far as Jessie could see, undiscriminating. 'But there is a mathematical element to playing with toy soldiers, you know. In fact, it would probably be possible to render the famous battles of the past into mathematics and extrapolate a theory of warfare from them.'

His eyes became distant, and Jessie hurried to ask him a question before he sank completely into thought. 'So what will you be doing at the university?'

He came back. 'I'll have some teaching to do, of course, but it isn't very onerous. And they've told me I shall have a completely free hand, and the use of any facilities I want.'

'You won't have to change lodgings,' Jessie remarked.

'No – I'm very conveniently placed in Gower Street.'

'So when you said you would have fewer women in your life, you meant because you are going to work in an all-male environment?'

'Yes. Mathematical physics is not a feminine pursuit. Though, of course, there is the work of Madame Curie on radium, without which my work wouldn't be possible.'

'Radium? Isn't that to do with Roentgen rays? I've heard

Cousin Venetia talk about them – wondering whether they'd be of any use in curing consumption. Is that what you're interested in?'

'In a sense. It's radiation theory I want to work on – that's what my paper was about.'

'What is radiation theory?'

He looked at her carefully. 'I don't think I could explain it to you.'

She picked up the teapot and refilled his cup. 'Try,' she invited.

'Hm,' he said. 'Well, you know that everything in the world is made of tiny particles called atoms?'

'Is it?'

'Yes. And we always thought that the atom was the smallest thing in the universe, the basis of all matter. Now we know that isn't true. The atom is itself made up of even smaller particles. Some atoms are unstable and give off the particles in the form of radiation. But, interestingly, it seems that they don't move individually but in clumps, which Einstein called quanta.'

'But what's that got to do with mathematics?' Jessie interrupted.

'Mathematics is the basis of all physics,' he said. 'Rendering physical phenomena into mathematical form allows them first to be understood, and then expanded, developed, and the formulae applied to other phenomena. Minkowski, Lorentz and Einstein – Max Planck – Hilbert – me, in my own small way – we are engaged in trying to understand the workings of the universe, of space and time. It's the most important work ever undertaken. There has never been a more exciting time to be a mathematician.'

Jessie smiled at him, moved by his enthusiasm and the visionary shine in his eyes, though she hadn't the slightest idea what he was talking about. 'Just tell me this,' she said. 'Am I going to be sister one day to one of the great names of science, like Newton, or – or—' She couldn't think of any other famous scientists. 'Is your name going to be in all the schoolbooks?' she concluded instead.

He smiled at her. 'Is that important to you?'

'Yes, if you aren't going to settle down and get married and make me an aunt.'

'I don't think that's going to happen.'

She thought how different all three of her brothers were from each other: Robbie, the domesticated husband and father; Jack, the flyer who could understand machines but was mutton-headed when it came to women; and Frank, the detached and monkish academic. She leaned across the table and clasped his hand affectionately. 'Dear Frankie! However did you get to be so very clever? The people who've offered you this – this readership, they think you are going to be another Newton one day, don't they?'

'Modesty forbids,' he laughed; but she thought she could almost feel via his hand the powerful surge of the thoughts running through him, and she was sure she was right. A brilliant career lay ahead of him, even though she would probably never understand what it was he had done.

There was no getting out of one visit of form that Jessie would rather not have had to pay. The Parkes did not move in the same circle of society as the Holkams, but as Maud and Richard at least were sure to be in London, she was duty-bound to call at their house. She was quite glad to be told they were out, left her card, and two days later received a formal visit in St James's Square from Maud alone. From her she learned that Bertie was in the country, at their place near Cheshunt.

'Is he well?' Jessie asked.

'Oh, yes, thank you, very well,' Maud said. 'He hardly ever comes to Town. He's going into cattle. It's a new interest and it keeps him busy.'

'And your father – is he well?' Jessie asked, feeling at a loss.

'Yes, very well,' said Maud, and glanced at the clock. 'I have to meet him in Bond Street, so I must not stay long. We are looking at a new painting for the hall.'

Jessie struggled to keep the conversation going, but she and Maud had too little in common, except the one thing that could not be mentioned, and she was relieved when her visitor rose to go. Afterwards she felt disturbed and upset, and had to seek the solitude of her room to compose herself before returning to Violet's company. How could Maud be happy to stay in London when Bertie was in Hertfordshire? She seemed to prefer her father's company to her husband's. If only Bertie had not married her – but she must not think *that*. She felt desperately sorry for them both, for she could not believe either of them could really be happy in the situation; but there was nothing to be done about it. Married was married. She had to sit by the window for quite a while before her disturbed feeling subsided and the inexplicable urge to cry had passed. It was a relief, in a way, she decided, to know she was not likely to bump into Bertie while she was in London – and then the thought that perhaps that was why he never came to Town disturbed her all over again.

Jessie had not forgotten her invitation to call 'any time' on the Darroways, and it was not difficult to persuade Oliver to escort her one evening, when Holkam was otherwise engaged and Violet had gone to spend the evening with her mother. Mark and Katherine greeted her with the same warmth, and absorbed her effortlessly into the usual group gathered around their dining-table. As she listened to the intellectual conversation going on around her, she realised that here, at least, Frank's success would be understood. When a suitable opening came she announced it rather boastfully. Everyone knew the value of his having been offered a readership on the strength of an original paper, but she discovered one of the guests, a man studying for his doctorate at King's, had actually read it. He had been impressed by it, and was quite excited to discover that Jessie was the author's sister. Her boasting was punished by the embarrassment that followed when he questioned her closely and enthusiastically about Frank's work, and the profundity of her ignorance was exposed. Oliver, in fits of laughter, was forced to rescue her at last by diverting the talk from doctor-*ates* to doctor*ing*.

At the end of the evening Jessie was exhausted from the

volume and speed of talk, and from all the new ideas thrust into her head and fighting for her attention. In the taxi-cab, Oliver saw she was disinclined for talk and let her be, and they stared out of opposite windows in companionable silence.

Traffic was heavy on Shaftesbury Avenue, and the taxi-cab crawled and stopped, crawled and stopped. Jessie stared idly at the brightly lit theatres and restaurants and the moving crowds, her mind disengaged; until, at a moment when they were stationary next to a small restaurant with discreetly draped windows, her attention was caught by a couple just emerging onto the street, right opposite her and only a pavement's width away. The woman was swathed in an evening gown of green and purple silk, much draped over the hips and narrowing at the ankle, shimmering with beads and spangles. She wore a turban of gold cloth with a stiff cockade two feet high, a ruched evening cloak of purple velvet, and there were sparkling jewels at her neck and ears. Her clothes were obviously expensive, but bright in a way that suggested she was not of the *ton*. Her hair was red, of a shade too intense to be natural, and she seemed to be wearing maquillage, such as Jessie had only seen on actors and dancers.

All these things made her moderately interesting to Jessie, though not terribly surprising, for she had been in London long enough to recognise the *demi-monde* when she saw it. Besides, a respectable woman would not be coming out of a restaurant in the first place, certainly not a restaurant like that, which evidently catered for assignations. But Jessie's idle interest was seized and pinned like a moth to a card when she saw the gentleman coming out of the restaurant behind her. He was in the usual black and white of evening dress with an overcoat hanging open and a dangling white silk scarf. He was just resuming his silk hat, and the light from the lamp-post struck his face before he had it in place. It was Lord Holkam.

In the same instant several thoughts dashed through Jessie's head – that perhaps it was not him but a stranger who resembled him, that perhaps he was not with the woman but just happened to have followed her out. But it was certainly him, and as soon as he was outside the restaurant door he offered his arm to the woman and she slipped her hand through it. Jessie's third thought was that he must surely see her, and that she would be mortified if he did. But his eye flicked over the cab without interest as he scanned the street for a taxi that was for hire. The window was down a little on her side, and she heard him say, 'Not a cab to be seen, as usual. Do you wish to wait, or shall we walk a little?' Jessie recognised his voice.

The woman said, 'I don't mind. But I can't walk far in these shoes. Too tight by half! I wish I'd never bought 'em.' Her accent proclaimed her not a lady, had there still been any doubt about it.

Jessie felt paralysed by the situation. She could not remove her eyes from the couple, nor shrink away from the window into the shadows. If he had really looked, he would have seen her; but having scanned the street again, he turned and walked away with the woman tottering beside him. A moment later the taxi moved forward and, hideous irony, brought her opposite them again. She ought not to stare – it might attract his attention – but she could not seem to help it. It was the fascination of horror. For a moment they kept pace with each other, and if Holkam had turned his head he would have seen his wife's intimate friend staring at him from a few feet away like a goldfish in a bowl; but then the couple turned down Denman Street and the taxi bore Jessie and Oliver away.

Jessie lay much of the night unsleeping in a turmoil of thought. When she arrived at St James's Square, Varden, the butler, told her Violet was not home yet, and she went straight to bed, claiming a headache, relieved at not having to face her friend just yet.

Her mind played over and over again the image of the couple emerging from the restaurant. That woman: young and probably attractive, but over-bright, and as vulgar as could be, with her painted face and dyed hair and her common accent. That was the woman he preferred to Violet,

419

sweet, beautiful Violet. She remembered the time she had caught him kissing the nurserymaid at Brancaster Hall. What was it about him? Was he especially attracted to low women? She remembered, with the heat of shame, how he had once hinted at an assignation with *her*.

It seemed to her that Holkam had not been taking pains to avoid discovery. It was bad luck on him that Jessie happened to be passing just at that minute, but Shaftesbury Avenue was a main thoroughfare, after all. A gentleman in a silk hat and evening clothes was an anonymous figure and a hat brim cast a useful shadow, but it was not beyond possibility that he could have walked slap into a couple of his acquaintance just emerging legitimately from a theatre.

She thought this through. Of course, couples in that sphere of life did not walk about much. Emerging from a theatre they would only cross the pavement directly to a waiting motor-car or taxi. Gentlemen alone might walk along the streets; but then, she thought bitterly, a gentleman alone seeing Holkam with his – his – *female* would probably pretend not to know him and walk on, and think nothing more of it. She did not believe all men were like Holkam, but she was old enough to know that even those who were honourable tended to shrug and turn a blind eye to such weakness in others, and not think it mattered much.

But, oh, Violet was her friend, and the thought of her being betrayed by her husband with such a female was agonising. Did she know? Surely she could not – she seemed so happy. An even more troubling question – should she be told? Jessie wrestled with the problem through to the small hours, until she finally fell asleep just as dawn was breaking, and the birds in the square's garden were reaching the peak of their racket.

The maids had no instructions not to disturb her, but at her usual time for waking she was so heavily asleep she did not stir for the curtains being drawn back, nor for Tomlinson's cheerful 'Good morning, madam,' spoken aloud before she realised that her mistress was still unconscious. What did wake her was a cool hand resting on her brow, and she grunted and flung her eyes open to find

Violet, in her dressing-gown, sitting on the edge of her bed, her lovely face, smooth as a pearl, so close that for an instant Jessie thought it was a dream.

'I'm sorry, I didn't mean to wake you,' Violet said. 'Tomlinson was worried that you might be unwell, so I was just seeing if you had a fever. How is your headache?'

'Headache?' said Jessie, vague with sleep. She heaved herself up onto her elbow. Lapsang and Souchong had evidently followed their mistress in, and were snuffling their way round this interesting room that they had not been in before.

'Varden said you complained of a headache last night. Is it still bad?'

'No – no, it's gone away. I'm just a little – fuddled. I didn't sleep well.'

'I'll go away and leave you,' Violet said, beginning to rise. 'Tomlinson shall pull the curtains again and you shall sleep as long as you like.'

'No, it's all right. I'm awake now,' Jessie said. 'I don't want to sleep again.' She studied Violet's face: so serene, always. She really seemed contented, but who could tell what she was concealing? Jessie knew a bit by now about concealing emotions.

Violet smiled, and said, 'What a long, earnest look! You've seen me in my *déshabille* before – no-one more often, in fact. Remember when we used to run in and out of each other's rooms in our come-out Season?'

The words struck Jessie. She was the most intimate friend in Violet's life – and did not a friend owe the truth to a friend? They were alone in the room now, Violet was close, relaxed, sitting on the edge of the bed and looking at her quizzically. There might never be a better moment for confidences. She had a sidelong, half-acknowledged feeling that once they were dressed they would be further apart, there would be barriers between them.

So she said, 'That was a happy time. Are you happy now, Vi? Do you regret anything?'

'Regret? No, of course not,' Violet said, seeming simply surprised by the question.

'You're happy now, with Holkam?' Jessie pursued.

'Why do you ask that?' said Violet. 'Because he and I have a different way of life from you and Ned? But I've explained to you—'

'Yes, you've explained that it's quite usual, but you've never said that you like it or that it makes you happy.'

'Don't I look happy?'

'That's evading the question.' She sat up, and captured Violet's hand, as if that would help to extract information. 'I know I probably shouldn't ask you this sort of thing. It's very personal and embarrassing, but you're my oldest and dearest friend and I care about you.'

'I know you do,' Violet said calmly. 'What is it?'

'You remember when we were having our come-out, how we talked about marriage and love and – so on?'

Violet laughed, but it was an unnatural laugh – a sign of embarrassment. Perhaps she guessed what was coming. She said, 'Oh, we were such children! We didn't know anything.'

'But love – and so on – it *isn't* the way you imagined, is it?'

Suddenly Violet spoke, and her hand gripped Jessie's in a sudden spasm that she was probably not aware of. '*Nothing* is the way we imagined. We thought love all happened in the mind, flowers and poetry and lots of gazing. But that's not what the world means by love, is it?'

'I don't know that—' Jessie began, but Violet did not want to stop now she had launched herself.

'They mean that awful, awful thing we have to do with our husbands. So degrading and – and revolting! We have to put up with it, I know, for the sake of having children. I'm just so grateful that it's all over now. I've got my three children and I won't have to do it ever again. And I'm grateful that Holkam is a perfect gentleman about it. I believe some husbands insist on it – well, from time to time – even when they have their children and there's no more need.'

Jessie thought of Ned and of herself, of her pleasure in him. Had Violet never felt like that, not even for Holkam at the beginning? Was there something wrong with her, Jessie, for feeling that way?

Violet suddenly realised she was clutching Jessie's hand like a lifeline, and detached herself gently. She said, 'I'm sorry, I shouldn't talk that way to you. You're not in my happy position. But when you've had your children . . .'

'Yes.' Jessie nodded, distracted, not wanting to go down that track. She made another attempt to get at the truth. 'But men – men don't feel that way about it.' It was almost a question, for she wanted to know whether Violet knew that.

Violet smiled, a pale little strained smile. 'I know,' she said. 'It makes it hard to understand them, doesn't it? But, as I said, Holkam is a perfect gentleman. As far as that goes, we have completely separate lives.'

'Separate lives,' Jessie said. 'That's true. Vi, have you ever wondered—'

Violet leaned forward to stop Jessie's lips with a finger. 'Is that what this is all about? Did someone say something to you? Did you see something? No, don't tell me. I'd rather not know the detail.'

'You know about it? You don't mind?'

'Why should I? My husband, out of consideration for me, takes all that elsewhere and doesn't trouble me with it. Why should I mind that?'

'It's usually considered something one ought to mind when – when one's husband takes an interest in someone else.'

'If it were a woman of one's own sort,' Violet said, a little stiffly, because she was talking about things she was not comfortable with. 'But he would never, never do such a thing to me. This is quite different. It's like – a visit to the doctor, I suppose.' Her cheeks burned at coming so close to forbidden topics.

'So you really are happy?' Jessie said.

Violet smiled, back on firmer ground. 'I'm very happy, Jessie darling. Believe it! I love my husband, I have three dear children, a house in Town and a house in the country. Holkam and I are the best of friends. My life is full of pleasant and interesting things, and now I can see my family again, I have nothing in the world to want for.'

There was no doubting her sincerity. 'I'm glad,' Jessie said. 'And I can't tell you how relieved.'

Violet laughed. 'Did you think I was making the best of a bad bargain? Oh, Jessie! I have all this!' She waved a hand, meaning to encompass, Jessie guessed, not the bedroom or the house, but her whole life of wealth, stability and freedom as a member of the upper levels of the *ton*. Souchong thought the gesture was for him, and came running over, tongue trailing in a happy grin, to ask to be picked up. Achieving his objective, the little dog gave a great yawn of content, which made Jessie yawn by contagion. 'I'd better go and leave you to sleep some more,' Violet said, and stood up.

'I'm not going back to sleep. I'm wide awake now,' Jessie said. 'And very hungry. Let's dress like lightning so we can have breakfast very soon. What are we going to do today? What should Tomlinson put out for me?'

'Well, if you're really not too tired, there's the exhibition of post-impressionist paintings I was thinking of going to. Billy Copthall has been talking about it so much, he's quite made me want to see for myself. And then there's lunch at the Savoy with the Damerels and Johnnie Wentworth.'

'It sounds lovely,' Jessie said, with an inward smile. Despite what she had said, she knew Violet never dressed 'like lightning', and liked a leisurely breakfast. As the visit to the art gallery would be terminated by lunch, there would not be very much time in between in which to appreciate post-impressionism, whatever that might be. But she liked Billy, Johnnie and the Damerels, who would seem very restful after the Darroways and their friends; and with the knowledge that Violet really was happy, and knew and didn't care about Holkam's *female*, she could look forward with a light heart to a day of frivolity.

Purvis was waiting on the station platform to meet Jessie, and Jessie's disappointment that it was not Ned told her that she really had been missing him.

'Mr Morland was unavoidably detained by business,' the chauffeur said. She let him handle everything, and followed him and the porter meekly out of the station to where the

Arno was waiting. She had half hoped he might have brought Brach with him, but seeing the empty motor realised that it had been a foolish thought: Purvis hardly even liked humans in his spotless interior, never mind dogs with a fondness for rolling in cow-manure. She worked off her disappointment by saying, '*I'll* drive,' knowing that he would hate it but would not be able to argue with her in front of a third party. He could only open the driver's side door for her in seething silence, then go to supervise the loading of the luggage.

She had only tooled the Arno a couple of times, as both Purvis and Ned thought it too heavy for a woman. But she managed it neatly. She always enjoyed driving, and this drive was even more fun, with the sense of forbidden fruit, the rigid disapproval of Purvis beside her. Maystone Villa looked nice and square and welcoming, very home-like after the grandeur of London, and as she stepped out of the Arno, the air smelt wonderful – so green! Brach must have been mooching about the grounds waiting for the motor to come back, for she came running up, her tail a semaphore of joy, her eyes shining with accomplished love as she butted her head into Jessie's groin, then tried to climb up her and put her arms round her neck.

'Silly old dog! Mind my suit! Ugh, don't lick my face, simpleton!'

Gladding came from the back of the house and helped Purvis with the luggage; Daltry opened the house door and smiled as though he was glad to see her.

'Welcome home, madam,' he said, as she approached, with Brach frisking first on one side, then on the other.

'I'm glad to be home,' she said, and meant it. 'It's seemed like a long time.'

'Yes, madam,' Daltry said, and then, surprising her, 'Everyone has missed you – not just the dog.'

'Are we alone for dinner tonight?' she asked.

'Yes, madam. The master ordered it, so there's no need for you to be troubled.'

'Good – because the thing I want most in the world just now is to saddle my horse and go out for a ride. London is very exciting, but rather confining.'

'I imagine so, madam. Shall I ask Gladding to saddle up while you change? Or would you care for a little luncheon first?' Jessie hesitated, her attention caught, as it always was, by the thought of food. Breakfast was a long way in the past and dinner a long way in the future, and she was *hungry*. Daltry watched her expressive face with inner amusement. 'I could ask Mrs Peck to make you one of her omelettes,' he said innocently. 'There are some mushrooms fresh picked this morning. A mushroom omelette and fried potatoes? Or there's pea soup left over from dinner last night.'

'Both,' said Jessie decisively, passing him on the way to the stairs.

Daltry bowed his head, following. 'Mrs Peck has been making gooseberry tarts this morning,' he mentioned.

'My favourite! I'll have some of those, too. Tell Gladding to have my horse ready at half past one, will you?' She ran up the stairs and he watched her go with a smile.

Jessie had a wonderful ride, came back ravenous again and had tea, examined the invitations on the chimneypiece, telephoned to Morland Place to say that she would be over the next day, and then went upstairs to bathe and dress for Ned's return and dinner. She felt nervous and excited about seeing him. She had been away a long time, and they had parted, not coolly, but awkwardly. The shadow of the lost baby had been over them, and the possibility of her guilt had been between them, keeping them apart, making it impossible for them to touch. How would it be when he came home? Would it still be awkward? Would he be reserved, or embarrassed, or indifferent? Oh, not indifferent! She was no Violet: she needed her husband close and warm. She knew that now with the vividness of a new discovery. Whether there was something wrong with her or not, she wanted Ned's body, wanted to sleep with him and be held by him and make love with him – all those things you couldn't do with a polite stranger. They hadn't made love since she lost the baby, and as she dried herself after her bath, she was taken with a nervous notion that if they didn't do it soon, they might never be able to do it again.

Tomlinson, a thought-reader like any good lady's maid,

had laid out one of her most attractive gowns, and dressed her and did her hair with care. She was just putting in the last pins when they both stiffened, Brach, lying under the dressing-table, lifted her head, and Jessie said, 'Was that the motor-car?'

'I think so,' said Tomlinson. They listened to the sounds of arrival, a male voice downstairs somewhere, and after a pause, steps on the stairs.

Jessie jumped to her feet. 'Go,' she said.

'Your jewels, madam,' Tomlinson remembered, though she was half-way to the door already.

'I'll manage myself,' Jessie said. Brach came out from under the dressing-table and began to sing. The footsteps had an eager sound to them – quick and light, not tired and dragging. Tomlinson opened the door and whisked out just as Ned came into view. He paused in the doorway, looking at Jessie appreciatively, his face not smiling but ready to smile if he were welcomed. Brach went to him, lifting her forelegs like a greyhound, pointing her muzzle up at him. Jessie had been thinking about Ned for the last hour, but his sudden reality made her feel absurdly shy. Her mouth didn't know what to do with itself and smirked foolishly, and then she chewed her lip and looked down, feeling herself blush.

'Well,' said Ned, 'here you are.'

It was a foolish thing to say, and she looked up, glad he was not as composed as he had appeared. 'Yes, here I am,' she said.

They looked each other over, eagerly, cautiously, hopefully.

'It seems a long time,' he said.

'Yes,' she said. She searched his face. 'I've missed you,' she blurted.

And at that he simply opened his arms, and she went to them.

All evening they talked, about what she had done in London, about how things had been here and at Morland Place, about Frank's success, and Jack's part in the *Daily Mail* prize attempt, about some of the ideas she had taken up at the Darroways, about the horses. Nothing was said about their past difficulties, no hint of a word about the lost baby and her possible part in it. That had been folded up and put away in a drawer, she understood, not to be opened again. She was – forgiven? Not that, since she had never officially been blamed. She was – they were – restored.

In the bedroom he dismissed Tomlinson, saying he would help Mrs Morland undress, and Tomlinson departed in haste with a red face at the implication. Jessie had expected a tumultuous rush once the door was closed, but Ned tended to her as efficiently as a maid, but with a tenderness and a lingering touch that was all his own, removing her jewels, unhooking her gown, taking out her pins, delicately divesting her of her underwear, until she stood naked but for her shift, the mild air of the night starting her flesh to awareness, so that she tingled all over, her stomach tight with longing for him. Then he took off his own clothes with a few rapid movements – no lingering there, not even looking where they fell – until he was naked. Her mouth dried at the sight of him, the hair rose on the back of her neck for his male, alien, desired body, the primitive hardness of him that neither of them controlled but which came from the dark stream of the earth's life, which flowed around and through all its creatures. Her legs felt weak and the backs of her knees ached with wanting him. She put her arms up to him and he caught hold of her and they met like flame, kissing frantically, and then melting together. Somehow they were lying down, and then they were coupling. Their passions met and merged, and it was an equal thing on both sides, not something one did to the other. It was wild and beautiful, like flying, like a team of fast horses, powerful and liberating.

Afterwards they lay together damply, hearts still drumming, getting their breath back. Ned pulled the counterpane from under him and put it over them both, in case the night air should chill them as their hot skin cooled. Jessie lay in his arms, her face against his neck, and felt content. Violet must be wrong, she thought. There was nothing unnatural in this, nothing sordid or wrong. It was – it was

428

wholesome, the word came to her. It made her laugh inwardly and add, *exciting*.

He felt the laughter through his skin, and said quietly, 'What? Why are you smiling?'

The train of logic that would have been needed to explain it to him was far too long and complex; and in any case, she didn't want to talk about Violet's arrangement with her husband; didn't want, just then, even to think about Violet. So she said, 'I'm glad to be home, that's all.'

And he said, 'I'm glad to have you home.' And that was that.

In October she thought that she might be pregnant; but when November came she bled again, so it seemed that she wasn't. She was glad then that she hadn't said anything to Ned about it, and he seemed not to have noticed.

CHAPTER TWENTY-ONE

The new season for the Suffragettes started on the 1st of October, 1913, when Miss Kerr and Mrs Sanders – two 'mice' who had been tried for conspiracy along with Anne – arrived at Lincoln's Inn to reopen the *Suffragette* office after the summer recess. A crowd of supporters gathered outside during the morning, as everyone expected an attempt to be made to arrest them. Nothing happened, however, until they left the building for lunch, at which point a body of police and detectives appeared as if from nowhere and tried to seize them. A violent struggle ensued between the police and the supporters, at the end of which the mice, much battered and with their clothing torn, were taken away into custody.

On the following Monday, the 6th, there was a regular meeting called an At Home at the Pavilion, at which Annie Kenney was due to speak. Police surrounded the building, but Annie Kenney had herself smuggled in in a costume hamper, and was able to get to the stage without being seen. But as soon as she stood up to speak, the wild cheering that greeted her alerted the detectives outside and they broke in and stormed the platform. They were armed with sticks, the uniformed police with their truncheons, and they lashed out on all sides as Annie tried to escape and her supporters tried to shield her. Heads were broken, blood flowed, and Annie was dragged out to a waiting taxi with her dress so badly torn it was almost off, so she had to clutch it together at the front to be decent. On the next day the management of the Pavilion announced that they would not allow any more militant meetings on its premises, and cancelled the hire contract.

Anne was not in London at that time. At the end of the summer holiday in France she was still feeling languid and unfit to resume the Cat-and-Mouse ordeal in London. Mrs Pankhurst was staying abroad and planned to go to America on a lecture tour until December, which would mean that all police attention would be directed towards Anne, a distinction she was not eager to embrace. She decided, therefore, that she would go to America too, not to lecture – though she would not refuse an engagement if it were offered – but to take up Lizzie's invitation, and recuperate in peace and quiet.

Vera was not pleased when she discovered these plans did not include her. She, with Mary Taylor, was to part from Anne at Cherbourg, and take the ferry back to England while Anne embarked for New York.

'Why can't I go too?' she cried angrily. 'I've always wanted to see America. I don't want to go back to England. Why should you have all the pleasure and me none?'

Anne was taken aback at the violence of her reaction. 'Don't shout at me like that,' she said quietly. 'You sound like a barrow boy.'

Vera was incensed. 'Oh, do I? I see it now, I see what you're thinking! You're ashamed of me! You don't want me meeting your precious relatives because you think I'm not good enough for them!'

'That's not it at all.'

'Oh, isn't it? Just because your father was an earl and mine is a cobbler—'

'Vera, stop! That has nothing to do with it. I would like to take you with me but I can't afford it. You know we moved to Chelsea because my finances were suffering. I can't afford two lots of travelling expenses at the moment.'

'Well, then, don't you go either,' Vera said sulkily. 'Wait until you can afford for us both to go. Why should I have to be stuck all alone in London with nothing to do while you're jaunting round the world enjoying yourself?'

'You have lots of friends in London, and I'm sure you'll

have plenty to do. You are not on a Cat-and-Mouse licence – you can go about freely. When I've retrenched enough, when I can afford it, I will take you to America, I promise. For the moment, I'm going alone to recruit my strength for the next battle.'

Vera grumbled on, and continued to complain right up to the moment she boarded the ship at Cherbourg. Anne parted from her with a final injunction that she should be careful and not get herself arrested. 'One of us under this curse is enough.'

'Oh, I shan't get caught,' Vera said. 'I'm too clever for that.' She flounced away, up the gangplank, but at the top paused and turned to look back at Anne and say gruffly, 'Don't stay away too long. I shall miss you.'

Mrs Pankhurst, when she arrived in New York, was detained by the authorities and taken to Ellis Island as an undesirable immigrant to await deportation. For two days she remained there while lawyers argued on her behalf, and the scandalised press mounted a campaign for 'this brave little old lady' who represented 'the rising democratic spirit of Europe'. Such was the degree of indignation in the papers that the President intervened at last and ordered her to be admitted.

Anne was not so famous in America, and – perhaps also because of her title – she had an easier entrance to the country. Even so, she was surrounded by pressmen as she left the terminal building, and was asked how she liked New York, what she had to say to the women of America, whether she intended to visit the Empire State Building, what she thought of rag songs and the tango, and whether she thought the Suffragette movement was responsible for the slit skirt and other symptoms of the decline in feminine morals. But when she had given her rather bemused, and amused, answers, she was suffered to get into a taxi-cab for the railway station, and there was no attempt on the part of the authorities to hinder her movements.

The railway journey she found restorative. The engine was massive, the carriages large and comfortable, the service impeccable, and having nothing to do but sit still and watch the vastness of the country reel by was very soothing. By the time she arrived at Flagstaff station she felt very much better; and the sight of Lizzie and little Rose – a sturdy young lady of four and a half – waiting to greet her on the platform was all she needed to convince her she had done the right thing in coming.

Lizzie clasped her in a fierce embrace and wet her neck with tears, and Anne found her own eyes unaccountably leaking too.

'You're my first visitor from home,' Lizzie said, when the first rather incoherent greetings were over. 'Oh, it's so good to see you! But it makes me feel even more far away than ever.'

'Dear Lizzie! You haven't changed a bit,' Anne said.

'You have,' Lizzie said frankly. 'Poor Anne, things must have been hard for you. But I shall soon have you fattened up with our good Arizona food and clean air and sunshine. I shall send you back a new woman! When *do* you have to go back?' she added anxiously.

'Not until December,' Anne said, 'if you can have me for so long. As soon as I appear in London they'll arrest me again, and then I'll have to serve three or four days before they let me out – probably on a seven-day licence. So if I want to be out for Christmas I shall have to be in London by about the eighteenth.'

Lizzie looked grave. 'What an awful way to have to calculate.'

'It's an awful business,' Anne said grimly. 'I had no idea when I began, all those years ago, how awful it would become. The Government is mad, I think – quite literally mad. To inflict such tortures on helpless women, merely for the sake of arbitrarily denying a right to half the population which the other half enjoys, is to my mind an insanity. But – don't let's talk about it now. I want to put the whole dreadful business out of my head while I'm here, and enjoy the sensation of being free to go where I like and say what I like.'

'I shan't bring the subject up unless you do,' Lizzie promised. 'Oh, but we shall have a lovely time! I've all sorts of things planned for you, once you've got your strength back. For one thing, I must take you to see the Grand Canyon. You simply can't imagine it until you've been there. It's something everyone should see before they die. And then there's a place called Sedona that has the most amazing rock formations you've ever seen – red, red rock cut by the wind into extraordinary shapes. And I thought we might go out and stay on one of the ranches for a few days, so that you can have some riding and see the country from the saddle.'

Anne laughed. 'It sounds as though I shall need a holiday to recover from my holiday.'

In England, meanwhile, the arson campaign was resumed. Vera Polk, along with others of the 'hot-bloods', avoided the difficulties of London, where they were known by too many detectives and likely to be caught as soon as they attempted anything, by travelling all over the country and striking at widely separated points. Every target had to be carefully chosen and the attack meticulously planned, because it was essential that no person was harmed, not even, as the WSPU put it, 'a cat, dog or canary'. Not many of the WSPU members were willing or able to undertake this kind of action, for it was a violation of a woman's nature, and against all their upbringing and centuries of social moulding. Even Vera, who spoke in the hardest language and liked to appear a care-for-none, found it a strain, and sometimes wondered what her father would think if he knew what sort of things she did for the Cause. Burning hayricks was the easiest, for they went up easily and were rarely guarded, though one always had to be careful of the farm dogs. A rick or two, together with cutting up golf courses, gave light relief between more serious burnings – a timber yard in Yarmouth, a football stand in Lancashire, an empty mansion in Kent.

This latter was to be Vera's last action for that year, for Anne was due home and she wanted to be in London and at liberty through Christmas. On the night, a dense fog rolled in over Kent, which Vera thought would help them to go undetected, but which unnerved her companion, Winifred Walton. She was a pale, slight girl who looked as helpless as a white mouse, but had taken part in a number of actions since her first stone-throwing in 1909 had brought her into contact with Anne. On this night, however, the fog frightened her, and she saw detectives in every swirl and shadow. Half-seen trees and bushes seemed to move towards her; muffled sounds were lurking attackers waiting to jump out on her. At last, when it came to climbing the wall of the mansion, she could not do it. Her hands and feet were numb from the cold, clammy fog, her knees were shaking with fear, and her spirits had sunk so low she was completely immobilised.

'We can't go back now,' Vera said fiercely. 'Come *on*, Winnie! We can't let the side down.'

But Miss Walton only whimpered and wrung her hands. 'I can't. I really can't.'

Vera tossed her head angrily and snatched her companion's fire package from her helpless hands. 'All right, I'll do it alone. Give me a boost up, will you? And for goodness' sake stay *here*. Don't go wandering off. Keep watch, and when you hear me by the wall again, let me know if the coast is clear.'

The rest of the plan went off all right, though Vera was more afraid than she had admitted to Winifred or herself. The fog made everything seem strange, and more dangerous rather than less, for though she could not be seen, she could not see either: anyone could have been lurking nearby. She broke a pane of the french window to the downstairs library, slipped her hand through and undid the catch, then stepped in, listening. The house was supposed to be entirely empty, but still her heart was pounding wildly. The white wall of fog moved gently outside the window, and wisps of it drifted in as if they were trying to catch and choke her. Her over-stretched nerves heard creaks, footsteps, breathing. She had to force herself to leave the shelter of the heavy curtains and cross the open floor of the room.

Reaching the bookshelves she pulled out books in a mad hurry, throwing them down, making a heap to set on fire. She tore out pages to make kindling, stuffing them into the heart of the heap, and then, her fingers shaking, set it alight.

435

The dry old paper caught at once, and a trail of oily rags about the room would get a good conflagration going: the floor and all the bookshelves were wood. When the heap was blazing and the first of the rags had caught, she made her way back to the french windows.

Outside, the contrast with the flames made the fog seem even denser, and she missed her way back to the wall and wandered helplessly for a while, groping about in a featureless murk, terrified every moment of being caught. After some time she bumped into a tree she recognised – a big redwood, unmistakable – and took a new bearing, remembering what she had seen in daylight when reconnoitring. But it seemed to be much further to the wall than it ought to have been, and despite the glow of the fire behind her giving her a direction, she was afraid she might be walking in circles. Her feet and ankles were soaked from the wet grass, the hem of her skirt flapped dismally against them, and she was shivering with cold and reaction. She found the wall at last, and with huge relief groped her way along it until she reached the tree by which she was to climb over. Standing beneath it she called out softly to Winifred, but had no answer. She could hear fire bells now, and with the muffling of the fog had no idea how far off they were. In desperation she climbed up the tree and onto the wall, and seeing nothing below her, swung over and dropped down.

She landed on a stone and fell, turning her ankle. Winifred was nowhere in sight. She must have wandered off, or run away, Vera thought with exasperation. She must make her own escape, before the police arrived, for they would certainly follow the fire brigade out here. Her ankle hurt her, and she hobbled along. This was a narrow, rutted lane that ran between the mansion's high wall and a wood. The ruts tripped her, the tussocky grass caught at her feet and caused her to stumble, the clammy fog filled her lungs and made her eyes sting. Then she heard something up ahead of her – it sounded like muffled voices. She stopped dead, her senses stretched. Someone coughed, ahead and quite close. She jumped in panic across the path, bumped into a bush, whipped round it and crouched down behind it.

She heard rustling footsteps, someone's heavy breathing, another cough. Not a man's cough – it must be Winnie. A moment later Winifred appeared through the fog, looking round helplessly. She stopped still, as if listening, then turned back the way she had come. Vera half rose, about to call her, when the sound of voices came again – male voices. Winnie stopped dead, turning her head this way and that, apparently unable to tell which direction they were coming from. Vera hissed, 'Winnie! Over here! Winnie! Hide, they're coming!'

But her companion showed no sign of having heard her. Peering through the leaves Vera saw her take a step in one direction, then the other, dithering on the spot; and then two large, dark figures loomed out of the murk. The shape of the helmets was too distinctive to mistake: they were policemen.

'Hello, what have we here?' said a deep male voice. Winnie gave a small squeak, like a caught mouse, and her hands flew up to her mouth. Vera felt exasperation – couldn't she at least *pretend* to be innocent? 'Aren't you out a bit late, Missy?' the man went on, not unkindly.

The other one said, 'We've been looking for you for half an hour. You'd better come along with us. All alone, are you? Or are there others?'

Vera had pulled back a little, so she didn't see what Winnie did or how she looked, but she heard her voice, sounding surprisingly calm. 'No. I'm on my own.'

Now was the time, Vera supposed, to jump up and take her share of the punishment. But she was damned if she was going to! If Winnie had stayed put, she wouldn't have walked into the police. If she hadn't been so feeble, she would have got behind a bush as soon as she heard them coming, and they'd have gone past in the fog. Vera had no desire to go to prison, especially when Anne was coming home soon. And there was no point in two of them going up the steps when it could be just one. Winnie wouldn't give her away, she was sure. So she held her breath and kept still until the oddly matched threesome had walked away. Of course, they might still come back to search some more, so she stayed put for a long time, listening, and then crept very slowly and carefully from bush to bush until she reached the road.

There seemed no-one about: all the activity must be taking place around the gates, on the other side of the property. She ran across the road and climbed over a gate into the field on the other side, then crept along behind the hedge until she got back to the village. There she made her way by cautious stages to the house of the local Suffragette, which had been their base for operations. By the time she was safe indoors, she was soaked, tattered, and chilled to the bone, and could hardly tell what had happened to Winnie for the chattering of her teeth.

She went back to London the next day with a cold beginning; Winifred Walton was by then on remand in Maidstone gaol until her trial should come on in January. The penalty for arson was likely to be heavy – she might get two years – but Vera felt it was her own fault for getting caught, and had no sympathy for her. Besides, she was feeling very ill. Back in Chelsea she took to her bed with a feverish cold, and felt too unwell to travel down to Southampton, as she had intended, to meet Anne off the boat. She was a very popular member of Anne's coterie and had made plenty of friends of her own since moving to London, so she did not lack for visitors or nurses in her sickroom.

On the day Anne was to arrive in London, she was in bed, in her room, surrounded by her rather Bohemian set, sitting on the bed, the floor, on every available piece of furniture. She chatted rather hoarsely to them as some arranged flowers they had brought, others made toast at the bedroom fire, and one perched on the window-sill playing the banjo rather inexpertly. There was a hasty banging at the street door below, and a moment later Miss Rogers ran up the stairs to announce that the Enemy, as they called the police, had somehow got wind of Anne's impending arrival, and had been waiting at Waterloo station for her train. Unwilling to allow another of those daring escapes that were making a mockery of justice, they had closed off the platform with a large force and arrested her as soon as she stepped down. She was now back in Holloway.

Everyone looked at Vera, who was blowing her nose on a large spotted handkerchief.

'Ah, well,' she said, when she emerged, 'we knew it was going to happen.'

The autumn was a lively season in York for the Ned Morlands, who found themselves completely rehabilitated after the *Titanic* business, and much invited. There were still those who regarded Teddy Morland as guilty, and Jessie would have nothing to do with them, would not invite them or accept their invitations, or attend, if she could help it, if she knew they would be present; but those who had indicated they realised they had been wrong about Uncle Teddy she forgave for Ned's sake – or for the sake of his business – though she felt she could never really like or trust them again.

She had plenty to do with her own work at Twelvetrees, her almost daily visits to Morland Place, regular bridge evenings with various friends, and other parties and dances. Ada Cornleigh turned seventeen in October, and the Cornleighs gave a dance to bring her out. Ada asked Jessie endless questions about her own come-out in London, and sometimes seemed to be anticipating a ball along similar lines for herself, complete with awning, red carpet, police directing the traffic, twenty-piece orchestra, two suppers and titled guests. Jessie wondered whether she was doing the right thing in answering the questions at all, and was afraid Ada was courting deep disappointment. But when it came to it, the Station Hotel, dinner for thirty in the dining-room, and afterwards fifty couples circling to a six-piece band in the hotel's Victoria Ballroom, seemed to answer every hope she had cherished.

Teddy had been invited to this occasion, and the Cornleighs had hoped that it would prove the thin end of the wedge with him. Mrs Cornleigh took a great deal of care over the wording of the invitation, sending a letter along with the card, couched in such flattering terms it all but said Ada could not be brought out without his presence. But still he refused, sending a polite but unrevealing letter in reply. He could not go into public, to be stared at. He liked the Cornleighs, but he was still the man who should not have survived, and he would not taint their party with his shame.

There was a big dance at the cavalry barracks in October, to which Jessie and Ned went, and which she enjoyed very much. She felt more at home with the regiment, many of whom had bought her horses and who had always been pro-Morland, than with most civilians. She danced a great deal – several times with Ned, but she was much in demand with the officers, too – and on the few occasions when she was not dancing, she walked arm in arm with Mrs Wycherley and enjoyed her conversation.

She was telling Mrs Wycherley about her visit to Dr Darroway, when she remembered the major's long-ago suggestion that she should take a first-aid course.

'I meant to do something about it, but somehow time has slipped away. It does seem like a good idea, though. When one works with horses there's never any knowing what might happen, and it could easily come in useful.'

'Yes,' said Mrs Wycherley. 'I hadn't thought about it, but it's true. Especially when one hunts.'

'I ought to look round and see whether there are any courses hereabouts,' Jessie said.

'Lady Surridge is head of the Red Cross Committee,' Mrs Wycherley said. 'I do know that.'

'I suppose I ought to have known it,' said Jessie. 'She's the head of every committee in York.'

'Well, not quite,' said Mrs Wycherley. 'But, really, one can't blame her. If I was married to Sir Philip, I'd take every opportunity to be out of the house, too.'

Jessie laughed, but said, 'Well, I'm not going to ask her about a course – or join one if she has anything to do with it. She cut Uncle Teddy, and I'll never forgive her.'

'Dear me, you are fierce,' said Mrs Wycherley. 'But I'm sure there must be more than one Red Cross committee in an area like this. What would you think about going into Leeds, for instance?'

'I suppose I could,' Jessie said reluctantly. 'But I hardly have the time to go investigating all that way.'

'I'll do the investigating,' Mrs Wycherley offered, 'and if I find a suitable course, I'll join it with you. How would that be?'

'Oh, yes, it'll be much more fun to do it with a friend,' Jessie said.

Mrs Wycherley made her enquiries, and found there was a cottage hospital just outside Wetherby that gave regular courses for ladies of first-aid principles and practice, so she enrolled them both, and it added another activity to that busy autumn. One of the best things about it, Jessie felt, was that, as it was only ten miles away on a direct road, Ned withdrew his objections to her handling the Arno and let her drive herself and her friend there and back each week.

Their circle received the addition, in November, of Emma Weston. After a very quiet spring and early summer in Scotland with the Abradales, she had gone on a round of some of her half-brothers and -sisters, staying a few weeks here and a few weeks there. She had enjoyed a two-month seaside visit with Fanny and her family at Weymouth in August and September, and had been bored to death for a month with Thomas and his family in Baldock in October, before a wistful letter to Henrietta had resulted in a warm invitation to stay at Morland Place for as long as she liked.

So Emma arrived, rejoicing, in time for the hunting. She came with an elderly servant, who had once been a nurse to some of Lady Abradale's cousins: she was no sort of use as a lady's maid, but it was necessary for Emma to be accompanied on her many railway journeys, and Mrs Fletcher was penurious and grateful for the position.

'I'm a sad sort of gypsy,' Emma said to Henrietta, as they watched her luggage being brought in, to make a considerable pile in the great hall. 'I'm sorry to inflict all this on you, but as I don't really have a home any more, I have to carry everything with me.'

Henrietta thought this a very pathetic state of affairs. 'What about your house in London?' she asked.

'Oh, Uncle Bruce has sublet it, and all the furniture has gone into store until I want it – if I ever do. Most of it's very old and heavy, and I can't imagine it anywhere but where it was. Well,' she said, seeing a question in Henrietta's eyes, 'there was no point in the house standing empty. There's another twenty years on the lease, Uncle Bruce says, but I'm not sure I shall ever want to live there again, even if I could. I couldn't live there alone, could I? I'll have to stay with some relative or another until I get married, and then I suppose whoever I married would have his own house.'

'So you're to be passed about from one relative to another?' Henrietta said.

'Like a parcel,' Emma said, with a sad smile, 'only not so welcome. At least a parcel gets unwrapped by someone, eventually.'

'But that's not right,' Henrietta protested. 'Someone must have responsibility for you?'

'Well, Uncle Bruce is my legal guardian until I'm twenty-one, and he's a dear, but I don't want to live in Scotland all the time. It was all right at first, just after Papa died. I was glad then that it was quiet. But the castle is absolutely miles from anywhere – honestly, except for the deer and the crows you never see a *thing* moving as far as the eye can see, not even from the turret with binoculars. Cousin Venetia says I can stay with her in London, but though she doesn't say so, I know she doesn't want me there all the time, because she's so busy. And so I thought I'd write to you. I liked it here *so* much, and I thought perhaps with so many people here already you might not notice another one too much.'

It was not long before Henrietta had put this story to Uncle Teddy, who reinforced her invitation, told Emma to regard the Place as her home, assured her that as far as he was concerned, the more was always the merrier, and instructed her to call him Uncle Teddy. Emma settled in, and under the benign Morland Place influence soon became less pale and thin and regained some of her effervescence. In bereavement she had grown taller and more than eight months older, but with Polly as her mentor she learned to romp again, though never quite with the same abandon. She would be eighteen in January, and a young lady had to remember her dignity. Teddy was already planning a birthday-party treat for her, and wondering whether, if he gave her a horse for her present, it would persuade her to stay permanently.

Jessie enjoyed Emma's company and, with her visits to Morland Place and Emma's to Maystone, saw her pretty much every day. Emma hadn't ridden much since the previous autumn, and Jessie gave her some lessons in advance of her first hunt. Emma had a natural seat and balance, and a little practice was all she needed. Jessie kept close to her the first few times out, but Emma took to it like a duck to water, and Jessie soon saw she had no need to worry about her. She graduated from a quiet old mare to Jessie's second horse, and by Christmas was riding one of the young horses, which Uncle Teddy had whispered to Jessie he might like to buy for her.

Emma, ready for anything new, went to the first-aid classes too, and brought a livelier element to the proceedings, for she could not resist play-acting when it was her turn to be the victim and submit to bandaging. Some of the older ladies disapproved, but Mrs Wycherley was enchanted with her, and invited her to tea at her house in Fulford most weeks after the lesson. It nearly always seemed to happen that there were a few young subalterns hanging around the house or dropping in at the same time, and Jessie noticed how they looked at Emma, and how she lowered her eyelashes prettily and didn't look at them. She had been enjoying having Emma as a sister – she who had grown up in a household full of boys – but after all, Emma was out, and almost eighteen, and very pretty. It looked rather as though she wouldn't keep her as a sister for long.

Three days' hunger and thirst strike secured Anne her release from Holloway on the 22nd of December on a five-day licence, and having spent two days in bed recovering, she decided to go down to the country, to Wolvercote, for Christmas, to avoid any disturbance and to extend the break, perhaps, until the New Year. The Aylesburys' house in Wolvercote had been her second home in childhood, and the present earl, her second cousin Ralph, invited her to stay for Christmas. She declined, though gratefully, and asked for the use instead of a small cottage in the grounds for herself, Vera and Mary. She'd have liked to join the family celebration, but she did not feel she could trust Vera to behave herself. Faced with more of Anne's 'precious relatives', she was likely to see slights where there were none, make a fuss, be rude, insult somebody and embarrass everyone. And there was also the question of Anne's own notoriety. Aylesbury Christmases tended to gather distant and aged relatives from all over the family tree, and they might not all be glad to welcome a gaol-bird in their midst. No, the cottage was the thing: they could be snug there, and private, and still have the grounds to walk in and enjoy the benefit of the game, eggs, cream and enormous logs for the fire the estate provided.

The only difficulty was in getting away, for the house in Paulton's Square was watched by detectives day and night. Anne's own particular set had formed themselves into a bodyguard for her, along the same lines as that which functioned for Mrs Pankhurst. They took lessons in ju-jitsu with Mrs Garrud; and a former army sergeant, who was a sympathiser with the Cause, had shown them the most effective ways to use the short, heavy sticks they had armed themselves with. But what was needed now was subterfuge. One of the Bodyguard, Miss Rogers, was a tall girl, as tall as Anne herself, and of a similar build: dressed in Anne's clothes and with a veil over her face she felt she could attract the detectives' attention to herself. So on the day of the departure, they set up a great deal of to-ing and fro-ing, in the middle of which Miss Rogers slipped out with a group of others, hurried to the end of the road and jumped into a taxi. The hounds were drawn off, and a little later Anne and Vera came out in disguise and made their way to a rendezvous where Mary Taylor was waiting with the motorcar.

Once they were down at Wolvercote, there was nothing to worry about, for even if it had been possible to trace them to the cottage, they would not be disturbed while on

444

the earl's grounds. In fact, the Enemy never did find where they had gone. It was only when they returned to London that Anne was picked up.

They had gone straight to a rally organised in protest against the forcible feeding, which was being used again, against some women on remand. Anne managed to get into the hall through a side door and made her way to the platform, but she had only been speaking for a few minutes when there was a commotion at the back of the hall, and a body of policemen with drawn truncheons burst in and tried to storm the platform. The Bodyguard jumped up and put themselves in the way, and a violent struggle ensued. More policemen broke in from the back and got onto the platform from the wings. Anne picked up a chair to defend herself, and managed to get in quite a few blows with it before it was snatched from her hands, and a truncheon crashed down on her head, stunning her. As she fell, Miss Rogers caught hold of her and Vera tried to get between her and the police, but the force was overwhelming, and they were beaten aside. Anne was dragged, half unconscious, down off the platform. Most of the audience was now involved with the battle, one way or another, and sticks and truncheons were flailing, chairs being thrown. By the time the police got Anne out of the hall her clothes were torn and she had sustained a bad cut on the forehead as well as the blow on the head.

She was taken back to Holloway, where her condition was alarming enough for her to be sent straight to the hospital prison. But her skull was tough, and was not fractured, and by the next day she was regarded as fit enough to be sent to a cell. She resumed hunger and thirst strike, and three days later was carried out on a stretcher, half dead, to a waiting Suffragette ambulance. This time she was not taken home but to the Brackenburys' house in Campden Hill Square, which had been set up as a convalescent home for recovering 'mice' – the women called it Mouse Castle. Though her skull had not been fractured, the concussion and the battering she had received worsened her condition and complicated her recovery. When her licence expired, a police doctor pronounced her unfit to go back to prison, and it was extended a further ten days.

Vera had gone back to Paulton's Square and her normal life. Anne thought of the months to come, of the dreary, painful, endless cat-and-mouse game to be played out until her sentence had been served – and how, when that distant day came, she would commit another illegal act, and it would all begin again. But the weariness of her thoughts never lasted long. Anger would come to buoy her up, anger and determination. She thought of all she had suffered, of the sufferings of all her colleagues, of the hideous, mad injustice of the situation, and she knew she could never give in, never. She would have the vote, or they would have to kill her. Those were the only alternatives.

Things were growing uglier. Three women, Rachel Peace, Mary Richardson and Phyllis Brady, who were on remand for arson, had been being forcibly fed for weeks. In mid-December, Rachel Peace had managed to smuggle out a letter, which said that she could not carry on with the hunger strike any longer because the forcible feeding was giving her such terrifying hallucinations that she was afraid of permanently losing her mind. She took food normally for a while, but in January resumed the hunger strike, and was again forcibly fed. A fellow inmate, released in mid-January, told of the hideous screams and tortured sobbing she had heard. She said that she believed Rachel Peace had been moved to a padded cell.

There had been another protest by the clergy against forcible feeding, and Mrs Dacre Fox now led a deputation to the bishops to ask them to investigate. After much urging the Bishop of London agreed to interview Rachel Peace, and obtained permission to visit her in Holloway. He reported afterwards that she had seemed calm and happy and had made no complaint about her treatment. There was an outcry at this, and accusations in the press that a 'whitewash brush' had been used. Under pressure, the Bishop of London arranged to interview the other two women, and reported that they had responded in the same calm, placid way to his questioning.

Suspicions became to form and circulate, and when Phyllis Brady was released on the 11th of February, she was asked if she would allow tests for drugs to be made. The tests proved positive for bromide. A few days afterwards, when she had recovered, she said that she had felt dazed and stupid during the interview with the Bishop, and too 'limp and feeble' to be able to answer him properly, or with the emphasis she knew in the back of her mind she ought to employ.

So now it was known that forcible feeding was being accompanied by drugging to make the victims docile – and this in a British prison at the heart of civilisation, and in the twentieth century! The women were outraged, but though the bishops were asked to intervene with the Government, and some were sympathetic, none was willing to speak out. Questions about the drugging were asked in the House, but the allegations were denied, and McKenna again announced, in his infuriatingly reasonable voice, that Suffragette prisoners could secure immediate release if they would only swear to renounce militancy.

'Never!' said Anne, when she read the report in *The Times*, and went straight out to Speaker's Corner. While she stood on a box and addressed the crowds, the Bodyguard stood around her, keeping watch, and as soon as the police approached they began swinging Indian clubs in a rhythmic way, as though performing a gymnastic exercise – something Mrs Garrud had instructed them in. While they kept the Enemy at bay, Anne jumped down and ran to another box across the other side, where she resumed her address. When the police saw where she had gone, they and the Bodyguard raced each other to reach her, but she jumped off the box and ran herself, and was able to get into a taxi and escape. She could not go home, so went to a friendly house for the night, but the next morning the police caught up with her again and she was arrested as soon as she stepped onto the street and taken to Holloway.

At the beginning of March 1914, Mrs Pankhurst was arrested with great violence while talking at a hall in Glasgow. Many of her bodyguard and the audience were quite badly hurt, and when the police caught hold of Mrs Pankhurst they seemed to go into a frenzy, shouting, shoving and dragging her, hitting her, tearing off her necklace, fountain pen, neck-ribbon and the velvet bag that was tied to her waist, and kicking her shins until they bled. It was reported in the papers the next day that the citizens of Glasgow were shocked at such behaviour; and in protest Mary Richardson slashed the painting of the Rokeby Venus. All the London galleries were closed after that, but it was the one incident that was reported all over the world.

Paulton's Square was not the sort of place that expected to see the likes of the Earl of Padstowe, but he thought it pleasant enough when he called one day to visit Anne, though the house was nothing like the surroundings he had been accustomed to seeing her in. He had been in love with Anne in her youth, and had asked her many times to marry him. Eventually he had married someone else, but they had remained friends – perhaps better friends than when he had still held ambitions with regard to her.

Now he had come on a painful mission. He had always supported the idea of votes for women, but the slashing of the Rokeby Venus was an act of a different order from burning railway stations or cutting golf greens. He needed to make sure Anne understood the difference and wanted her to promise that she would ensure the WSPU spoke out against it and forbade anything like that from being done again. Works of art belonged to the whole of mankind, and should be sacrosanct. What good would it do the women to obtain the vote in a world that was irreversibly debased? He rehearsed his arguments as he walked from the main road, examining the house numbers. It was a mild March day, and most of the houses had windows open, or partly open. As he proceeded he realised he was walking into a noise issuing from one of them, and guessed from the progression of the numbers that it was going to turn out to be the house he was seeking.

His footsteps slowed and stopped. Yes, it was Anne's house, and the noise was rag music, played inside very loudly, and coming out through the top of a downstairs sash, along with a clatter of voices and a quantity of smoke. A man leaning on a lamp-post opposite straightened up as Padstowe halted, threw away his cigarette butt and took a step forward, his face sharpening with interest. Padstowe guessed he was a detective. He knew enough about the business to know that the leaders of the Movement were watched all the time. He turned to look fully at the man, and after scanning him once over very quickly, the man resumed his lounging position and drew out another cigarette.

Padstowe's first knock on the door was not answered, and he guessed he had been too feeble about it, and banged as hard as he could. After a pause the door was flung back by a tall young woman with a mass of curly hair and a cross look on her face. 'Who are you?' she demanded. 'What do you want?' She stared him up and down quite rudely. 'You're not police – not in that outfit.'

Padstowe glanced down at himself. In Town he usually wore a frock-coat, but he had put on a lounge suit and a soft hat for this visit to the suburbs, and had thought himself perfectly dressed for the occasion. A little hurt, he lifted his hat and said, 'My name's Padstowe. I came to see Lady – to see Anne Farraline.'

The young woman gave him another hard stare, but she said, 'You'd better come in.' She stood back to allow him into the hall, took a quick glance up and down the street, and slammed the door behind him. 'Vera!' she bellowed, so loudly and suddenly it made him jump. He was not accustomed to people – especially ladies – raising their voices indoors. The noise inside the house was great, not only the rag music, but a number of high, female voices, and various clatterings and bangings from somewhere, as though a large meal were being prepared. The air was full of smoke, some of it from cigarettes, some with a strange, spicy, Oriental kind of tang to it, and some that, bluer and fattier, was frankly from sausages being burnt.

'Vera!' the young woman yelled again, and then with a tut and a shrug she laid a hand on his upper arm, turned him towards a door, and said, 'In there. Vera will tell you,' and went the other way herself.

He pushed open the door with some reluctance and entered the source of most of the atmosphere in the house. The music was issuing from a machine on a table by the far wall, being tended lovingly by a girl in a flowing red dress. Despite the cramped space, two couples of women were attempting to dance to it. The sausage smoke was coming from the chimneyplace where two women were kneeling and trying to cook sausages on toasting forks in front of a fire that was making the room horribly hot. The other smoke was coming from a variety of cigarettes and pipes held in the fingers or between the lips of the large number of females who were crowded into the room, standing, sitting or semi-recumbent on a variety of chairs and sofas. They all seemed to be rather oddly dressed, in flowing, brightly coloured, pre-Raphaelite sort of clothes, except that two of them seemed to be men – until they turned their heads and he saw that they were not.

Everyone turned to look at him, and all the conversation stopped, so that the only noise was the ragtime, the slight hissing from the machine that accompanied it, and the sound of a sausage falling off its fork into the hearth. Then one of the figures reclining on a sofa said, 'Who are you?'

He looked towards her. She was lounging with her legs stretched out, one elbow propped on the sofa's arm, with some kind of cigarette between her fingers, the other arm round the shoulders of the red-haired woman lounging beside her.

'I'm Peter Padstowe,' he said.

'I'm Vera Polk,' the woman said. She disengaged herself from her companion and stood up. 'What do you want?'

She was wearing Turkish trousers of red cloth – rather shocking to Padstowe, for he had never seen a woman in trousers, though these were so baggy and voluminous he might have mistaken them for a skirt had the woman not stood with her legs apart in an aggressively male posture. She also had on a white shirt, very full in cut and with voluminous sleeves – something like a buccaneer's in a pantomime. Her hair was cut very short, and she wore a red and gold scarf bound round her brows like a headband, the fringed ends falling over one shoulder. Her eyes were lined round with black paint like a ballet dancer's, and the thing she was smoking was pungent and did not smell at all like tobacco.

'I came to see Anne – Anne Farraline,' Padstowe said, feeling very uncomfortable and wishing he hadn't come. The other women had resumed their conversations, but in lower voices, and with covert and sidelong glances at him, as though he were a wild animal that might turn dangerous at any moment.

'She's not here,' Vera said. 'I know your name – you're an old friend of hers, aren't you?'

'Yes, a very old friend. Can you tell me where she is?'

'She's at the Mouse Castle.'

He had no idea what or where that was. He said, 'Will she be coming back later? I'd like to speak to her.'

Vera shook her head. 'You can leave her a note, and I'll see she gets it. Or you could write to her. But I don't know when she'll be here next.'

Padstowe felt himself becoming light-headed, though whether that was the smoke, the noise, or the strangeness of everything he couldn't be sure. 'I'll write,' he said, and began to back away. 'I'm sorry to have disturbed you.'

Vera gave an ungracious shrug. He looked towards the music machine, and then back to her. He had to know. 'Is that a phonograph?' he asked. He had heard of them, but never seen one.

'No, it's a gramophone,' she said. He thought for an instant she was making fun of him, the words were so similar, but then she expanded, with some pride, 'It's like a phonograph but it plays flat discs instead of cylinders. It's much better. It's absolutely the latest thing. Anne brought it back from America for me at Christmas.'

'Oh,' Padstowe said blankly. He bowed awkwardly and backed out, aware that they were all looking at him, probably laughing at him. Gramophone, phonogram, gramograph – by the time he was out in the street and breathing clear air again, he couldn't remember which word was what.

The detective gave him a terse nod of acknowledgement from across the street, and picked a shred of tobacco daintily from his lips. 'Queer lot of people in that house,' he remarked. 'You're well out of it.'

Padstowe heartily agreed.

CHAPTER TWENTY-TWO

In April 1914 Jessie received another visit at Twelvetrees from John Forrester, the army's horse-buyer. On this occasion, however, he had not come to buy. He looked rather apologetic as she greeted him in her usual friendly manner, and said, 'I'm afraid, Mrs Morland, you won't be so pleased to see me when you know why I have come.' And he showed her some official-looking papers. 'It's for the War Book, you see. A census of horses.'

'A census?'

'Yes. We have to count all the horses in the country, so that if there should be a war, we'll know exactly what we have and where they are. So that we can – requisition them.'

That was the horrid word. Jessie felt it like a dig from a sharp point 'Oh,' she said. 'Does that mean you would just take them? For nothing?'

'Not for nothing,' Forrester said hastily. 'The Government would pay compensation. But it would be compulsory. I'm afraid,' he added, with a sigh, 'the requisitioning officers will not be popular. It's not just horses like yours, you see, bred for the purpose, but all horses. Privately owned riding horses too.'

Now she was alarmed. 'You wouldn't take my own Hotspur? Not my hunters?'

'They wouldn't be exempted,' he said. And, to take her mind off it, he added, 'And the army will need heavy horses. Plough horses, carthorses, bus and tram horses, they all have to be registered.'

'Railway horses?'

'We'll count them, but they won't be taken except in extreme need. It will be important to keep the railways running.'

She noticed that he had changed from the conditional to the future tense. 'You think there really will be a war.'

He hesitated. 'It's right and proper for the Government to make preparations and for everyone to know exactly what to do if ever the situation should arise. But—'

'But?'

'Between you and me, there's a lot of talk at the Horseguards. It's thought – this year or next.'

Jessie was very quiet that evening, and Ned, having addressed several remarks to her and received little more than grunts for acknowledgement, finally asked her what was wrong.

'You're not . . .' he began hopefully; but when she looked up, frowning, he thought better of risking the question and changed it to, 'You're not worried about anything, are you?'

So Jessie told him about Forrester's visit. 'But, Ned, he said they'd take all the horses, not just the ones we're breeding for them. People's own riding horses. The polo ponies. My Hotspur and your Compass Rose, the hunters – everything.'

'Hotspur's – what – eleven? And Compass Rose is twelve. I dare say they'd take the younger horses first,' Ned said.

She was not comforted. 'The hunters are younger. And first or last, my darling Hotspur to go to war! He might be injured or killed. My father gave him to me! He's not just a horse, he's a—' She didn't know how to finish the sentence.

Ned knew how she was feeling, but he could offer no help. 'If it came to war,' he said, 'there would be no helping it. When everyone is called on to make an effort or a sacrifice in the cause of right, you can't hold back.'

Jessie acknowledged his words with a slight nod, but she did not speak, grieving inwardly. Her horses – her lovely horses! They were like her children to her, and she could not bear to think of them being hurt. Even the army remounts she had bred had been sold to a peace-time army. Her imagination was active enough to be able to picture

454

what might happen to her darlings in a battle area, with bullets and shells flying about, and she couldn't bear it.

Ned could guess pretty much what she was thinking. When it came to it, he thought sadly, Jessie liked horses a lot more than babies. He said, 'If there was a war, a lot of men would be hurt too, you know.'

She looked up with a flash of passion in her eyes. 'But they go knowingly, and willingly! The horses – they just do – do what they're told, and they never – never understand why—' She couldn't go on for the tears rising up her throat to choke her. She jumped up and ran out of the room, and sought the privacy of the bedroom to cry.

Later, she was roused by sounds of arrival downstairs, and after a while the door opened and Ned was there. She sat up – she had been sprawled face down on the bed – and reached for her handkerchief to blow her nose.

'Bertie's here,' he said.

'Bertie?'

'He just dropped in. I think he'd like to see you too.'

She wiped the tears from under her eyes with the back of her hand. 'I must look terrible.'

He smiled. 'A little red about the nose and eyes, that's all. In any case, I'd have thought he's the one person who'll understand. But don't if you don't want to.'

She swung her legs off the bed. 'Of course I'll come down, if he's come all this way,' she said.

'Take your time,' Ned said. 'We've plenty to talk about.'

She poured water into her basin and splashed it on her face, then straightened her clothes and tidied her hair. Looking into the dressing-table glass, she said to herself, 'Not bad. A bit white-mouse-ish, but – not bad.'

Bertie was in the wing-backed chair by the fire nursing a glass of whisky, and he rose to his feet when she appeared in the doorway. His eyes scanned her face swiftly and piercingly as she came forward and held out her hand. 'Were you asleep? I hope I didn't disturb you?' he said gently, pressing it.

'Tactful,' she said. 'You can see perfectly well that I've been crying.' She sat down on the sofa and he sat too.

'Well, it wouldn't have been polite to mention it,' Bertie said.

'What are you doing here, Bertie?' she asked.

'Not that it isn't a pleasure to see you,' Ned added.

'Of course it is,' Jessie amended, 'but unexpected.'

'I came up on the train to see to some business, and I couldn't be so close without calling in,' Bertie said.

'Ask him to stay the night,' Ned urged. 'I have, but he might say yes to you.'

'Stay the night, Bertie,' Jessie said obediently. 'Stay as long as you like.'

'Thank you, but I have to go back tomorrow, and I've already booked a room in the Station Hotel.'

'You can cancel that.'

'I'm catching a very early train. Really, thank you, but I'd sooner leave it as it is,' said Bertie. He was still looking at Jessie, feasting his eyes while he could, but he had never slept under this roof and never wanted to. It would be too painful. When Ned had said Jessie was upstairs resting, he was afraid that might mean she was with child. He would try to be glad for her if – when – that happened, but he knew he would suffer agonies of jealousy. But now he could see she had been crying, and he supposed they had been quarrelling. That was painful in its own way, and for more than one reason. He was afraid if he stayed too long he might find himself feeling glad about it.

'I did call in with a purpose,' he said. 'I've had a visit from John Forrester.'

'He came to Twelvetrees today,' Jessie said.

'Ah. I'm sorry. I had hoped to be able to give you warning. I knew it would upset you.'

'Oh, I've had my weep, and I'm over it now,' Jessie said, trying to be brisk. 'It's foolish to rail against what can't be helped. It's just—'

'I know,' said Bertie. 'Horses are not just animals.'

Jessie nodded, glad he really did understand.

'As it happens,' Bertie said, 'I'm getting rid of all my horses anyway, except for two road horses. Forrester's taking the remounts right away, and I'm finding buyers for my hunters and the other hacks, and I'll put the yearlings and two-year-olds up for sale on the open market.'

'Getting rid of all your horses?' Jessie said 'Are you going out of the business? Maud said you were going into cattle.'

'Yes,' said Bertie. 'When the war comes, you see, I shall be called up straight away. I'm in the reserve. I shall want two horses for myself, but for the rest – well, cattle are one thing, and my agent and bailiff can keep the estate going between them, but I can't leave the horses to anyone else.'

Jessie stared, trying to absorb the idea. 'But – need you sell now? Surely it isn't that close?'

'I think it is,' Bertie said. 'I talk from time to time to fellows closer to the centre than I am, and the feeling is that it may well happen this year – next year at the latest. So I have to be prepared. I can't leave Maud and Richard with the problem, and it will take time to place all my horses. I don't want to send them to open market and not know where they'll end up.'

Jessie said, a little bitterly, 'According to what Forrester says, they'll all end up in the same place anyway.'

There was a silence, and then Bertie said, 'There is one thing – the particular reason why I came. It's the Bhutias.'

'Oh, yes. I was going to ask you about them,' Jessie said.

'I've six mares with foals at foot,' he said. 'I was wondering if you'd like to have them – run them with your own.'

'You want to give them to me?' Jessie asked in surprise.

Ned said, 'Won't they be requisitioned as well?'

'They're too small for officers' mounts, and not strong enough for draught horses. Of course, if there's a need for baggage horses at some point – one can't tell . . . But they're very special to me, as you know. I would sooner you had them than anyone else.'

'I'll buy them from you,' Jessie said, and looked at Ned. 'We could afford to buy them, couldn't we? If Bertie wouldn't mind our not paying the money all at once?'

Fortunately Ned, who was looking alarmed, wasn't required to answer this. Bertie said firmly, 'No, I don't want to sell them, I want to give them to you. It would be hard to find a market for them other than you, so their financial

457

value is limited. I just want them properly taken care of, that's all.'

'Well, then, that's easy,' Jessie said. 'I'll keep them until you come back. It won't be long, surely?'

Bertie said, 'It may be. I was talking to a fellow at Horseguards, who said that Kitchener is saying if there is a war it will last three years.'

'Three years!' Ned said. 'Surely not?'

'Look at the Boer War,' Bertie said. 'We kept thinking that would be rolled up in a few weeks more, and it went on and on.'

'Three years?' Ned said, frowning. 'It puts a different complexion on things.'

'On what things?' Jessie asked. They both looked at her cautiously, as though estimating her ability to take bad news. It made her nervous. 'What is it? What are you keeping from me? Ned?'

'I'm not keeping anything from you. I was going to tell you anyway,' said Ned. 'It was just something we were talking about – Bertie and I – before you came downstairs. You see, the army is short of officers – the reserves particularly.'

'Public-school men will be very much in demand,' Bertie went on. 'They have the right qualities of leadership, judgement, hardihood and so on.'

'I went to Eton,' Ned said. 'And besides that, I can ride, and I'm used to handling firearms.'

'You mean – you'd have to go?' Jessie said. Ned nodded. 'But wars are fought by the army, by soldiers. You're not a soldier. You're just a private gentleman. They can't make you go.'

'I wouldn't wait to be made to go,' Ned said. 'As Bertie says, they're short of officers. It would be my duty to go.'

Bertie took it up. 'The German army is massive,' he said. 'Twenty times the size of ours. If war comes, I'm afraid a great many private men will have to go.'

Jessie looked from one of them to the other. This had given her something to think about. It was one thing to part with her horses, and had she thought about it she would have anticipated that Bertie, the soldier, would go – but for

Ned to go too ... There were so many aspects and ramifications to that, it would take her some time and a great deal of solitude to understand all that she thought about it.

On the 15th of April, 1914, there was an important WSPU meeting in Lowestoft, at the Hippodrome. The date had been chosen to coincide with a conference of women teachers being held in the seaside town, and a great deal of publicity was expected from it. Annie Kenney, Mrs Drummond and Anne were all to speak.

Anne took the train down there from Liverpool Street, travelling alone and in disguise. She was out on licence, and she and Annie had both had to escape from the Mouse Castle, which was being closely guarded. To increase their odds, they had left separately and were travelling to Lowestoft by different trains. Vera was going to create a decoy in the motor with Miss Rogers pretending to be Anne. They had left early and were going to drive westwards out of London in the hoping of drawing pursuit. Mary would leave Vera and Miss Rogers at a railway station to make their way back to London and thence to Lowestoft, while she drove the motor back to Chelsea.

Anne sat in the corner of a second-class compartment, pretending to be deep in a book; but in fact though she occasionally turned a page she had not read a word of it. She had examined covertly the other people in the carriage and did not recognise any of them, and felt reasonably sure none of them was a detective or anything to do with the Movement. The train was fast only as far as Ipswich, where she had to change onto the local train, which made its way up through Suffolk, running parallel to the sea and calling at all the little towns and villages on the way. She did not see anyone suspicious as she hurried across the platform at Ipswich, and when she was settled again in another carriage, she turned her body slightly towards the window, as though to get the light on her book, and thus with her head averted felt safe to stare broodingly out of the window at the passing countryside.

Her thoughts were not happy. She felt no exhilaration any

more in the cat-and-mouse game, no pleasure when she managed to outwit her pursuers, no triumph in escape. She was tired and always felt ill, but these things in themselves would not have been enough to daunt her. Her mind went back, as it always did when it slipped her control, to the day that Peter Padstowe had come to visit her at the Mouse Castle.

She had been sitting in the conservatory, resting, when he was shown in, and his eyes had shown clearly what she must look like to him. He had tried to be gallant, bowing over her hand, but she had said bluntly, 'Forgive me, I cannot rise. Sit down, Peter. I can see you think I look a sketch.'

'Not at all,' he said quickly.

'Don't talk nonsense, please,' she said.

He sat, and looked at her earnestly. 'You look as though you had been ill; but you are as beautiful as ever. It takes more than illness to eradicate true beauty.'

'Oh, Peter,' she said. 'You are hopeless of reform. How is Caroline?'

'She's well, thank you.'

'And the children?'

'All well. But what about you, Anne? Is it really worth it, what you're doing?'

'*I* think so,' she said firmly. 'Let's leave it at that, shall we? You can't have come here just to make the old arguments again. How did you find me here, anyway?'

'I went to Paulton's Square,' he said, 'and they told me there that you were at the Mouse Castle. I had no idea what that was, but I applied to Lady Overton, and she told me.'

'Ah! And why did you go to Paulton's Square to see me? Not really in your way, is it? It must have been a deliberate visit for some special purpose.'

'It was,' he said. He hesitated, looking uncomfortable. 'I went there to ask you to use your influence to prevent any more incidents like the slashing of the Rokeby Venus.'

'Mary Richardson acted on her own impulse when she did that. It was not planned or discussed,' Anne said.

'But if the leaders, like you, condemned it – warned the members against ever doing anything like that again?'

'Why is it so important to you, Peter? It's only a painting, after all – not flesh and blood.'

'Flesh and blood will heal. A work of art destroyed is gone for ever.'

She gave him an odd smile. 'Why, Peter, what a strange philosophy.'

'I thought, coming from your background, you would understand,' he said, a little stiffly.

'I understand,' she said. 'But when you have seen your friends kicked and beaten until they bleed, when you've witnessed the horror of forcible feeding, when you've seen frail women tortured to the edge of madness – yes, I understand, but it's hard to care.' He was silent, and she said, 'Is that all? No rejoinder? You disappoint me, Peter dear. I thought you would make more of a fight of it, especially as you came all this way to do it.'

'I had another purpose in coming.' He looked uncomfortable now.

'Well?' she prompted, and then, 'Speak up. We are old friends. You can say anything to me.'

He met her eyes, and took a breath. 'Very well. I went to your house—'

'In Paulton's Square, yes, so you said. You are making hard work of this. Spit it out – what happened?'

'There was a party going on,' he said. 'Music – very loud music. A great many women, very oddly dressed, smoking, drinking, dancing. The smell of hasheesh. It was a very Bohemian scene. Everyone seemed to be making extremely merry.'

'Well, what of it?' she said indifferently; but he could see he had shaken her.

'And here you are, obviously ill, too weak to stand up,' he said gently.

Her brows drew down. 'Make your point, Peter,' she snapped.

'Goings-on of that sort,' he said awkwardly, 'in your house, even though you weren't there – even in Chelsea – that sort of thing gets talked about. I have heard gossip.' Still she scowled at him. 'Anne, there were two women there, embracing.'

461

The scowl disappeared. She smiled at him, though it seemed to him a forced smile. 'Oh, Peter! Can't women be friends? Can't friends embrace each other?'

He looked at her a moment longer, then sighed a little, and stood up. 'Well, I've told you. I hope you don't hate me for it, Anne. I meant it for the best.'

He bowed slightly and was walking away, but when he was at the door she called quietly, 'Peter!' He turned his head. 'I know you act as a friend. But you mustn't worry about me any more. It's far too late for that.'

He bowed again, and left her. When he had gone, she remained staring at nothing, thinking. She knew what sort of a party he had been describing. She had heard of parties like that – had even been to one or two, though briefly, for they were not to her taste. A party of that sort, at her house, while she was here recovering from her latest fast! Vera had not been to visit her at the Mouse Castle. They had agreed before she was arrested the last time that she would recover here and that Vera would keep away, for her own sake, so that she should not become too familiar to the detectives. They would take a person up on the least excuse these days, and she had no wish for Vera to become a mouse, and go through all this hideous suffering. But why would Vera hold a party? Would not her absence, and thought of her suffering, make Vera too miserable to want such entertainment?

Then she thought about the other thing he had said. Women embracing? She wished she had asked him to describe them. No, she didn't. She didn't want to know. But it wouldn't be Vera, anyway. Some of Vera's friends – as opposed to Anne's particular circle – were rather odd, rather more *outré* and ungoverned. Probably one of them had urged the party onto Vera and she had been unable to resist.

But as the slow days of recovery passed and she was often alone, she found her thoughts returning to the theme. She had noticed, since she came back from America, a difference in Vera. She was more impatient, sharper in her speech; she criticised more. She had always been quarrelsome and easy to take offence, but underneath there had been a warm passion that showed itself when they made up their differences. Since December that had not been in evidence. Vera was more off-handed. When they argued, she was more likely to toss her head and walk out with a cold look, rather than flying into a tantrum that ended in tears and kisses.

And there was that new friend of hers, Evelyn Shaw. Anne couldn't like her. She was a thin-faced, smart girl with freckles and red hair, given to what Anne thought a vulgarly bright way of dressing – but it was not for that, or for her rather grating voice and lack of polished manners, that Anne disliked her. It was from a feeling that Miss Shaw did not like *her*. Often when they happened to be in company together, she would catch Miss Shaw staring at her; and when she caught her eye she would look away with a sniff and a toss of the head. In fact, Anne suspected that was where Vera had caught the gesture, for they always seemed to have their heads together, talking in low voices, breaking off hurriedly when Anne came near. And if Anne spoke to her, Miss Shaw would answer in a manner that verged on the impertinent, a kind of open-eyed, staring, disagreeable way that suggested Anne had no right to be asking *her* anything.

Anne had never felt she was entitled to choose Vera's friends for her, or object to those she did make, but it was not nice to be disliked in one's own home. She did on one occasion say, very mildly, that she wished Miss Shaw did not have to be there every time she came home, or be included in everything they did. But Vera had flown up in the boughs at once, and cried that she had to put up with Anne's boring, stuck-up friends, so it was rather much that she could not have a *single* person she liked about the house without Anne objecting.

When she had left the Mouse Castle, she had gone home for a while. Vera had seemed pleased to see her, Miss Shaw was not in evidence, so Anne had decided to leave sleeping dogs lie, and had said nothing about Peter's visit, even though Vera did not mention that he had been at the house while she was absent. It was not long before Anne was arrested again, and her hunger and thirst strike was followed by another spell in the Mouse Castle; a few days at home

463

and the pattern was repeated. But the last time she had gone home, she had gone a day early and had made her way there without announcement.

It was around ten in the morning when she reached Paulton's Square, and let herself in with her door-key. No servant came to meet her, and the house was in silence. There was a heavy smell of cigarette and other smoke in the air, which made Anne frown. She disliked excessive smoking, not being a partaker herself, and she thoroughly disapproved of hasheesh, which was well known to cause insanity, as well as inducing stupid behaviour that she found tiresome. She had told Vera she would not have the stuff used in her house, and Vera had said she did not care for it herself. Yet *someone* had been smoking it.

She went to the drawing-room door, which stood open, and looked in. The curtains were still drawn, though they had not been pulled efficiently and there was a gap through which the light was streaming. The scene thus illuminated was not pleasant. The room was desperately untidy, with overflowing ashtrays and dirty plates and glasses on every available surface. The fire had burned out and the grate had not been cleaned, and there was a large quantity of orange peel and eggshells lying on the hearthstone, together with a saucepan in which something had burned to a volcanic black residue, and a pair of shoes Anne did not recognise. There were cushions on the floor, the rug had a cigarette hole burnt in it, a scarf was lying abandoned across the arm of a chair, and one of the sofas had something glutinous spilled on its seat – fat or candle-wax, she couldn't be sure in this light. And on another sofa, someone was fast asleep. She was curled up with her face buried in a cushion, so Anne could not see who it was, but she did not recognise the back.

She left the sleeper and walked upstairs, her heart heavy. It was not that she had doubted Peter's word, just that she had hoped it had been an isolated incident. She crossed the landing and opened the door to her bedroom, went across to the window and pulled the curtains. At the sound and the light, Vera stirred, grunted, then struggled up on one elbow, putting an arm across her eyes and muttering crossly, 'Oh, must you? It's too early. Go away.'

'Wake up, Vera,' said Anne. Vera's shoulders were clad in her usual striped pyjamas, her short hair was wildly ruffled, and there was smudged maquillage around her eyes and mouth. What was making Anne's heart beat so hard that it was an effort to speak steadily was that next to her, on Anne's side of the bed, was another sleeping figure, a hump under the bedclothes. A naked female shoulder appeared at the top, a head rested on the pillow, turned away from the window. The hair was long, tangled and very red.

'What are you doing back? I wasn't expecting you until tomorrow,' Vera said.

'Evidently,' said Anne. 'Put your dressing-gown on and come downstairs. I want to talk to you.' And she turned and went away.

Vera took her time about getting up, and eventually trailed down the stairs looking sulky and aggrieved. Anne met her at the foot of the stairs and led her into the dining-room, which was slightly less devastated than the drawing-room and, more importantly, did not contain a comatose reveller.

'The house looks as though a battle's been fought through it,' she said, turning to face Vera.

Vera yawned. 'You aren't going to be disagreeable, are you? You won't have to clean it up. The girl will do it.'

'She's not here.'

'I told her not to come in until midday. Didn't want to be woken up at some unearthly hour. And now you've woken me anyway!'

'Vera, what in God's name is going on?' Anne asked, and heard her voice tremble with emotion.

'I should have thought that was obvious,' Vera said. 'There was a party here last night.'

'From the debris left, I should think it was nearer a riot than a party.'

'A few friends came to see me and we enjoyed ourselves, that's all.'

'While I was recovering at the Mouse Castle?'

'Why not? It wasn't going to do you any harm, was it?'

'Is this the way you've been carrying on all the time I've been away?'

'Carrying on?' Vera scowled. 'If you mean, have I carried on with normal life, the answer's yes. Why should I go into mourning just because you've got yourself put in prison again?'

The words were like a blow. Anne felt her temper rising, but beneath that there was a feeling of terrible harm, as though something had been severed or torn out, the pain of which would be felt later, when the shock had passed.

'And is it part of your normal life to have someone else in bed with you?' she asked, in a shaking voice. 'I presume it's Evelyn Shaw?'

'What if it is?' Vera said, walking away to the fireplace. She hunted along the chimneypiece and said, 'Damn. I thought there were some cigarettes here.'

'Don't turn your back on me!' Anne cried.

Vera half turned. 'I don't want to look at you when you're like this. You just want to start a quarrel, and I'm not in the mood for it.'

'*Start a quarrel?* Vera, answer me: what was Evelyn Shaw doing in bed with you?'

Vera turned and stared at her, a mixture of that poke-chinned defiance she had recently learned, and a sort of calculation. 'What kind of a question is that?' she said. 'Do you really want me to answer it?'

Anne was stunned. She had expected some attempt at explanation; she had even thought that it *might* have been innocent; but Vera only faced her down, and dared her to object. She had been caught *in flagrante*, but she was not going to apologise, or evince any shame or regret. Anne could only stare at her, her lips moving helplessly as she felt the pain begin to flower inside her.

'What?' Vera said. 'Have you got something to say? No, I didn't think so. I've a right to have friends of my own, people who don't look down their noses at me.'

'Vera, don't,' Anne said weakly. 'I can't stand it.'

'We're not married, you know! I'm not your chattel. That's the men's trick, to think you can own someone. I'd have thought *you*'d be above that sort of thing. Isn't that what we're fighting for, the right to do what we want? To make a different kind of world for women?'

Anne's legs were turning to rubber, and she grabbed the back of one of the dining chairs to steady herself, then slowly sat down on it. She bent her head towards her lap. 'I feel faint,' she muttered. Then she must have swooned, for she remembered only a confusion of swooping blackness, a feeling of nausea, voices and hands.

When the world cleared again, she was sitting on the floor, and someone was holding a smelling bottle under her nose. She sniffed and gasped, then brushed it feebly away. Pale hands and red hair. She recoiled. Vera and Evelyn Shaw were both kneeling in front of her. Miss Shaw said, 'Better? You went right off there, for a minute.'

Anne felt cold with horror that she had been exposed, not only before Vera, but before this outsider. She pushed them away and managed to get to her feet, swaying a little, trying to control herself.

The two women stood as well, and Miss Shaw said, not unkindly, 'Don't try to do too much too soon. Just sit quietly until you feel better.'

'Miss Shaw, would you please leave,' Anne said, with all the dignity she could muster.

'Now wait a minute—' Vera began angrily, but Miss Shaw put a restraining hand on her wrist.

'No, no, she's quite right. Leave well alone, Vee. I'll push off.' And with a curious look and a nod to Anne, she left them.

After a moment, Vera said, a little awkwardly, 'You don't look well at all. I think you'd better go straight to bed.' She must have seen something in Anne's eyes, because she added, 'I'll put clean sheets on for you, if you're so particular. You just sit here and I'll call you when it's done.'

Anne remembered all this, as the wooded and gentle rises of Suffolk rolled past the train windows. That had been ten days ago. No more had been said between them since that day about the parties, or about Miss Shaw. They had resumed what on the surface appeared to be normal life.

467

They had talked together, eaten together, met others of the group, discussed future plans. Everything had seemed as before, except that they had separate rooms now, and that Vera had been less irritable, more considerate towards Anne. Miss Shaw had not come to the house since then, and Anne did not think Vera had seen her.

But something had been broken that could not be mended. Anne could never forget that red head on the pillow, or Vera's words, 'Why should I go into mourning just because you've got yourself put in prison again?' She had taken certain measures, and when she had leisure and privacy enough, she would make the break with Vera. She had faced many things in her life and would not have called herself a coward, but that was one thing she dreaded. She dreaded the rage, the vituperation; and she dreaded the loneliness afterwards. There was a part of her that wanted to accept the compromise and go on as they were, take whatever comfort she could get, on Vera's terms. She was not young any more.

She felt tired and ill, and so alone. She was on her way to speak at a meeting, and probably by tonight she would be back in Holloway, facing another fast. At a few days at a time, it would be years before she finished her sentence and was free. Perhaps there would be no need to have the confrontation: perhaps in her absence Vera would just drift away. She didn't really know any more why she stayed.

Anne sighed and shook her thoughts away. She must not allow anything to come between her and the Cause. She had an important speech to make today, and in order to deliver it she must avoid the police, who would doubtless be looking for her. She must have her wits about her, and not allow herself to be distracted by her personal unhappiness.

Lowestoft was a large terminus with several platforms and exits, and it was crowded when she got off the train, which allowed her to hide herself in a crush of bodies and look about without being obvious. She spotted the detectives at once but, with her dull, shabby clothing, elderly hat and her old cloth shopping-bag, she looked much like everyone else returning from a day in Ipswich and perhaps hurrying home to get the old man his tea. She remembered to walk slowly and with her shoulders hunched in a weary, downtrodden way. As she neared the barrier she sniffed and bent her head away a little as if to rub her nose on the back of her hand, which got her past the detective. He did not, in any case, seem to be making much of an effort to scan the faces as they passed him. Near one of the arches onto the street she saw Miss Rogers, and made her way towards her. Miss Rogers did not look at her, but as she walked out she fell in behind her and they hurried away from the station lights into the dimmer streets.

The air was keen, blowing in off the sea, and smelt faintly of fish.

'I almost didn't recognise you,' Miss Rogers said. 'Your disguise is so good.'

'Any trouble?' Anne asked. 'Did the decoy work?'

'Perfectly,' said Miss Rogers. 'We were followed. We had a taxi-cab behind us all the way to Ealing, and then we lost it in the traffic, so Mary was able to double back and drop us at the Underground station.'

'Where's Vera?' Anne asked. A gust of wind brought a prickle of dampness with it. Anne licked her lips and tasted salt.

'I'm not sure where she is,' said Miss Rogers. 'She didn't come down on the train with me.'

'But I thought you said—'

'Oh, we got on together at Ealing, all right. But she got off at South Kensington. She said she was going to meet Miss Shaw, and that they'd come down together and meet me here. But I haven't seen them yet. I expect they got delayed. Or perhaps they're caught up with the crowds at the Hippodrome,' she concluded.

'Yes, perhaps,' Anne said. That must be it. Surely Vera would not miss this meeting? It was one of the biggest and most important of the year, and even had Anne not been speaking, she would have wanted to be there.

Before they reached the Hippodrome, they were met in the street by one of the Bodyguard, Miss Rowe, who said,

'The police and detectives are out in force. They're shining an arc lamp into everyone's faces as they arrive. But they've got all the back and side entrances covered. It will be better to go in the front with the public.'

'It's all right,' Miss Rogers said. 'I don't think I would have recognised Anne if I hadn't known her. That putty nose and the glasses – and the hat!'

Miss Rowe said, 'We've borrowed a schoolgirl for you, just in case. They won't be looking for a woman with a child.'

'Have you seen Vera?' Anne asked.

'No,' said Miss Rowe briskly. 'She hasn't turned up yet. Did she miss the train?'

The streets were gradually more crowded as they drew nearer the Hippodrome and they joined other people walking in the same direction. There were movable barriers up, gradually funnelling people into the entrance, where the police stood with the arc lamp and four detectives examining each face, referring now and then to pictures of wanted women. Beyond the barriers mere onlookers had gathered, perhaps in expectation of a spectacular arrest.

Anne, pressed in now on either side, her walk slowed to a shuffle, was not so sure that her disguise would pass muster. In poor light a putty nose would look all right, but the harshness of an arc lamp would show up both the colour and the texture as unnatural. She might be better off without it; but it was too late to remove it now. Someone might see the action; and she would need a looking-glass to do the work properly.

'Here are the others,' Miss Rowe said. Anne turned her head eagerly, but though there were four more of the Bodyguard, plus a strange woman and child, Vera was not there. 'This is Mrs Good, and her daughter Edie,' Miss Rowe introduced.

'I'm very grateful to you,' Anne said, shaking her hand. 'How do you do, Edie?'

'Very-well-thank-you, m'lady,' the little girl said, and all but dropped a curtsy.

'All you have to do is hold Lady Anne's hand, and if she

talks to you just pretend it's your auntie Bet,' Mrs Good said to her daughter. 'I'll be right behind you all the time.'

But things did not go quite as planned. As they came close to the inspection point, Anne recognised one of the detectives. His name was Kemp, and she had had several run-ins with him, and felt that there was no hope that he would not recognise her if he laid eyes on her. She explained this quickly to the Bodyguard. 'You'll have to try to make a diversion just as I reach the front. I'll get on the other side from him, but you'll have to make him look away. Even in profile he'll recognise me.'

'All right, I'll stumble against Charlotte and we'll both nearly fall,' said Miss Rowe. 'That'll make him look, even if it's only for a moment.'

Anne's hands were beginning to sweat, and she was glad she was wearing gloves, or it would have been very unpleasant for little Edie. Closer, closer. She tried to keep an eye on Kemp without actually looking at him. She had edged her way to the other side of the funnelling crowd. Three or four people were passing through abreast, so it looked as though she might make it.

And then, almost at the last moment, she saw something that made her turn her head the wrong way, towards Kemp. Among the spectators beyond the barrier Anne had caught a glimpse of a white face under red hair, blowing in the sea breeze, and beside it another face she would have noticed anywhere. Catching her eye, Vera grinned and waved a hand; her other arm was round Miss Shaw's shoulders. And even as she looked at them, Anne saw Kemp's head come round like a pointer's, his eyes widening as he recognised her.

'Stop that woman!' he shouted. 'You – Farraline! Stop there!'

Everyone was looking round. The detective nearest Anne looked at Kemp and then back to see who he meant. 'Get her!' Kemp shouted. 'Blue hat and spectacles! Don't let her get away!'

It was hopeless. Anne let go of little Edie's hand, turned, and tried to force her way through the bodies hemming her in. It was a good scheme, she thought, to funnel them to the entrance, making it impossible to go back against the stream. The other detectives had jumped into action, and at the same time the Bodyguard had flung themselves into the breach, getting between them and Anne. A large, heavily built man was blocking her way, and she thought it was all up with her, but she saw he was guiding her to the side, to the barrier, and with a wide grin he picked her up as though she weighed nothing and dumped her over it. 'Goo on, run for it!' he advised her.

She almost stumbled as her feet met the ground, but she staggered and regained her balance. The detectives were after her, vaulting over the barrier. Faintly from behind them, over the general noise of the throng, she thought she heard Vera's voice calling her name. People were shouting, 'Go it!' or, 'There she goes!' or 'Stop her!' according to their sympathies. Beyond the spectators the street was clearer, and she began to run. There were people around in ones and twos, and mostly they just stared, though one or two tried half-heartedly to grab her, and one stuck out his foot. It touched her ankle and she only just managed to keep upright.

The police were behind her – she didn't know how many, but the sound of boots suggested half a dozen. And now there were two more in front of her, uniformed men, blocking the pavement. They had their truncheons out, and were ready to use them. There was an unbroken terrace of houses on her left, moving traffic on her right. But across the other side of the road there was a lane, or alley, leading off the street. She thought perhaps if she could reach it she might throw them off. She darted to her right, between two slow-moving motorcars, flinging a quick look back to see how close the pursuers were. She saw that Kemp was among them, his hand up gesturing, his mouth wide open, shouting something.

She didn't see the lorry coming in the other direction; in fact, she never saw what hit her. There was only a scream from somewhere, a confusion of lights, and a great, painless explosion inside her head. She felt herself flying, falling, caught a glimpse of wheels and legs, and boxes showering down into the road with her. Her head hit the tarmac, and she saw nothing more.

The vehicle was a fish-lorry, and though the boxes were empty, they were impregnated with the odour. Lying where she had fallen, just for an instant Anne caught the smell of fish, and was faintly puzzled by it as the voices all around her faded away into the blackness.

CHAPTER TWENTY-THREE

Anne's brother, the Earl of Batchworth, came up from his estate near Manchester to claim the body. As soon as Venetia had telegraphed him the news, he sent urgent telegrams both to her and to the police insisting that no Suffragette was to have anything to do with it. He also sent messages to the newspapers requesting them not to report the manner of her death.

That was a demand never likely to be met. It was too much of a tasty morsel for any editor to pass up, and all the papers reported the death of the Lady Anne Farraline, sister to the Earl of Batchworth, in a road accident while fleeing the police. The more dignified papers left it at that; the popular ones made the most of it. Pages of background on the peer's daughter turned Suffragette contrasted her presumed upbringing of comfort and privilege with her life as a militant, her spells in prison, the hunger strikes and her latest incarnation as a mouse.

It was not long before the *Daily Mail* unearthed her relationship to Venetia, who then had the dubious privilege of seeing her own history as a pioneer woman doctor recounted for the titillation of clerks and domestic servants. Overton was very phlegmatic about it, and said, 'My dear, does it matter? You have done nothing to be ashamed of. It will soon blow over.' He knew that her anger with the newspapers was only a reaction covering her grief for her cousin. Anne's very public death precluded any truly private mourning.

Batchworth dealt with everything, interviewed the police,

instructed an undertaker. He was infuriated to learn that he could not at once remove the body for burial because there had to be an inquest. Venetia advised him not to be present, because she was sure that Anne's hot-bloods would attend it, which would only upset him more. But he said it was his duty to go, and he went; and when the Bodyguard approached him afterwards he drove them off with bitter words and threatened to have them put in charge if they did not leave him alone. His picture appeared in the newspapers the next day under the headline 'THE PEER AND THE SUFFRAGETTES'.

What the Bodyguard had wanted to talk to him about was the funeral. They, and indeed the WSPU, wanted a Suffragette funeral for Anne, with full procession, as they had done for Emily Davison. Since Batchworth would not talk to them, it was natural for them to regard Venetia as a go-between, and she received several letters, and a number of callers whom she refused to see. But when Mrs Pankhurst herself risked a visit, heavily veiled, Venetia felt obliged at least to hear her.

'I am *certain* it is what Anne would have wanted,' Mrs Pankhurst said. 'She was so dedicated to the Cause. We ought to give our sisters the opportunity to express their grief – she was such an important figure in the Movement, and so much beloved. And besides that, it would help our campaign enormously. She was as good as murdered by this government, and we must tell the world so.'

'You do your cause no credit by using such extreme language,' Venetia said, with distaste. This tiny, thin, elderly lady with the burning eyes – what was she? It was like madness, she thought – a madness that had infected and then killed Anne. 'Intercession by me would serve no purpose,' she said. 'Lord Batchworth is adamant. And I certainly would never intercede for such a purpose.'

The gleaming eyes surveyed Venetia's face keenly, and with evident disappointment. 'You used to be such a supporter. In your own life you have struggled against the insane prejudice of men against us. What happened to turn you to their side?'

'Please leave,' Venetia said, reaching for the bell.

Mrs Pankhurst turned obediently to go, but at the door she made one last appeal. 'Don't let her death be in vain.'

'It *was* in vain,' Venetia said stonily.

She couldn't cry for Anne – not yet, at least, while all this was going on. But she grieved bitterly. She remembered the high-spirited child, so dainty her nickname had been 'Fairy'; she remembered the lovely, ardent young woman; and she wondered how it could have come to this, the sudden and pointless death of a battle-hardened campaigner. The thing she had feared for years had happened. Anne had said many times that martyrdom was the logical end of what she had set herself to do. Had she – Venetia did not want to wonder, but could not help it – had she killed herself deliberately? The police had said that it was an accident, and bystanders had reported that she had been looking back as she ran into that fatal conjunction with the lorry. If she had meant to do it, surely she would have been looking towards it? And surely if she had decided on martyrdom, she would have made more of it, chosen a great public occasion and a large audience, as Emily Davison had done – not died under the wheels of a fish-lorry in a dark street in an obscure seaside town?

No, on reflection she felt satisfied that it was not suicide; and in the watches of sleepless night she wondered whether that made it better or worse. Better, of course, that the shame and sin and crime of suicide were not on her cousin's troubled soul; but it perhaps made the pointlessness of the death harder to bear.

Batchworth, grey and old and haggard, looking much more than his sixty-one years, was in no doubt that the Cause – 'those damn' Suffragettes and their wicked ideas' – had killed his sister. His eyes, dry but red-rimmed, burned with a slow anger as he sat by Venetia's fire and fulminated against them. 'I tried to talk to her. God knows I tried. Offered her a home with me. She used to like the country – riding, fresh air. But she wouldn't come. If she'd only married, she'd have been too busy to worry about that pernicious nonsense. She had offers enough, God knows. Why wouldn't she take young Padstowe? Dangled after her for years. But no, she needs must make a spectacle of herself – and me. A gaol-bird in the family! A Farraline for ever in the newspapers! And now look – look where it's ended! Dead, my sister dead – and so young!'

Anne had been fifty, but to him, as he rocked slightly in his grief, she was still the golden girl he had helped to bring up after their father died.

He did not linger in London. As soon as the formalities were taken care of, the body was moved without ceremony directly to Euston station, where Batchworth met it and accompanied it back to Manchester for a private interment at Grasscroft.

'You needn't come,' he told Venetia. 'I shan't be asking anyone. I just want to be done with it now.' And as he left he said, 'London was never good for her. It's where she got all her bad ideas.' And he gave Venetia a bitter look, which told her that, in his deepest heart, he blamed her for the way Anne's life had gone.

Overton feared Venetia might blame herself, and tried to put it into context for her. 'Anne did just what she wanted, her whole life. I doubt whether, even if she had known how it would end, she would have had anything different.'

'Only one thing,' Venetia said. 'She never had the vote.'

At the time of Anne's death, Emma Weston had been staying at Manchester Square. She had come up at the beginning of March to have a Season. Now eighteen, with her father's death a year behind her, she was ready to enjoy herself and test the matrimonial market. She was extremely pretty, she had a decent fortune and good connections, and Venetia saw no reason why she should not make as good a marriage as she wanted, either this year or next.

Venetia worried a little that such a high-spirited girl might have her head turned by her popularity; but after observing her closely for a month, she came to the conclusion that Emma had a native shrewdness to her that would keep her safe. She managed the young men who flirted with her with a light hand, and seemed more committed to enjoying herself

477

than to finding a mate. Everyone said it was a brilliant Season, one of the best in memory, and Emma, pretty, likeable, and with Venetia as her patroness, was invited everywhere.

Anne's death was like a bombshell. Venetia reacted to the first news by dispatching Emma with all her baggage to Violet, who had been back in Town since mid-February. Venetia was going to order a month's mourning for her household, but though Emma stood in the same degree of relationship as Venetia herself to Anne, she had hardly known her, and Venetia felt it would be a great nonsense for Emma to go into mourning. It would not only spoil her Season and prevent her going out and about, but it would attract attention to Emma's connection with Anne. The militants were not well thought of in the drawing-rooms of the great hostesses, and any shadow on Emma might spoil her prospects. There were always plenty of people jealous enough of pretty, well-dowered girls, and it was as well not to give them any ammunition.

So Emma went to stay with Violet, where there was no question of mourning. Violet might grieve privately for the cousin she had known all her life, but she could not put on blacks in Lord Holkam's house for a woman who had died fleeing the police while demonstrating for female emancipation.

Emma had been shocked by the news, and confided to Violet that she did not quite like to go into company at once. Violet suggested they go down to the country for a week, until things had blown over. It was her custom to go down and see the children from time to time during the Season, so it presented no strange appearance to Holkam.

The two young women took the train and descended on Brancaster Hall, to the delight of young Robert, five, who welcomed any interruption to his lessons. Richard, three years old, adored his pretty mother, and saw all too little of her. Charlotte, who was almost two, was running about everywhere, and loved above all to be chased so that she could demonstrate her amazing turn of speed, a procedure that would provoke her delicious, fat and infectious chuckle. Emma found Brancaster surprising after Morland Place, for she could not conceive how anyone could be rich and in the country and not ride. But with the children and the dogs, the grounds to walk in, and Violet's garden to help with, there was enough to do for a week to pass quickly. Emma even felt she wouldn't have minded staying longer when they said goodbye to the children and were taken to the station to catch the train back to London.

Venetia was not sorry to have a respite from the demands of supporting Emma's Season. It gave her a chance to catch up with her work, to read in the evenings by her own fire and to go to bed early every night.

'You are a sad excuse for a fashionable woman,' Overton teased her. 'The most brilliant Season in memory is going on all around you, with balls and parties and I don't know what, and you prefer cocoa and –' he lifted the book from her fingers to look at the title '– *Nicholas Nickleby.*'

'When was I ever a fashionable woman?' she objected.

He gave her back her book. 'You're all the woman I ever wanted,' he said. He touched her cheek and said, 'You're tired. Would you like to go out of Town for a while? I might contrive to be absent for a few days, escort you down to Brighton or somewhere of the sort.'

Venetia laughed. 'What would I want with Brighton?'

'Wolvercote, then.'

'No, darling, thank you. I'd sooner stay here. I find getting on with my work much more restful than resting would be. I never did lounge gracefully.'

'Whereas lounging is what I do best. How ever did we get together, when we're so different?'

'You're not so different. For a man who claims to be idle, you get an awful lot done,' she said. 'You don't fool me for a moment, Beauty, my love. When this War Book is finished, it will be largely due to your efforts.'

'The War Book will never be finished,' he said. 'It's a continuous process. Shall we go to bed?'

'It's only nine o'clock,' she said in surprise. A particular smile from him was the only answer, and she put her book aside, stood up and placed her hand in his, feeling ten years younger for knowing he still found her desirable.

Anne's death brought one more unpleasantness in its train. One day in May Venetia was on the point of going out when there was a violent and prolonged knocking at the door, and the butler came up to say that a Miss Polk was below, demanding to see Venetia and refusing to be denied, or to leave until she had had her way.

Vera had obviously made a bad impression on Burton. His face trembled with outrage and he said, 'Should I call a constable, my lady, and have the young person removed?'

Venetia was tempted, especially as Burton had called her a 'person', but she considered that it might be better to see Miss Polk this once rather than have a fuss made at the door and perhaps attract the attention of the press. She told him to send Miss Polk up.

Vera appeared moments later in such a fury that Venetia thought it better to get her word in first. 'I suppose you have something to say to me about Lady Anne,' she said coolly.

Vera attacked at once. 'Lady Anne, Lady Anne! That's what it all comes down to, doesn't it? She had a title and you've got a title. You never liked me, because I wasn't a nob like you and her.'

Venetia decided on frankness. 'I never liked you because you are rude and selfish. Why aren't you in mourning, by the way?'

'We don't believe in it,' said Miss Polk, momentarily distracted.

'I see. Well, I *am* in mourning, so I'd be obliged if you'd say what you have to say and then leave.'

Miss Polk obliged, with waxing fury. 'I went to see Anne's lawyer this morning. He said she's left me nothing – not a penny! It's all gone to her brother. And I suppose that's *your* doing!'

'I know nothing about it,' Venetia said, taken aback.

'Oh, really?' Miss Polk said, with heavy sarcasm. 'I know what she was leaving me, because she told me. Half of everything – half to me and half to the Cause. Then suddenly she changes her will without telling me, and leaves it all to her brother! She never cared twopence for him. She never saw him from one year's end to the next. She called him a prig and a booby. But she's left him everything! Don't tell me you had nothing to do with it.'

'She did not confide her dispositions to me,' Venetia said, trying to keep calm. 'If what you say is true, you must be best placed to know whether you have done anything that might have caused Lady Anne to change her mind.'

A flaming blush rushed through Miss Polk's face, and her eyes glittered with anger. 'That's none of your business! Anne loved me. She'd have done anything for me. It was you and your sort that turned her against me. You and that brother of hers. All you nobs stick together.'

Venetia had had quite enough. She drew herself up. 'Miss Polk, you seem to be under the misapprehension that I have the slightest interest in you or your affairs. I admitted you because I thought you might have some legitimate business with me, but I see you have none. You will leave now, and you will not come here again.'

'Oh, won't I?' Miss Polk retorted furiously.

Venetia spoke quietly: 'If you come here again I will call the police and have you put in charge. Do I make myself clear?'

Vera glared, her face working, but Venetia had the advantage of age and authority, and faced her down. 'I don't want to come here again. I'd rather die than set foot in your precious house!' she cried. She turned and flung the door open, almost cannoning into Burton, who was lingering on the landing in case of trouble. At the last moment she turned and, with fine dramatic effect, fixed Venetia with a glittering eye and cried, *'Traitor!'* Then she pushed past Burton, ran down the stairs and out of the house.

'Burton,' Venetia said, 'that young woman is not to be admitted again. I am never at home to Miss Polk.'

'No, my lady,' Burton said, and in his tone was the distinct suggestion that it had not been his idea to admit her in the first place.

481

The details of Anne's will were published in *The Times* the next day. Venetia was surprised. She had thought Anne's fortune had been squandered, but evidently she had had better sense than Venetia had given her credit for, and not touched the capital, for she left a considerable sum. It was no wonder Miss Polk was so incensed at losing it.

But what an unpleasant young woman! The violence of her language, her rudeness, her complete disregard for social usage were deeply upsetting, even to one who had doctored in the slums. The poor who had come to Venetia's free dispensary had had more social grace than Anne's friend. It made her wonder what the relationship had been between them that Anne could have put up with it. Vera must have had some powerful hold over her. Well, it was all over now; and at least Venetia was released from the unpleasant duty of ever thinking about Miss Polk again.

The beginning of June brought a visitor to Morland Place: Lennox Manning arrived to fulfil his grandmother's lifelong desire to see England. He was a tall, pleasant-faced young man with soft brown hair and tawny eyes. He had the easy, open converse and good manners of the well-brought-up American, together with a charming smile, and quickly recommended himself to everyone.

Henrietta was delighted to receive anyone who had seen her darling Lizzie more recently than she had, and he obliged her by giving her every tiny detail he could dredge up of his visit to Flagstaff. Teddy, in his expansive way, invited the young man to stay as long as he liked. Robbie and Ethel were impressed by his charm and how easy he was to talk to. Alice liked his gentleness when he talked to her. Polly, fascinated from the beginning by his accent, admired his tall, strong figure and approved his love of the outdoor life and the way the dogs came to him straight away. She liked the way he didn't treat her as a child, and since at fourteen she was just of the age to fall in love for the first time, she very soon fell in love with him, and thereafter followed him around and hung on his every word in a way that would have embarrassed a less well-balanced young man.

Henrietta had several pleasant evenings going over family documents to determine Lennie's exact relationship to everyone, and showed him old photographs and paintings of the various relatives who came into the narrative. He was especially interested in a photograph of her father Benedict Morland, taken in the Crimea as he stood proudly by the railway he had helped build, because this was one name he recognised. Benedict had been Dan and Nat's grandfather through their mother Mary, and he had once visited the old family plantation at Twelvetrees.

Teddy showed him round the estate, and he took an intelligent interest in the new plans. Lennie's father, Lennox Mynott, had been a land agent, and he was toying with the idea of going into that line when he finished college. He took a great many photographs for his 'people back home', particularly of Twelvetrees, after which Ruth's childhood home had been named. He won Jessie's heart by admiring her horses and by proving a good rider when she lent him a mount. His seat was rather odd to her eyes, and he thought the saddle 'darned uncomfortable', but he was gentle on her horses' mouths.

He was very interested in the polo ponies, never having seen the game played before. She and Ned took him to a match, and thereafter he often turned up when she was training. He begged her to let him try, and under her instruction soon picked up the rudiments.

'This would go down really well back home in the States,' he said. 'I wonder you don't export the game. There are plenty of rich folk looking for a new thrill, and if you got them interested, you could sell 'em your horses too.'

It was a glorious summer, with day after day of brilliant, clear sunshine: the harvests would all be early and abundant. Lennox's visit brought a new interest to Jessie's days, and kept her mind off the thought of war and of parting with her horses. Perhaps it would never come, after all, she thought. It was impossible to think about war when the weather was so fine, the world around her so beautiful. The only shadow in her life was that there was still no sign of a baby, though there had been two more false alarms. The second year of her marriage was half-way through, but Henrietta told her not to worry, that babies would come in God's own good time, and that only He knew when that would be. Jessie didn't worry, or not very much. She wanted children, but in the abstract, knowing they would disrupt, perhaps even end, her life in the saddle. But Ned wanted them, more than anything in the world. He didn't say anything, but she couldn't help knowing that month after month she disappointed him.

During the winter of 1913–14, Jack had been kept so busy at the Kingston works that he had decided to move to new lodgings in Kingston itself, to be nearer both the factory and Brooklands. The journey to and from Oakley Street had become a drain on his time, and seemed pointless now that he was rarely needed in London itself.

He found rooms in a pleasant house overlooking the river, with a good-tempered landlady who did not mind his irregular hours. From there he could walk to the skating rink in a few minutes. It took him away from Miss Monkton, but he was not sorry to allow that relationship gently to die. Though she was pretty and good-natured, he was finding her rather a bore to be with for any length of time, and he suspected she found him rather too hard work to keep up with.

He had taken over all the testing previously undertaken by Harry Hawker, who had gone back to Australia for a long stay to demonstrate the new single-seat racing biplane they had developed, called the Tabloid. The factory was busy building Tabloids, three-seater tractor biplanes for the army, and Bat Boats, floatplanes and a torpedo-carrying seaplane for the navy. In February 1914 they received a visit from the First Lord of the Admiralty, Winston Churchill, to inspect the works and in particular a new aeroplane they were developing for the navy, a cross between the three-seater and the Tabloid, which was a two-seater with the seats side by side. They called it the Sociable. The First Lord, who was an air enthusiast, was taken up for a spin by Jack in a Sociable at Hendon in February, which provided useful publicity for the company. Hendon was a popular Saturday resort for the public, who flocked in their thousands and paid a shilling entry just to watch whatever might be going up and coming down.

In March came the Olympia show, and the Sopwith stand, number forty-four, displayed the new version of the Bat Boat, which had a powerful 200 h.p. engine, and was fitted with wireless. The company was doing so well that it was able to purchase new premises in Canbury Road, about a hundred yards from the skating rink, for the necessary expansion of works; and at the same time it was reconstituted as a limited company with capital of £26,000 in £1 shares, of which Jack bought a number. His salary was generous and his living expenses few, so he felt quite well-to-do.

In April the summer competition season started, and attention turned first of all to the second contest for the Schneider Trophy, held in Monaco. The Sopwith company entered a modified Tabloid, fitted with floats and a 100 h.p. engine. It won the prize, and a great deal of glory both for Britain and the Sopwith company. Through May Jack was testing all sorts of new aeroplanes ordered for the services, plus Tabloids for private customers, and in between giving passenger and exhibition flights at Brooklands and Hendon. He also gave Miss Ormerod a lesson whenever it could be squeezed in. She was getting on so well that he thought she would have been ready to take her ticket if he had been able to take her up more regularly. The move to Kingston put him within easy reach of Weybridge, and he spent a lot of time at Fairoaks, dining, playing tennis, joining bridge parties, going out for drives, and walking round Mrs Ormerod's garden with her, discussing her plans for it, while Rug and the dachshunds romped in a way that suggested any new planting would have to be robust in nature.

It had become customary by now to enter a Sopwith aeroplane in every competition, so when the 'Race From London to Manchester and Back' was inaugurated in June, a Tabloid was put down for it. The race, to take place on Saturday the 20th of June, was sponsored by Pratt's, of Pratt's

485

Petroleum, and the prize was a gold trophy and £750. As always there was a great deal of coverage in the press, and huge crowds would gather at Hendon to see the fun.

Jack took off in the early morning from Brooklands in the Tabloid. It was evidently going to be another fine day, but there was a lot of thick white summer mist about. For a time he could not see the roads he normally followed, and he got lost – not an uncommon experience. He flew in wide circles for a time, waiting to see something below that he recognised. At last the fog thinned out, sucked up by the sun, and he spotted the unmistakable glitter of the Welsh Harp away in the distance, and was able to take direction from there.

When he landed, the crowds had already begun to gather, and one of the first people he saw as he jumped down from the Tabloid's wing was Miss Ormerod. Rug barked a greeting to her, and she came over to him, with the large shape of her brother Freddie behind her.

Miss Ormerod reached him first. 'You're looking extremely smart,' he said, returning her smile. 'I do like that hat.'

'It's new,' she said. 'Probably a great deal too good for an airfield, but Freddie brought me in his motor, and he does like his female passengers to be smart, so I thought I had better wear it.'

'I'm very glad you did,' said Jack. The June morning sunshine was illuminating her face, and he thought suddenly how its very familiarity was something delightful. No-one judging her by her features alone would have called her a beauty, but there were few people he would sooner look at – or be with. He smiled, and said, 'That colour suits you,' and she seemed pleased.

Freddie joined them, shook Jack's hand, and asked about the aeroplane and his prospects of winning the prize.

'Pretty good, I think,' Jack said. 'She's a fine little bus. We've fitted a more powerful engine – a hundred h.p. – so she goes a bit. Had a little trouble with the carburettor the other day—'

'Too much petrol in the jet again?' Miss Ormerod put in.

'Yes, and we had a little fire, but no harm done, and I think we've sorted out the problem now.'

Freddie Ormerod looked at his sister with faint impatience. 'What do you know about carburettors, Helen?'

'As much as you, I dare say,' she answered him.

'More, I shouldn't wonder. But it's not ladylike,' he said. 'It's no wonder you're not married. You're too old still to be a tomboy.'

Jack was sorry for her discomfiture. Evidently Freddie regarded him as near enough one of the family to talk to his sister openly in front of him. He intervened quickly by saying, 'I was hoping you would come to watch today. I need someone to look after Rug.'

'You're not taking him with you?' Miss Ormerod said. She tried to speak naturally but her voice wavered a little with vexation at her brother.

'It's a little snug in the Tabloid for the two of us, and there's no-one else I'd rather leave him with.'

'Of course I'll take him. We're old friends, aren't we, Rug, old boy?' Rug agreed with this sentiment so enthusiastically he put dusty pawprints on Miss Ormerod's nice hyacinth-blue skirt, setting Freddie off into a salvo of tuts. Jack caught Miss Ormerod's eye and winked, taking the sting out of the moment, and she smiled gratefully at him.

They were interrupted at that moment by one of the newspaper photographers who were always at such events. Pictures of aeroplanes and flyers were very popular in the press, and Jack knew most of the cameramen by name now.

'Would you mind, Mr Compton?'

'Not at all,' Jack said. It was all good publicity for Sopwith's. 'Where would you like me, Joe?'

'Over by the aeroplane, if you would.' He glanced at Miss Ormerod, who still had the remains of the smile lingering on her lips, and said, 'Would you be in it too, Miss? The readers always like to see an airman with a pretty young lady by his side.'

Miss Ormerod laughed at his choice of words, but Jack thought that, yes, when she smiled, she did look almost pretty. She seemed about to agree when her brother spoke

487

up. 'My sister declines,' he said firmly, to the photographer; and when Miss Ormerod raised her eyebrows at him, he said quietly, 'Your picture in a newspaper? Father wouldn't like it. What are you thinking of, Helen?'

'Sorry, Joe,' said Jack. 'Would a dog do instead?' He posed by the Tabloid with Rug wriggling indignantly in his arms. Then he put the dog's leash on, handed him over to Miss Ormerod, and went off to the starter's tent to announce his arrival and find out his number and the order of take-off.

The competition attempt was not a success. The weather was fine, the visibility perfect, the wind very light, but as soon as he took off he could hear that the engine wasn't right. It must be that damn' carburettor again: he thought he had solved the problem. And before he had got very far, shortly after he had flown past Northampton, he began to feel very sick and slightly lightheaded. Spent fumes from the engine must be getting back into the cockpit, he thought. It had happened before, with other models, and he knew that if he carried on he might lose consciousness and crash. There was nothing to be done but look about for a flat field and put down.

He landed safely, and walked about in the fresh air until he felt better. A labourer who had been working in the next field came over to him, his eyes round with wonder. It was the first airy-o-plane he had ever seen in real life, he confided – Law, wait till the old woman heard about this! He chuckled with anticipatory pleasure as he helped Jack turn the machine and prepare to take off again. The fumes seemed even worse on the return journey, and he was very glad to see Hendon airfield appear ahead of him. He made a rather bumpy landing, switched off and clambered out, staggering a little, and in a moment was helped by two stewards to the St John's Ambulance tent.

The doctor on duty examined him, but Jack assured him that it was nothing but the fumes, and he would be fine in a few minutes. He only needed to sit down by the open tent flaps until it went off. One of the nurses brought him a mug of tea, and he sat cradling it, gazing out at the bright sunshine pouring down onto the field and the dabs of colour of the spectators walking about.

He must have closed his eyes for a moment, for he was startled by something cold touching his hand, and flung them open to find the mug at a perilous angle, the tea ready to overspill, and Rug in a frenzy of greeting, trying to climb into his lap. Behind him was Miss Ormerod, alone, having outstripped her brother in her anxiety. She was panting slightly from having run, and her eyes were bright with anxiety. 'I was on the other side of the field,' she said. 'I saw them help you away. What happened? Are you all right?'

'It's nothing,' he said, putting the mug down on the trampled grass so that he had two hands to fend off Rug.

Miss Ormerod pulled the dog sharply away, hunkered down in his place, and took one of Jack's hands in both hers in what was evidently an unconscious gesture. 'It's not *nothing*. I know you. You wouldn't let them bring you here unless it was *something*.'

'Just fumes,' he said. 'That carburettor's playing up again, and the fumes got into the cockpit and made me dizzy. But I'm fine now. I was just going to get up when you arrived.'

She scanned his face. 'Are you sure?'

'I'm sure,' he said, and then, looking over her shoulder, 'Your brother's coming.'

She dropped his hand and got at once to her feet, as Freddie Ormerod arrived. 'Are you all right, Compton?'

'I shall be in a moment,' Jack said. 'Just a dizzy spell.' He hoped that Freddie would go away and leave them be, but he drew his sister just outside the tent and told her off, quietly, for running. Jack heard some parts of it. 'People were looking at you.' And, 'You must try to have some dignity, Helen.' Finally he did walk off, and with the coast clear, Jack was just about to get up and join his friend, when a young woman came into view.

She was small and slender and dainty, exquisitely pretty, dressed in a killing pink skirt and jacket, with a mass of red-gold curls under a very frivolous hat, large blue eyes, a tender mouth. She was holding a small boy by the hand, and as she stepped into the tent she said to the receiving nurse,

'My little brother has a horrid splinter in his hand. Do you think you could take it out? He won't let me touch it.'

The nurse led him to a seat, and at that moment the golden female caught Jack's eyes on her, turned her head towards him, said, 'Oh!' in a little gasp, and blushed adorably.

'I'm sorry,' Jack said at once. 'I didn't mean to stare. Most rude of me.'

'No, no,' she disclaimed, making a little flapping movement of her lavender-gloved hands. 'It's just that I recognise you,' she went on, in a breathy little voice that quickened Jack's interest. 'You're an airman, aren't you? I've seen your picture in the papers ever such a lot of times. You took one of the aeroplanes up today, didn't you?'

'Yes, but I didn't get far, I'm afraid. Engine trouble.'

She clasped her hands together under her chin. 'Oh! I do hope you didn't crash! Are you hurt?'

'No, not at all,' he said.

'You must be so *very* brave. I could never go up in one of those things, never, never!'

She was as beautiful as an angel, and so sweetly concerned about him, how could he resist? Jack was about to stand up and ask if he might have the honour of introducing himself, when there was a strange sound from just outside the tent, and he turned his head to see Miss Ormerod glaring at him, holding Rug inadvertently so tight that the dog had coughed. As he met her eyes, she thrust the end of the leash at him, snapped, 'Here, you take him,' and turned on her heel and stalked away.

'Excuse me,' Jack said to the angel, 'I must just . . .' And dragging Rug after him he hurried after Miss Ormerod. 'Hey, wait!' he called. She did not turn back, but broke into a run, her head slightly bent so that he thought for a horrifying moment that she was crying. He had to run to catch up, had to grab her arm before she would stop. Rug, excited by the chase, jumped up and tried to lick her, and Jack saw that she was not crying, but that her face was red and her expression strange. 'What's the matter?' he asked, utterly perplexed.

'You don't know? You honestly don't know?' she cried.

'No, not at all. Aren't you well?'

'Of course I'm well. When am I ever ill? Let me go!' she said, shaking her arm free. She stood square on to him, and he saw now that she was far more angry than upset: if she cried it would be from frustration or fury rather than sorrow.

'Is it something I've done?' he asked, more gently.

'No, it's something you *are*!' she snapped, as though goaded beyond endurance. 'You're a fool, Jack Compton! What were you about, back there? That girl—'

'The pretty one?'

'Yes, the pretty one! You were about to introduce yourself, weren't you? Make her acquaintance. Say a few flattering things. Edge towards making an assignation with her.'

'Assignation?' he protested, almost laughing at her choice of word. But underneath he was smarting a little. What business was it of hers, anyway?

'What else would you call it? Next thing you'll be falling in love, telling me she's as beautiful as an angel—'

'Well, she is!'

'And an absolute simpleton as well! I saw the way she did *this*, and *this* with her hands, how she looked at you with her head cocked like a little bird. I've seen it all before – Miss Fairbrother, Miss Monkton, I don't know how many others in between and before. Why do you *do* it? Why do you infallibly pick on pretty idiots and then convince yourself you're in love with them?'

'I don't "convince myself" as you put it,' he began.

'Yes, you do!' she cried. 'Underneath, in your heart of hearts, you *know* they're idiots, that they won't do. They may be pretty, but that's all they are. They're all falseness.'

'That's a pretty stiff criticism of your own sex,' he tried to protest, but she rolled over him, too angry to mind what she said.

'My sex? I'd be ashamed to acknowledge them, with their simpering and fluttering and pretending to be helpless *ickle girls*! Why do you *like* it? Does your mother behave like that? Does your sister? Do you *really* want to marry someone like that and have to listen to their empty twitter every day?

Someone who'll never understand or care a thing about what you're doing, someone you could never talk to? There are plenty of rational women about, but you just don't seem to see them.'

'Well,' he defended himself stiffly, 'perhaps I've never yet met a rational woman I could love.'

'Haven't you?' she retorted. And then all the fire seemed to go out of her. Her face seemed to melt with misery, its taut lines sagging, and for a moment there was nothing but stark unhappiness in her eyes. 'I never want to see you or speak to you again,' she said, in a low voice, and turned from him and walked away.

In a blinding flash, like a physical pain in his head, he saw what his life would be like if he never saw her again. In a tumble of images he remembered all the things he had shared with Miss Ormerod, the comfortable conversations at the sheds, the times she had been waiting with a mug of tea when he landed with frozen hands, the times she had collected him in her motor after a crash, the flying lessons, the drives, the games of tennis, the walks – but, above all, the talks. She always understood what he was saying, she was interested in the same things, she made him think, she made him laugh. He stood, stunned, as she walked away from him. Her face came before his mind's eye, smiling, as it had been that morning, when he had thought how familiar it was – and, yes, to him, how beautiful. How could he not have realised? She had been so close to him all this time and he had never really seen her at all.

Rug whined, and he snapped back to the present and realised he had been standing like a gaping idiot while she got further and further from him, disappearing into the crowd. He broke into a run, with Rug bouncing beside him – he was having a *splendid* time today! He brushed past people with gasped apologies and saw their startled looks. She had become one of a crowd gathering to watch a take-off, and he had to pull and push people out of his way to get through, and was tutted and hissed. But there was her blue suit ahead of him – her pretty blue suit: had she put it on for his sake? – and he grabbed her arm desperately and turned her.

'You're hurting me,' she complained, trying to prise his fingers loose. Now there were tears on her cheeks, he saw. She was not of an age to cry easily, and he knew it must hurt her pride if anyone saw her do it.

'Please,' he said, 'please don't go.' She stared at him, and aware of all the people looking at them, he drew her gently but firmly back through the throng. When they were out he stopped and turned to her, though he dared not let her arm go. There was no-one else very near; it was all the privacy they were likely to get here.

'What you said about me was right,' he said earnestly. 'I'm an idiot. I'm the worst and most damnable fool that ever lived, and when I think about how I've behaved it makes me sick. It's been staring me in the face ever since I first went to Brooklands, and I've been too stupid and – pig-headed and – blind—'

She had been reading his face, and now a gleam of something warmer than misery was in her eyes – the dawn of hope, perhaps. 'Abuse of yourself is all very well,' she said, 'and I agree with every word of it, but what then?'

'I don't only mean I was an idiot to fall for those empty-headed females,' he said. 'I was a far worse idiot for not noticing that the most wonderful woman in the world was right there all the time, just under my nose.' He scanned her face, feeling his heart beat more quickly. 'I think I must have loved you all along and just didn't realise it. It was so easy and comfortable and good being with you, and I never knew that love could be like that. I thought it had to be difficult, and hurt.'

She made a strange sound, which was a laugh fighting its way through a sob. 'Don't say you love me if you're not sure. Not just because I'm different—'

He saw how he had hurt her, how she was afraid he would hurt her again – think he loved her just for the novelty, and then go off after someone else. 'How can I convince you?' he said. 'Have you ever thought you saw someone you knew in the street? You call to them, and they turn round and it's not them at all. And then you really see the friend, and you wonder how you could ever have mistaken the other person

493

for them? The feeling I have for you is nothing, *nothing* like what I thought I felt for those—'

'Angels,' she put in.

'*You*'re the angel,' he said firmly.

'No, you must never call me that,' she said, and she was smiling now, and he wondered why people did not turn and stare at her, she was so dazzling. 'If you ever call me an angel I shall—'

'Marry me,' he said. 'Please, will you marry me? I know I don't deserve you, but now I know how much I love you I can't bear to think of not having you near me every day.' He thought he saw resistance in her face, and hurried on, 'Please, at least think about it.'

'You really want to marry me?' she asked, scanning his face earnestly.

'Would you like me to go down on one knee?'

'Not really. I see my brother heading this way, and he'd be scandalised. He doesn't know I've seen him. Can we be very naughty and avoid him?'

'With pleasure. But will you marry me?'

'Yes, of course. Oh, hurry, this way – come on.'

Behind them, they heard Freddie's voice raised to the nearest thing a polite person could manage to a shout. 'Helen! I say, Helen!'

Miss Ormerod gasped with laughter, and they both broke into a run, Rug frisking along beside them, until they were out of breath and far enough away to stop.

Jack took both her hands, and gazed down at her. 'You did say yes? I didn't imagine it? You will marry me?'

She laughed up at him, all joy now, where a short time ago it had been despair. Oh, he was a villain for having put her through it! 'Yes, I will marry you,' she said.

Triumph filled his heart, a happiness so intense it hurt. 'Come on, then,' he said, pulling her after him.

'*Now* where are we going?'

'Hendon has sheds like any other airfield,' he said. 'I'm going to take you behind one of them so I can kiss you.'

At the end of June, the heir to the throne of Austria-Hungary and his wife were murdered in Bosnia by a Serb nationalist. The news was in all the papers, but it did not impinge much on people's consciousness. There was always trouble in the Balkans, and foreign rulers not infrequently had bombs thrown at them. Much more interesting was the word from Paris that black was to be the new, smart colour for women's fashion. This was daring, innovative, exciting. Black had been *de rigueur* for men ever since Beau Brummell, but women wore black only in mourning, and the idea that the colour could become a tool of fashion was really quite shocking.

The King had ordered Court mourning of a week for the Austrian heir, and Venetia said to Lord Overton, 'I suppose it eases the sting a little to know one is following the latest trend; but really, if it keeps up, how will one ever know whether people one meets are in mourning or not?'

'It won't keep up,' said Overton. 'Fashion can't last, otherwise it wouldn't be fashion.'

'I never thought of that,' said Venetia.

But as June turned to July, and Lord Overton was called to ever more and longer meetings, his wife became aware that he was worried.

'What is it?' she asked him.

'It's an international crisis,' he answered. 'There are talks going on between Austria and Germany, and it's pretty clear that Austria means to make a *casus belli* out of this assassination.'

'What do you mean?'

'You know, don't you, that Austria wants to expand eastwards and absorb all of the Balkans, which means Serbian territory? The fear is that they are going to use this as an excuse. But if Serbia is attacked, Russia is sworn to protect her.'

'Yes, I understand that – because they are Slavs.'

'And if Russia attacks Austria, Germany may feel inclined to come in on Austria's side. If Austria and Germany go to war with Russia, France is bound by treaty to support Russia. That will give Germany the excuse it needs to attack France.'

'It sounds like a game of chess. Do you think this might be the start of the war everyone's been talking about?'

495

She had hoped he would say no, but he was thoughtful for a moment, and then said, 'It needn't be. Grey is convinced Germany doesn't want it – not yet, anyway. He thinks diplomacy can get us over this. Russia doesn't really want war, and the Tsar and the Kaiser are cousins and friends. It's all Austria, really. Grey wants a conference, mediation between Austria and Serbia. If Austria feels Germany isn't really behind her, it will all blow over.'

The glorious summer weather continued, the Season drew towards its end. Emma was enjoying every minute of it. She had even danced with the young Prince of Wales at a ball at the Tonbridges', and again at the Londesboroughs', and had had the felicity of hearing that he had described her afterwards as 'a very nice girl'. Violet had agreed, with Holkam's permission, to take her with them on their country-house circuit that summer, and Venetia was hopeful that she might get her married off before the end of the year. There was a promising something between Emma and Peter Hargrave, a young man of good family and reasonable fortune, which had started up at a ball in May.

In mid-July there was a giant meeting of Suffragettes in Holland Park. Mrs Pankhurst was carried into the hall on a stretcher and immediately arrested. The size of the audience and the collection that was raised proved that support for the Cause was not failing as the Government had hoped, and there were signs that Asquith was prepared to soften his language towards them, if not his actions. Instead of saying 'never', he now said, 'possibly', though he offered no timetable or proposals. But trouble broke out in Ireland, with shooting in the streets of Dublin, and the women found themselves eclipsed again by more important events.

By the end of July, the international situation was so tense that even the trouble in Ireland seemed small by comparison. Despite the increasingly urgent attempts at mediation, Austria had issued a challenge to Serbia, a series of demands so outrageous they were clearly intended to provoke. Astonishingly, Serbia had acceded to all but two; but on the basis of the two, Austria declared war on Serbia on the 28th of July.

Even so, the Tsar and the Kaiser exchanged telegrams

swearing eternal friendship and promised each other not to mobilise, and France declared that even if it mobilised, it would not move any troops within ten kilometres of the German border, so there could be no provocation. Asquith said that if war came, Britain's role would be confined to that of a spectator.

But on the 29th of July Russia ordered partial mobilisation, and Germany warned that unless it was cancelled, she would mobilise too. On the 31st, Russia and Austria-Hungary both mobilised fully. Britain asked Germany and France for a guarantee of Belgian neutrality. France agreed, but Germany did not reply.

'We can't ignore a violation of Belgian neutrality,' Overton said to Venetia. 'It's not war yet, but things may have gone too far to pull back.'

And on the 1st of August, Germany ordered full mobilisation.

August Bank Holiday weekend was traditionally the moment when all the foreign royalty, in London for the Season, went down to Cowes. But on the Saturday, Cowes Week was cancelled, and the King announced he was staying in London. It was enough of a hint for the royalty to rush off for the Channel ports to make their way home before it was too late.

The Holkams cancelled their plans, and on the Sunday, when the earl had gone off to the House, Violet and Emma went over to Manchester Square.

'London's very odd,' Violet said to her mother. 'It's crowded with the strangest people. Everyone seems to be rushing about to no real purpose.'

'There's a demonstration planned in Trafalgar Square,' Venetia said. 'Socialists demanding there should be no war – Keir Hardie's to speak. And I expect a lot of people have come in from the suburbs as well, just to see what's going on. Whatever's known will be known first in London.'

'Everyone seems very cheerful,' Emma observed. 'Lots of people with Union Jacks, singing the national anthem, and there were crowds and crowds in front of Buckingham Palace. It was rather like Coronation year.'

The young women were still there when Lord Overton

came in from the War Office, grey with weariness, and said, 'Well, that's that.'

'Papa, what do you mean? You do look grim,' Violet said.

'Germany demanded to be allowed to march her armies through Belgium. We've just had a telegram from the Belgian government to say that they have refused, and we know what will happen next.'

'Germany will invade Belgium,' said Venetia.

'Just so. Belgium has asked us for our help. Tomorrow we mobilise – the orders are going out tonight, though it won't be announced until tomorrow afternoon. Everything's ready, everything's in place.' The War Book had it all planned, to the last detail. 'We may still get out of it – Germany may back down – but if they don't, we'll be ready.' He passed a weary hand over his face. 'I shall have to go back to the War Office, and I dare say we shall be working all night. Can dinner be brought forward?'

Emma said timidly, 'Does this mean all the summer plans will have to be cancelled?'

'War doesn't concern you young ladies,' Overton said.

'But the young men will go,' Venetia said. 'It will disrupt all the house parties.'

'Cowes is already cancelled,' Violet said. 'I expect other things will be.'

'Peter Hargrave was in the cadet training corps,' Emma said, in a small voice. 'He told me so at the Salisburys' ball.'

Bank Holiday Monday dawned bright and clear, and the morning papers carried the news that Germany had declared war on Russia, had invaded Luxembourg, and was hovering on the brink of invading Belgium. From early in the morning, crowds arrived at the various railway stations: family parties, the women weighed down with bags full of sandwiches and oranges and towels, the children carrying buckets, spades and shrimping nets. It was the Bank Holiday, and war or no war, they were going for their annual jaunt to the seaside.

But all the excursion trains had been cancelled. Disappointed, the crowds milled around, complaining, arguing with the porters, agreeing that it was all that there Kaiser's fault. Some paid the extra fare to take the regular train, but for the rest, who could not afford it, it was either go tamely home, or have a day in London instead.

Most opted for the latter. Hyde Park was soon packed with picnickers, rugs were spread on grass instead of sand, and boats taken out on the Serpentine instead of the sea. Hundreds went to the zoo, hundreds more to the 'Wild West' exhibition at the White City. Madame Tussaud's was another traditional entertainment, and the managers used their wits and opened early, with a special display of the Crowned Heads of Europe, moved from their usual positions to make one tableau. Every restaurant, café and public house was packed to the doors, the crowds spilling over onto the pavements in the August sunshine. Card sharps, organ grinders, jugglers and bands of every sort set up hurriedly wherever they could find space to entertain the masses. And not a few of those who had been seaside-bound stayed on in the great termini to watch the fun as the excursion trains they should have taken were filled with soldiers and sailors, hurrying off to join their units.

There was a flying display at Hendon, which attracted larger crowds than usual because of the cancellations; and one at Brooklands, where Jack, along with the other Sopwith pilots, had given a flying display in the morning, and in the afternoon was engaged in taking up passengers for spins. Miss Ormerod was there, of course, looking after Rug. In between flights Jack took every opportunity to jump down and spend a little time talking to her, marvelling at the fact that he was now licensed to call her Helen. In a few weeks they would be married, and he would be able to wake beside her every day of his life from then on.

'I'm so happy,' he said, more than once. 'What a glorious day this is.'

She had been there all day. In the afternoon her parents came, with Molly, and shook Jack's hand and beamed at him. He might not have a great fortune, and he and Helen would have to start off in a small way, but they liked him, and had known for a long time that their daughter was hopelessly in love with him. It was all they had dreamed of for months, that he would wake up and rescue their girl from misery. Mr Ormerod was so genial he was even persuaded to let Jack take him up for a circuit or two, though Mrs Ormerod firmly crushed Molly's pleas to be allowed a 'go'.

They had brought a large hamper with them in the motor-car, and spread out a blanket in a quiet corner of the field and invited Jack to join them for a picnic tea. It was pleasant relaxing in the sunshine, while the aeroplanes droned gently round and round above them, up in the big blue sky. Rug got rather over-excited about the sausage rolls and almost disgraced himself, but a prolonged, friendly tussle with the Dackies, as Molly called them, used up his energy, and all three dogs flopped down panting on the grass, and fell into a doze. Mrs Ormerod and Helen discussed wedding matters, with Molly adding her suggestions, helpful or otherwise. Mr Ormerod had some polite manly talk with Jack, but soon abandoned the effort in favour of smoking his pipe and squinting up at the sky in peaceful silence.

Jack was just thinking that he ought to get back to his duties, when there was some kind of commotion across the field. A crowd of people had gathered and were talking and gesticulating; then they parted enough for it to be seen that the centre of the fuss was a newspaper-boy with a stack that was diminishing as fast as people could struggle their pennies out of their pockets.

Jack jumped up. 'It must be important news. I'll go and get one.'

'I'll come too,' Molly said, and ran after him.

They came back together more slowly a few minutes later, Jack reading as he walked, his hands stained with ink. The paper was so fresh it was still wet. Reaching the group, he offered it to Mr Ormerod, but it was Helen's eyes he met. 'Germany has declared war on France. German troops are massing on the Belgian border ready to invade. If they cross the border – if they don't withdraw . . .'

'They won't withdraw,' said Helen.

'No,' Jack agreed. It seemed, now it had happened, always to have been inevitable. A restless sea was about to overwhelm them all. 'It's war.'